Praise for *Love Sa...*

"Prudence [is a] sassy but sensitive feline heroine."
—*Time*

"Unforgettably moving . . . a hard one to put down."
—*Modern Cat*

"If you are the Most Important Person to a cat, you will hold them much tighter by the book's end. If you don't have a cat, Prudence will have surreptitiously lured you into the danger zone: Falling in love with a cat because they need family, too."
—*The Vancouver Sun*

"Cooper brings readers a fictional tale that cat lovers will treasure. . . . This book will make most readers laugh and cry, and probably lead them to wonder more often what, exactly, their pet is thinking."
—Fredericksburg *Free Lance-Star*

"The interspersed viewpoints . . . enrich Cooper's sensitively told novel that unravels a story (based on actual events) about a century-old tenement building—and the inhabitants therein. That story ultimately serves as the basis to understanding the emotional subtexts of these authentic, well-drawn characters."
—Shelf Awareness

"*Love Saves the Day* is a charming story of love lost and found, both in human hearts and that of one very special cat. Prudence's voice is as simple and honest as that of the child who sees things adults miss. At its heart, this book is an exploration of unconditional love between mother and daughter, as seen through the eyes of a creature who lives for just this. In that sense,

Love Saves the Day eloquently explains why so many of us would do anything at all for our pets."
—BARBARA DELINSKY,
New York Times bestselling author of *Escape*

"Finally, publishers are realizing cats can write. You go, Prudence!"
—SNEAKY PIE BROWN
(via her spokeshuman, RITA MAE BROWN)

"Once again Gwen Cooper shines her light on the territory that defines the human/animal bond. In *Love Saves the Day,* she creates an emotional landscape so beautifully complete that we can't help but share in the heartbreaks and triumphs of her characters, regardless of their species. That, in itself, is a reason to stand up and cheer."
—JACKSON GALAXY,
star of *My Cat from Hell* and author of *Cat Daddy*

"If you love cats, music, or New York City, you'll love Gwen Cooper's *Love Saves the Day.*"
—NANCY THAYER, author of *Island Girls*

"Prudence's voice is so hauntingly fragile and raw it will break your heart a million ways while simultaneously piecing you back together. A beautifully told story of loss and love and recovery, and how the animals in our lives connect us to our own humanity."
—AMANDA KYLE WILLIAMS,
author of *Stranger in the Room*

"Cooper's beautiful words tell a moving story of the sometimes fragile relationship between mothers and daughters as well as speaking on the special love that forms between a pet and its owner."
—RT Book Reviews

"[Cooper] once again demonstrates her compassionate fluency in felinespeak and proves equally adept at conveying complex human emotions with flair and sensitivity."
—*Booklist*

"Hauntingly beautiful, heart-touching, and at times painfully raw, this is a story about grief, hope and healing. It's a story about the importance of memories, and of preserving a part of one's past. . . . But ultimately, this is a book about love, and how one small cat, through her mere presence, can change multiple lives. This book will stay with you long after you turn the final page. And it already makes me look forward to Gwen Cooper's next book."
—The Conscious Cat

"*Love Saves the Day* has taken Gwen Cooper to a whole new pinnacle as an author. The writing is superb. The storyline is riveting. . . . There's no doubt *Love Saves the Day* is a winner. It's a book that everyone, whether you're a cat lover or not, should read."
—BJ Bangs, Paws for Reflection

"*Love Saves the Day* is sometimes funny, sometimes heartbreaking, sometimes devastatingly tragic, and it holds your attention all the way through to its happy ending. For both cats and humans, it is one of this year's must-reads."
—Sparkle the Designer Cat

LOVE SAVES THE DAY

BY GWEN COOPER

Love Saves the Day

Homer's Odyssey

Diary of a South Beach Party Girl

LOVE SAVES
THE DAY

a novel

GWEN COOPER

BANTAM BOOKS TRADE PAPERBACKS
NEW YORK

Love Saves the Day is a work of fiction. Names, characters, places, and incidents either are the product of the author's imagination or are used fictitiously. Any resemblance to actual persons, living or dead, events, or locales is entirely coincidental.

2013 Bantam Books Trade Paperback Edition

Copyright © 2013 by Gwen Cooper

All rights reserved.

Published in the United States by Bantam Books, an imprint of The Random House Publishing Group, a division of Random House, Inc., New York.

BANTAM BOOKS and the HOUSE colophon are registered trademarks of Random House, Inc.

Originally published in hardcover in the United States by Bantam Books, an imprint of The Random House Publishing Group, a division of Random House, Inc., in 2013.

Grateful acknowledgment is made to Sony/ATV Music Publishing LLC for permission to reprint an excerpt from "Dear Prudence" written by John Lennon and Paul McCartney, copyright © 1968 by Sony/ATV Music Publishing LLC. All rights administered by Sony/ATV Music Publishing LLC, 8 Music Square West, Nashville, TN 37203. All rights reserved. Used by permission.

Library of Congress Cataloging-in-Publication Data
Cooper, Gwen.
Love saves the day : a novel / Gwen Cooper.
p. cm.
ISBN: 978-0-345-52695-3
eBook ISBN: 978-0-345-52696-0
1. Mothers and daughters—Fiction. 2. Cats—Fiction. 3. Human-animal relationships—Fiction. 4. Married people—Fiction. 5. Life change events—Fiction. I. Title.
PS3603.O58263L68 2013
813'.6—dc23   2012026135

Printed in the United States of America

www.bantamdell.com

2 4 6 8 9 7 5 3 1

Book design by Susan Turner

For Scarlett, the original Prudence

———

For Homer, the Original

———

For Vashti, sweeter than Honey

———

And for Laurence, always

Like all pure creatures, cats are practical.

—WILLIAM S. BURROUGHS

PART ONE

1

Prudence

THERE ARE TWO WAYS HUMANS HAVE OF NOT TELLING THE TRUTH. The first used to be hard for me to understand because it doesn't come with any of the usual signs of not-truth-telling. Like the time Sarah called my white paws "socks." *Look at your adorable little socks,* she said. Socks are what humans wear on their feet to make them more like cats' paws. But my paws are already padded and soft, and I can't imagine any self-respecting cat tolerating something as silly as socks for very long.

So at first I thought Sarah was trying to trick me by saying something that wasn't true. Like the time she took me to the Bad Place and said, *Don't worry, they're going to make you healthy and strong.* I knew from the tightness in her voice when she put me into my carrier that some betrayal was coming. And it turned out I was right. They stabbed me with sharp things there and forced me to hold still while human fingers poked into every part of my body, even my mouth.

When it was all over, the lady who did it put me back into my carrier and told Sarah, *Prudence has such cute white socks!* She was smiling and calm when she said it, so I knew she wasn't trying to trick Sarah like Sarah had tried to trick me about going there in the first place. I thought maybe I should lick my paws or do something to show them that these were my real feet, not the fake feet humans put on before they go outside. I thought that maybe humans weren't as smart as cats and wouldn't understand such subtle distinctions unless they were pointed out.

That was when I was very young, just a kitten, really—back when I first came to live with Sarah. Now I know that humans sometimes best understand the truth of things if they come at it indirectly. Like how sometimes the best way to catch a mouse that's right in front of you is to back up a bit before you pounce.

And later at home, looking at my reflection in Sarah's mirror (once I realized it was my reflection and not some other cat who was trying to take my home away from me), I saw how the bottoms of my legs did look a bit like the socks Sarah sometimes wears.

Still, to say that they *were* socks and not that they *looked like* socks was clearly untrue.

The other way humans have of not telling the truth is when they're trying to trick one another outright. Like when Laura visits and says, *I'm sorry I haven't been here in such a long time, Mom, I really wanted to come sooner . . .* and it's obvious, by the way her face turns light pink and her shoulders tense, that what she really means is she never wants to come here. And Sarah says, *Oh, of course, I understand,* when you can tell by the way her voice gets higher and her eyebrows scrunch up that she doesn't understand at all.

I used to wonder where the rest of Laura's littermates were and how come they never came over to see us. But I don't think Laura has any littermates. Maybe humans have smaller litters than cats, or maybe something happened to the others. After all, I used to have littermates, too.

But that was a long time ago. Before I found Sarah.

* * *

The Bad Place is a short walk from where we live in a place called Lower East Side. (Technically, it was Sarah who walked there, because I was in my carrier. Still, it didn't take her very long, and cats can walk faster than humans. That's a fact.) The lady there told Sarah that I'm a polydactyl brown tabby. Sarah asked if that meant I was some kind of flying dinosaur? The lady laughed and said, no, it just means I have extra toes. I'm not sure which of my toes are supposed to be the "extra" ones though, because I'm positive I need them all. And it's not really true to say I'm brown because parts of me are white—like my chest and my chin and the bottoms of my legs. Also, my eyes are green. And even the parts of me that are brown have darker stripes that are almost black. But I've noticed that humans aren't as precise as cats are. It's hard to believe they feel safe enough to sleep at night.

The stabbing lady also told Sarah that I was too skinny, which was to be expected because I'd been living by myself on the street. She said I'd probably fatten up quickly. I've gotten much taller and longer since then, but I'm still pretty skinny. Sarah says I'm lucky to stay that way without having to try. But the truth is I'm skinny because I never eat all the food Sarah gives me. That's because even though she feeds me every day, she never feeds me at exactly the same time. Sometimes she feeds me first thing in the morning, sometimes she feeds me when it's closer to midday. There have even been times when she hasn't fed me until after it's dark. That's why I always make sure to keep some food left over, in case one day Sarah forgets to feed me altogether.

And it turns out I was right to worry. Sarah hasn't been home to feed me—hasn't been home at all—in five days. The first two days I had to get by on what was left over in my food bowl. I even jumped onto the counter where my bag of dry food is kept and used my teeth and claws to make a small hole in it so I could get some food out myself. (I would normally never do that because it's bad manners. But sometimes there are things more important than manners.)

Finally, on the third day, a woman I recognized as one of our neighbors came over and opened a can of food for me. *Prudence!* she called. *Come and eat, poor kitty, you must be so hungry.*

I had been waiting under the couch for her to leave, but I came out when I heard the can open. The woman tried to stroke my head, though, so I had to go back under the couch again and twitch the muscles on my back very fast until I felt calm. I don't like to be touched by humans I don't know well. So I waited until she left before I came out to eat, even though I was starving after two days with hardly any food.

The woman has been back to feed me every day since then, although I still won't come out from under-the-couch until she's gone. Maybe she's trying to trap me with the food. Maybe she's already trapped Sarah somewhere, and that's why Sarah hasn't been home for so long.

To pass the time while I wait for Sarah to come back, I sit on the windowsill—the one that overlooks the fire escape Sarah says I'm never, *ever* supposed to go onto—and watch what's happening on the street. This also gives me a clear view of the entrance to our building, which means I'll see Sarah as soon as she comes back.

To get to the windowsill, I jump from the floor to the coffee table, and then from the coffee table to the couch. Then I climb to the back of the couch and step right onto the windowsill. I can jump directly from the floor to the windowsill, of course (I could jump much higher than that if I had to), but this way I can check to make sure everything is safe and exactly the way I left it. If the little, everyday things don't change, it makes sense that the bigger and more important things won't change, either. If I keep doing things the way I always do, Sarah will have to come back the way she always does. Probably I made a mistake of some kind a few days ago—did something in a different·order than I'm supposed to—and that's what made her go away.

Sarah and I have been roommates for three years, one month, and sixteen days. I would tell you how many hours and seconds we've been together, but cats don't use hours and seconds. We know that's something humans made up. Cats have an instinct that tells us exactly when the right time for everything is. Humans never know when they're supposed to do anything, so they need things like clocks and timers to tell them. Twice a year, Sarah sets all the clocks in our apartment forward one hour or back one hour, and that just proves how made-up hours are. Because it's not like you can tell everybody to move the world one whole day back or one whole year ahead and have it be true.

You might think Sarah and I are a family because we live together, but not everybody who lives together is a family. Sometimes they're roommates. The difference is that, in a family, everybody does things together, and they do those things at the same time every day. They all eat breakfast with each other, and breakfast is always at the same time in the morning. Then they have dinner together, and that always happens at the same time, too. They take each other to school or work and then pick each other up from those places a few hours later, and both the picking-up and the dropping-off happen on a schedule. I learned all about it from the TV shows Sarah and I watch together. Even the TV shows about families always come on at the same time, every day.

(I used to think that the things on TV were *really* happening, right here in our apartment. Once I tried to catch a mouse that was on the TV screen. I clawed and clawed at the glass and couldn't understand why I couldn't get the mouse. And Sarah laughed and explained that TV is like a window, except it shows you things that are happening far away.)

With roommates, it's more like you have separate lives even though you live in the same place. Things happen when they happen and not at any specific time. Also, families live in houses with an upstairs and a downstairs. Roommates live in apartments. Sarah and I live in an apartment, and our schedule is always different. Sarah says this is because they always change the times she's supposed to work. She types things for a big office in a place called Midtown, and she's so good at typing that sometimes they need her to type early in the morning, and sometimes they need her to type later in the day. Sometimes they pay her a lot of extra money to type all night and not come home until after the sun comes up, which is when most other humans are first *starting* to work.

Money is what Sarah uses to get food for me and to keep our apartment. She always says you have to get it when you can get it, even if you wish you didn't have to. I know just what she means, because sometimes a cat has to chase her food when it runs by, even if she's in the middle of a really great nap. Who knows when the next time food runs by will be? That's why smart cats spend most of their time napping—to save their energy for when they suddenly need it.

But even on the days she doesn't work, Sarah doesn't do things on anything like a regular schedule. Sometimes I have to meow in my saddest voice and paw at her leg to remind her it's time to feed me. I feel bad when I have to do that, because I can tell from her face how unhappy it makes her when she forgets to do things for me. But she usually laughs a little in the way that humans do when they're trying to make something sad into something funny, and says she supposes the reason she's so forgetful is because she has an artistic temperament, even though it's been years since she's done anything creative.

I'm not sure what a "temperament" is. Maybe it's something an artist makes. Or maybe it's something an artist uses to make something else. Whatever it is, though, I've never seen anything like that around here.

You might think from all this that I'm complaining about living with Sarah, but that's not true. Living with Sarah is actually pretty great. For one thing, she's always willing to share her food with me. When she sits down to eat, she usually puts some of her food on a little plate off to the side, and I sit on the table and eat with her. Although sometimes Sarah eats things that are just plain gross. There's one kind of food, called "cookies," that Sarah especially loves even though they don't have any meat or grass or anything in them. Sarah laughs when I turn up my nose in disgust and says I don't know what I'm missing. I think Sarah's the one who doesn't know what's supposed to be eaten and what isn't.

There are two rooms in our apartment. In the room with our kitchen is also our couch and television and coffee table. This is the room people are allowed into when they come to visit us, although people hardly ever come to visit us except for Laura and, sometimes, Sarah's best friend, Anise. Anise only comes over two or three times a year because her job is going on tours in a place called Asia. Laura won't come over if she knows Anise will be here, but Sarah and I are always happy to see Anise because when Anise smiles she smiles with her whole face, and she never says anything even a little untrue. Also, as Sarah likes to say, Anise is a person who understands cats. (As much as a human can, anyway.) When I first came to live with Sarah, she brought home a "self-cleaning" litterbox that would make a terrifying *whirrrrrr* noise whenever I tried to use it. (I think it planned to keep itself clean by never letting me use it.) It scared me so much that I started going on the living room rug just to avoid it, which made Sarah very unhappy with me even though it *clearly* wasn't my fault. This went on for weeks until finally Anise came over and wrinkled her nose at the smell from the rug that now filled our whole apartment. *Ugh,* she said, *doesn't Prudence have a litterbox?* Then she saw the "self-cleaning" monster Sarah had brought home and said, *Sarah, you're scaring the piss out of her with that thing.* (Although really the piss was getting scared *into* me until I couldn't hold it anymore.) She took Sarah right out to buy me a regular litterbox, and we didn't have any problems after that.

The other room in our apartment has our bed and a dresser for Sarah's clothes and—my favorite place—our closet. There's all kinds of fun stuff for me to play with in both rooms, like old magazines that feel like the dry leaves I used to lie on sometimes when I lived outside, and framed posters on the walls that I can jump up and hit with my paw until they go in a different direction. There are shoe boxes of little paper toys that Sarah calls matchbooks, and Sarah says she has a matchbook from every club and bar and restaurant she's been to in New York since she moved here thirty-four years ago. Even though Sarah has a lot of stuff, she's careful to keep everything neat and put-away so there's plenty of room for me to run around. It's the one thing Sarah's good at being organized about.

Way in the back of our closet are a lot of clothes she never wears anymore—she wore them a long time ago, she says, back in her "going-out" days. Some of her clothes have feathers on them, so of course I thought they were birds and tried to catch them with my claws. That was the only time Sarah ever got really mad at me. But if a human doesn't want her clothes chased by a cat, then she shouldn't have clothes that look like birds.

It took me a while, but I've finally gotten the whole apartment to the point where it has a comfortable cat-smell. It's not anything a human would be able to smell, but if some other cat were to come here and try to move in with us, she would know that another cat already got here first. The back of the closet especially has a very homey and safe aroma. Sarah put some old things of hers there for me to sleep on, and it's the closest thing I have to my own private cave.

And, best of all, our apartment is filled with music. Most of it lives on round, flat, black disks that Sarah keeps in stiff cardboard holders. All the cardboard holders have pictures or drawings on them, and some of them look exactly like the posters hanging on our walls. The wall where the music lives, though, doesn't have any posters hanging on it. That's because that whole wall is nothing but music, from floor to ceiling. Sarah tells me I'm not allowed to mark any of it with my claws, which means it belongs just to her and not to both of us. Still, I get to listen to it with her. The black disks don't look like they should be able to do anything, but Sarah puts them on a special silver table that can hold two black disks at one time. Then she presses some buttons and moves some things around, and the disks sing their music. Sometimes we only listen to one or two songs, but there are times when Sarah makes the black disks sing all day. Sometimes, although not very often, Sarah sings with them. That's always my favorite.

It's because of music that I adopted Sarah in the first place.

This was when I was very little and had been living outside with my littermates. We were running away from some rats one day, which are the most disgusting creatures in the whole world. They have horrible long teeth and claws, and they smell bad, and if they're not chasing you to hurt you then they're trying to steal whatever bits of food you've managed to find. Then it started to rain—a huge, terrifying thunderstorm that I was sure would drown every living thing that couldn't find a hiding place. My littermates and I, between running from the rats and then trying to hide from the rain, got separated. I ended up tucking myself under a broken cement block in a big empty lot. I was scared to be alone for the first time in my life, and I started mewing in the hope my littermates would hear me and come find me.

Instead, Sarah found me. Of course, I didn't know she was Sarah then. I just knew she was a human—taller than most of them, with brown hair to her shoulders. She looked older than a lot of the humans who live in Lower East Side, but not *really* old.

Usually, I'm very good at staying hidden from humans when I don't want them to find me. Most people would walk right past my hiding places without ever seeing me. I don't think Sarah would have seen me, either, except that she stopped in front of the lot and stared at it for a long time. She stared so long that the clouds went away and the sun came out, and that's when she spotted my hiding place.

I thought she was just going to walk away and leave me alone. Instead she came closer and squatted down to hold out her hand to me. But I'd never been touched by a human before and didn't trust any of them. Plus, I couldn't understand what she was saying because I didn't understand much of human language back then. I backed up until I fell into a puddle, shivering at how cold the rainwater made my fur.

And that's when Sarah started singing. It was the first time I'd ever heard music—almost everything I'd heard until then were ugly and scary sounds, like machines, and things shattering on the sidewalk, or humans yelling at my littermates and me when they chased us away.

Sarah's music was the most beautiful thing I'd ever heard. I'd *seen* beautiful things before, like the plates of perfect food that people ate at outside tables in warm weather. Or the shady grass under trees in the park that humans go to, which meant my litter-mates and I could do nothing but hide from the humans and look with longing at how pretty the sunlight was and how cool the shade looked.

But when Sarah sang, it was the first time something was beautiful just for me. Sarah's music was *my* beautiful thing, and nobody was going to chase me away from it or try to take it from me.

I couldn't understand the words she was singing, but there were two words her song kept saying: *Dear Prudence.* She sang *Dear Prudence* right to me like it was my name. And it turns out Prudence *was* my name. I just didn't know it yet.

But Sarah knew it all along. That's how I knew I could trust her, even though she was a human. I decided then and there to adopt her, because it was clear we were supposed to be together.

Mice hardly ever find their way into our apartment, but whenever one does I catch it and present it to Sarah, to show her that I'm willing to do things for her in exchange for her doing things for me. And I practice very hard at catching mice even when there aren't any around. I train on empty toilet paper rolls or crumpled-up balls of paper, leaping on them and rehearsing my fighting techniques so that when a mouse does come in, I'm ready. If I work hard, I hope that Sarah and I can be a real family one day, instead of just roommates.

It's as I'm thinking this that I see, from my perch on the windowsill, Laura across the street. She's getting out of a car with a man I don't recognize. Laura and the man are carrying a bunch of big empty boxes.

And I couldn't tell you how I know it. Maybe it's because Laura so rarely comes over even when Sarah *is* here. I get a tight feeling in my belly that spreads up to my back and makes my fur stand up higher than it usually does. My whiskers pull back flat against my cheeks, and the dark centers of my eyes must be bigger because everything suddenly looks too-bright and startling in its clarity.

Even before Laura gets to the front door of our building, every part of my body knows already that something terrible has happened.

2

Prudence

AURA AND THE STRANGE MAN BRING THE SMELL OF OUTSIDE IN WITH them. They also smell like each other. Not *exactly* like each other, because male humans smell different from female humans, but enough so I can tell they live together.

If Laura had come in by herself, I would greet her at the door with a loud demand for explanations. Although humans aren't as good at understanding cat language as I am at understanding human language, a firm and direct *meow* usually prompts a response. For example, if Sarah hasn't remembered to give me a cat treat, I'll stand next to the kitchen counter and meow pointedly. This always makes Sarah either give me a treat or explain why she hasn't by saying something like, *Oh no! We're out of treats! Let me run across the street and buy you some more.* Sarah says this means I have her "trained." Training is what humans have to do to dogs, because a dog doesn't even know when to sit or lie down unless a human tells it to first. (The humans who keep dogs must be *very* patient and kind to burden themselves with such simple-minded creatures.) That's not how I think of Sarah at all. It's not that I *train* her, it's just that sometimes I have to *gently remind* her.

But Laura is here with a man I don't know, so I decide to wait under the couch until I'm sure coming out will be completely safe. Humans can be unpredictable. Sometimes they lunge at me and rub my fur the wrong way, or even (this is so demeaning) *pick me up off the ground*! So all I can do is watch and wait while Laura props the front door open with her foot to allow the man to enter in front of her, then kicks it shut behind her and turns the three locks.

A long time ago Sarah gave me a red collar with a little tag attached to it that Sarah says spells PRUDENCE in word-writing. Sometimes, if I move too quickly, the tag makes a jingly sound. So I creep very slowly to the edge of under-the-couch, where I can get a better look at the strange man with Laura.

He's taller than she is, with light brown hair and dark blue eyes, and he's skinnier than a lot of humans. What I can see most easily, though, are his feet and ankles. He's wearing the kind of feet-shoes called "sneakers" (because they help humans sneak quietly, the way cats do), and they must be old because they're covered in black smudges and dried mud, and there's a little hole he probably hasn't noticed yet just under his left big toe. He hasn't been around any cats lately, because there isn't any fur or cat-smell on his ankles—which is the first place a cat would rub her head to mark him with her scent. One of the laces from his sneakers dangles over the side of his foot. As I watch it wave in a tantalizing way while he walks, the temptation to attack it is almost irresistible. But I force myself to remain still, crouching so low that the fur of my belly brushes the floor and tickles my skin uncomfortably.

Laura is also wearing sneakers, except hers are all white and look much newer. I can tell by the little bumps in the tops of her sneakers that her toes are curled up, which means Laura is tense. She smells tense, too. Even more tense than she usually smells when she comes to visit us. The man with light brown hair must be able to smell her tension, too, because he sets down his own boxes and puts his hands on her shoulders. Sarah always strokes my back when I'm upset about something, like when I think I have a fly cornered but it buzzes out of my reach, or when a car outside makes an unexpected *boom!* sound and frightens me. Laura seems to relax at the man's touch, but when he asks, in a kind voice, "Are you okay?" her toes curl up again and she says, "I'm fine." Then she pushes her fingers through her hair the way Sarah does. "Let's just get this over with."

"We could wait," the man says. "I'm sure the super would understand if . . ."

But Laura is already shaking her head. "Thursday's the first of the month," she says. "If we wait we'll have to take over the rent."

My right ear turns forward so I can hear better when Laura says this. If Sarah's not paying rent money to live here anymore, that means she's decided to live someplace else. The anxious feeling in my belly gets stronger as I try to understand why Sarah would go and not tell me or take any of her favorite things with her. On TV, when two humans are living together and one of them decides to move away, first she tells her roommate why she has to leave (usually it's either because of Her Career or The Man She Loves). The two roommates get angry and fight about it, until they start remembering all the fun they had together. Then they cry and hug each other and they're friends again, and that's when the second roommate, even though she's sad to lose her friend, says she understands why the first roommate has to go and tells her she hopes she'll be happy.

Roommates have to tell each other before they move away. I'm almost certain it's the Law.

Laura has a way of moving that says she knows exactly where she's going and wishes she'd gotten there earlier. That's the way she tries to walk into our bedroom, but she doesn't quite succeed. Her steps are the smallest bit slower than usual, and if she were something I was stalking, I'd probably think this was a good time to pounce.

She tells the man that she'll take care of the bedroom and he should start on the kitchen. She hands him some old newspapers, and at first I think maybe they're going to play one of my favorite games, where Sarah crumples up newspaper and throws it for me to chase so I can practice my mice-fighting. But instead the man is using it to wrap up our dishes and glasses before putting them into the boxes. He even wraps up the big ceramic bowl that lives on the little table next to the front door. That's the bowl I like to sleep in when my body tells me it's almost time for Sarah to come home, so I can be right there at the door when she walks in. Once, when I was especially excited to see Sarah, I jumped out of the bowl so fast that it fell on the floor and broke. The sudden crashing sound drove me all the way into the bedroom and under the bed, where I stayed twitching my fur for a long time. But Sarah was very patient and calm as she glued the bowl back together. There were cracks in it after that, but Sarah said that was okay, because cracks are how the light gets in.

Laura and the man work silently, except when Laura tells him that the Army is coming over later to pick up our furniture and kitchen things and some of Sarah's clothing. I don't know what the Army is going to do with a bed that smells like me and Sarah sleeping together under the covers on cold nights. Or a couch that smells like the time I accidentally spilled a glass of milk all over it (it was the glass's fault; it was pretending to be shorter than it really was), and I got so startled because the milk splashed on me so suddenly, and because I thought maybe Sarah would yell at me, but she only scooped me up and pressed her cheek to the top of my head and said, *Poor Prudence!* Then she hugged me tighter and said, *Oh, Prudence, life would be so boring if you weren't here.* (Which was so obvious she didn't need to point it out.)

I don't understand what use the Army could have for those things, but there's a lot happening right now that I don't understand. Sarah once knew a man who lost his cat and everything else he'd ever had, all on the same day. After that, Sarah said, he didn't want to live anymore. Maybe Sarah left because she knew Laura was going to come here with this man to take all our beautiful things away and she couldn't stand to see that happen. And now it occurs to me for the first time that if Sarah is going away, along with all our furniture and everything else we need, I might have to go away, too.

I crouch down lower under-the-couch and wish Sarah would come back and explain things. She could have told me before she left, even if the reasons why she had to leave were frightening or confusing. She *knows,* more than any other human, how much I understand.

Cats always understand things. That's why we make such good roommates.

Laura and the man with light brown hair are in opposite sides of the apartment, which means I can only watch one of them at a time. Even though my whiskers will let me follow the general movements of whichever one of them is behind me, I can't decide who I should follow with my eyes. Then Laura finds the floorboard in the bedroom that sounds like a human voice crying out when you step on it the wrong way. This brings my attention instantly to her. The doorway to the bedroom is exactly opposite the right arm of the couch, and by creeping all the way to the edge of the space underneath the couch, I can see into the bedroom and watch Laura work.

She and Sarah don't look exactly alike, but enough so you can tell Laura must have come from one of Sarah's litters. Their hair is the same color and length. Laura's not quite as tall as Sarah, but she's stretchier, and when she stands on her tiptoes to reach something on a top shelf she can reach as high as Sarah can. Her eyes are lighter than Sarah's and not as round, and her jaw is more square-shaped, and the makeup she usually wears when she comes over makes these differences more obvious. Laura isn't wearing any makeup today, which is unusual. The skin under her eyes is darker than normal, which makes her eyes look almost as dark blue as Sarah's, and her skin is so pale that it's even lighter than

Sarah's. She and Sarah have the exact same hands, though—surprisingly big for such slender humans, with long fingers.

Laura's hands are shaking a little now, but they still manage to make precisely folded and ordered stacks of things. She pulls Sarah's clothes from our closet with the kind of efficiency I use when burying something in my litterbox. From the clothes Sarah wears to the office, Laura creates a tidy, four-cornered pile. She uses a fat black pen to put word-writing on one of the brown boxes, which she then fills with Sarah's work and everyday clothes. Sarah's other clothes, the ones with shiny stones and fringes and feathers that I used to think were birds, go into a less tidy pile, and then Laura puts the pile of bird-clothes into a garbage bag.

Sarah doesn't wear the bird-clothes often, but I can tell (at least, I thought I could tell) that they matter to her like everything else in our apartment does. *It's important to keep your past organized,* Sarah likes to say.

One night three months ago, Sarah was on the phone with Anise and kept using the word *remember* a lot, like when she said, *Remember the first time I came to hear you guys play Monty Python's? That place was such a pit!* or *Remember the night that crazy woman chased us down Fourteenth Street with a knife? And we had to beg that cabbie to get us out of there even though we didn't have any money?*

That didn't sound funny to me, but Sarah laughed until she couldn't breathe. I'd only heard Sarah laugh that long and loud when I had one of my *very* rare clumsy moments. Like the time I tried to run straight through a closed window (how was I supposed to know that you could *see* through something but not necessarily *run* through it?), or once when I reached up to a paper plate on the kitchen table to try a *tiny* bit of the food on it, but instead the plate and all its food fell on my head. (I still say that was Sarah's fault; she should *never* have left a plate of food on the edge of the table like that.)

After Sarah hung up with Anise, she pulled a bunch of boxes and bags from the big closet in the living room. She took some black disks off the shelves and the apartment filled with music while the two of us looked through the matchbook toys. (Actually Sarah looked through them and I batted them around, because what good are toys if you don't play with them?) She kept saying things like, *I completely forgot about* this *place!* or, *This was the very first club that ever let me spin, and I had to do it for free. It was so much harder for girl DJs.* She showed me newspapers and magazines so old they don't make them anymore, full of word-writing (which I can't understand, but Sarah read some of it to me) about the music she used to listen to and the places she used to go to hear it. Then Sarah went into the bedroom and put on the outfits she hasn't worn since she as young.

She was so happy while she looked at herself in the mirror in those clothes! Except that after a while her face turned a light pink, and finally she shook her head and murmured the word *stupid* under her breath. Then she changed back into her regular nighttime clothes, silenced the black disks, and tidied up the apartment before getting into bed.

The best thing about all that old stuff isn't that it helps Sarah organize the past. The best thing is that it smells like the two of us, here together in this apartment. And now all those clothes and everything else in our closet is disappearing into that bag and those boxes. I twitch the fur on my back to try to stay calm.

Maybe if I get to go with the bag and boxes, the things in them will still smell like me. But unless Sarah comes back, little by little the Sarah-smell will disappear from them. And then one day there won't be anything left in the whole world that smells like the two of us together.

By now the bedroom looks empty, the bed naked the way it is on laundry-doing days when I help Sarah dress it in fresh sheets by running from corner to corner of the mattress to make sure the sheets don't go anyplace they're not supposed to. Laura is holding one of the Army boxes, to carry it into the living room, when the sound of a door slamming in an apartment upstairs startles her and makes her drop it. *"Dammit!"* she mutters under her breath. Water rushes to fill her eyes, and she wipes it away impatiently with the sleeve of her sweater.

"Laur? Are you all right?" the man with light brown hair calls from the kitchen.

"I'm okay, Josh," she calls back. Her voice sounds shaky, and she takes a deep breath. "I *hate* these old walk-ups," she adds. "You can hear everything."

I realize now that I've heard about this man. The last time Anise visited us was seven months ago, and Sarah told her then that Laura was getting married to someone named Josh. Anise seemed surprised Laura was getting married at all, and Sarah said she was surprised at first, too, but that Josh was a Good Man. Anise said Laura's marrying a Good Man was pretty miraculous, all things considered. Then they started talking about the man Sarah used to be married to, and I fell asleep eventually when I realized nobody was saying *Prudence.*

Josh has made the kitchen empty, too, and everything that used to live there is in a box or a garbage bag. It doesn't look like our kitchen anymore, and the only way you could tell a human and a cat ever used it is because my bag of dry food is still sitting on the counter. When Laura comes out to wipe down the counters with a spritzy bottle and paper towels, she looks at the food and then looks around the apartment, as if she's trying to see where I am. But then she just pushes the food bag to one side and keeps cleaning.   •

I've never seen Laura look sad before, but today she seems sad. Her eyes fill up with water again as she moves into the living room, although she quickly blinks the water away. And the sadness is there in the way she talks, too. Usually Laura forms her opinions quickly and sticks to them, and you can tell, when she and Sarah disagree about something, how impatient she gets when Sarah hesitates and says, *Well, maybe you're right . . . I don't know . . .* And even though I always sympathize with Sarah, because she's my Most Important Person, privately I agree with Laura that Sarah just needs to make up her mind. That's part of the reason why

Sarah and I get along so well, because I have strong opinions even when she doesn't. Sarah always, for example, asks what I think about what she's wearing before she goes out. If I like it, I stare at her with my eyes very big and put all my wisdom and approval into them. And if I don't like it, I close my eyes slightly and turn my head off to the side, like maybe I'm just sleepy, but Sarah knows what that means. And she'll say, *You're right, this skirt needs a different jacket,* and change into something better before she leaves.

But when Laura tells Josh she guesses they should get started on the big closets in the living room, she almost sounds confused. Instead of saying, *We should get started on the big closets in the living room,* she asks, *I guess we should get started on the big closets in the living room?* Even saying *I guess* instead of just *we should* is more uncertainty than Laura usually shows.

I'm not sure what's so confusing to her about this room. Everything in here seems ordinary to me. Maybe it looks and smells a little dustier than usual, with Sarah not having been here to clean for almost a week. My litterbox smells bad all the way from the bathroom and that's embarrassing, especially when there's a stranger here who doesn't know how tidy I usually am.

But I don't think it's dust or the litterbox that's making Laura hesitate. Then it comes to me: Laura feels the way I do. She didn't expect Sarah to leave any more than I did, and now she's confused and sad because she has to decide what to do with Sarah's and my stuff. I've been waiting for her to say something about where Sarah went and why, but she's been left behind by Sarah just like I have.

Realizing that even Laura didn't know Sarah was leaving makes me feel for the first time that I really might never see Sarah again. It feels like my stomach is trying to squeeze all the way through the top of my throat. It feels worse than when humans used to shout at me on the streets, or the day I lost my littermates in that thunderstorm.

Now I want desperately to come out, to tell Laura that maybe Sarah *will* come back if only we don't move all her things that smell familiar and make her recognize this as her home. But Laura hasn't called to me the way Sarah would, or tried to introduce me to the strange human in the way it's supposed to be done. Too much is unusual today already, and the thought of coming out from under-the-couch the wrong way, without anybody even saying, *Prudence, come here and meet so-and-so,* the way Sarah always does, makes my stomach squeeze even harder.

It's Josh who first goes to the big closet and starts pulling things down. The shoe boxes of matchbook toys spill over his head. I expect him to be mad the way most humans would be if all those matchbooks fell on them, but he just says "D'oh!" and rubs his head in an exaggerated way, pretending the matchbook toys hurt him. From the way his eyes flick over to Laura I think he's hoping she'll laugh, because humans think it's funny when things fall on other humans.

Laura smiles, but that's all.

"Look at all these," he says, crouching down to scoop up a handful of matchbooks. "Paradise Garage, Le Jardin, 8BC, Max's Kansas City." He puts them back in their box. "The writers I work with would kill to have spent five minutes at Max's Kansas City."

Laura has finally started on the other closet, the smaller one near the front door. She's going through boxes of papers, some of which she puts into folders that disappear into a big brown box. The others go directly into a garbage bag. "Just throw all that into trash bags," she tells Josh. "The Salvation Army won't want it."

Maybe the Army won't want those things, but *I* do! How could Laura not even *ask* me what I want to do with my own (well, Sarah's and my) things?

Josh pauses when Laura says this, his hand in the middle of reaching up to pull things from the top shelf. He continues moving his hand in that direction, although he does it more slowly, the way you move to keep from startling a small animal. "You don't want to throw it *all* away. Your mom wouldn't have kept all this stuff if it didn't mean something to her. Someday, when you're ready, you'll want to go back and look through it."

Laura sounds exasperated, just like she does whenever Sarah objects to what Laura thinks is a perfectly logical plan. "Where would we even put it all?"

"There's the spare bedroom," Josh says in a quieter voice than the one he's been using. "We could put everything there, temporarily at least."

Laura's face changes just enough to let me know she doesn't like this idea. If it were Sarah's idea, Laura would keep arguing until she made herself right. But now she mutters, "Fine," and keeps going through papers. Josh puts the matchbook toys back in their shoe boxes, then puts the whole thing into one of the big brown boxes. They're both quiet again, until Josh struggles with a buldgy paper bag all the way in the back of the big closet. Once he's freed it he peers inside and says, "Oh, wow!" Pulling out some of Sarah's old newspapers and magazines, he says, *"Mixmaster, New York Rocker,* the *East Village Eye."* His eyes go up and a little to the left, which means he's remembering something. "My sister used to go into the city with her friends and bring these back for me. I still haven't forgiven my mother for deciding they were 'trash' one day and throwing them all out."

Laura has been stacking up Sarah's coats and jackets, which smell more like her than anything else. Why does she have to make *everything* of Sarah's go away? Sarah once told me that if you remember someone, they'll always be with you. But what if the opposite is true? What if getting rid of everything that reminds you of someone means they'll never come back to be with you again? I feel the muscles around my face whiskers tighten and pull back again.

Laura doesn't know this, of course. She turns to face Josh, and when she sees the bag he's looking through, she squints and walks over to where he's sitting on the floor. She picks up the bag and looks at the script-y word-writing on its side. Then she says, "Love Saves the Day."

"Hm?" Josh says. He's still flipping through the old newspapers.

"Love Saves the Day," she repeats. "That's where this bag is from. It was that vintage store on Seventh and Second." Now Laura's eyes slide up and left. Her voice sounds softer, the way Sarah's does when she's telling me about something nice that happened to her a long time ago. "My mother and I used to go there sometimes when I was a kid. We'd spend hours trying on ridiculous outfits and then go up the block to Gem Spa for egg creams."

Josh grins up at her. "Do you have pictures?" I can tell he's imagining Laura, except much smaller than she is now, wearing clothes like Sarah's bird-clothes. He looks around the room. "I keep hoping to find your baby pictures, but I don't see them anywhere."

The black centers of Laura's eyes widen a little and her face colors, which is how I know what she's about to say will be at least partly untrue. "We lost them in a move."

"Oh." Josh sounds disappointed and unconvinced. But all he says is, "That's a shame." He looks toward the table next to the couch, where Sarah and I keep a lamp and some framed pictures that I've learned to maneuver through without knocking them over. Josh says, "Well, at least there's a picture of your mom and her cat." He looks around the room. "Hey, where *is* the cat?"

Laura's head doesn't move. "Hiding under the couch."

I'm not "hiding"! I'm waiting! Of course, I could never expect a human to understand a subtle difference like that. Still, this is probably as close as Laura is going to come to requesting my presence for a proper introduction. So, partly to give Laura a chance to do things the right way, and partly to make it perfectly clear to these humans that I was *not* "hiding," I crawl out from under-the-couch and announce myself with a curt *mew*. Then I begin an elaborate stretching-and-grooming ritual, as if to say, *Oh, is somebody here? I didn't even realize it because I was napping so deeply. I certainly wasn't hiding, if that's what you were thinking.*

It's easy to fool them, because humans have a much harder time detecting untruths than cats do.

"Well, hey, Prudence," Josh says, turning to face me. "You look like a sweet girl. You're a sweet girl, aren't you?"

The condescension in his tone is unbearable. I fix him with an icy stare and swish my tail to remind him of his manners, and then I go back to cleaning my face with my left front paw. Josh slowly reaches out a hand toward the top of my head, but I stop him with a warning hiss. Talking to someone you haven't been properly in-troduced to is rude, but *touching* someone you haven't been prop-erly introduced to is far worse. Laura laughs for the first time since she's been here and says, "Don't take it personally. Prudence isn't a 'people cat.'"

Josh and Laura watch as I begin cleaning behind my ear. Why are they paying such close attention to how I wash myself? Then Josh says, "I'm happy to have her come live with us, Laur, but if you wanted to find another home for her, I'd understand. Every-body would understand."

Laura is silent for a moment as her eyes look into mine. I keep my face carefully expressionless, not wanting her to know how nervous I am thinking of all the unbearable change that would come from having to live in a new place with strangers. "It was important to my mother that Prudence stay with us," Laura finally says. "She was very specific about it in her will."

I think about the day I met Laura. I was still small then, and I'd only been living with Sarah for four weeks and three days. Sarah said, in the voice she only uses when she's talking to me, "Pru-dence, this is my daughter, Laura." Laura stiffened when I ap-proached her the way I knew I was supposed to when Sarah spoke in that voice. She didn't bend down to get closer to me, she didn't move at all, but her eyes followed me. "I'm sure she'd like it if you pet her," Sarah said, and although I dislike being touched by hu-mans I don't know well, Laura smelled enough like Sarah to make me think that maybe I'd also adopted her when I adopted Sarah. I rubbed against her ankles and even purred for her. Not as much as I purr for Sarah, but enough to let Laura know I accepted her.

She and Sarah shared a smile when they heard me purr, and I didn't know back then how unusual it was to see the two of them smile at each other happily like that. Then Sarah said, "Animals have always liked you. I remember how crazy the Mandelbaums' cat was about you."

And just like that, Laura's whole face changed. One time, when I was still very small, Sarah didn't see me in front of her and she stepped on my tail. The pain of it spread all the way up my back. And the sharp suddenness of that pain made me angry, so angry I hissed and whapped out at Sarah with my claws. That's what Laura's face looked like in that moment. First there was a fast and terrible pain, and then there was anger, just as fast and terrible, at Sarah for causing it. Laura stopped smiling and her shoulders got stiffer.

"Honey," Laura told Sarah. "The Mandelbaums' cat was named Honey." And then, using her voice the way I'd used my claws, Laura said, "I don't even know why *you* want a cat, Mom. I didn't think you cared about them all that much."

Sarah's face looked sad then, although she didn't try to defend herself. She knew she had said the wrong thing, even though I could tell she hadn't meant to.

I don't want to go live with Laura. I don't want to live anywhere with anybody except right here with Sarah. But if Sarah isn't paying money to live here anymore, that means I can't live here anymore, either. Apparently Sarah knew she was leaving and wanted me to live with Laura. Maybe she's planning to come back and wants to be sure she knows exactly where to find me. That must be it!

The relief I feel as I realize this is wonderful—so wonderful it's all I can do to keep from collapsing into a deep, luxurious nap as the tension leaves my body. Still, I can tell by the way Laura is looking at me that she's thinking about what Josh just said, how he would understand if Laura wanted to send me to live somewhere else. I remember how happy her face was for a moment when she heard me purr that first day, and I think she must like cats more than she's willing to say right now. (What's *not* to like about living with a cat?)

So, ignoring Josh with his bad manners, I walk over to Laura and pat her leg with my paw, claws sheathed, the way I do when I want Sarah to pay attention. Then I rub my head against her ankles, to mark her with my scent and make her understand that she has no choice about whether or not to take me with her.

Laura doesn't reach down to pet me, but she does sigh in a resigned-sounding way. The tightness in my stomach relaxes even more, and I rub my head harder against her legs.

Josh may never have had a cat to teach him proper manners, but spending only a few minutes with me has already made him smarter. He doesn't say anything, but when he hears Laura sigh he can tell as plainly as I can that it's been settled.

The sun is getting lower and the apartment is almost empty. The closets have been cleared out, the rugs rolled up so the Army can take them when they come for the furniture. The posters on the wall that I used to love batting in different directions have been taken out of their glass frames and rolled up so they fit into the boxes of things that are coming with us. It looks and smells so different that, already, it's getting harder for me to remember the life Sarah and I had together here. My plastic carrier is waiting by the door, and even though I usually hate getting into it (because the only time Sarah puts me in it is when she's taking me to the Bad Place), I crawl in now voluntarily. I know I'm not going to the Bad Place today. And, besides, it's almost the only thing left here that smells like Sarah and me at the same time.

When Laura and Josh rolled up the rugs, they found the old squeaky toys Sarah used to bring back for me when I first came to live here. She always said how bad she felt that I had to be alone while she was out working, and she wanted to make sure I had something to play with and to make sounds for me when I was by myself. She never understood that I *liked* having my own quiet space and being alone sometimes. Maybe that was because Sarah never really liked being alone.

Those toys weren't as interesting to me as the matchbook toys or the newspapers Sarah crumpled up (it's no fun to play with things you think you *have* to play with; it's much more fun to play with stuff you just find), and I lost track of where they were a long time ago. But I remember how happy it made me when Sarah first brought them home. That was how I knew, even though she was never good at keeping to feeding schedules or things like that, that she was thinking about me even when she wasn't here to see me. Just like I thought about her even when she was gone. It meant I was right that day when I decided to adopt her.

I'm still angry with Sarah for leaving me without saying goodbye. Mostly, though, I just hope I get to see her again someday. She's the only human I've ever loved.

The only things still unpacked in the whole apartment are Sarah's collection of black disks and the special table she plays them on. Josh washes his hands before he touches them, and from the way he approaches I can tell how badly he's wanted to look through the black disks since he first walked in. I don't like it, because those are *Sarah's* black disks and even *I'm* not allowed to touch them. But Sarah doesn't live here anymore. She must have had her reasons for leaving them, and that must mean that wherever she's living now, she still gets to hear music.

"I can't believe how many there are," Josh says to Laura. "I don't think I've ever seen a vinyl collection this big."

"I never noticed how big it was, either," Laura says. "She must have kept more than I realized after she sold the record store."

"There's such a range." The way Josh sounds makes me wonder if maybe not all humans have a wall of black disks like Sarah does. From behind the metal bars of my carrier I can see Josh in pieces, the way I used to see the world in pieces when I'd crouch beneath our big window and look up through the fire escape bars. He sits down cross-legged in front of the records. "Look at all this."

"My mother was mostly into dance music," Laura says. "But her roommate was in a punk band and the two of them swapped records a lot."

Josh grins. "I guess that explains why she's got the Dictators' *Go Girl Crazy!* shelved next to Disco Tex and the Sex-O-Lettes."

"Let's pack them up. We can look through them later at home," Laura says. When Josh hesitates, she turns her mouth up at the corners and says, "Scout's honor."

Josh nods. Then he says, "Oh!" He stands and walks over to an open brown box and pulls something from it. "I didn't wrap this because I thought you might want it for the apartment."

Laura walks over to see what Josh is holding. It looks like one of the framed photographs that used to live on the table next to the couch.

"How old was she here?" Josh asks. "She looks so young."

Laura takes the picture from his hand. "She was nineteen. This was right before she had me."

"She was beautiful." Josh looks at Laura and smiles. "Like you."

"No," Laura says. "I'll never be as beautiful as my mother was."

At first I think she's doing this thing called modesty, which is when humans pretend not to be as special or good at something as they know they really are. (This is something a cat would never do.) But there's too much sadness in her smile when she adds, "When I was little, I always used to think how lucky I was to have the prettiest mommy."

"Our kids will feel that way about you someday." When Laura doesn't respond, Josh puts his arm around her shoulders and says, in a gentler tone, "They will, Laur. I promise."

It seems like a nice thing for him to say. Especially since it's hard for me to judge human beauty (anything stripped of its fur and forced to walk on its hind legs looks naked and awkward to me). It doesn't seem like there's any reason for Laura's eyes to fill with water again because of what Josh said. But they do.

I think Josh wants to give Laura privacy to make the water go away, even though she swallows hard a few times and blinks it back before it can fall. He goes over to the black disks again, takes one out, and puts it on Sarah's special table. Music fills the apartment one more time. It's so much like the kind of thing Sarah would do that, for the first time, I think maybe I could get to like Josh. He even sings along with the music, the way Sarah sometimes used to.

Love is the message, love, love is, love is the . . .

* * *

Most of the big brown boxes stay in the apartment for the Army to come and take them. The rest are carried down by Laura and Josh to the giant metal box on wheels that's attached to the car. Laura carries the garbage bags down the outside hallway to Trash Room. She leaves the front door open when she does this, and through the open door I hear her footsteps pause on her way back from Trash Room. Then I hear her go back and pull one of the garbage bags out. Her footsteps get faraway sounding, like she's taking the bag outside, and I guess she's adding it to the boxes we're bringing.

I stay in my carrier the whole time. I have to. Laura has closed and locked it, which is just plain rude because didn't I get in here of my own free will? Is there any good reason to treat me like some stupid dog trying to run out of a kennel? I think humans don't even realize how much they insult cats' dignity sometimes. But I don't have long to be angry about this, because Laura quickly comes back inside and picks up my carrier. I catch one last glimpse of the apartment through its bars and wonder if I'll ever live here again.

Laura takes me outside, and I have to close my eyes halfway because the sun is getting so bright as it comes through the crisscrossed bars of my carrier. She climbs into the car and settles my carrier on her lap, and Josh gets into the car through the other door, so he can sit behind the big round thing that makes the car go.

I've never been in a car before. The feeling of it isn't so bad once I get used to the sensation of something other than legs moving me forward. It's even soothing me into drowsiness, and I have to fight to keep my eyes open, because I don't want to miss anything. I had no idea how much I'd never seen before until now, watching everything that moves past the windows of the car.

The farther away we get the wider the streets are, until I'm positive we're not in Lower East Side anymore. Some of the streets are so wide I can't believe they're real. And the buildings! I can't even see the tops of all of them, although I stretch my neck as high up as my carrier will allow me. I never saw buildings this tall in Lower East Side. In some of their windows I see other cats, lounging in the late-day sunlight or batting at curtains that try to block their views. I wonder if they'll get to live in their apartments forever, or if maybe one day they'll have to move away like I am because their humans stop coming home. I wish I could ask them. Maybe one of them knows what you're supposed to do to make a human return after she's left you.

Josh tells Laura he's going to take the West Side Highway. We drive past a wide river, which holds more water than I ever imagined seeing in real life. There are boats on the water, and people in other kinds of strange, smaller machines that let them move on top of the water as if they were running on it. (I've always felt sorry for humans because they have to get all the way into water to get clean, but here are these humans doing it for no good reason!) The sidewalks near the river are a swarm of humans holding food, shopping bags, or the hands of smaller humans. One of them is throwing bread crumbs to an enormous flock of pigeons and—oh! How wonderful it would be to jump into the middle of that flock and show those silly birds who's boss!

Laura rolls down the car window on our side, and all kinds of smells come rushing to my nose. The mixture of aromas makes me think of the time before Sarah, when I lived outside with my littermates. I can smell other cars, and birds, and humans sweating in their coats, and the scent of new, fresh dirt. It's that time of year when the cold starts to go away, so I can smell flowers, too, and other things I can't name because I'm too overwhelmed. I wish I could stay where we are long enough to identify every single thing I smell and give it its proper name.

And if I did get to stay here—right here on this very spot—I would never have to go to Laura and Josh's apartment. I would never have to start the life I'm going to have to live, at least for now, without Sarah in it.

3

Prudence

THE HUMAN WORD FOR SOMEONE WHO MOVES FROM ONE COUNTRY to another is *immigrant*. I moved from Lower East Side to Upper West Side, which is obviously all the way on the opposite side of the world. And if it's on the other side of the world, then it must be a whole different country. This means I'm an immigrant, too. (Sarah used to talk about the immigrants in Lower East Side who had to move away because apartments got expensive, just like I had to.)

TV says that immigrants sometimes get homesick. I've been here sixteen days so far, and I was sick for the first five of them. That's how long it took just to get used to how different the food is in Upper West Side. I was nervous about *everything* being so different, and having different food, too, was more than I could bear. I heard Josh tell Laura that they should buy me something "better" than the "cheap" food Sarah used to feed me. (Oh, I loved that food! I wish Sarah was here to tell Josh to buy me the food I like.) He brought something home in a can and told Laura it was "organic." That's a word humans use to describe food that comes from a farm instead of a factory. Except the food came in a can, and cans only come from factories, so how could it be in a can *and* be organic?

Trying to figure out what exactly was in my food that smelled so different from the good food I'm used to made my stomach sick and nervous. The only time I came out of the closet in the upstairs bedroom (which is where they put all the Sarah-boxes) was when I had to throw up. This made Josh worry and tell Laura that maybe they should take me to the Bad Place, which only made my stomach clench tighter. But Laura went out and bought a can of the food I'm used to and mixed some of it with Josh's new food. Even though it wasn't as good as just my regular food by itself would have been, at least it smelled familiar enough for me to eat without feeling nervous.

Now Laura mixes some of my old food with the new food every morning, except each day there's more of the new and less of the old. I think Laura's trying to trick me into not noticing, so that one day soon she can put down just the new food and none of the food I like. As if that would fool a cat!

When I lived with Sarah, my first feeding of the day was always a happy time. I would stand next to her at the kitchen counter and meow for her to hurry up (humans tend to dawdle when they're feeding cats) while she emptied the food into my special Prudence-bowl. Then I'd run in excited circles in front of her feet while she carried the bowl to the kitchen table where I could eat it.

I can't do the same thing with Laura, though. For one thing, Laura is never in a happy mood when she comes into this room with all the Sarah-boxes to put my food down. She doesn't like it here, in a way that has nothing to do with my living in here most of the time. I can tell by the way the tiny hairs on her arms rise slightly when she enters, or just walks past the doorway. And even if I wanted to run around in circles (which I don't), the floor in here is so crowded from the Sarah-boxes that there isn't room for me to run without bumping into things.

Also I can't eat in front of Laura the way I did with Sarah, because I don't want Laura to know too much about my eating habits. For example, I have to drink three laps of water for every five bites of food. When I lived outside, I learned that water that's been standing still for a long time usually tastes bad. Now I like to rattle my water bowl with my right paw before I drink from it, so I can see the water move and keep it tasting fresh. Sarah understood this and only filled my water bowl up halfway. But Laura fills it all the way to the top, so some of it sloshes onto the dark, polished floor and leaves light spots on the wood when it dries. Laura's mouth presses into a straight line when she sees those spots, and I think she'd be mad if she saw me sloshing the water bowl on purpose. Yesterday she brought home a blue rubber mat with ridiculous cartoon drawings of smiling cats all over it (is this what Laura thinks cats are *supposed* to look like?), and she put it under my food and water bowls so nothing spills onto the floor anymore. Probably it would have been easier to just stop filling the water bowl so high, but even if I had a way of suggesting this to her, I doubt she'd listen. *Laura has to do things her own way,* Sarah always says. I guess I should be grateful she still lets me eat in here, with all of Sarah's and my old things around me, instead of insisting I eat someplace else. I don't think I'd be able to force much down without having safe, familiar smells around me.

I haven't been getting enough sleep, which also makes me feel less healthy and alert than I used to. Sleeping is usually one of my favorite things to do, and this is something humans would be wise to learn from cats. Humans never seem to get enough sleep, and Laura and Josh haven't napped *once* since I've been here! (The last few months I lived with Sarah, she was smart enough to follow my example and started napping with me more frequently.) But sleeping is harder for me now, because every time I wake up I get confused about where I am and why everything smells different. I have to remember all over again that I live with Laura and Josh now instead of Sarah, and when I remember it hurts from my chest all the way down to my stomach. It's gotten so I'm afraid to fall asleep because it hurts so much to wake up.

Sometimes, though, I get fooled for a few moments, and that's the hardest of all. Like right now. It's early in the morning, before anybody's left for work, and I'm in the back of the closet having just opened my eyes. I smell the can of my old food opening and see a woman with Sarah's hair bending over my bowl. *Good morning, Sarah,* I meow. Sarah looks up in surprise, and when her hair slides back from her face I see it isn't Sarah at all. It's Laura who's looking at me, wondering why I just meowed when I've been quiet most of the time since I've been here. It was Laura's hair, so much like Sarah's, that tricked me.

Besides her voice when she sang, just about my favorite thing about Sarah was her hair. I loved to rub my face against it and bury my nose in it. I could spend hours batting at it with my front paws, or watching Sarah twisting it in and out of ponytails, or noticing the way each strand sparkled and turned a slightly different color from the other strands in the sunlight that came through our windows. Once I was sitting behind Sarah's head on the back of our couch with my nose and mouth nestled in her hair, and I chewed off a big mouthful. Sarah got mad (although she couldn't help laughing when she saw me sitting there with a chunk of her hair in my mouth as if it were a mouse I was carrying back to my den). I don't know why I did it, exactly, except I was thinking how nice it would be if I could have some of Sarah's hair to take with me to my little cave in the back of our closet.

One of the times when Anise came over to our apartment, she cut Sarah's hair for her. Anise's hair always looks different every time she comes over. Sometimes it's very short and straight, and other times it's long and curly. Sometimes she even puts streaks of different colors in her hair, like green or pink.

Anise always tells Sarah that she's been wearing her hair the same way for thirty years—long and straight—and that she should change it now and then "just for fun." (What's *fun* about change?!) This one time, though, she actually talked Sarah into it. Anise sat her down in one of our kitchen chairs with a towel around her neck, and attacked Sarah's head with scissors until her hair was much, *much* shorter. While Anise worked they talked and laughed about The Old Days, when they were young and too poor to afford new clothes or professional haircuts, so Anise made their clothes and cut their hair for them.

I was miserable when I saw Sarah's beautiful hair falling in sad little clumps to the floor, and for the first time I didn't like Anise very much. But Laura's reaction was even worse. When she came over three Sundays later and Sarah opened the door, Laura's face froze. Her eyes widened and got shinier than normal. "Your hair!" she cried. "What happened to it?"

"You don't like it." Sarah made this a statement instead of a question.

"No, I just . . ." One hand moved up from Laura's side as if she was going to touch the side of Sarah's head, although it stopped before it got there. "I'm surprised, is all," Laura finally said. "What made you decide to do something so radical?"

"I was ready for a change. Do you like it?" Sarah almost looked shy. "Anise did it for me."

Laura made a sound like a snort. "That's Anise," she said. "You can always count on her for the little things." She emphasized the word *little*.

Laura's hair looks and smells like Sarah's, although she spends more time straightening it in the mornings with a loud hair dryer than Sarah ever did. Laura cares about hair a lot. That must be why she got so upset when Anise cut Sarah's off.

Sarah let her hair grow back long and never tried cutting it short again after that. When Laura visited, her eyes would travel to the top of Sarah's head and down the length of Sarah's hair while Sarah chattered at her. I think she was waiting for Laura to notice and say something about it. But Laura never did.

Laura doesn't usually linger in this room, but sometimes—like now—she'll spend long, quiet minutes after she feeds me looking out the windows, watching a flock of pigeons on the rooftop of the building across the street. You can see these same pigeons from the tall living room windows downstairs that go from the floor to the ceiling and make up two whole walls of the room. The pigeons are the same color as coffee when you add cream to it, which is an unusual color for pigeons. Other than that, though, I don't see what's so interesting about them. But Laura can't seem to move her eyes away. She even winds a single strand of hair around one finger, the way Sarah always does when she's thinking deeply about something.

I've tried watching the pigeons also, to see what Laura finds so fascinating, but all the pigeons ever do is fly around in big circles for an absurdly long time, and then come back to land on the rooftop. Naturally I hadn't really expected to see much because pigeons aren't even as smart as *dogs,* if you can believe it.

The room is silent while Laura watches the pigeons and I crouch in the closet waiting for her to leave. Upper West Side is quiet in ways that Lower East Side never was. In Sarah's and my apartment, when the windows were open, I could hear squirrels and large bugs turning in the earth, birds singing while they nested in trees. People would walk along the sidewalk, their voices talking into tiny phones and the sounds drifting up to the third floor where Sarah and I lived. Cars drove past with music flying out of their rolled-down windows to announce that they had arrived. Like the way the man who lives in the lobby of this apartment building calls Laura and Josh to announce when their pizza or Chinese food is on its way upstairs. In Lower East Side, even when our windows were closed, you could always hear people talking in other apartments or water moving through pipes in the wall. Sometimes I would hear loud *crack!* sounds without being able to tell where they came from. It used to startle me until Sarah explained that it was just our building "settling."

There are neighbors and cars and birds here in Upper West Side, too, but the street is so far below us that you can't hear any of its sounds. I never hear people talking or playing their televisions loudly in their own apartments next to this one. Most days, after Laura and Josh have left for work, the only thing I hear is the jingle of the Prudence-tags on my red collar as I walk from room to room. Sometimes, if I've been sitting still for a while, I meow loudly and send the sound of it echoing from the walls and ceilings, just to make sure I haven't gone deaf.

Sarah never liked it when things were too quiet. Maybe that's why she played music and watched TV all the time. She would chatter and chatter at Laura whenever Laura came over to visit, afraid of the silence she would hear if she stopped because Laura never had much to say in return. Sarah told Anise once that Laura had built a wall around herself with silence. I used to imagine Sarah's chatter going *chip, chip, chip* at this wall, even though I couldn't see where the wall was. It must be different for Laura in Upper West Side, though, because she and Josh talk all the time.

Josh walks past the doorway now, in the nicer clothes and dark feet-shoes he wears to work. Laura's own work clothes match each other a lot more than Sarah's. Today she wears a black jacket and matching black pants with shiny high-heeled black shoes. The only thing that isn't black is the white blouse she wears under her jacket.

Josh pauses when he sees Laura standing in front of the window and says, "Everything okay?"

"I'm fine." Laura smiles a little and turns to face him. "Just daydreaming."

Something about the way Josh's eyes narrow and widen makes me think he notices more than most humans do. Whenever Laura's talking to him, his eyes zip all over her face, and you can tell how interested he is in what she's saying. It's not like when Sarah's eyes stayed focused anxiously on Laura's face without moving, or when Laura would look off to the side while Sarah was talking to her. Sometimes, though, when Sarah would turn her eyes to watch me do something, Laura would look into her face with an expression that was hard to describe. The skin at her throat would tighten, as if she was about to say something. But by the time Sarah looked at her again, Laura's face would be wearing its normal expression, and she would say something unimportant to Sarah like, *This is good coffee.*

Josh's eyes leave Laura's face now just long enough to look around the room once. "Where's Prudence?"

"Hiding in the closet." My tail swishes when I hear Laura describe what I'm doing as "hiding" instead of what it really is—waiting for her to leave already.

"She sure does love that closet," Josh says.

"She just needs some time." Laura plucks a strand of my fur from the sleeve of her jacket. "I don't think she's very comfortable yet. It doesn't seem like she's sleeping much."

Josh walks toward Laura and brushes his hand gently across her cheek. "There's a lot of that going around these days."

Laura touches his hand with her own, but takes a small step back so he's not touching her face anymore. "I'm fine," she repeats. Then she looks down at the watch on her wrist and says, "We're going to be late if we don't get a move on."

I listen to the sound of their feet-shoes going down the stairs and wonder how much longer I'll have to live here before Sarah comes to take me back to Lower East Side.

Every morning, after Laura and Josh have left for work, I wander around the apartment trying to find a place where I can feel comfortable enough to settle into the kind of long, good sleep I need more and more desperately as the days go by. It's hard to sleep well, though, when nothing smells the way it's supposed to. Laura makes this problem worse because she's always cleaning and wiping things down with foul sprays and polishes that smell the way humans think things like lemons and pine trees are supposed to smell when they grow naturally outdoors. She especially hates it when there are any crumbs or bits of food on the kitchen counters or floor. Crumbs are how you end up with roaches and mice, Laura says (although she really doesn't have to worry about that while *I'm* here), and I remember Sarah saying how they always had to be careful about that in the apartment they lived in together when Laura was a child.

I crawl in and out of the Sarah-boxes, looking for a way to get comfortable among the smells I know. I press my cheeks on the things in the boxes, rubbing Sarah's smell into me and my smell into the Sarah-things, but the boxes are too full for me to find a place to lie down and sleep. Yesterday I tried burrowing into the big Love Saves the Day bag that was lying on its side in one of the Sarah-boxes. I thought that, since it already smells like Sarah's and my apartment, if I could dig all the way into it I could surround myself with that wonderful Sarah-and-me-together smell, as if it were a cave.

It took a while to drag all the newspapers and magazines out of the bag to make enough room for me to squeeze in. But once I got all the papers out, I realized there was something made of cold metal—completely uncomfortable to lie against—at the bottom of the bag. Even using my "extra" toes, I couldn't pry it out. When Josh came home and saw all the old newspapers scattered on the floor, he chuckled and said, "Looks like somebody had a good time today." I don't know what made him think that (I'd had anything *but* "a good time"), but he must have liked that idea because he was smiling while he put the newspapers and magazines back together. It took him longer than it needed to, since he was reading them while he straightened everything out. He stuffed the magazines and newspapers back into the Love Saves the Day bag, then took the bag into Home Office, which is the room right next to this one. I guess that's sensible. There are already lots of magazines in that room anyway, because Josh works for a company that makes magazines.

Now I creep slowly into Home Office, listening for footsteps—just to be sure—even though I already heard Laura and Josh leave for the day. Home Office is far too crowded with what Josh calls "memorabilia" and what Laura calls "junk" (although she smiles teasingly whenever she says this) to be a truly comfortable room for me. But there *is* a wonderful heated cat bed that rests on the desk in front of a small TV screen. Attached to the bed is a toy mouse on a leash, which just goes to show how little humans like Josh know about mice. In the first place the toy mouse looks nothing at all like a *real* mouse, and in the second place no mouse would ever let a human put a leash on it, because even mice are smarter than dogs.

Josh likes to use this cat bed as a scratching post, exercising his fingers on it without stopping for hours on end. They make a *clackety-clack* noise and not the clawing sounds that usually come from a scratching post. If he sees me sleeping on it—using it the *right* way—he chases me off so he can take over and use it the wrong way. So now I come in here to nap lightly for brief stretches during the day while he's gone. The first few times Josh saw me sleeping here, he told me that my having to stay off it was a "rule." If I weren't so tired from not sleeping enough, I probably would have thought Josh giving me "rules" was funny. All cats are born knowing that there's no point in paying attention to unreasonable rules made by humans. Besides, what humans don't know won't hurt them.

I'm able to sleep for a little while, but everything still smells too foreign for me to relax very much. I step carefully from the cat bed to the desk, from the desk to the chair in front of it, and then leap from the chair to the floor. Then I make my way back to the room Laura feeds me in. The room with all the Sarah-boxes.

Laura might not like coming into this room very much, but I do have to admit that she's very good at keeping to a schedule—much better than Sarah. She feeds me at the same time every morning except on Sundays, which is the only day when Laura doesn't go to her office. She works in a law office like Sarah, and Laura must do something even more important than typing because the humans in her office need her to do her work just about every second she's awake. When she comes home at night she brings big stacks of paper with her so she can do even more work here in the apartment. She wears glasses while she reads her work papers, and probably she wears the glasses in her office, too. There are always faint pink marks on the sides of her nose from where they press into her skin.

Laura's workdays are much longer than Sarah's ever were, and it's usually long after dark before she comes home to give me my nighttime feeding. Most nights Josh goes out with friends from his own work, but even so he still gets home before Laura. Sometimes he tells her that he wishes she could come home earlier, and Laura explains how her clients' businesses would fall apart if she didn't do as much work as she does, and then her bosses would give her even less work in the future. Getting less work sounds just fine to me, but Laura obviously thinks this would be a bad thing. It seems like the more work some humans do, the more work they *have* to do, which doesn't make any sense. But very little of the way humans think about things makes sense to me.

The walls in this room are painted yellow, and the paint in here smells new. The floor is made of smooth wooden boards that have been polished until they shine in the sunlight like water. The first few days I was here, I thought maybe the floors really were made of water, they were so slippery. It took me days to learn how to walk here without my hind legs sliding out from under me if I ran or turned too quickly.

These same slippery wooden boards cover all the floors in the rest of the apartment, and even Laura and Josh slip a little on them sometimes. The other day Laura slid right into Josh as they were walking down the hall, and he reached out and grabbed her before she fell. I would have hated having a human grab me that way, but Laura squirmed and laughed. She laughs at a lot of the things Josh does. Sometimes he crumples a paper napkin in his hand, brings his hand to his mouth, and then coughs—making the crumpled paper napkin fly out. *Oh, excuse me,* he'll say. *I don't know how that happened.* It looks ridiculous to me, but Laura always rolls her eyes and laughs. This hardly seems fair. When *I* cough up a hairball for real, Laura doesn't roll her eyes affectionately while she cleans it up and say, *You're so funny, Prudence!*

This room is mostly empty aside from the Sarah-boxes and four dark brown wooden chairs with black leather seats, which live stacked up in one corner. I tried marking just *one* of the chairs in this room with my claws the way I'd marked our couch in Lower East Side (all I wanted was to make this room feel more like my own), but Laura saw me and said, "*No!* No, Prudence!" in a sharp voice. I don't see why she had to get so excited. She could have calmly said something like, *Prudence, marking chairs is bad manners in Upper West Side,* and I would have understood her just as well. Maybe even better.

I don't really need the chairs anyway, though, because the two big windows have sills for me to lie on while I look at things outside. This apartment is so high up that from the windows I can see all kinds of things I never thought about before. Like what the tops of buildings look like. Some of them have black tops, and some of them are white, and some have little brick areas where humans grow flowers and sit outside in the sunshine. A few of the roofs have these giant, pointy-topped round things I once heard Josh call "water towers." All around us is more sky than I've ever seen, and when the sun is very bright and the sky is very blue, I see little squiggly things behind my eyes if I stare at it too long.

If Sarah lived here with me, she would probably carry one of those chairs from the corner next to the window, so the two of us could sit and look out at the sunshine together. She'd hum and stroke my fur while I sat in her lap, and maybe she'd even sing the Prudence song to me until I fell into a deep sleep.

But I'm alone in here almost all the time, and the only music anybody has sung to me since I left Lower East Side is the memory-music Sarah sings inside my head.

I hear a key turning in the lock of the front door downstairs, and from all the jingling I know it's Josh. Laura must always have her key ready as soon as she steps out of the elevator. I never hear her jingling keys around, looking for the right one, before she comes in.

The sound of Josh's feet-shoes comes up the stairs, and the faint scent of his cologne that smells so much stronger in the mornings drifts past as he walks toward his and Laura's bedroom. After he changes out of his work clothes into socks and sweat-clothes, he spends a little while clackety-clacking on the scratching post in Home Office. Then he goes downstairs to listen to music in the living room while he waits for Laura. I hear the muffled sounds of it coming up through the floor of my room.

Most of Josh's music lives on small silvery disks that go in a different kind of machine than the table Sarah uses to make her black disks sing. He also has a few black disks, although not nearly as many as Sarah. Even Sarah didn't have more than a few when I first adopted her. Her posters and black disks and the special "DJ" table she plays them on were living by themselves for years and years in a place called Storage. It was only after I'd been living with Sarah for nearly two months that she went out one day and brought them home. *It was you, you know,* Sarah murmured later, when we were on the couch listening to the black disks together. *You brought my music back. I thought I'd lost it forever.* I rolled onto my side and purred, because I could tell from Sarah's voice and hands how much love there was between us in that moment. But I didn't know what I'd done to give Sarah back her music. Maybe I'll do whatever it was again. Maybe (if I have to be here that long) in a couple of months Laura and Josh will drive out to Storage one day and come back with hundreds of their own black disks.

Josh likes music almost as much as Sarah. If he's listening to music and Laura is in the room, he'll pucker his lips and put his hands on his hips and pretend to strut around. He looks pretty foolish when he does this, but it always makes Laura laugh. Or he'll take Laura's hand and put his arm around her waist, and the two of them dance for real. It makes me wonder if Sarah would have liked to have another human to dance with when she used to listen to music in our old apartment.

Sometimes lately, because I haven't slept well in so long, I get confused about what's really happening *now* and what's a memory or part of a dream I might be having if I were asleep. A breeze from the open window in my room makes the white curtains move. When its shadow on the opposite wall moves, too, I think for a moment that I see Sarah here in this room, bending down to stroke the fur of my back and saying, *What should we listen to tonight, Prudence?*

I stretch for a long moment, pushing my front paws all the way out in front of me and arching my back. My tail stretches, too, pointing straight up and curling at the tip. I have to get up and move around, or else I'll just lie here not really sleeping and not really awake, thinking I see Sarah everywhere. The hurt I feel when I remember Sarah *isn't* here starts to spread from my chest to my belly again. Trying to make the hurt leave me alone, I stand up and walk toward the stairs.

I used to wish Sarah and I lived together in a house with stairs, but it turns out stairs are tricky if you're not used to them. I'm trying to figure out if it's better to move each of my four legs individually to the step above or below me, or if I should move both of my front paws at the same time and then sort of hop with my back ones. I try to practice the stairs when Laura and Josh are out of the apartment so they won't see me. That would be embarrassing. *Poor Prudence doesn't know how to use stairs!* they might say, and chuckle at my ignorance. Two days ago, I happened to walk into Josh and Laura's bedroom and saw the two of them rolling around on top of each other in the bed, making odd noises. It was the least dignified thing I'd ever seen in my entire life. I have no intention of making myself look equally foolish in front of them.

There's a spot exactly halfway down the stairs where the floor gets flat for a little way before turning back into steps. When Laura and Josh are home, I can still practice walking up and down the top half of the stairs and then rest on the flat spot, peeking around the wall to watch what they're doing in the living room.

The smallest part of the living room is the dining room next to the kitchen, which has a long table of dark wood and four matching chairs that look exactly like the ones that live stacked up in my room. The only time I've seen Laura and Josh in the dining room is when they pay bills and talk about money. Laura worries that they're not putting enough into savings, and Josh says Laura worries about money too much. Once I heard Laura tell Josh he only thinks that because he doesn't know what it's *really* like to have no money at all.

Even though this apartment is much bigger than Sarah's and mine, Josh and Laura don't have nearly as much stuff in it as we did. There's nothing hanging on the walls, and none of the "knick-knacks" Sarah loves so much, like beautiful little glass bottles or the prisms she hung in our windows to make the sunlight sparkle and dance in different colors. Sarah used to keep plants, including a special kind called "cat grass" that was good to eat when my belly was upset with me. Here there's only one plant that lives in a corner of the living room, and it's made out of silk.

There are some framed photographs on shelves—mostly pictures of Josh at different ages, doing things like standing outside in the snow (which is just cold water!) holding up a pair of big wooden sticks or on a stage somewhere with lots of other young-looking humans, wearing funny costumes. There aren't nearly as many pictures of Laura, and none from when she was younger. There are a few of Laura and Josh together on the day they got married, and also from their honeymoon in a place called Hawaii. (There's a lot of water in the background of the honeymoon pictures, so Hawaii must be near that river we drove past on our way to Upper West Side.)

There's also one from their wedding day of just Laura and Sarah. Laura's wearing a plain, short white dress with a little white jacket and holding a cluster of long, beautiful white flowers. Sarah's dress is light purple. This is my favorite photograph, because I remember when I helped Sarah decide that this was the outfit she should wear to see her daughter get married. It makes me happy to look at it, even though Laura and Sarah don't really look comfortable, posed stiffly, each with one arm around the other.

Now Josh stands up from the couch and walks past the shelves with the photographs on his way into the kitchen. I hear the sound of heavy pans being jostled free from a cabinet, and after a few moments the smell of cooking floats toward the stairs. It smells like Josh is making eggs, although that can't be right. Josh only makes eggs on Sunday mornings, and Laura goes out to get bagels for them to eat with the eggs. Laura says Josh makes the best scrambled eggs ever, although I wouldn't know because nobody's thought to offer me any the way Sarah would if she'd cooked something for breakfast.

It's always bad when things happen in a different way than they're supposed to, but when the thing that's different is with your food, that's the worst of all. I think maybe, even though she likes Josh's eggs, Laura is going to be upset when she comes home and finds out Josh is making them on a Tuesday night instead of a Sunday morning. But what actually happens when Laura finally comes through the front door, and then walks into the kitchen to see what Josh is doing, is that she says, "What's all this?" in a voice that sounds surprised and pleased.

"Breakfast for dinner," Josh says. "I had a jones for scrambled eggs. And I thought it might help you sleep. You usually go right back to bed after breakfast on Sundays."

"I don't go back to bed *alone*." Laura isn't laughing, exactly, but her voice sounds like she's smiling.

"Hey, I'll try anything if it helps you relax."

"Thanks," Laura says, in what Sarah would call a "dry" voice. Then I hear the wet, puckering sounds Josh and Laura make when they put their mouths together. After a moment, when the sounds stop, Laura says in a quieter voice, "You don't have to worry about me, Josh. I keep telling you. I've just got a lot on my mind, with work and everything."

There's a clatter of plates and silverware, and then the sounds of Laura and Josh walking from the kitchen to the living room couch, where I can see them again. The two of them talk about what they did at work all day while they eat. When the music that was playing stops, Josh walks across the room to where his music lives. This time he takes out a black disk instead of one of the small silvery ones.

The song that starts playing sounds like one Sarah and Anise used to listen to the two or three times a year when Anise came over. Something about a "personality crisis." The two of them would act silly, singing into things like hairbrushes and empty paper towel rolls as if they were the microphones that singing humans on TV use. Anise has a nice singing voice (even though her regular speaking voice is deep and scratchy), and I can tell Sarah likes Anise's singing better than her own. After all, Sarah says, Anise is famous for her singing.

Humans and cats must like different things in singing voices, because I think nobody has a nicer voice than Sarah. Anise would always say how Sarah should have tried being a singer professionally. I would rise up on my hind legs, butting my head against Sarah's hand because it made me so happy when she sang. And Anise would bend down to scratch behind my ears the way I like and say, *Look—even Prudence agrees with me!*

But Sarah says she never had that Thing Anise has that lets her perform on a stage in front of other people. That's what she liked about being a DJ, she says, and about the record store she opened after she stopped being a DJ. She could still give people music without having to stand in front of them. *And anyway,* Sarah would say to Anise, *I was never as talented as you.*

All I hear for a few moments is this song and the sound of one fork scraping across a plate. Josh is still eating, but Laura's fork is hanging halfway between her plate and her mouth. Then Josh says, "Is everything okay?"

"Hm?" Laura shakes her head slightly, the way Sarah does when she's trying to "clear her thoughts." "I'm sorry," she says. "I got distracted."

Josh's face flushes pink, although I can't tell whether this is because he's embarrassed or because he's about to say something that isn't true. "*I'm* sorry," he says. "I wasn't thinking. I saw this same record in your mom's collection when we were cleaning out her apartment."

"Probably," Laura answers. "She liked the New York Dolls."

Josh is watching Laura's face, which is trying to look the way it normally does, and would almost succeed if not for the crease between her eyebrows. Finally, Josh says gently, "Why don't we go upstairs when we're done and go through some of her boxes,

We can do the records over the weekend. I really think," he adds in a hurried way, as if he's afraid Laura might cut him off, "you'll sleep better once it's done. And if we cleared a few out of the way, we could make life a little better for Prudence. I see her pacing around that room all the time. She hardly has space to turn around in."

The muscles around my whiskers tighten. If Josh *really* cared about me, he'd know that the very last thing I want is to see even one of those boxes go away.

Also, if he really cared about me, he'd have let me try some of his eggs.

"Prudence is still getting used to being in a new place," Laura says. "She'll be fine. And I've got a ton of paperwork to go through tonight." She stands, holding her plate.

"Don't worry," Josh says. "I'll clean everything up."

"Thanks," Laura tells him, and stoops to kiss him on the cheek.

The apartment is silent, except for the scratch of a pen against paper from where Laura works on the living room couch. Josh went to bed a long time ago. From my spot halfway down the stairs, I can see that Laura is tired, too. Every so often she pauses to push up her glasses and rub her eyes. She doesn't go upstairs to bed, though. Probably because she knows that even when she does, she'll spend hours flipping from side to side and kicking at the sheets, the way she seems to every night.

Something has been tickling at my left ear, and twitching it back and forth doesn't make the tickle go away. Finally I reach my back left paw around to scratch at it with my claws. This makes my Prudence-tags jingle, and Laura looks up, startled. Our eyes meet. It's the first time she's seen me in this spot. My body tenses, waiting to see if she's going to do anything.

"Hey, Prudence," she says softly. "Can't fall asleep?"

I've heard Laura and Josh talk *about* me since I came to live here, but this may be the first time Laura has talked *to* me. This makes me feel nervous, for reasons I don't quite understand. Rising to a crouch, I turn and take the top half of the stairs at a hop, then scurry down the hallway, staying close to the wall, back into my darkened room with all the Sarah-boxes. My Prudence-tags ring the whole way and only stop when I dart into the back of my closet.

Laura comes into my room and pauses. Even though she can't see me hidden back here without turning the light on, I can tell she knows that this is where I am.

The dark outline of her shape crosses the room and kneels in front of one of the Sarah-boxes. There's a bang and rustle of things moving around, and then the crinkling noise of a heavy bag being pulled out from beneath heavier things. I remember, now, Laura going back to Trash Room to get one of the plastic garbage bags she threw out the day they brought me to live here.

Laura approaches the closet and I scurry backward, my backside in the air as I keep my nose pressed tightly to my front paws. "Here you go," she whispers as she hunkers down onto her heels and thrusts something into the closet toward me.

It's one of Sarah's dresses from her "going-out" days, dull gold with a white diamond-shaped pattern on it. I remember thinking, that day when Sarah tried on all her fancy bird-clothes, that I'd never seen Sarah look prettier than she did in this dress from when she was younger than Laura is now.

I creep cautiously toward the dress, kneading at it with my front paws to make it into a more comfortable shape. Already I can tell that having something soft with that good, familiar, Sarah-and-me-together smell to lie in is going to make it easier for me to sleep tonight. Laura continues to crouch in front of the closet, and when I look up from the dress, her eyes are looking into mine again. We look at each other, and then, very slowly Laura closes her eyes and opens them again. This was something Sarah did, slowly close and open her eyes when I was looking at her, and I feel a rush of exhaustion wash over my body. As my eyelids droop Laura slowly blinks at me again.

My eyes close into sleep so quickly that I don't even hear when she leaves the room. It isn't until the next day—when I wake up after having slept late into the morning for the first time since I can remember—that I realize some things are the same everywhere. Even here in this foreign country, all the way on the other side of the world from the home I was raised in, somebody has taught Laura the correct way to speak cat.

4

Prudence

JOSH AND LAURA KEEP SAYING HOW UNUSUAL IT IS FOR THERE TO BE snow so late in April, but that's just what happened this week. A giant snowstorm came in with such hard wind that it blew the snow sideways. Back in Lower East Side, you would have been able to hear the wind howling through the cracks between the window frames and the wall. It was odd to see so much wind outside while inside, the apartment stayed silent.

Sarah used to laugh when I would press my nose against the windows during snowstorms, trying to catch some of it on my paw. Even knowing I couldn't get to it through the glass—and even knowing how cold and nasty the snow would be if I *could* get to it—the urge to catch some as it fell was irresistible. Laura and Josh went to their offices anyway, even though it was snowing so hard. With nobody here to laugh as I batted at the windows, trying to catch snowflakes, suddenly didn't seem like as much fun as it used to be.

The day it snowed, Josh came upstairs to my room with the Sarah-boxes to pull out his and Laura's heavy winter coats from the back of my closet. He'd thought they'd put them away for the year and wasn't expecting to have to wear them again so soon. He also wasn't expecting to find so much of my fur clinging to the wool. He complained to Laura about it, which just seems unreasonable. After all, my fur is what keeps *me* warm, so having some of my fur on their coats could only keep Laura and Josh warmer, too. Really, Josh should be *thanking* me, if you think about it.

Not that most humans know how to show cats the gratitude we deserve.

Josh asked Laura if maybe they should start closing the closet door to keep me out, and the fur on my back twitched hard at the thought of losing my favorite dark, cozy sleeping place. But Laura laughed and said it would be easier to move the coats to another closet than to get a cat to change her habits.

Two weeks after Laura gave me Sarah's dress to sleep with, things between us haven't changed a lot. It's true that I'm sleeping *much* better than I was, now that I have something that smells like Sarah and me together to curl up with. I also spend a lot more time downstairs, now that I'm more used to things. Laura's eyes have a way of following me whenever she looks up from whatever work papers she has in front of her. Sometimes her fingers bend and straighten, and I can tell that she's thinking about touching me. She hasn't tried to pet me so far, though.

Nobody has petted me at all since Sarah went away, which seems like a long time ago now—five weeks. When I think about that, it doesn't make me miss being touched by a human. It just makes me miss Sarah all the more.

Even though, with all the snow, it doesn't feel like springtime, Josh and Laura are having his family over to the apartment tonight for a springtime holiday called Pass Over. Sarah and Anise used to talk sometimes about the casual "potluck" holidays Sarah would have in her Lower East Side apartment when Laura was young. Neighbors and friends and people who worked in Sarah's store would come in and out all day whenever they felt like it, bringing food with them and eating foods the other humans had brought while Sarah played music on her DJ table. Christmas was one of only two days in the whole year when her store was closed. The other was Thanksgiving. Thanksgiving wasn't so bad, Sarah said, but there would always be at least one person who would call her at home on Christmas Day, begging her to open the store just long enough to sell him one last black disk he needed to give some other human as a gift. When you're raising a daughter alone, according to Sarah, you have to get your money when you can. So she would run over to her store long enough to sell that one black disk to that one human, and then it was good there were so many people in her apartment to keep an eye on Laura while Sarah was gone.

I don't know how Upper West Side humans celebrate holidays, but it doesn't seem like there's anything "casual" about Josh's family coming over. It's Monday morning now, and Laura spent all Sunday attacking our apartment like she was mad at it. She's always cleaning things whenever she has a few extra minutes, but yesterday she *cleaned* everything from the floors to the ceiling until every speck of dirt was gone and the apartment smelled unbearable from cleansers. She even cleaned under the bed in her and Josh's room. Josh laughed when he saw her doing this and told her that his mother wasn't going to inspect under their bed. But Laura said it was the first time his parents were coming over for dinner since they'd gotten married, and she wanted everything to be "immaculate."

While Laura was busy cleaning, Josh went out to buy special foods to serve to his family. Everything went into the refrigerator when he got home, and now whenever Laura or Josh opens it, the smell of wonderful meats and other things I've never tasted before drifts all the way upstairs. I hope Laura remembers to be generous when she arranges my special Prudence-plate of food at dinnertime tonight.

I don't know who exactly in Josh's family is coming over, but the one person I know *won't* be coming is the man who used to be married to Josh's sister. That's because yesterday I heard Josh say, "At least I don't have to look at that Dead Beat at holiday dinners anymore."

I'm not sure what a "Dead Beat" is. Anise used to say that Laura's father was also a Dead Beat. But Sarah always used the word *beat* in a positive way when she was describing the music she loved. Anise also said that Laura's father was a talentless good-for-nothing. He tried being in a band, and then he tried being an actor, and he was even a photographer for a little while, but he never stuck with anything long enough to become good at it, although he took that picture of Sarah that Josh brought to live with us here, and I see Laura looking at it sometimes when Josh isn't in the room with her.

I know what *dead* means (it's what happens to mice, for example, when cats catch them), but I also know how unusual it is for humans to say anything bad about dead people, because they can't help being dead. So maybe being a Dead Beat means a human who makes really awful music and then forces everybody to listen to it until they *wish* they were dead. That doesn't seem exactly right, though. I almost wish the Dead Beat *was* coming over tonight, so I could see what one looks like.

The thump of Josh's feet coming into my room distracts me from my thoughts. He must be waiting for Laura, because he doesn't do anything except stand there in the middle of the floor next to the Sarah-boxes. His eyes make a quick circle of the room without seeing me in the back of the closet, and they come to rest on the boxes of Sarah's black disks. Crouching down, he starts to flip through them. My ears flatten against my head when he takes one out to look at the back of its cardboard cover. Those are *Sarah's* black disks! It's one thing if *Laura* wants to look at them (I guess), but for Josh to go through them by himself seems wrong.

Josh must be thinking the same thing, because he seems cautious at first, keeping one ear tilted toward the door, but it's like he can't help himself. And he's forgotten all about his caution when

Laura's footsteps approach. "Look at this!" He turns his head up to her. "There's a picture of your mother on the back of this Evil Sugar album! Right here." He holds the black disk in its cardboard cover up to Laura, pointing to a spot I can't see from where I am. "There she is with Anise Pierce in front of the Gem Spa awning."

"She and Anise were roommates." Laura's voice sounds like she doesn't really want to talk about this. "Before Evil Sugar moved out to LA."

It's funny to hear Josh call her "Anise Pierce," because Sarah always calls her "Anise's to Pieces." Back before Anise was famous, crazy things always seemed to happen to her. Sarah teases Anise that she couldn't even go out to buy a can of tuna for her cats without getting hit by a car or having her purse stolen or a tree branch fall right onto her head, or making some poor guy fall desperately in love with her at first sight—and usually all those things would happen in the same day.

"This was my favorite album in junior high," Josh says. "I was obsessed with that whole generation of New York bands recording at Alphaville Studios." He laughs. "I was devastated when Anise Pierce married Keith Amaker. That's when I tried to convince my mother to buy me a drum set. I figured if drummers got girls like Anise Pierce, then I'd be a drummer, too." Josh turns the cardboard cover over in his hands. "I never realized how tiny she was until I saw her standing next to your mother." He looks up at Laura, his eyes shining with excitement but also looking confused. "How could you not tell me your mom knew her?"

"It never came up." Laura shrugs. "Come on, let's get these chairs down to the dining room before we're late for work."

Josh seems reluctant as he puts the black disk back into the box with the others, but he walks with Laura over to the black chairs that live in the corner without saying anything else. "There'll be seven of us tonight, right?" Laura asks.

Josh puts one hand on her shoulder. "It's not too late to call it off," he says gently. "My parents would understand if you weren't ready yet for a houseful of people."

"Don't be silly. We've been planning this forever." Laura turns her head around so she can smile up at him, although her nostrils widen slightly the way humans' do when they're irritated. "And I keep telling you, I'm *fine*. Honestly."

Laura carries one chair and Josh carries two as they pick their way around all the boxes on the floor. This is the only room Laura didn't clean yesterday. She still doesn't like coming in here, and I notice how her eyes don't look into the Sarah-boxes on her way out, just around them to make sure she doesn't bump into anything.

I think about that man Sarah talked about once—the one who lost his cat and all his reminders and didn't want to be alive anymore after that. I wonder why Laura doesn't want to look through these boxes and remember Sarah with me, so both of us can make sure she has a reason to come back.

The day seems to go by more slowly than usual while I wait for Laura and Josh to come back so tonight's wonderful holiday dinner can get started. I try to pass the time by sleeping in the places I don't get to sleep in when Josh is home, like the cat bed on the desk in Home Office and the spot on the couch where Josh likes to sit and watch TV sometimes while he waits for Laura to get home from work. I've learned, though, that if I roll onto my back and pretend to be deeply asleep, Josh isn't as likely to make me move. "She looks so comfortable," he says to Laura. "I feel guilty." Whenever he says this it makes me feel sorry for humans, who are forever doing the wrong thing and then having to feel guilty about it.

I'm also drawn again and again into the kitchen, even though none of the holiday foods have started cooking yet. I should probably spend more time here, because kitchens are where some of the best things live. In Lower East Side, the kitchen was where I sometimes found things that are lots of fun to practice my mice-fighting with, like the twisty-ties that keep bread closed in its bag, or the plastic straws that Sarah sometimes uses to drink her sodas through. (I could never make Sarah understand what straws are really supposed to be used for, although I tried to show her many times. Finally I started hiding my straws under the refrigerator or the couch, so she wouldn't try to take them back from me to use the wrong way.) And there are delicious things to eat and drink in the kitchen even when there isn't a holiday dinner, like tuna fish from a can, or the thin pieces of turkey meat that live inside crinkly paper in the refrigerator. Sarah had to stop keeping things in the kitchen like cream for her coffee and cheese when the doctor said dairy products would be bad for her heart. Maybe if I come in here more often when Laura and Josh are here, I could get some of those little treats again.

The day may have *felt* long, but I can still tell that it's much earlier than usual when I finally hear Laura's key in the lock. It isn't even dark outside yet. I knew Laura was anxious about tonight, but I didn't realize she was *so* anxious that it was worth leaving work early for.

Laura and Josh did something this morning to the dining room table to make it long enough to fit seven chairs. Now Laura reaches up to the highest cabinet in the kitchen for cloth mats (which are much nicer than the rubber mat she put underneath my food and water bowls and don't have insulting cartoons of smiling cats all over them). Then she goes to the front-hall closet and drags out two huge, heavy boxes. From these she starts taking out fancy plates and glasses that are nicer than the plates she and Josh usually eat off of. Laura's hands move slowly, and she lingers to look at each plate as she sets it out. Once everything is on the table, she looks out the tall windows behind the table and watches the coffee-colored pigeons across the street. She stares at them so long that I turn to stare, too, but as usual the pigeons aren't doing much of anything except flying in pointless circles.

It isn't very long until Josh comes home. He comes up behind Laura to give her a big hug. "I can't believe you got home so early!" he says happily.

"Pass Over is a time of miracles and wonders," Laura tells him, using her "dry" voice.

Josh goes upstairs to wash his hands, and when he comes back he starts helping Laura, pulling platters down from the higher cabinets and taking bottles out of the refrigerator while Laura turns the oven on. "Do you think your mother will be offended we got all the food from Zabar's instead of making it myself?"

Laura sounds worried, but Josh laughs. "She'll respect you for it. Zelda hasn't cooked voluntarily in years."

The air in front of the oven isn't even hot yet, which means it's still going to be a while before the food is ready. I decide that napping in the closet upstairs is the best way to make the time shorter between now and when I can eat. As I'm leaving, I hear Josh tell Laura, "I'm going to vacuum in the spare bedroom. I was noticing this morning how dusty it is in there."

"Sounds good," Laura says, in a distracted-sounding voice. My Prudence-tags ring softly against my red collar as I climb the stairs, and I hear the dull thud of Josh's footsteps following me.

I've just settled down comfortably in the back of the closet when Josh flicks on the light in the ceiling. There's so much extra light all of a sudden that I can't see much—just the blurry shape of Josh standing in the doorway, pushing what looks like a tall triangle with a handle at the top and a flat square thing on wheels at the bottom. It's attached to a leash, which Josh plugs into a socket on the wall right next to the door.

My eyes adjust to all the new light, and now I see Josh leave this strange object so he can walk over to the Sarah-boxes. He starts moving them around and pushing them into arrangements different from the one they're supposed to have—the arrangement I've spent days memorizing. I rush out from the closet to leap onto the boxes, thinking that maybe the extra weight of my body will make them too heavy for him to move. But I don't slow him down at all. He just says, "Come on, Prudence, out of the way," in what he probably thinks is a friendly voice, nudging me gently on my backside with his foot until I'm forced to jump out of one box after the other.

Once the boxes have been lined up in two rows on either side of the floor next to the rug, Josh goes back to the strange thing standing in the doorway. He kicks its base and a white light comes on. Then it begins to scream!

It screams and screams without stopping even to catch its breath. It doesn't scream like something in pain, but like something that's vicious and wants to hurt somebody. Maybe even a cat! It's a monster—just like the monsters I've heard about in TV movies that everybody says aren't real. Except this one is! It roars in anger because Josh holds tight to its neck and won't let it get free, even though it gnashes and pushes itself back and forth trying to break away from him—glaring fiercely right at me from its one awful eye that lights up near its mouth. It gobbles up all the spilled litter from my litterbox and the little bits of my fur that have rubbed off over the last few weeks. It has to move over the litter a few times before it gets it all, but it sucks my fur right up. It's trying to find me! It's not satisfied with just the scraps of my fur—now it wants to eat a whole cat!

I knew Laura didn't like having all the Sarah-boxes up here, but I never thought she'd send Josh to *kill* them—and me at the same time. I try bravely to defend at least one row of Sarah-boxes from this terrible monster. I puff up all my fur, to make myself look much bigger than I really am, and I hiss at it and rake its smooth head with my claws as a warning. Humans are usually intimidated by this, but The Monster is obviously much stronger than any human—except Josh. He just says, *"Shoo!,"* waving his hand in my direction as if I were a dog he was chasing away. That he can control this horrible beast with *only one hand* must mean he's the strongest human in the entire world. Finally I give up and run to hide deep in the closet, my heart racing. I can hear The Monster roaring near the closet door, but it doesn't come in after me. Probably it can't see very well because it only has the one eye. Still, I don't know how well it can hear, and my heart is beating so loud! I concentrate on trying to quiet my heartbeat, and soon I hear The Monster's roar get fainter and fainter, until I know it's gone to look for cats in another room.

I wait until I can't hear it at all anymore before I dare to creep out of the closet again. None of the Sarah-boxes seems to be hurt, although everything's in the wrong place.

I crouch in my upstairs room for a long time, so long that the sun is coming in low through the windows the way it does when it will be dark soon. The aroma of meat cooking in the oven is what finally draws me down the stairs again.

I walk cautiously through the living room and dining room. The meat-smell in the kitchen is so powerful that I hardly know what to do with myself.

I'm usually in perfect control of everything I do, but today the meat's will is stronger than my own. It uses its scent to pull me to the spot right in front of the oven and hold me there, with so much power that I couldn't resist it even if I wanted to.

So this is where I curl up and fall into only a half sleep. I want to stay at least a little alert, because as soon as that meat comes out of the oven, I'm going to demand that Laura or Josh feed some of it to me. Otherwise I won't get any, just like with the eggs.

I had thought that I'd be able to circle around the food until it was ready, the way all my instincts are telling me to do. But it turns out that I won't get to. That's because the moment Josh's family finally gets here, I'm forced—most rudely—out of the kitchen.

Josh's family are his mother and father. They're older than any humans I've seen in real life (other than on TV, I mean). They drove a car here from a place called New Jersey. Josh's sister also comes and brings her litter with her, a small girl and an even smaller boy. They're the *youngest* humans I've ever seen up close and not on TV. *They* took a train here from Washington Heights. I know this because when Josh opens the front door, everybody says how funny it is that they all got here at the same time, even though they came from different places.

"*Chag Pesach*," Josh says as he kisses them all on their cheeks. Then he says to the little girl and boy, "That means *Happy Pass Over* in Hebrew."

The little girl says, "I *know*," in a voice of such offended dignity that, for a moment, I think I'm going to like her. "They taught us that in Hebrew school. Actually," she adds, "you're *supposed* to say, *Chag Pesach sameach.*"

"Duly noted." Josh sounds amused. "I keep forgetting how smart ten-year-olds are these days."

I decide the little girl is like me—somebody whose intelligence is underestimated by humans just because she's small. But when she and the little boy walk past the kitchen and spot me guarding the food, they squeal, "Oooh, a *kitteeeeee*!" Then they both run at me with their hands outstretched, not even giving Josh a *chance* for an introduction. And when I turn and flee from this attack, the little wretches *chase after me*! I race for under-the-couch as fast as I can. The two of them kneel and plunge little hands that smell like fruit juice and snack chips after me, trying to grab at my tail and bits of my fur!

I'm in so much shock from this display of horrible manners (has *nobody* bothered to teach these littermates *anything*?) that I can think of no better way of handling the situation than to hiss and swipe at their hands with my claws. My breath becomes loud and rapid as my fur twitches, what Sarah called "chuffing." I don't like reacting this way, but the whole thing is simply more than dignity or patience can bear. Finally, Josh's sister says, "Abbie! Robert! Leave the kitty alone. She'll come out and play with you when she's ready."

Not likely, I think, twitching my tail back and forth as I try to calm down. "I'm sorry," Laura tells Josh's sister. "Prudence isn't really a 'people cat.'" Hearing Laura try to pass this story around again just makes me madder. If she was telling the truth, what she'd say is, *Prudence will only play with humans who have good manners.*

Josh's parents come into the living room where Laura stands in front of the couch pouring wine into glasses. "There's my gorgeous daughter-in-law!" Josh's father says in a loud voice. They each hug her, and Josh's mother murmurs, "We're so sorry your mother couldn't be here with us tonight." Laura hugs them back a bit stiffly and says, "Thank you," in a polite but brief way that means she doesn't want to talk about Sarah right now. Then she and Josh's sister kiss each other on the cheek.

The couch has a long side and a short side, and I'm crouched beneath the shorter part. The littermates come to sit right above me, kicking their legs and playing with a kind of small black plastic box that has buttons and moving pictures all over it. Sometimes they try to grab it away from each other, saying things like, *You're taking too long,* or, *It's my turn now.*

Josh and his father sit all the way on the other side of the couch, where I can just see their faces if I peek out far enough. Josh's father wears shiny black shoes with laces on top and black socks that slide down his ankles when he crosses one leg over the other. Laura is sitting between Josh's mother and Josh's sister on the other side of the coffee table. Josh's mother is sparkly all over with more jewelry than Sarah ever wears. The rings on her hand catch the light as she keeps grabbing Laura's arm while she talks, which makes Laura look uncomfortable. Sarah once said that Laura and I were alike, because neither one of us could stand being petted unless it was our idea first.

I notice how carefully Laura is watching everybody. It's like she wants to make sure nothing happens that she isn't prepared for or doesn't know how to react to. I realize that Laura grew up in Lower East Side with Sarah, where holidays were celebrated differently than they are in Upper West Side. Laura's an immigrant, like I am. She must also be trying to understand the way things are done in this country.

Not that I feel any sympathy for her. She did, after all, send Josh upstairs with The Monster to try to destroy me and the Sarah-boxes.

I've never been in a room with so many humans at one time, and with everybody talking at once it's hard to hear everything. I can't tell what Josh's mother is saying, but I do hear Josh and his father talking about Josh's work. Josh's father sighs and says he never understands what young people do anymore, so Josh explains (in a voice that sounds like he's explained this to his father

already) how he does something called "marketing and public rela-
tions," which means he talks to reporters and writes sales presen-
tations for humans called "advertisers" and helps create awareness
so other humans know they should buy the magazines his company makes.

"Eh," Josh's father says. "That's too complicated for me. I still
don't know what it is you do all day."

Josh laughs a little and says, "You know, your job seemed pretty
complicated to me when I was a kid."

"What complicated?" Josh's father answers. "I sold electrical
supplies. I had the electrical supplies, I sold them, and then the
other guy had supplies and I had money." Josh's father sighs again.
"That was when you could describe a man's job in one word. Sales-
man. Contractor. Accountant." From underneath the couch, I can
see the tips of his fingers as he gestures in Laura's direction. "Now,
a *lawyer*," he says. "*That's* a job I can understand."

"Really, Dad?" Josh sounds amused, but also exasperated.
"You know what lawyers do all day?"

"How should I know what a lawyer does all day?" Josh's father
replies. "If I knew that, *I'd* be a lawyer."

If Sarah had ever talked to Laura like this, Laura's face would
have gotten tight, and she would have left Sarah's apartment without saying another word. But Josh bursts out laughing and says,
"One of us sounds crazy right now, and I'm honestly not sure
which one it is."

"It's your mother," Josh's father says. "She always sounds crazy.
I think we should rescue Laura."

"What's that?" Josh's mother calls from the other side of the
coffee table. Her voice is loud and what Sarah would call "raspy."
"Are you two talking about me?"

"We were just wondering what the ladies were talking about,"
Josh's father says.

"I was telling Laura and Erica about Esther Bookman. She's
getting married again, you know."

"Ah, Esther Bookman!" Josh exclaims. "The sexual dynamo of
Parsippany. What is this, husband number five?"

"Oh, stop," his mother says. "You know perfectly well this is only her third marriage." Turning to Laura, she adds, "Do you see how they make fun of me?"

"One time, when I was nine or ten, I had to call Mrs. Bookman's son Matt about a school project," Josh tells Laura. "Mrs. Bookman answered the phone and I asked to speak to Matt. After I hung up, my mother said, *Did Mrs. Bookman answer the phone?* I said yes, and then she said, *Well, did you say hello, Mrs. Bookman, how are you?* I said no, and she told me, *You call her back right now and apologize for being so rude.*" Josh laughs again. "I *really* didn't want to. I begged and cried, but Zelda was relentless. Finally, after an hour of fighting, I called Mrs. Bookman and said"—Josh pretends to sound like he's crying—"*I'm s-sorry I d-didn't say hello, how are you, Mrs. Bookman.*"

Laura laughs, too. "At least I know why Josh is so polite," she tells Josh's mother.

Humans aren't nearly as good at being polite as cats are. But even I have to admit that it was very smart of Josh's mother to try to teach him the proper way to greet someone by her name. I wonder why he didn't remember that the first time he met me.

"I have no idea what he's talking about," Josh's mother says. "He's making that up."

Laura just smiles. "Would anybody like another glass of wine? More soda?"

"You don't need another glass of wine, Abe," Josh's mother says, before his father can answer Laura.

"It's a holiday," Josh's father says. "I can live a *little,* for God's sake."

"A seventy-five-year-old man shouldn't drink so much," she tells him.

"Mother loves reminding me how old I am." I see his hand reach for the bottle on the coffee table. "As if she wasn't only five years behind me."

"Five years is five years," she says. I wonder why some humans, like Josh's mother, like to talk so much that they think they have to point out perfectly obvious things.

"How old are you, Mom?" It's the little boy who asks this.

"I'm forty-two," Erica answers.

"And how old is Uncle Josh?"

"Thirty-nine," Erica says.

Now Abbie speaks up. "How old is Aunt Laura?"

"A lady never tells," Josh's mother says. But the corners of Laura's mouth twitch into a smile, and she says, "That's okay. I just turned thirty."

With everybody talking about their ages (I had no idea they were all so old—I'm only *three*!), this seems like the perfect opportunity for me to creep out from under-the-couch and into the dining area without the littermates noticing me. The food smells unbearably delicious, and everybody else must be able to smell it, too. I even hear the sound of a human stomach growling. It can't be too much longer before they eat.

Laura must be thinking the same thing, because she puts her glass of wine down and says, "Why don't we head over to the table?"

"Hooray!" the littermates yell. They run over so fast that I have to crouch down into the shadow next to the couch to keep them from seeing me. Josh's father and mother struggle a little when they stand up from the couches, but soon everyone is at the table. My mouth has so much water in it that I have to lick my whiskers a few times while I wait for the eating to begin.

I was sure that, once everybody was sitting in their places, the food would come out of the kitchen right away. Any smart cat knows you should eat the food you like as soon as it's available, because who knows what might happen later to prevent you from eating?

But now I understand that a Seder, which is the meal we're having tonight, is a very specific thing that's different from other kinds of dinners. (I know because at one point Robert had to read something called the Four Questions, and the first question was, *Why is this night different from all other nights?*) A Seder takes a long time, and a lot of things have to happen in a very specific order before you're allowed to eat. And even though I'm so hungry for that wonderful-smelling meat by now that I can hardly stand it, I understand how important it is to do things the exact right way, especially when it concerns food.

First they have to say something called "blessings" over the wine they're drinking and a kind of flat cracker. Then everybody around the table takes turns reading from a book that tells the story of a group of people called the Hebrews, who were forced to be slaves in a place called Egypt. A man named Moses tried to convince another man called Pharaoh to let the Hebrews go live someplace else. Every time Pharaoh said no, a *third* fellow, called God, made bad things happen to Pharaoh and his humans. Each time a bad thing happened, Pharaoh decided to let the Hebrews leave. But then (and this is the part I *really* don't understand), God would force Pharaoh to *change his mind* and make the Hebrews stay, just so Moses could go to all the trouble of asking him again to let the Hebrews go, and God could go to all the trouble of making one more bad thing happen to Pharaoh. They went through this back-and-forth *ten whole times*!

This just goes to show that humans aren't nearly as smart or efficient about figuring things out as cats are. Anise liked to say that a cat might touch a burning stove once, but after that she'd never touch any stove ever again.

At long last, when all the cracker-eating and storytelling are finished, *finally* Laura and Josh start bringing out the food. There's the delicious-smelling meat (called "brisket") that I've been salivating for all day, and a soup made from chicken, and something called chopped liver that looks and smells so wonderful, I can't believe Sarah never thought to have it in our old apartment. There are lots of other things, too. Everything looks beautiful and perfectly arranged, like on one of those TV shows that tell humans how to cook things.

Of course, as soon as the food is out I jump onto the table, ready for Laura or Josh to put together my little Prudence-plate of food. Sarah always sets aside some food for me when she eats at the kitchen table, so I can eat with her. I put one paw lightly on the brisket, which is the food I want to try first, so that Laura and Josh know that's the first thing they should serve me.

Well! Never in your whole life have you heard such a commotion! Laura and Josh yell, "PRUDENCE, NO! Get down!" And Josh's mother yells, "What is the *cat* doing on the table?" in the same kind of voice a human might use if they found a cockroach in their food. And the littermates shout, "It's the *kitteeeeee*!" and lunge at me again with their sticky hands while Josh's sister tries to hold them back.

There's so much yelling and confusion that even all that good food-smell isn't enough to keep me here. The only problem is that I can't find a place to jump down from the table. Everywhere I look, there's a human trying to touch me or grab me. I turn in fast circles, looking for an empty spot I can slip through and escape, and I hear a glass tumble over. "Mom, the kitty spilled on me!" Robert cries. I try backing away, but my left hind paw steps into something hot and liquid. It's Josh's father's bowl of soup, and when he jumps up and says, "Hey!" I pull my paw back so fast that the entire bowl flips upside down. Now the table is slippery and wet. I'm skidding around, and the more I try to run the more things I knock into. My ears and whiskers flatten against my head and my fur puffs up, and when somebody stabs their finger right at me and yells, "Stop it! Bad cat!" I hiss and whap at it with my claws, because the rudest thing in the world is when somebody puts their finger in your face.

Finally Laura stands and says, "Everybody be quiet!" The whole table gets silent as they all turn to stare at her. Laura's face is a bright, bright red. It's as red as the little tomatoes that were on top of the salad bowl that got knocked over. Her hands are shaking a bit, but she nevertheless strokes the back of my neck calmly. Then she scoops one hand underneath me and lifts me up the way you're supposed to pick up a cat when you absolutely have to, and she puts me on the floor, very gently. For a moment, I can't move. I feel the shock of human hands touching me for the first time in so long. Hands that aren't Sarah's. Hands that are warm and not cold the way Sarah's always were the last few months I lived with her. The table that was so beautiful with food only a little while ago now looks like a pack of dogs ran over it.

This time I don't run to hide under the couch. This time I run as fast as I can upstairs and into the back of the closet in my room with the Sarah-boxes, burrowing deep beneath the dress with the Sarah-and-me-together smell. I twitch my back muscles so hard I almost give myself a cramp.

I don't think anybody has ever been treated as cruelly as I've been treated tonight. Whenever Sarah used to be upset about something bad that happened to her, she would cheer herself up by saying, *Worse things have happened to better people.* But I don't think anything worse than this has ever happened to anybody. Even that long story about what the Hebrews went through seems like nothing in comparison.

I hear Laura's footsteps coming up the stairs, but they pause when Josh follows her. "I just want to check on Prudence and make sure she's okay," she tells him in a low voice.

"I'm sure she's fine," Josh says in an equally low voice. "She's just a little rattled. Come back down and help me straighten out the table."

"I will," Laura tells him. "I'll be back in a minute."

Josh's footsteps start to go back down the stairs when I hear Laura say, "Josh?" She's silent for a moment. "I'm sorry about this. I really wanted everything to be perfect."

"It *is* perfect. Well," Josh adds, "maybe we got a bit of unexpected dinner theater." He chuckles. "But everything can be salvaged. No harm done."

"I know, but . . ." Laura falls silent again. "It's the first time we've had your parents over for dinner," she finally says. "I don't want them to think that . . . I just don't think Prudence knew any better. Letting her eat on the table is exactly the kind of thing my mother would've done."

"Prudence is a *cat,* Laura." Josh's voice is gentle when he makes this (obvious) statement. "Of course she didn't know any better. Nobody thinks it reflects on you or your mother."

As if *I* were the one with bad manners!

"I'll be down in a minute," Laura says again. Her footsteps continue up the stairs and down the hall until she's standing in the doorway of my room. "Prudence?" her voice whispers into the darkness. "Prudence, are you okay?"

I can tell she's waiting for me to meow in response, but I have nothing to say to Laura right now. "Prudence?" she whispers again. I turn around three times in Sarah's dress and wait for Laura to leave so the room will be silent and I can fall asleep— even though I never did get anything to eat for dinner except for the dried chicken soup I lick off my left hind paw.

5

Laura

LAURA DYEN'S FAVORITE PLACE IN THE WORLD, WITH THE EXCEPTION of her own bed on a Sunday morning, was found on the forty-seventh floor in the Midtown offices of Neuman Daines. The forty-seventh floor was assigned to the Corporate group, and Laura frequently had a quick lunch of deli sandwiches with her fellow fifth-year associates in what was grandly referred to as the forty-seventh-floor conference room—although in truth it was no more than a smallish meeting space. They'd spread newspapers and legal pads over the surface of the round table, where reflected globes of white light from the overhead fluorescents floated like water lilies in its cherrywood depths.

Often they used these group lunches as an opportunity to solicit one another's unofficial input on opinion or adversary letters they were working on. But the lunches were primarily about camaraderie. Once they'd been a group of thirty first-years who'd started out as summer associates together. Now they were eight, the rest having left for other firms. Laura had gotten the same early-morning phone calls from recruiters as the others—still got them, in fact—but she'd also understood, in a way few people her age did, that those who jump around early usually end up jumping around forever. All she'd had to do to recognize the truth of this was look at her mother.

As much as Laura appreciated the fraternal spirit of these impromptu lunches, it was the early-morning or late-evening hours, when the conference room was empty, that she enjoyed most. She could look through the windows and all the way down onto the silent diorama of the city streets below, and the very silence of it soothed her. The Empire State Building was more than ten blocks away, but the illusion created by the height of her own building made it seem as though she were level with its peak. On hot summer nights, Laura would watch as its pinnacle was repeatedly struck by heat lightning, a display of kinetic energy rendered mute by the thick, reinforced windows of her office building. She'd grown up in a neighborhood loud with the twenty-four-hour cacophony of dance music blared from boom boxes, of police sirens and domestic arguments and glass shattering on pavement, the all-night hum of after-hours partiers that gave way each morning to the rumble of overcrowded buses and the metal clank of store grates rolling up. In the five-story walk-up she and Sarah had lived in, these sounds had been a constant assault, even with the windows closed. And they'd been intensified by the noise from their own building, babies wailing and neighbors flushing toilets or walking on the floors overhead.

People talked about the views to be had on higher floors, but Laura knew it was the silence, the serenity of heights, that one paid obscene sums for in a city like New York. Noise was one of a thousand indignities visited upon the poor. Money was the only thing that could buy the illusion of peace.

Perry had learned to look for Laura in the forty-seventh-floor conference room when the rest of the office was quiet. It was here that she came to think, to give her mind the break from computer screens and buzzing BlackBerrys and allow it to formulate creative solutions to knotty problems.

Perry poked his head in now and said, "It's almost nine o'clock. You should get home to your husband like a good newlywed."

Laura turned her face from the window. "I can't. Clay just dumped this project for Balaban Media on me." Clayton Newell was Neuman Daines's managing partner, and a figure of terror to all the firm's associates. "He says he needs it turned around by seven o'clock Monday morning."

"Yes, but you and I both know Clay won't be in Monday before ten thirty. It'll keep." Perry smiled. "The key to having a life in this business is training people to expect the best of you, not all of you at once."

Perry Steadman was Laura's "rabbi," a senior partner who had recognized Laura's potential early on and taken her under his wing. He was a short man in his fifties with thinning hair and a laid-back approach to his practice and his negotiations that belied the sharp mind at work behind them. And even though Perry's "rabbi" designation was strictly metaphorical, he had a true rabbi's fondness for quoting the Talmud. *"Two cripples don't make one dancer,"* he'd told Laura more than once. "Everybody's a cripple to some extent. The trick is never putting together two parties who are equally crippled, or crippled in the same way. Otherwise you'll be up to your eyeballs in paperwork when they realize they can't dance together."

Not every associate was fortunate, or strategic, enough to find a rabbi, particularly one as influential within the firm as Perry. Perry was an acknowledged rainmaker, a partner who landed large corporate clients for the firm and then distributed the work to Corporate group associates. He'd noted Laura's quick mind and rigorous approach back when she was still a summer associate, and when she was a first-year he'd made a point of routing her way the more complex of the memos and briefs first-years were expected to spend the majority of their time hammering out. Laura, who had attended Hunter College and Fordham Law in the city, noted with inward satisfaction how much more quickly she was rising than some of the Ivy Leaguers she'd started out with, although she was careful never to let her sense of her own success show outwardly.

She had come to specialize in contracts, and she was more at home among the language of contracts than anywhere else. There was something profoundly comforting in having all worst-case scenarios accounted for and resolved ahead of time, nailed down in the black-and-white precision of a signed and witnessed document. In a perfect world, Laura thought, all of life's surprises would be anticipated and disposed of with equal ease.

It was Perry who'd decided a little over a year ago that Laura was finally ready to go to client meetings. She'd met Josh at the first of these meetings, which had lent the early days of their romance an air of the clandestine. She'd known how it would look to the rest of the firm, and to Perry in particular, if the fact that she was dating a client became general knowledge. Sometimes Laura wondered if maybe she'd agreed to marry Josh after only a few months of dating because marriage recast the whole thing in an indisputably respectable light. When she'd announced her engagement, Perry had hugged her warmly and said, *"When love is strong, a man and a woman can make their bed on a sword's blade.* May your love always be as strong as it is now." It had sounded nice at the time, although later Laura thought it was rather more portentous than an expression of congratulations ought to be.

Now, in the face of Perry's admonishment that she finish up for the night, Laura found she wasn't as eager to return home as she'd been in the earliest days of her marriage, only six months ago. Sarah's things—mostly items salvaged from the record store she'd owned and then sold sixteen years ago—remained unpacked in the boxes stored in their spare bedroom. Still, the smell of old records and yellowing newspapers, the smell of Laura's childhood, had invaded the entire upstairs of their apartment. Even the faint odor of a litter box threatened to unearth long-buried images and associations.

This displacement between *then* and *now* created an ever-present sense of unease, like a low-frequency sound she couldn't hear clearly enough to identify, but that was disturbing nonetheless. Laura found herself using the downstairs guest bathroom whenever possible and avoiding going upstairs to bed until the moment when she literally couldn't hold her eyes open anymore. Even so, her sleep was restless these days, leaving her almost more exhausted when she woke up than she'd been when she'd gone to bed.

She knew how eager Josh, a self-described music geek, was to go through all of Sarah's posters and listen to recordings of songs on their original vinyl that hadn't been available in nearly a generation. Josh was in love with the past. Stored in their home office were stacks of photo albums and summer-camp swimming awards and school report cards and even the twenty-year-old fraternity roster listing all the names and phone numbers of his pledge class. Laura knew he was wondering why she hadn't looked through everything yet, even though over a month had passed since they'd cleaned out Sarah's apartment. So far, however, he hadn't pressed the point.

The only one who had spent any time going through Sarah's things was Prudence. That her mother, of all people, should have decided to adopt a cat was something Laura still couldn't understand. But it was clear that Prudence missed Sarah terribly. The cat had spent her first days with them both refusing food and vomiting, and her obvious distress had made Laura wonder if they'd made the right decision, or if perhaps Prudence would be happier living in a more cat-friendly household someplace else, despite her mother's will. Only some deep reluctance to part with this final living link to Sarah had held her back.

At their Passover Seder three nights earlier, when Prudence had made such a mess of their carefully laid table, Laura had felt both deeply embarrassed by Prudence and deeply sorry for her. Like Laura, Prudence had been raised by Sarah. How could she be expected to understand the way normal families behaved at a holiday dinner? It had taken Laura years of careful observation as an adult to figure it out herself.

Still, it had been nice, these last few weeks, to see Prudence finally begin integrating herself into the general flow of life in their apartment. Digging out one of Sarah's old dresses from the bag she'd salvaged from the trash room at the last minute had been the right idea. Prudence was starting to act like a normal cat again (as if, Laura thought wryly, there was any such thing as "normal" when it came to cats). Laura couldn't help watching her, couldn't help smiling at the way Prudence sprawled out on her back sometimes, four white paws in the air, in the patches of sunlight that fell through the windows. What would it be like, she wondered, to give yourself over so entirely to something as simple as that, to have no thought in your mind beyond, *This sunlight is warm. It feels good.*

Laura had noted Prudence's fascination with the same flock of amber-and-white pigeons across the street that she found herself watching at times. Such unusually colored birds would have been prized in the neighborhood she'd grown up in, would have been kept and coddled in rooftop coops and eyed wistfully by young boys who would have tried to steal a few. Once, when she was twelve, Laura had sneaked onto the rooftop of the apartment building next to her own to cradle a young pigeon under the watchful eyes of its owner. The world before her was an uneven patchwork quilt of white cement and black tarpaper roofs, seamed by heavily laden clotheslines. Laura had never touched the warm feathers of a living bird before, never felt the intricate symmetry that molded the soft fluff into a resilient shell. The only feathers she'd touched were those found on sidewalks. Sarah had been furious when she'd found out Laura had gone onto the roof next door; two weeks earlier, a fourteen-year-old boy had plummeted to his death trying to leap from one rooftop to another.

Laura liked to watch Prudence looking out the window. At such moments, she wanted to stroke Prudence's fur, to breathe in the cinnamon-and-milk smell of her neck and hear the low rumble of her purring. It had been a long time since she'd sat with a cat and listened to it purr, or felt the kind of peace that comes when a small animal trusts you enough to fall asleep in your lap.

But whenever she reached out to Prudence, she saw—no matter how hard she tried not to—an old man in tears, kneeling on a cracked sidewalk and crying out, *She's all I got!* There was a terrible danger in loving small, fragile things. Laura had learned this almost before she'd learned anything else.

Laura knew her face must have taken on a faraway expression, because now Perry was repeating, "You should go home for the night." And then, with a look of concern that was almost harder for Laura to bear than a direct reprimand would have been, "I wish you'd taken some time off when your mother died."

"It wasn't the right time," Laura said. "I'd just taken off three weeks." In fact, it was Perry, claiming that the directive came straight from Clay (who sometimes tried to mitigate his own capriciousness with equally random acts of generosity), who'd insisted that she take a full three weeks for her honeymoon. "And, anyway"—she paused to smile in a way she hoped would be convincing—"I'm fine. I really am."

It had been a Tuesday in March, the first legitimately gorgeous spring day of the year—and an illusion of sorts, because the following week would be as cold and rainy as the depths of February—when Laura had gotten the call from her mother's office. Even though Sarah had worked as a typist for the small real estate law firm in the East Thirties for over fifteen years, Laura had never met any of her mother's co-workers. So when she'd heard a voice other than Sarah's on the other end of the line, she'd known instantly that something was wrong, known it even before the woman's hesitant voice had said, "Is this Laura? I worked, *work* I mean, with your mother . . ." She'd known before the woman went on to say things like *heart attack* and *didn't suffer.*

Laura must have told a co-worker, must have told somebody what happened and where she was going, although afterward she could never remember. The next thing she knew, she was squinting in too-bright sunshine. *I should have worn sunglasses today,* she thought, and then wondered if she ought to be thinking about sunglasses now. Women in unbuttoned winter coats and men in suits with their ties loosened, people whose mothers hadn't just died, walked at a more leisurely pace than they had in the brisker weather of the day before. They strolled past small cafés where people whose mothers hadn't just died sat outside for the first time in months, and past the Mister Softee trucks that always seemed to spring up like fresh grass the instant the thermometer climbed above sixty-five. Laura had a sudden flash of memory, of Sarah bringing armfuls of fresh fruit on breathless summer nights to the hookers who walked Second Avenue, Laura hiding behind Sarah's legs as the hookers thanked her and bent down to tell Laura, *Ainchou a pretty girl.*

By now Laura was aware that her scattered thoughts were a way of distracting herself, of avoiding the knowledge of her new reality (*I have no parents*) even as she hailed a cab and directed it to the morgue at 32nd and First, deep beneath the ground mere blocks from the desk where Sarah had died, high in a glass tower not unlike the building Laura had just left.

It was on a day much like this—when Laura had been, what, six? seven?—that Sarah had picked her up outside of her elementary school one Friday afternoon and announced, with a kind of happy mystery, "I got Noel to cover the store. We're going someplace else today." And Laura, still wearing her red backpack with the Menudo pin she'd begged Sarah for at the Menuditis store, had clasped Sarah's hand and followed her to Eldridge Street and Adam Purple's Garden of Eden.

There were dozens of community gardens on the Lower East Side in those days, but the Garden of Eden was far and away the grandest of them all. Adam Purple, a squatter and neighborhood eccentric, had spent a decade reclaiming what had been five lots of burned-out tenement buildings with plant clippings and compost he made himself by filling wheelbarrows and grocery carts with manure he collected from the horse-drawn carriages of Central Park. The result was a fifteen-thousand-square-foot formal garden bursting with roses, pear trees, climbing ivy, flowering bushes, and hundreds of other plants Laura couldn't begin to name. At its precise center was an enormous foliage yin–yang circle.

Laura, with the limited perspective of childhood, had thought she'd known everything there was to know about New York City, especially her small corner of it. Then, seemingly out of nowhere, there was *this*! She felt staggered by the realization of how much beauty, unsuspected by her, had lived hidden within the bleak, shabby cityscapes she saw daily.

The afternoon sun had played mischievous tricks in Sarah's hair that day, crowning her in a red-gold blaze. To Laura's dazzled eyes, her mother had never seemed more beautiful. She looked like a fairy queen from one of Laura's much-loved picture books. What magic was this that her mother had conjured? One moment they'd been walking down a glass-and-rubble-strewn urban street, picking their way carefully over crack vials and crumpled soda cans, and then suddenly they were overwhelmed by the spicy-sweet scent of roses and crocuses. Feral cats lazily opened and closed their eyes in the sun-dappled shadows beneath fruit trees, too serene to bother with the birds chattering in branches overhead. Laura thought of *The Secret Garden*, a book she had just begun to struggle through. Surely, she told herself, this very spot must be the most enchanted place in the entire world.

"Most people, people who live in other places, only think about dirt and noise when they think about New York and where we live," Sarah had said as the two of them strolled, still hand in hand, through the alternating coolness and warmth of the garden. "They don't know it like you and I do. They don't know that we live in the most wonderful place in the world." In an echo of Laura's earlier thoughts, Sarah had winked and added in a stage whisper, "It's our secret."

They were standing beneath a cherry tree that had not yet begun to blossom, and Laura stopped Sarah to pull a sheet of paper from her backpack. Her teacher had made everyone in the class write a poem about springtime that day, and Laura was suddenly moved to read hers aloud to her mother. Blushing, because Laura hadn't been a child who "performed" for adults, she read:

Winter is over
Gone is the snow

Everything's bright
And all aglow

Birds are singing
With greatest cheer
Expressing their joy
That spring is here

Animals awaken
From their long winter sleep
Spring is like a treasure
We all wish to keep

Sarah had been charmed. "That is the most beautiful poem I've ever heard," she'd said. "Did you know that some of the best poems are songs?" And Laura, who hadn't known that but did know that her mother knew everything about music and songs, had nodded with what she hoped passed for the solemn wisdom of somebody much older, perhaps ten or eleven. "I think your poem is a song," Sarah had told her. Then she and Laura had practically run all the way back to Sarah's record store, where Sarah had selected a few albums from her enormous personal collection and made a phone call to a friend. Then they'd walked over to Avenue A and entered what looked like a perfectly ordinary twenty-story apartment building.

But it turned out there was a recording studio in the basement. Funny-looking block letters etched into the glass-door entrance proclaimed it Alphaville Studios, and Sarah said it was a famous place. A man Laura had never seen before, with a scraggly long beard and deep dimples, appeared from some hidden back office and greeted Sarah with a hug and a warm rubbing of cheeks. "It's been a long time since we've seen the likes of you around here, girl." He sneaked them into an unoccupied recording studio where Sarah put her records on a kind of machine that let her filter out the vocals until all they could hear was the music. Laura had been deeply impressed with Sarah's knowledge of this complicated-looking equipment. Clearly, she'd spent a lot of time here once. With this realization came the insight, always shocking for a small child, that Sarah must have had an entire life all her own before Laura was born.

Sarah played around with various knobs and buttons until the percussion was a heavy, insistent *thump thump-thump thump*. That was when she had started to sing Laura's poem. She'd made Laura sing along with her. And even though, in Laura's opinion, it wasn't a very good song, there was little in the world more delightful to her in those years than the sound of her mother's singing.

Sarah had made a tape recording of the two of them singing together in the studio, which they'd listened to again at home that night before Sarah ceremoniously placed the cassette in a small metal box she'd shown Laura once, claiming it held her most treasured personal belongings.

The City bulldozed the Garden of Eden a few years later, and the metal box disappeared in 1995, the day Laura and Sarah lost their apartment. And now, Laura thought, there was nobody left except her to remember what Sarah had sounded like when she sang, nobody left alive who even remembered (because Laura realized that she didn't) what Laura's own voice had sounded like when she was a child.

Where did tapes go when they died? Did they go to a Tape Heaven? Laura felt herself on the verge of a giggling fit as this idea weaved through her thoughts, but she quelled it because by now she was standing in the lobby of the Morgue. Above her head was a motto inscribed in Latin. Laura drew on the Latin she'd picked up in her law studies to translate.

Let conversation cease, let laughter flee. This is the place where death delights in helping the living.

Perry wasn't the only one who thought Laura hadn't taken enough time to grieve. She was starting to feel like one of those dolls, the kind with a string in its back that, if you pulled it, forced the doll to repeat the same litany of phrases. *I'm fine,* she'd said when she'd returned to work the next day. *I'm fine,* she'd said after coming back from the half day she took for her mother's funeral. *I'm fine,* she'd been repeating to everybody, to Perry, to her fellow fifth-years, to the hard-faced blond woman who answered her phone and filed her papers. *I'm fine. I'm okay. You don't have to look at me that way because I really am fine.*

She remembered when she was younger and had started noticing that seemingly every pay phone in New York—not just the ones on the Lower East Side, but all the way up to Grand Central and beyond—had the words WORSHIP GOD etched into its metal base. Laura had wondered about the person who'd poured so many hours and days—months, even—into seeking out each and every pay phone in Manhattan. Had it been religious zeal? A sincere, if skewed, belief that repeating those two words so many times would actually induce others to worship God? Or had it been that the whole weight of this person's soul had come to rest on those two words, endlessly repeated, and the act of inscribing them was the only way to exorcise the thought?

Laura was inclined to think it was the latter, because if she'd been able to take one of the dozens of paper clips she systematically unfurled over the course of a workday and use it to scratch the words I'M FINE on every desk, phone, and wall in the office, she would have done so. She appreciated everybody's concern. But the burden of appearing to be fine, so as to keep others from worrying about her, was almost worse than simply allowing herself to feel bad would have been.

She was especially glad now that she hadn't told anybody when, unexpectedly (and despite taking the appropriate precautions), she'd found herself pregnant only two months into her marriage. Of course, it wasn't strictly necessary to tell anybody right away—in fact, it was accepted that you weren't supposed to tell anybody until your first trimester was safely behind you.

Josh had been overjoyed at the news; he'd actually had tears in his eyes. But Laura had to spend a few hours composing herself

before she could even get the words out, because her own first reaction had been panic. The best time for her to have gotten pregnant would have been four years ago, when she was a first-year
associate and therefore more expendable to the firm—or it would
be seven years from now, when she would (hopefully) have made
partner. The fifth year was the worst possible time to take mater-
nity leave. Now was the time to put in the hours, to take on the
caseload, to wine and dine clients after hours and cultivate the relationships among partners that would—after a grueling, decade-
plus slog—lift her to the heights of success she'd always striven
toward. She'd seen other female attorneys who'd gone on reduced
schedules once they had children. The idea was something of a
grim joke among women in the firm, because what a "reduced
schedule" meant in reality was that you ended up doing the same
amount of work for less money. Most of them never regained their
pre-pregnancy standing in the firm. Laura realized, too late, that
questions like when they'd have children, and how many children
they'd have, were among a million things she and Josh hadn't discussed before rushing into marriage.

And she'd had deeper fears even than that. There were an infinite number of ways to be unhappy. Laura had learned from Sarah
that marriage and children were no guarantee of avoiding any of
them.

Still, it was impossible to ignore Josh's happiness or remain
untouched by it. One Sunday afternoon they'd painted the walls of
their spare bedroom a soft, sunny yellow—perfect, as Josh had
noted, for a boy or a girl. She thought about this peanut-sized
thing—something made of her and Josh—traveling with her wherever she went, a secret sharer who sat in with her on meetings and
rode with her on the subway and inhaled the same smoky-sweet
smell of early winter that she did. She felt a kind of tender pity for
it sometimes, so small and defenseless. *Poor thing!* she would
think, and then wonder why she pitied it so much.

So the pregnancy had remained their secret, hers and Josh's,
which made things infinitely easier when, one Friday night in mid-

February and just before the official end of her first trimester, the pain had started in her lower back and blood began to flow.

She'd returned to work on Monday, a bit pale and tired but otherwise not noteworthy in any way to her co-workers. Because she hadn't told anyone she was pregnant, she didn't have to go through the ordeal of telling everyone she no longer was. Not even Josh's parents had been told. ("Let's give Abe and Zelda a couple of months before they drown us in parenting advice," he'd said.) The only exception they'd made—or, at least, that Josh had thought they'd made—had been telling Sarah. "Of course you'll want your mother to know right away," he'd said. Laura hadn't bothered to correct him, because what could be more expected, more perfectly normal, than a young woman, pregnant for the first time, sharing the experience with her mother and leaning on her for advice and support?

But Laura hadn't said anything to Sarah. She wasn't sure why. Maybe it was because when you told your mother you were pregnant with your first child, she was supposed to tell you how you don't even know what love is until you hold your baby for the first time, or how you'll never love anything in life the way you'll love your child. Except that Laura already knew this hadn't been true in Sarah's case, and Sarah knew that Laura knew. So what could Sarah have said? *You'll love your baby, but only as much as you love some things and less than you love others*?

Perhaps if Laura had told Sarah about her pregnancy, Sarah would have told Laura about the bottle of nitroglycerin pills Laura had found when she'd cleaned out Sarah's bathroom. Sarah had been keeping her own secrets. And even though Laura was angry now, angrier than she allowed herself to realize, she could guess that Sarah's reasons for saying nothing to Laura about her heart condition had been similar to Laura's reasons for saying nothing about her pregnancy to Sarah. Because when your mother told you she was sick, you were supposed to tear up and hug her and beg her to do everything the doctor said because you absolutely couldn't bear to lose her.

Sarah must have known that Laura couldn't and wouldn't have said any of those things. Not because they weren't true. But because she and Sarah had already lost each other years ago.

Josh never tried to get her to talk about the miscarriage. But he did keep trying to get her to talk about Sarah, to remember things. When they'd driven down to the Lower East Side to clean out Sarah's apartment, he'd insisted on a "nostalgia tour" like his parents had always given him and his sister when they used to drive through Brooklyn as a family. "Come on," he'd urged. "Tell a sheltered boy from Parsippany what it was like growing up in Manhattan. How often are we down here?"

And Laura had tried. She tried to re-create for him the open-air drug markets that had flourished on Avenue B and 2nd Street, ignored by the authorities for far too long because what could be done in the face of such large-scale—and lucrative—dedication to vice? When they drove past Tompkins Square Park, with its cheerful playgrounds, flowered pathways, and pristine basketball courts, it was impossible to make Josh visualize the Tompkins Square Park she'd grown up with, taken over almost entirely by tent cities erected by junkies and the homeless, and frequented by punked-out teenagers in dog collars and Sex Pistols T-shirts. Million-dollar condos and trendy restaurants had once been burned-out tenements where squatting artists lived, or SRO hotels that, for all their seediness, were still preferable to the violent squalor of the city's official homeless shelters. "And—oh!—right there." Laura pointed to a spot on the pavement. "That's where my friend Maria Elena and I used to play Skelzie with bottle caps. Whenever we went out to play together, her mother would yell after us, *Cuidado en la calle!*"

The whole time she was talking, Laura found herself wondering why Sarah all those years later, had moved back to the Lower East Side. Had she thought she could rewrite the past? Play out the same scenarios but tack on a different ending? Hadn't she realized that the Lower East Side she'd haunted these past few years had borne only the most passing resemblance to the place she'd landed in as a teenager, armed with nothing more than her high school diploma and a determination to see the world the way she wanted to?

Nevertheless, Laura's memories made Josh smile. And nothing had ever made her feel like a whole person—had given her the same sense of belonging that the intimidating, shiny-haired women she worked with clearly felt—the way making Josh smile always did.

It wasn't until he insisted on doubling back to drive down Stanton, where Laura and Sarah had lived, that Laura felt her throat tighten. "My mom used to pick me up after school every day and bring me back to the record store to do my homework," she told him, "and I was fourteen when we moved away. I really don't know this neighborhood as well as you think I do."

Josh's interest in all this was to be expected. He was chief marketing officer for a magazine publishing group whose flagship publication was a music-industry glossy, and the Lower East Side had once been ground zero for seminal movements in rock and pop. Of course Laura's old neighborhood would seem like a theme park called Punk World or Disco Land, where tastefully "distressed" buildings re-created a semblance of the grittiness of yesteryear, and if you squinted hard enough you could almost see Joey Ramone or Wayne County lugging their gear down the Bowery after a set at CBGB. Laura herself had thought for a fleeting moment that she'd seen Adam Purple, an old man now, pushing a battered grocery cart filled with compost up Avenue B.

Josh hadn't been one of the people in the meeting that day when Laura had gone to his offices with Perry for the first time, but he'd seen her struggling outside the conference room with two oversized briefcases while Perry lingered behind to schmooze. Josh had hurried to her side and said, "Let me help you with those," taking the briefcases over Laura's protests and walking toward the elevator with them. This had embarrassed her; it was an associate's job to carry the briefcases when she went to a meeting, or to court, with a partner.

When he'd called her at her office four days later, she was even more embarrassed. He must have asked someone who'd been in the meeting what her name was and where she worked. She'd refused the first time he asked her out, not wanting to be *that girl* who got hit on at the first meeting she went to. But the second time Josh called, inviting her to a party his company was throwing to celebrate their April Latin Music issue, she'd said yes. She didn't plan on being an associate forever, she reasoned. It couldn't hurt to start showing her face at client events. Most associates who considered themselves partner-track made a point of doing so.

Josh's magazine had taken over SOB's, a Brazilian nightclub in the West Village, and hired a live salsa band. The swoop and swirl of strobes overhead transformed the women's dresses and flowing blouses into shimmering beacons of iridescent light. Laura felt like an undertaker in the black pantsuit she'd worn to work that day. Trays of mojitos crossed the floor and she drank three in quick succession near the bar, then felt so light-headed she had to sit down. Gratefully accepting an empanada from a passing waiter, she looked around the room for Josh.

He was in a corner near the back, conferring with underlings in headsets. Laura hadn't remembered, perhaps hadn't realized, how good-looking he was. His hands gestured as he spoke, his long fingers blunt at the tips. Laura ran her own fingers through her hair, trying to remember if she'd styled it that morning or simply let it hang loose to air-dry. She thought, *What am I doing here?* Josh looked up then and saw her. She watched him give a final instruction to the people wearing headsets, then lope across the room toward her. "You made it!" He smiled warmly and lightly bussed her cheek, the crowd behind Laura preventing her from backing up and offering her hand instead for a more decorous handshake. Shouting to be heard over the band, Josh asked, "Do you dance? Latin dancing is easier than it looks—promise!"

Perhaps it was the implied assumption that somebody who looked like her, an island of suit in a sea of business casual, wouldn't know how to dance that propelled her onto the floor when normally she would have refused. At nearly five foot ten Laura was taller than a lot of men, but Josh was just tall enough to make her feel feminine. She found herself acutely aware of the smooth skin of his palm pressed against her own, of his breath on the top of her head whenever he twirled her in before releasing her. It had been fifteen years and at least six inches of height since Laura had last danced like this. She was pleasantly surprised to discover that her hips still remembered how to find the rhythm, that her movements still felt as fluid as if she'd done this only last week. The only difference was that she didn't remember feeling quite this dizzy or short of breath dancing when she was younger. *It's the mojitos,* Laura thought, and then she stopped thinking.

They danced through four straight numbers, Josh's questioning look at the end of each (did she need a rest?) met with a reassuring squeeze of her hand (no, no she didn't). She was surprised at what a strong partner he was. Laura knew her own dancing must look as good as it felt, because people were actually standing back to watch the two of them bevel their way across the dance floor.

Maybe if she hadn't already been doing so many things that felt unlike her regular self (and yet, conversely, more like her genuine self than any other self she'd allowed herself to be in years), maybe then the rest of the night would have turned out differently. Maybe she wouldn't have been so quick to tell Josh things she worked to keep hidden from her colleagues who, when they heard she'd been raised in Manhattan, assumed she meant one of the wealthier uptown enclaves around Park Avenue. Maybe she wouldn't even be married to Josh now. Could a life truly turn on such things? On the electricity of fingertips on the small of her back, or a moment of swift elation that came from knowing a crowd of strangers admired her on a dance floor?

When they eventually collapsed, breathless, into a banquette, Josh's blue eyes glowed. "You're *amazing.* Where'd you learn to dance like that?"

"I grew up on the Lower East Side, and there was a huge Puerto Rican community," she answered. "There'd be these enormous block parties with music and food. My mother says the first time she brought me to one, I was three years old and I slipped away from her in the crowd. It was an hour before she found me, in the middle of a group of older kids teaching me the steps. Everybody would dance, from little kids to grandmothers." She smiled. "It was nice, seeing different generations dancing the same dances and enjoying the same music like that."

Josh had been impressed. "When I was a kid, I would've given anything to grow up in the city," he told her. "Living here was all I ever wanted. I had it all planned out. I was going to write music reviews for an alt-weekly and live in one of those shabby old downtown tenements with a futon on the floor and milk crates for furniture."

His self-deprecation had made her laugh. "Somehow it doesn't seem like that's how things turned out for you."

"No," Josh agreed, in a way that struck Laura as a touch rueful. "I don't even know if those ratty little apartments I was so excited to live in still existed by the time I got here."

"I grew up in one of those ratty little tenement apartments. Believe me, there's nothing romantic about poverty. Or bad plumbing, for that matter."

Josh's eyes took in Laura's suit, which—for all its staid propriety—was clearly expensive. "Were you very poor?"

"Poor enough. Although I didn't realize it until we . . . until I was fourteen."

"What happened when you were fourteen?"

"Oh, you know." Laura made a vague gesture and felt her cheeks grow warm. What was wrong with her? Why couldn't she just chatter and flirt like any other woman talking to an attractive man in a nightclub? "One day you have to grow up and understand how the world really works."

The band, having launched into a Celia Cruz number, sounded louder in the momentary silence that fell between them. Laura smiled in recognition and, wanting to dispel the solemn mood that had sprung up, said, "I love Celia Cruz. The family that lived on the top floor of our building used to play her records all the time."

Josh's face caught Laura's smile. "So it wasn't *all* terrible."

"Of course not." She was relieved that the conversation had resumed on a lighter note. "I mean, the heat and the plumbing never quite worked the way they were supposed to. Our building went up at the turn of the century, so things were always breaking, but there was also always this sense of how many people had lived in our apartment before we did. My mother and I would find things from time to time, like a scorch mark on the floor from an old flatiron. Or once when we were scraping off wallpaper, we found out that one room had been papered in nineteenth-century sheet music. My mother was very into music, and she was a bit of a romantic like you are, so she forgave a lot of what was sometimes uncomfortable about living there."

"And you didn't feel the same way?" he asked.

"I liked the people," Laura said. "I think *that* part of it was actually a lot like what you used to imagine. We had a few performance artists as neighbors. The family upstairs had five kids, and their daughter who was my age was my best friend. And then there were the Mandelbaums in the apartment right above ours. They used to watch me sometimes when my mother was busy." Laura's smile held a hint of sadness. "They were married for over fifty years, and they were madly in love right up until the end."

"True love!" Josh exclaimed. "Was it love at first sight?"

"Oh no." Laura laughed. "They met through a mutual friend one summer at Rockaway Beach. Mr. Mandelbaum was short and already balding, but very hairy everywhere else. Although supposedly he had quite a way with the ladies." Laura found herself slipping into the cadence and phrasing that Mrs. Mandelbaum had always used when telling the story. *Max used to go with Rockettes before he met me*, she would say, still proud some fifty years later of having vanquished these statuesque rivals for Mr. Mandelbaum's affections. "Mrs. Mandelbaum was only eighteen and eight years younger than he was. So when their friend tried to fix them up, Mr. Mandelbaum said, *I'm not going out with that child!* And Mrs. Mandelbaum said, *I'm not going out with that hairy baboon!* But somehow they let themselves get talked into it, and they had an

awful time. He took her to a roadhouse and left her sitting by herself in a corner while he danced with every other woman there.
But later, when he was walking her home, he felt so sorry for the
way he'd treated her that he started talking to her. They didn't stop
talking until they got to her door. Mrs. Mandelbaum used to say,
And that's when the love bug bit us both!"

Laura fell silent. She was inexplicably happy to talk about them
now, with Josh, but lingering beneath the memories was always the
pain she felt when she thought of the Mandelbaums. She was lost
so far in the past that she was almost startled when Josh asked,
"Did they have any children?"

"A son, Joseph. He was killed in Vietnam. They had a picture
of him in his army uniform that they kept next to his Purple Heart
in their living room. When I was little I used to think he looked so
handsome, just like a movie star." Laura looked down at Josh's
hands. "He looked a little like you, actually."

The corners of Josh's mouth turned upward in a way that accepted the compliment while also turning it aside. "Do any of the
people you knew still live there?"

"No." Laura would have given anything to sound less abrupt,
but she couldn't help it. "The building was condemned and we all
had to move."

Another silence fell. Josh lifted his drink to his lips, and Laura
blushed deeply as she realized she was wondering what his mouth
would taste like, or how it would feel to have him press her back
against the plush of the banquette and put his hands on her. He
slung his arm casually across the top of the banquette, and to
Laura he smelled like rum and shampoo, like the warmth of dancing in a crowded room and freshly laundered clothes that could
bear the strain. Laura's nose even caught something that reminded
her of the spikenard flowers Sarah had once tried unsuccessfully
to cultivate in a small box hung from their apartment window. She
found herself leaning subtly closer to him, the edge of his sleeve
brushing against the back of her neck.

He looked at her then, and their eyes held. "Why don't we grab some food?" Josh asked. "Raoul's is somewhere around here." And when Laura started to protest, thinking decorum demanded his presence until the party was over, he added, "I've been here long enough. They can wrap things up without me."

They were together nearly all the time after that first night, whenever they weren't working. Josh worked as hard as Laura did, although his hours weren't as long. Since finishing law school and going to work for Neuman Daines, Laura's first and only commitment had been to the firm. But now she found herself ducking out as early as seven o'clock some nights, because she literally couldn't wait to see Josh. Life in the office, with its demanding hours and crushing workload, had started to feel like her real life, and everything else was just the blurry stuff around the edges. With Josh, though, her after-hours life suddenly stood out in sparkling relief. She remembered what life had felt like before she'd entered high school, when everything had become about the *next* test, the *next* grade, the *next* accomplishment. Josh had an easygoing charm, a goofiness so at odds with his good looks. His ability to make her laugh felt like a tonic for things she hadn't even known were wrong with her.

Laura had always struggled to suppress an inner conviction that she was an imposter in this life she'd built for herself. A long time ago, when she'd still lived with Sarah, things had happened to them that would be unthinkable to the people she knew now. Things like the nearly unbearable humiliation and heartbreak of being fourteen and watching your mother pick through a waterlogged mountain of personal belongings flung into the street for the world to gawk at, in the hope of finding *something*, anything— a pair of underwear, a shredded childhood diary—that had been yours and private only the day before. Was it possible that anything like that could ever happen to Perry? Or to the other fifth-years at her firm? Or even to Mrs. Reeves, the woman who sat behind the firm's mahogany reception desk where she'd answered phones and greeted clients in undisputed authority for the past thirty-four years?

Sometimes Laura imagined what Sarah's life would eventually become, shuffling alone among the flotsam and jetsam of her former life crammed into that small, overheated apartment. The sadness she saw in Sarah's face, whenever she brought herself to make one of her increasingly rare visits, made her feel both guilty and terrified. She felt like yelling at Sarah, *It's not my fault that you're sad now, that you're lonely. You made your choices. It took both of us to make our relationship what it is.*

But the things Laura imagined might someday happen to herself, or to Sarah, were things that would never happen to Josh. One only had to look at him, to spend five minutes in his presence, to know that he was one of the anointed—him and all those belonging to him. Meeting Josh's parents and sister for the first time in New Jersey over Sunday brunch, Laura had said politely, *It's nice to meet you, Mrs. Broder.* And Zelda Broder, formidable in chunky diamonds and frosted hair, had grasped Laura's hand and exclaimed in her raspy voice, *Josh, she's lovely!* Laura had looked around at the comfortable faces, listened to the loud conversations about work or eager exchanges of gossip that weren't about the quixotic sorts of things that had formed the background of her early life with Sarah—discussions about the meaning of art in music, or painting banners for rallies that proclaimed HOUSING IS A HUMAN RIGHT—and she'd thought, *This is where I belong.*

Josh was simply a person who enjoyed his life and his work. He was passionate about music and books, the way Sarah had been, but he viewed them as smaller gifts that made everything else better rather than ends in themselves. He could make something as minor as a spontaneous afternoon movie or midnight pizza order seem like a holiday, a treat they'd earned by working so hard. For Laura, the idea of hard work being rewarded with anything other than money and the security of knowing more work and money would follow was so foreign as to come as a revelation.

She would think about him all day, imagining Josh's hands and

Josh's legs wrapped around her own, and her knees would tremble beneath her desk. Innocuous office talk, like, *Laura, could you please come in here?* or, *The meeting is starting now,* reminded her of the urgency of a *please* or *now* whispered in the dark. In her bed alone on the nights when she didn't see Josh, her legs contracted and kicked restlessly, keeping her up for hours, as if they were desperate to walk away with or without her, desperate to walk back to him.

To fall in love in New York is to walk, and she and Josh spent hours walking all over the city, although when they were downtown Laura made sure they never went any farther east than Soho or the Village. Their long legs naturally took rapid strides, but they deliberately slowed their pace to save their breath for the conversations that went back and forth and around and around, never ceasing, like an endless game of tetherball.

Once, only a few months into their relationship, they'd walked past a store on the Upper East Side, one of those tiny boutiques whose window mannequins wore heartbreakingly lovely, stunningly expensive gowns. One of the dresses in the window, a floor-length spaghetti-strapped number, was made of silk the exact color of the soft inside of a peach. Laura had stood contemplating it for a moment and said musingly, "I've always wanted to wear a dress like this."

"Then we should go in so you can try it on," Josh had replied.

Laura had glanced down at her faded jeans and light sweater— her typical nonwork uniform—and laughed. "What's the point? Where would I even wear something like that?"

"Trying on isn't buying," Josh had pointed out, and so the two of them went into the shop.

Looking at herself in the dress in front of the store's three-way mirror, Laura had felt transformed. Her pale skin looked creamy and rose-tinged next to the soft peach of the dress, and her hair gleamed against the delicate fabric like jewels in a velvet case. She didn't look like a lawyer with 150 pages of contracts to read through that night before returning to work in the morning, trudging to the subway with a shoulder bag so heavy that she was already developing back problems. She looked like someone who went whirling across polished floors before collapsing gracefully into a delicate chair with a glass of champagne and perhaps the smallest finger sandwich for refreshment.

"You should buy it," said Josh's voice, behind her.

"Are you crazy?" Laura whirled to face him. "Do you know how expensive . . . ?" But her protest trailed off when she saw Josh's face.

He looked at her as if seeing some version of herself she hadn't met. It was a look Laura had seen sometimes on Mr. Mandelbaum's face as he'd watched Mrs. Mandelbaum do the simplest things, like stand on her toes to pull a book from a high shelf, or pour boiling water from a kettle into a teacup. It was a half smile, stronger in the eyes than it was around the mouth. And even though Laura was very young when she'd seen it, even then she'd thought it was a smile that contained a lifetime of books and teacups, of sleepless nights next to a feverish son's bedside and clasped hands years later at that same son's graduation, months when the checkbook refused to balance and years of holiday dinners that were festive nonetheless. But, always, there had been this. This room. This woman.

"Marry me," Josh said. "Will you marry me?"

He reached out to take her hand, but Laura took an instinctive step back. "Are you serious?" She felt perspiration collect beneath her arms and thought, *Well, now I guess I have to buy this dress.* "Do we even know each other well enough to get married?"

"I know how I feel," Josh replied. "This is something I've been thinking about for a while."

His voice was firm, his eyes clear as they looked into her own. *He really has been thinking about it,* Laura realized. A wisp of an idea curled around the edges of thought: That you never knew, truly could never know, what another person was thinking. And yet what was love if not the possibility—the promise, even—of perfect understanding?

"I've never been this happy with anybody else," Josh continued, "and I can't imagine ever *being* this happy with anybody else. Can you?" His hand remained outstretched. "If you can, then I have nothing else to say."

Laura had always known that the world was made up of two types of people. There were those, like Josh (and Sarah, for that matter), who felt that life existed to be enjoyed for its own sake. It wasn't that such people were necessarily irresponsible (Laura again thought of Sarah), but that the point of the responsibility and hard work and worrying over bills and all the rest of it was so that, in the end, you could enjoy your life. If all those things didn't get you to the joy, then all those things didn't matter.

And then there were those who knew that life was something to be battled and survived. If you were very careful, and if you worked very hard, you could get through it without anything truly terrible happening to you. That was the most it was reasonable to hope for.

Laura was the second type of person, but she hadn't always been. She had been happy these few months of dating Josh, had remembered what it had felt like when she was young and any small thing—like the promise of visiting the Mandelbaums and spending long, uninterrupted hours with Honey the cat purring in her lap—had made ordinary days alive with the promise of joy to come. But she'd never really expected it to last. She'd been shoring up the happy days against the inevitable time when all she'd have left of them was the memory of what it had felt like, and the reality of struggling forward regardless.

Laura felt a stab of guilt now at the thought of saddling Josh with somebody like her for the rest of his life. But the thought, the half-suggested promise that maybe, just maybe, she could get it back somehow—that the silly songs Sarah had always listened to and sung about love and happiness and all the rest of it could be true, not just for a moment, but forever—was too much for her.

"Yes," she'd said. She let Josh take her hand, and as he pulled her into his arms she repeated against his ear, "Yes, I'll marry you."

Sarah had finally met Josh, not long after their engagement, over lunch in a small East Village sandwich place. If the suddenness of their courtship had alarmed her, she'd hidden it well. She and Josh had talked music for a solid hour, and Sarah's eyes shone in a way Laura hadn't seen in years. For the span of that hour, Laura had seen the Sarah she remembered from childhood, the Sarah who spoke confidently and had interesting things to say. Not the Sarah of recent years, who chattered at Laura so relentlessly that calling her or going to visit felt like being taken hostage. After so many years of keeping her distance, Laura would think resentfully, it hardly seemed fair.

She had worried what Josh would think when he saw how strained her relationship with Sarah was. (Because how could anyone fail to notice how uncomfortable they were in each other's presence?) Would he think there was something wrong with Laura? Reconsider the wisdom of entangling himself with someone whose family wasn't as healthy as his own?

But Josh had been enthralled. "Your mom is the *best*," he'd enthused afterward. "You have no idea how lucky you were, growing up with a mother who knew so much about music and *cared* about so many things."

Laura had always imagined that someday, at some hazy point in the future, after she and her mother had forgiven each other for all the unforgiven things that stood between them, they would sit in Sarah's apartment and talk across the battered kitchen table about Josh. Laura would say how falling for him had reminded her of the community pools Sarah had taken her to in the summers of her childhood, when Laura would allow herself to fall backward into the water and sink weightlessly to the bottom, the circle of sunlight reflected on the water's surface above her expanding as she sank. That was how love felt, like sinking into light.

Sarah would smile ruefully and say something like, *That's just how it was with your father and me.* And then Sarah would tell her what had gone wrong with Laura's father. She had wanted Sarah to offer some tangible explanation that could be logically applied to Laura's relationship with Josh, so Laura could say, *Well, that's something that would never happen to us.* Sarah used to say that Laura tried to wear logic like an armor, but Laura knew that everything that had gone wrong for Sarah, and therefore for Laura, had been the result of bad logic, a willful ignorance of the basic laws of cause and effect.

She'd thought about having a discussion like this with Sarah, but whenever she'd tried opening her mouth to begin it, it had seemed to her that the inevitable pain and exhaustion, the excruciating dredging-up of things long dormant (what an attorney might call the "opportunity cost"), couldn't possibly be worth it. Someday, perhaps, the right moment would present itself naturally.

Except that now, of course, that moment would never come.

Still, it was of some comfort to Laura that her mother had lived long enough to see her wedding. She and Josh had been married on a Thursday morning in the middle of September, in a Tribeca restaurant with only a handful of friends and family looking on. Laura was grateful they'd kept things small, as she wasn't sure who she would have invited beyond a few co-workers. Perry in his suit and yarmulke, properly restrained and joyful for the occasion, had made her think of Mr. Mandelbaum. How he would have loved to have been at her wedding! *My little ketsele a grown-up lady!* he would have said.

Sarah, now forty-nine, had been as beautiful as Laura had ever seen her, still tall and elegantly slim, the lilac silk dress she wore turning her eyes a vivid shade of indigo. Laura and Josh had both been walked down the aisle by their parents, in the Jewish tradition. While they were waiting for their cue, Sarah had pulled Laura's arm through her own. Laura could feel it tremble. Sarah looked as though she were about to say something, but instead she looked down at Laura's bouquet.

"I carried lilies at my wedding, too," was all she said.

* * *

Laura heard the sound of the TV from the living room as she pushed open the door of the apartment she shared with Josh, carefully hanging her coat and stowing her bag in the front-hall closet. A bit farther down the hall, she spied Prudence. Although she was lying down, the cat's entire body was a coil of tension. She leapt up when Laura entered, took a few steps toward her, and then, seeming uncertain, turned and started back in the direction of the living room. Laura paused to wonder at this, even as she went into the kitchen to pour the two glasses of red wine she brought into the living room where Josh sat watching the TV with fixed attention.

"Sorry it was such a late night again," she said, dropping a kiss on his cheek and handing him a glass. "How was your day?"

Josh clicked off the television and turned to face her. Something about the abrupt silence and Josh's expression sent a flicker of panic darting through Laura's stomach.

"Not so great." Josh took a deep breath and exhaled loudly through his nose. "I lost my job."

PART TWO

6

Prudence

THE NEWSPAPER JOSH DROPPED ONTO THE KITCHEN FLOOR HAS turned vicious. At first I only darted into its folds to make sure there weren't any rats or snakes trying to hide inside it (when I lived outside, I noticed them nesting in old newspapers all the time). But now it's trying to fold itself completely over me, even when I roll onto my back and kick at it with my hind legs. So I stand, crouch down with my tail straight out for balance, and take a flying leap onto it—to show it that *I'm* boss. It sees how much stronger I am and slides all the way into the kitchen wall as it tries to get away, taking me along with it. But I refuse to give up the fight so easily.

The newspaper stops moving once we both hit the wall, knowing that it's been beaten. Triumphantly, I tear a few pieces off with my teeth. Josh and Laura, who are eating breakfast at the kitchen table, are so relieved to see my victory over the newspaper— and to know for sure that there are no rats or mice or snakes hiding in it—that they burst out laughing. I return to my post by the table, rubbing my head against it and also the chair legs, so that anything else (like a rat or another vicious newspaper) that tries to get in here will know this territory is protected by a cat. Josh reaches down with one hand to pat my head, but I quickly pull back from his fingers, wrinkling my nose with distaste. He sighs and goes back to eating his breakfast.

Even though it's a Thursday, Josh isn't wearing his work clothes or shiny black feet-shoes. That's because the humans at his office won't let him go there to do work anymore. Now Josh is "working from home," although mostly what he does is talk on the phone and exercise his fingers on the cat bed in Home Office. (Is this what humans think "working" is?) Ever since this past Friday, when Josh told Laura he lost his job, Laura has been feeding me my breakfast in the kitchen. Josh says it's too hard to concentrate on his "work" with the smell of cat food drifting in from my room next door. Obviously, Josh doesn't know *half* of all the ways his suddenly being home inconveniences *me*.

I was nervous at first about eating my breakfast where Josh and Laura eat theirs, because of what happened that night of the Seder dinner. But it turns out that it isn't so bad. I've learned that if I *gently remind* them—by standing next to the kitchen counter and meowing—to let me have little bits of milk or eggs or the cheese they melt on top of bread in the toaster, I'm more likely to get to try new things. Sarah says my meows are irresistible. Actually, what she says is that some cats have meows that are almost musical, but I, sadly, am not one of them. I have a voice like a Lower East Side fishmonger, according to Sarah, and nobody can listen to *that* for too long before giving in. I think Sarah was afraid I would be offended whenever she called me a fishmonger, because she would always scoop me up in her arms and kiss my nose and say, *Don't worry, Prudence. I love your lovely atonal meows.* I don't know why she thought I'd be insulted, though. I'm not exactly sure what a fishmonger is, but it sounds like a *wonderful* thing to be.

Josh goes over to the counter now to get some more coffee, and when I meow at him he also pours a little of his coffee cream into my Prudence-bowl to mix with my breakfast. Just as I suspected would happen, Laura hardly mixes any of my old food in anymore with the "organic" food Josh buys for me. But I'm not as nervous about eating as I was that first week, and mixing the "organic" food with coffee cream makes it taste much better. Still, I use all the toes on my right paw to tilt my Prudence-bowl and spill just a little cream onto the blue rubber mat with all the cat drawings, because I hate that stupid thing.

Josh returns to the table and sits down again across from Laura, who drinks her coffee black with no cream or even sugar. I follow and rub my head against his ankle, as a reward for good behavior, and note with satisfaction that along with my scent I've left a few strands of my fur on the bottom of his jean leg.

"So what's on the agenda for today?" Laura asks him.

"The usual," Josh replies. "Phone calls, emails. And I guess it's time for me to break the news to Abe and Zelda."

Laura makes a sympathy-face. "Yikes."

Josh shrugs. "I don't think it'll be so bad. I've been working since I was fifteen, and this is the first job I've ever lost. They'll probably tell me I was overdue." He sips from his coffee mug. "And I have a call with that headhunter who tried to recruit me a couple years back."

Sarah and Anise used to talk about losing jobs. Back in The Old Days, they had something called Day Jobs, which was where they worked to get money in between doing something else called Gigs. Sarah had lots of Day Jobs, like selling fruit at a farmer's market that traveled all over the city and made Sarah show up for work before the sun was even up, which was especially hard when Sarah'd had a Gig that lasted all night. She also waited for tables and clerked at a record store. Anise only had one Day Job, as a bartender, but she ended up having to do that same job in lots of different places. The reason they changed Day Jobs so much was because sometimes Gigs happened at the same time as Day Jobs, and if they had to choose which one to go to, Sarah and Anise always picked Gigs—even though lots of times Gigs didn't even pay them. That's why Sarah and Anise were Flat Broke almost all the time. Sarah finally stopped doing Day Jobs *and* Gigs when Laura was three and Sarah's husband went away. That's when she knew she really had to get serious, so she opened her own record store. By then, Anise was famous and getting Gigs all the time. She didn't have to worry about Day Jobs after that.

It sounded like Sarah and Anise spent more time losing jobs than keeping them, so if it's true that this is the first time Josh ever lost a job then he really *has* been lucky.

Laura reaches across the table to take Josh's hand, and even though there's a slight crease in her forehead from tension, she smiles. "Something'll turn up," she says softly.

"I'm not worried." Josh is built with eyes that are turned just a little bit down and a mouth that's turned just a little bit up, so it always looks like he's right on the verge of being happy and also right on the verge of being sad. Now he turns the corners of his mouth all the way up until he's smiling. But his eyes don't smile at all.

As soon as I saw Josh last Friday, I knew that something unusual and bad had happened to him. I was napping on the cat bed in Home Office when he came home from work (inconsiderately) early. He noticed me there when he walked upstairs, and came over like he was going to shoo me off like he always does, but then he seemed to change his mind. He didn't smell sweaty, exactly, but he smelled like he *had been* sweating more than he usually does— not exercise-sweaty, but scared-sweaty. He also smelled like he'd stopped somewhere before coming home for a few gulps of the evil-smelling liquid that Laura and Josh keep on a special cart in the dining room. After he left Home Office—without even turning the light off the way he normally does on his way out—he went downstairs, and I heard the sound of the TV going on.

I didn't know yet what terrible thing had happened to Josh. But the smell of something terrible having happened made me nervous. Then I thought about Laura, who was going to walk right into the apartment after work without knowing she should be on her guard. Against my better judgment (because Laura and I aren't exactly friends after that horrible holiday dinner), I decided to wait downstairs and try to warn her. That's what Sarah would want me to do. After all, Sarah loves Laura almost as much as she loves me.

But Josh ended up telling Laura right away what had happened, before I got a chance to convince her to approach him cautiously. He said that magazine companies everywhere were losing money, and when that happens the first thing they do is get rid of the people who work in marketing. Josh said they gutted his entire staff, which is *horrible*! I once saw a TV show about a human gutting a fish he caught. First he cut the fish open right up the middle, and then he pulled out all its insides and threw what was left into a big container. And even though watching that made me hungry for fish (I wish I had some fish right now), hearing that Josh's office did the same thing to *humans* made all my fur stand straight up. How evil the humans at Josh's office must be! It sounded like Josh was lucky to escape that place with his life, and it made me understand why he looked and smelled so awful when he got home. If I saw a thing like that with my own eyes, I don't think I'd be able to sleep for at least a month.

I expected that Laura would throw her arms around Josh like in TV movies, and say something like, *Thank God* you're *okay!* Instead, a crease appeared between her eyebrows. When she finally did put her arms around him, she was gentler than I would have thought she'd be (seeing what a narrow escape Josh had) and she said, "I'm so sorry, honey."

Josh's eyes over Laura's shoulder looked worried, even though what his mouth said was, "I don't want you to worry about anything. I know how rough things have been for you these past few months."

Josh was still hugging Laura, so he couldn't see her face the way I could. He couldn't tell that it got that tight expression Laura always gets whenever Sarah is mentioned. It's like there's too much happening in Laura's head for her face to show it all, so she holds all her face muscles as still as she possibly can so they won't reveal anything. (This is something cats can do naturally without having to practice the way humans do.) "Josh, I'm *fine*," Laura said, and her voice sounded almost annoyed. "You don't need to worry about me right now."

Then Josh pulled back to look into Laura's face, and he pushed the corners of his mouth up until his own face looked more happy than sad. "The good news is that I'll be getting five months' severance. They're emailing me the agreement next week, and once I've signed it they'll mail the check. And in the meantime I'll start making calls first thing Monday morning."

The crease in Laura's forehead smoothed out, and she smiled. "That *is* good news. Five months should be plenty of time for you to find something else. You have such a great résumé."

"I think so," Josh said, and he smiled, too.

The days have been getting longer, and when Laura or Josh pushes open the top half of one of the long windows in the living room, I can feel how much warmer the air outside is. Still, it was cool enough inside the apartment. There was really no reason for the tiny beads of sweat-water that popped up on Josh's forehead.

At first I almost felt sorry for Josh, because it sounded like what happened at his office was even worse than the things that happen at the Bad Place. That was before I knew how disruptive to all my usual routines it would be to have Josh home all the time. If I'm upstairs in my room with all the Sarah-boxes, trying to spend some quiet-time alone with my memories, Josh is also in that room, walking around in circles—like those pigeons Laura likes watching so much—while he talks on the phone. I don't know why talking into the phone should have to involve walking around. I, for example, am perfectly capable of meowing as clearly and frequently as I need to from a still, sitting position. But Josh likes to walk when he's talking on the phone. Every time I try to walk over to one spot, Josh is pacing around that same exact spot, and I have to dart over and around the Sarah-boxes to get out of his way. I'm paying extra attention to what my whiskers tell me these days just to keep from getting stepped on or tripped over. (Maybe Josh's balance is so imprecise because he shaves off his own whiskers every morning.)

When I decide to go downstairs to the living room, where I could *always* count on being alone during the day, Josh comes downstairs, too. He's still talking on the phone, opening and closing the refrigerator and kitchen cabinets without taking anything out of them (or even really looking into them) as he talks. This is particularly frustrating because a cat has every right to expect that when a human opens the refrigerator or a kitchen cabinet, he'll pull out some food and share that food with the cat. Even sitting directly in front of Josh and meowing while staring pointedly at the cabinets does nothing except cause him to walk around me without any acknowledgment, as if I were no more than a couch or coffee table in his path. Sometimes he presses down on the handle of the can opener, which then makes the whirring sound that usually means a can is being opened. And even though I've realized that Josh isn't really opening cans when he does this, I *still* have to run in to check—just to be *completely* sure—because what if the one time I *don't* check, Josh *is* opening a can of tuna or something else I'd want to try and I've missed it?

Finally, when I can't bear *that* frustration anymore, I go back upstairs to have a short, restful nap on top of the cat bed in Home Office. And wouldn't you know it, Josh comes back into the room just as I've started to doze and says, "Prudence, I *told* you, stay off the computer!" and shoos me away without so much as a *please* or a *thank you*. And of course I *know* that he's told me before to "stay off," but I thought he meant only at night when *he's* home to use it as a scratching post. It seems perfectly obvious to *me* that something so warm and springy and cat-sized was intended to be used by cats for napping. If Josh is looking for something to exercise his fingers on, he's more than welcome to share my scratching post downstairs. I think he'll find he gets better results anyway, because that's what the scratching post is meant for. And it's quieter, too.

Sudden change is always bad. Change of any kind is something to be avoided if at all possible. Even humans understand this instinctively as well as cats do, which is why they follow our example and fall into sensible habits, like always sleeping on the same side of the bed, or sitting on the same spot on the couch, or eating the same breakfast every day at the same time. As unpredictable as Sarah can be, she always does certain things the same way. Like the way she counts exactly to one hundred when she brushes her hair before getting into bed at night.

Josh's being at home all the time is a *very* big, and very sudden, change. It's disrupted all my routines, and I can't remember ever having spent so much time with one human. Even Sarah, who doesn't have nearly as many human friends as Josh seems to (what with his endless phone-talking), never spent more than one full day a week at home without leaving the apartment at all, and that was only on days when she didn't have to go to work.

Don't misunderstand me. It's nice having a human or two around the house. Even though no other human will ever be as important to me as Sarah is, a well-mannered human can be a pleasant companion. They're very useful for things like opening cans of food, or cleaning a litterbox, or running a brush over your back when your fur gets too itchy (like Sarah used to do for me at least once a week), or making a spot on the couch nice and warm so that, when they stand up, it becomes the most comfortable spot in the whole room to sleep on.

But even the most useful companion can wear away your patience if they spend *too much* time just walking around and getting underfoot.

Josh settles into the chair that lives in front of the desk in Home Office. I follow and squeeze behind the desk to bat at some of the dangling wires that live back there. Josh doesn't like when I do this, either, but he's too distracted right now to notice, and it's important for me to practice my mice-fighting skills. (I got used to practicing them at exactly this time of day long before Josh started spending all his time in the apartment, and I'm trying to keep my routines as close as possible to what they're supposed to be.) He presses a few buttons on the telephone. It rings a few times and then Josh's mother answers. After they've said hello to each other, she says, "Do you have me on speaker? You know I hate being on speaker."

"I'm sorry, Ma," Josh says. "I've been on the phone all morning and I think my hand has stiffened into a claw."

Josh's hand doesn't look even a little like a claw, but his mother can't see that from the other end of the phone line. So she laughs and says, "Why are you calling from home in the middle of the day? Are you sick?"

"That's actually what I called to tell you." Josh takes a slightly deeper breath. "I lost my job last week."

"What happened?" She sounds alarmed, and instinctively my left ear turns in the direction of the phone, listening for any hint of sudden danger.

"Nothing, really," Josh says. "The company was having financial trouble and they made staff cuts. I was one of them."

There's a silence. "You've never lost a job in your whole life," Josh's mother finally tells him. "You'll find something else again before you know it. A smart boy like you has nothing to worry about."

"Thanks, Ma." Josh is smiling a little.

There's a muffled sound, and what sounds like a conversation in the background, and then Josh's mother says, "Hold on. Your father wants to talk to you."

"Josh?" his father's voice shouts from the speaker. Josh's legs shift slightly and he sits up straighter in his chair. Suddenly I'm trapped behind the desk with no way to get out until he moves. "Sorry to hear what happened. Listen, you've been putting away fifteen percent of your take-home every month like I told you, right?"

"More than that until this past year." Josh runs one hand back and forth over the top of his head. "Although I took a big hit back when the market tanked. I haven't fully recovered yet."

"Don't worry about that now. You just keep that money right where it is. Laura's job is still good?"

"Oh yeah. Laura's busier than ever."

"Good, good," his father repeats. "The two of you will be fine." Then there's another muffled pause, and he says, "Mother wants to talk to you again, so I'll say good-bye. Give Laura our love and try not to worry too much. You're a smart kid. You'll find a new job in no time."

Josh's mother's voice comes out of the speaker again. While the two of them talk about Josh's sister and how she's hoping to send the littermates to a place called Summer Camp next month, I try to figure out exactly how long "no time" is. It's hard to be sure, because the way humans think about time is so different from the way cats do. Waiting for someone to feed me tuna from an open can, or standing on the metal table at the Bad Place while they stab me with needles, is a long, *long* time. Sitting in my ceramic bowl in our old apartment until Sarah comes home from work to play with me is longer than anything. But sleeping in Sarah's lap while she brushes my fur or sings to me is always too short—even when Sarah says something like, *I'm sorry, little girl, but I have to stretch my legs. We've been sitting like this for four hours.* (This just proves again how made up human hours are—because if hours were real, sleeping in Sarah's lap for *four* of them wouldn't go by so quickly.)

"No time" sounds like it should happen right *now.* But when Josh and his mother say good-bye, it doesn't seem like Josh has found a new job yet. "I'm supposed to call a headhunter in a few minutes," Josh tells her. "I'll talk to you and Dad later."

There's a difference between saying things that aren't true, and saying something that's part of the truth but not all of it. Josh tells Laura how he's looking for a new job, and that's true. He also says he doesn't want her to worry, and I can tell that's true, too.

But the whole truth that Laura doesn't know is how nobody Josh talks to will ever be able to give him a new job. That's because Laura isn't here all day like I am and doesn't hear the phone conversations that Josh has.

Josh talks on the phone with lots of different humans, but the conversations all sound pretty similar. They begin with Josh saying how great it is to talk to the person again after so long. He asks how the other person is doing, how their kids and wives have been, and then I guess the person he's talking to must ask how Josh is, because that's when he says, *Well, I don't know if you've heard, but . . .*

Josh sounds and looks genuinely happy at the beginnings of these conversations. But as the conversations go on, even though his voice sounds the same, his face starts to look different. He goes from having the look of a human who's hoping for good news to the look of a human who's still trying to sound happy even though what he's hearing has made him feel just the opposite. By the time he gets to the part where he says things like, *If you hear about anything . . .* or, *I'm thinking of taking on some consulting projects, so if you know anyone who's looking to outsource . . .* there's no happiness left in his face.

Now Josh is talking to a type of human called a "headhunter." This sounds like a strange thing to be, because why would somebody only hunt heads? Even if you could catch just a head, that's the least-good part to eat!

The headhunter tells Josh that people are getting the ax all over town, which I guess explains how he's finding so many heads. This sounds even worse than the humans who got gutted at Josh's old job. I had no idea human jobs could be so violent. Then again, if so many people can't do their jobs anymore because their heads are getting chopped off, you'd think that would make it easier, rather than harder, for Josh to find a new one.

But what the human on the other end of the phone line says to Josh is, "Even if I could find you something, the money wouldn't be anything close to what you were making."

"How much less are we talking about?" Josh asks.

"Half, maybe. If that."

This is the first time I realize that human jobs all give people different amounts of money. I'd never really thought about it, but I just assumed that money was money, and any human who had a job got the same amount of money as any other human with a job. I guess it makes sense they'd be different, though. Jobs are what humans use to get food, like hunting is what cats use. And every cat knows that sometimes you catch a mouse that's plump and juicy, and other times the mouse you catch is so small and stringy you're hungry again almost right away.

"It's possible," Josh says slowly, "that I would consider something at a reduced salary. If the opportunity for growth was there."

"The problem is that anybody in a hiring position will figure you'll take the lower-paying job for now and then leave as soon as things pick up again. Which, let's be honest, you probably would." The headhunter pauses, and I hear a *glug glug* sound, like he's drinking from a glass. "The world isn't what it was when I first reached out to you two years ago, Josh. Frankly, there were never that many publishing jobs at your level to begin with. Your business is shrinking, and I don't see it expanding again anytime soon. I wish I could give you more hope, but those are the facts."

"I know it's bad out there," Josh says. "I guess I didn't realize how bad."

"You don't know the half of it," the headhunter says. "I talk to people every day who are out of work and whose husband or wife also lost *their* job. They've got kids in college and mortgage payments, and there's no money coming in. Do you and Laura rent or own?"

"We rent," Josh says.

"Well that's good, at least. How's Laura doing, by the way?"

"She's great." A smile flits across Josh's face. "She's been a rock, actually."

"You're a lucky man." The headhunter lets out a noisy sigh. "I'll keep my ears open. But, Josh . . ."

"Yes?"

"If I were you, I'd start thinking about how I could take my skills and experience and apply them in a different direction."

* * *

I'm sleepy by the time Josh finishes talking to the headhunter, so I go to curl up in my favorite napping spot with Sarah's dress in the back of my closet. It still smells like her, but I've noticed lately that the Sarah-smell is getting fainter. What will I do when her smell is completely gone? Sarah says that as long as you remember someone, they'll always be with you. But I remember Sarah all the time, and she still hasn't come back for me. What if that's because I'm not remembering her enough? What if I can't remember her at all anymore when I don't have anything with her Sarah-smell on it?

Lately Josh has been listening to Sarah's black disks while Laura is away at her office, always turning the music off and putting everything back into the Sarah-boxes before she comes home. It's the sound of Sarah's music that draws me downstairs after I wake up from my nap. Josh is sitting in the big chair in the living room, and as soon as I round the corner in the stairs I can tell he's upset about something by the way his shoulders are set. Resting on the coffee table is a thin stack of folded white papers held together with a paper clip.

I settle into my favorite spot on the short side of the big couch and listen to Sarah's music with Josh. From time to time he looks over at the papers on the table. After the music stops and he's returned the black disk upstairs, he takes the papers in his hand and looks through them. From the little creases around the edges, it seems like he's looked through them a few times already.

Even though the days are getting longer now, it's still dark outside when Laura finally comes home from work. Usually Josh's face changes as soon as he hears Laura's key in the lock. He looks the way I probably look when Laura is putting food down for me, and I know it will be one of the best times of the whole day. But now his face doesn't change at all when Laura calls out her usual greeting and he calls back to say, "I'm in here."

Laura walks into the room with two glasses of wine, and she hands one to Josh. That's when she sees the odd look on his face. "Is anything wrong?" When Josh doesn't say anything, she asks him, "Did something happen?"

Josh is quiet for a long moment while he drinks from the glass Laura handed him. Then he says, "Why didn't you tell me, Laur?" He picks up the folded stack of papers and hands them to her. "I got my severance agreement today. It's dated from a week before they let me go. Somebody at your firm must have known what was going on. I thought *you* worked on contracts."

Laura's face gets as red as it did the night of that Pass Over dinner. She takes the papers Josh is holding out to her, but she doesn't unfold them or try to read them. "Josh, I had no idea." I know she's telling the truth, because the black centers of her eyes stay the same size and nothing about her posture stiffens the way it usually does when a human isn't telling the truth. "I never saw this. Nobody said a word to me."

It's odd, because humans don't normally look this upset when what they're saying is true. And that's when I know. Laura is upset *because* she's telling the truth. That doesn't make any sense, and yet I feel sure I'm right.

"Well, maybe you can help me out with a couple of questions I have, your firm being the attorney-of-record." Josh's mouth twists into a shape that's trying to be a smile but isn't quite. "I've looked over the vacation pay and expense-account money they owe me. And I'll get another three months on my insurance until COBRA kicks in."

"That's boilerplate, standard," Laura tells him. "We just fill in the numbers based on the information the client provides." The skin of her knuckles curls and tenses around her wineglass until it's whiter than the rest of her hand. Maybe she's afraid of the kicking cobras Josh is talking about. Sarah is afraid of snakes, too, which is why I always check newspapers so carefully.

"What about on the third page? It says something about waiving my rights in perpetuity and throughout the universe." Josh tries again to smile. "Is that supposed to be a joke?"

"That's also standard. They're just trying to cover all their bases to avoid a lawsuit. Which was nothing you were planning to do, anyway. A nice, clean break—that's all they want."

Josh winces when Laura says this, although I don't think she notices. "Everything might be standard, but I'm not going to call it *nice* or *clean*," he tells her. "So I'm okay to sign it? Should you take a couple of minutes and look through the whole thing? You're my lawyer, after all."

Laura continues to hold the papers without unfolding them. She takes a long swallow from her wineglass. "I can't do that," she finally says.

"Really?" Josh sounds like he thinks Laura is saying something not-true. "*Really?*"

"Your company is my client, Josh. Forget all the ethical issues and conflicts of interest. The people at my firm had to go pretty far out of their way to keep me from knowing about this. There were meetings and memos that I didn't know anything about—about one of *my* clients—and nothing ever crossed my desk. And you really don't have to worry," she adds quickly, seeing how Josh's eyebrows come together to make an angry line across his forehead. "These severance agreements are—"

"Yeah, I know. *Standard.*" His voice gets louder. "And I guess I don't meet the standards to get some legal advice from my wife. Maybe I should call your buddy Perry—he seems like a nice guy."

"Josh, if I send you back with this thing all marked up, Perry will *know* it was me. He's not an idiot." Laura's voice is also getting louder. "And even if somehow he didn't figure it out, I couldn't look him in the face and lie."

"It didn't seem to bother Perry to look you in the face and lie."

"He didn't *lie.* He kept client information confidential. That's Perry's job. It's my job, too." Laura's eyes look hurt. Sarah says that Laura has her father's eyes, but Laura looks like Sarah now as she runs her fingers through her hair. "This is the kind of thing that could get me fired, Josh. And for what? It's not like we can afford for you to walk away from five months' salary, anyway."

"You know, I think I've heard enough legalese for one day." Josh takes the papers back from Laura.

"Let me call a friend at another firm. I'm sure I can find—"

"Don't worry about it." Josh's voice doesn't sound angry any-more. It has no expression at all. "There's nothing to worry about, right? It's standard."

"I'll make some calls first thing tomorrow morning," Laura says.

"I said don't worry about it. I wouldn't want to see you get your hands dirty." Josh is completely right about *that*. There's nothing more disgusting than a human with dirty hands trying to touch you. He gets up and says, "I'm going upstairs to check email."

Josh hands his glass back to Laura. She just stands there for a long time, holding two glasses of wine without drinking from ei-ther of them.

Most nights, Laura stays up much later than Josh. She likes to read her work papers when the apartment is quiet. But tonight, Josh is still awake in the living room when Laura gets into bed and turns on the TV. The only times Sarah ever watched the little TV in our bedroom, instead of the bigger one in the living room, was when she was too sick to get out of bed. Laura never watches TV in the bedroom, either. Not usually, anyway.

I remember one night, a year and three months ago, when Sarah came home very late from work. It was unlike her to spend so many hours in a row away from our apartment, and I was worried by the time she finally got back. Our neighbor from the building—the same one who came to feed me when Sarah stopped coming home at all—was with her. Sarah was pale and her face was pinched, as if she were in pain. But when the neighbor helped Sarah get settled on the couch and hovered over her, asking if there was anything else she needed, Sarah said, "I'll be fine, Sheila. Thanks so much again for everything."

Sarah stayed in bed watching TV for the next four days, and those were probably the happiest four days I've ever known. I had Sarah to snuggle under the covers with, and she didn't have to go to work or anything. I'd never had Sarah all to myself for so long.

But I wasn't happy that first night. Sarah didn't turn on any lamps after the neighbor left. She just sat on the couch with me in her lap until the sun came up. Even though she didn't say anything, I could tell that something was very wrong, and that she needed me close. In the darkness I could still see the tiny cracks in the skin around Sarah's eyes. And when the water from her eyes flowed into those cracks, that was where I licked her gently. To let the light in.

Now I follow the sound of the TV up the stairs and see Laura in bed like she's asleep, but her legs keep kicking. They kick so hard, she almost kicks the covers right off the bed. That's something else Sarah used to do—kick the blankets in her sleep when she was upset.

When Sarah was worried about something in her sleep, I used to curl up tight right next to her left ear and stretch out one paw to rest, very gently, on her shoulder. I didn't want to wake her, but I did want her to know that I was there with her. Sometimes my lying next to her was what made her able to fall into a deep enough sleep that she wasn't kicking anymore.

Josh is in the living room listening to one of Sarah's black disks. He's playing the song Sarah sang to me the day we found each other, the song that has my name in it. *Dear Prudence,* the song says, *won't you come out to play . . .*

I've been trying not to get *too* close to Laura and Josh. After all, only one person can be your Most Important Person. For me, that person is Sarah. And when she comes back, I don't want anybody—including me—to be confused about the way things are supposed to be.

But Laura looks so much like Sarah, lying there with her eyes closed and her legs scrunched up, that I find myself jumping onto the bed. The ache in my chest from Sarah's not being here, which I've been living with for so long, eases a little. Moving stealthily, so my Prudence-tags don't jingle and startle her, I settle onto the pillow next to Laura's left ear. Curling into a ball, with my tail wrapped around my nose to keep my face warm, I reach out one paw and let it rest on Laura's shoulder.

Laura rolls over so that she's facing me, with her eyes still closed. Her breathing gets deeper, the way Sarah's does when she's finally falling into a real sleep, and her arm curves out so that my tail and nose rest in the bend of her elbow. Alone in her bedroom, wearing her sleep clothes and without Josh lying next to her, Laura smells more like Sarah than ever. The TV isn't very loud, and I can still hear the *Dear Prudence* song playing downstairs.

Hearing it now, with all the little crackles and popping sounds in the exact same places I remember, just the way it was when Sarah played this black disk in our old apartment, I drift off to sleep. In my dream Sarah is there, smiling at me and saying, *Who's my love? Who's my little love?* When a hand falls onto my back to stroke my fur, I don't know if it's real or if it's Sarah's hand in my dream. I purr deeply anyway and think, *I am, Sarah. I'm your love.*

7

Sarah

I T'S HARD TO IMAGINE IT NOW, BUT DOWNTOWN NEW YORK USED TO BE
dead quiet at night. You could walk down Broadway from Prince
to Reade without hearing anything other than the sound of the
occasional taxicab and your own footsteps echoing off buildings.
You could walk down Elizabeth Street at four AM with nothing to
keep you company but the aroma of fresh-baked bread from mom-
and-pop bakeries.

It was silent, that is, unless you knew where to go. Even back
then—before it became big, and then commercial, and then finally
the playground of middle-class college kids and the bridge-and-
tunnel crowd—there were pockets and places where the noise
went on all night. Soho lofts where an invitation and password got
you into underground parties that played the kind of music you'd
never hear on the radio. Bars where jukeboxes hummed all night
and clubs where bands didn't start their first set until two AM. The

shattering-glass sound of beer bottles, the inevitable thud of a person too drunk to stand who eventually falls down, the *thump thump thump* of someone's bass turned all the way up.

I've always hated silence. I've always thought silence was like death. Quiet as death. Silent as the tomb. Dead men tell no tales. Nobody ever says the opposite. Nobody ever says *noisy as the tomb.*

That's what I loved so much about disco. Disco used *all* the sounds, *all* the beats, *all* the instruments. The *noise* of it was always there for you. It would pick you up and spin you around and whirl you and dip you until you were almost too dizzy to stand on your own, but it never once let you fall.

You're probably thinking to yourself how silly disco was. Maybe you were even one of those people who wore a DISCO SUCKS T-shirt back in the day. But you only remember it that way because, by the end, the major labels thought they had a formula for it and cranked out by-the-numbers fluff, trying to make a quick cash grab. Disco never died, though. It just changed forms. And even today, if you're at a wedding and the DJ puts on a song that gets every single person—no matter how old or young—out onto the floor, chances are it's a dance song written sometime between 1974 and 1979.

It was 1975 when I first discovered the New York music scene. When you start coming into the City by yourself at fifteen to sneak into parties and clubs, when you move there permanently at sixteen and live in an unfinished loft above a hardware store, people assume you're fleeing a troubled home life. Abusive parents, maybe, or some unnamed family tragedy, possibly even a grabby stepfather. When people keep making up the same story for you, it becomes easier and easier to believe it's true. That's why it's so important to keep your past organized. Your past is the *real* truth. Your past is who you are now.

Prudence comes to sit in front of me. Little lady with her dainty white socks and black tiger stripes. "It's important to keep your past organized," I tell her. She regards me from rounded green eyes, then meows in an apparently thoughtful way.

I hadn't heard music in so long before Prudence and I found each other. Not just the music in my records, which sat for years in a storage unit, but the music in my head. It just stopped one day. I lost it. And then there was Prudence. After that, it was like floodgates opened and all that music I'd hidden away came pouring back out.

Prudence, standing on her hind legs to swipe at dust motes in a sunbeam, is a conductor leading a symphony. Prudence curled in my lap while I stroke her little back is "In My Room" by the Beach Boys. Prudence sneaks into the bathroom and unrolls the toilet paper, spilling it all over the floor, in rhythm to "Soul Makossa" by Manu Dibango.

Pru-dence kit-*ten*, *Pru-dence* kit-*ten*. That's what I hear in my mind whenever I look at her. A perfect rhythm in four/four time. The sound of a heartbeat times two. The motor of a life.

What I remember most about the house I grew up in is the silence. We had wall-to-wall carpeting in every room except the bathrooms and kitchen, so even the sounds of us walking around doing everyday things felt more like sleepwalking than living.

By the time I was a teenager, my parents hardly spoke to each other anymore except when necessary. *What are you making for dinner tonight? When is the plumber coming? Sarah, could you pass the peas?*

They had been desperate for a second child. When I was eight, my mother gave birth to a baby boy who lived only ten hours. After he died, it was as if it was painful for my mother to be reminded that she'd ever had any children at all. The only thing she wanted was a quiet home. When my junior high music teacher said I had a good voice and should maybe take private singing lessons, my mother declined on the grounds that she didn't want noise in the house all the time. Trying to stop my "endless chatter" once (I'd been asking her questions about her own childhood), my mother told me I'd better get past my need for constant conversation, or someday when I grew up and got married myself there'd be no end of fighting in my house. The funny thing is, I never did fight with my husband until one day just after Laura turned three. He said, *I don't think I can handle this anymore.* And then, the next day, he was gone. Just like that.

Eventually I got used to the silence that emanated from my mother like smoke to fill the rooms of our house and choke our words. I spent most of my time trying to disappear into it. Still, I remember nights when I'd lie in bed and pray for rain just so I could hear the sound of it, like a round of applause, beating down on the roof above my head.

All that changed for me the day my parents gave me permission to take the train by myself to Manhattan from where we lived in White Plains. All I had to do was promise I wouldn't go farther downtown than Herald Square, where Macy's was. But the subway system, which had seemed so easy to understand when I went into the City with my mother, confused me hopelessly when I tried to figure it out on my own. I took the wrong train from Grand Central, and then another wrong train at 14th Street, and somehow I ended up on Third Avenue. The streets were mostly empty. I saw only a few bums huddled miserably in doorways, and clusters of tough-looking girls standing on street corners. Buildings, even the ones that didn't look so old, were crumbling from the disrepair of neglect.

By the time I reached Second Avenue, I knew beyond a doubt that I was nowhere near Macy's. Up ahead I saw what looked to be a newsstand with a yellow awning that inexplicably proclaimed GEM SPA (inexplicable because it didn't seem like you'd find either gems or a spa inside) and, farther down, a store whose black awning extended out onto the sidewalk. The words LOVE SAVES THE DAY were written along its side in multicolored block lettering. The store's window was a riot of color, a delta of ruckus jutting into a sea of gray and dull brick-red. It held exotic-looking clothes and magazines and toys and more than my eye was capable of taking in all at once. I could tell that it was a secondhand store, and I knew how appalled my mother would be at the thought of my buying used clothing. But against the gunmetal silence of the street, the colors of that store window were like shouts calling me in.

I took the first dress I pulled off the rack, made by somebody called Biba, into the dressing room. It was a muted gold, interwoven with a cream-colored diamond pattern. The sleeves were long and elaborate, blousing away from tight cuffs. The body of the dress fell in pleats, in a baby-doll fashion, from just above my still-flat chest to a hem so far up my thigh that, when I exited the dressing room to look at myself in the mirror, I blushed.

"You should buy it," I heard a voice say. A girl, barely five feet tall and weighing maybe all of ninety-five pounds, looked at me admiringly. I guessed that she was two or three years older than I was. Beautiful in an impish sort of way, with enormous hazel eyes, a snub nose like a cat's, and a mouth so small it just made you look at her eyes again. Her hair was short and chopped off unevenly in a careless way that nonetheless looked deliberate. It was mostly blond except for where it had streaks of green and pink.

The girl noticed where my eyes went and, touching one of the pink streaks, she said, "Manic panic." Later I'd learn that Manic Panic was a store on St. Mark's Place where they sold offbeat hair colors in spray-on aerosol cans. At the time, though, I had no idea what she was talking about. She added, "I go there a few times a week to let Snooky spray my hair, but I think I have to stop. Too many other people are doing it now."

I nodded, because I wanted to look like I knew what that sentence meant. An entire trend had apparently taken root and flourished here in the City. And I'd known nothing about it out in White Plains, where nothing ever changed except to get drabber.

"You should *definitely* buy that dress," the girl repeated.

"I'm not really sure it's me," I said. "Don't you think it's much too short?"

The girl laughed, loud and harsh. She had a voice like a chain saw, too gritty and hard-edged to belong to someone as young and delicate-looking as she was. How many sleepless nights of cigarettes and shouting over music had gone into the making of that voice? Eventually I'd hear her sing and come to know just how hypnotic and blissed-out she could make it sound when she wanted to. "Girl, that dress is more you than anything you've ever had on." She aimed a dimpled smile at me. "And I don't even *know* you."

I laughed, too, at the absurdity of her logic.

"What kind of music are you into?" she asked unexpectedly.

"The usual stuff, I guess." I tried to think of something to say that would be truthful, but that also might impress her. "I've been listening to *Pet Sounds* a lot lately." Then I blushed again, because what could be less impressive to this girl than *Pet Sounds,* which had come out way back in 1966, nine years earlier?

She looked at me appraisingly. "You sound like you can probably sing."

"I used to," I said. "But my parents didn't like it."

The girl's face registered deep understanding, and I saw that I'd unintentionally passed a test I hadn't realized I was taking. "I'm going to a party tonight that'll have some really great music," she told me. "Stuff nobody else is playing. You should come. I'll meet you somewhere at midnight and we can go over together."

I imagined all the insurmountable obstacles between me and a midnight party in the City. I'd never been to a party that *started* at midnight. The girl must have sensed something of this because she asked, "You're still living at home?" I nodded. How old did she think I was, anyway? I waited for her to decide I was just some kid, unworthy of her time, but she said, "Look, call your parents and tell them you're spending the night at a friend's house. You can hang out with me the rest of the day if you don't have anything else to do. I'll figure out something for you to wear."

I looked at her dubiously. Not only was she a foot shorter than I was, but nothing she wore was anything I would ever wear. She had on a black leather jacket with a glitzy, faded panther on the back, whose metal-studded paw reached over her left shoulder. Beneath that she wore a magenta-sequined party dress over skinny black jeans and a pair of unlaced black motorcycle boots. Around her neck was a silver pendant shaped like a holster dangling from a slender silver chain. She looked tough and sexy and surprisingly girlie, but to my suburban eyes she also looked outlandish. "Something that's *you*," she reassured me with another warm smile. "And for God's sake, buy that dress. You look incredible in it."

There didn't seem to be any way to get out of buying the dress now, so I began digging around in my purse to make sure I had enough cash. "Hey," I said. "What's your name?"

"Anise." It was a name I'd never heard before, and it was perfect for her.

"I'm Sarah."

"Pleased to meet you, Sarah." She made a show of solemnly shaking my hand, her own hand feeling larger in mine than it should have. "Tonight'll be fun," she said. "Trust me."

The party Anise took me to was held in a loft on lower Broadway, in a building that had once been a warehouse. We had to check in with two girls holding clipboards and hand over two dollars before we were allowed to climb the stairs and enter a cavernous space filled with multicolored balloons, like a child's birthday party. The balloons were shot through with winking silver sparkles reflected from a mirrored ball that hung from the ceiling in the center of the room. The mirrored ball also caught and refracted colored lights glowing from unseen sources, lights that brightened and dimmed in time with the music. The people who packed the room were even more gorgeous than the lights, glittering in outrageous outfits reminiscent of a carnival. I felt like I'd stumbled into the heart of a prism.

Later I would come to understand the technical aspects of what David Mancuso, the man who threw this party, had done. Most speakers back then had only one tweeter to transmit high-end frequencies. But David had eight JBL tweeters for his two speakers, grouped to hang from the ceiling in each of the four corners of the room. All I knew when I first walked into that loft, though, was that whatever I'd thought I'd been listening to, it wasn't music. At least, not the way music was supposed to sound. It was like I'd been listening to music all my life with cotton in my ears. I felt like one of Plato's cave dwellers (we were reading *The Republic* in my social studies class) who thought fire was sunlight—until they stepped outside and saw the real sun for the first time.

Everybody there felt the difference in the sound, even if they didn't know they did. You could see it in the way their bodies reacted with varying levels of tension to a hi-hat versus a cymbal versus a guitar line. You could see it in the way David controlled the mood of the room with what he played, in the way he told stories with the music he chose. I'd never known that "Woman" by Barrabás could be followed by "More Than a Woman" by the Bee Gees and tell you things you didn't already know about what it was like to fall in love. That night was the first time I had the sense of a record as a living thing. Seven inches of God. All that *sound* and all those voices compressed into its ridges and grooves, each song's pattern unique as a set of fingerprints, awaiting only the lightest caress from that tiny needle to set its music free.

David gave us what we wanted before we knew we wanted it, except that we did know it with our bodies—when we wanted to speed up, when we wanted to rest. The music changed depending on how we felt, and how we felt changed because of the music. It was like being at a concert or in a crowded movie theater where everybody reacts as one—laughing, shouting, standing up to dance—except we couldn't see the person who was making it happen for us. He didn't have to stand, exposed, in front of a crowd the way somebody like Anise would have to when she played with her band. From his hidden booth, David performed without performing.

And before I knew it, I was dancing. I'd never really danced before, always feeling like I'd rather make my too-tall, too-skinny, and too-boyish body disappear than show it off in any way. But within seconds, the impulse to dance became irresistible. Anise and I danced together and then with strangers who swayed over to join us before dancing away again to form the core of a new group somewhere else. My idea of dancing was the way it was at the handful of school dances I'd gone to, always waiting alone in a chair against the wall for someone to ask me to dance, because dancing meant one boy standing up with one girl. Here there were no partners. Here everybody danced however they wanted with whoever they wanted, yet somehow each one of us was a part of the same whole. For the first time in my life, I fit somewhere. I'd never been much for dating, but I finally understood what girls at school had been talking about when they described the way boys they liked made them feel. It was the same way the music made me feel now—a hot-and-cold fever rush of tingles down my body that took the air from my lungs and made my brain buzz. I was hooked.

Like the store where I'd met Anise, the party was also called Love Saves the Day. Later Anise showed me her crumpled invitation that bore the inscription, along with images of Dalí's melting clocks. She said there was no connection between the party and the store where we'd met. I never believed her. "Love Saves the Day" was obviously a code of some kind, a sign of recognition talked about among people who understood things I'd never imagined.

I'd been waiting my whole life for someone to talk to me.

I heard everything in disco's four/four time after that. Walking down the street, I'd set the heel of each foot down before the toe to create a four-count that always sounded in my head like, "One two *three* four, one two *three* four." But it wasn't just what I heard, it was also what I *saw*. A chair was four legs with four beats, and the seat was a hi-hat crowning the third beat, for flourish. This was what I was always doing in my mind—counting words, syllables, windows, TV screens, people's faces (which broke down conveniently into two ears, two eyes, two nostrils, and two lips—two full four/four measures). And where I couldn't make something break down into a perfect four, I'd imagine anything extra as additional sound and texture—French horn, timpani, clarinet, trombone, harp, violin, anything at all—that transformed a four/four beat into a full, orchestral song.

Laura, a few years later, lying in her crib beneath the red ribbons Mrs. Mandelbaum had festooned it with to ward off the Evil

Eye, was the most beautiful music I could imagine. I would sing "Fly, Robin, Fly" as she drifted off to sleep, wanting her to dream of the two of us flying together up, up to the sky. Her faint, tiny eyebrows were the quaver running alongside the four/four rhythm of her face, and the thin wisps of her baby curls were an open hi-hat on the off-beat. Her delighted gurgles were the strings, sounding more beautiful than anything. With Laura, I didn't just hear music. Laura *was* my music.

I began spending every weekend in the City with Anise—ready with an invented new social life to tell my parents about if they asked why I was suddenly out all the time, even though they never did—until I graduated high school a year early. (Because I was tall and somewhat shy, my elementary school teachers had thought I might "socialize" better with older kids, although it hadn't seemed to work out that way.) Once I had my diploma, it wasn't even a question what I was going to do. I moved to the City to live with Anise, where I could try to be a DJ while Anise and her band, Evil Sugar, tried to be rock stars.

For two years, Anise and I lived together in her loft on the Bowery. Music lived on the streets of New York in those days, and every neighborhood had its own rhythms. Way uptown, in Harlem and the Bronx, there were boom boxes and block parties, and DJs were playing around with sampling and remixes of disco and funk to create a new thing called hip-hop. Down on the Lower East Side, there were salsa musicians on what seemed like every street corner, and a stripped-down rock called "punk" spilling out of the doorways of places like CBGB and Monty Python's. Disco was everywhere. It lived downtown at David Mancuso's Loft, and farther uptown—all the way into Midtown—at places like Paradise Garage, the Gallery, New York New York, and Le Jardin. Anise and I went to Studio 54 a couple of times, but we didn't like it much. Nothing new ever happened musically there. You would never have the wild and utterly enlightening experience of hearing Arthur Russell's "Kiss Me Again" for the first time at a place like 54. I picked up a matchbook from every place we went, knowing even then that this kind of life was ephemeral at best, and that I'd never remember it later without something to anchor my memories to.

I was into disco and Anise was into punk, which probably should have made us natural enemies. But what Anise and I always had in common, right from the beginning, was that we both loved *noise*. Actually, what Anise loved even more than noise was trouble. She'd moved to New York from a farm in Ohio when she was sixteen, three years before I did, except Anise told her parents before she left that she was pregnant. It wasn't true—she was still a virgin—but it wasn't enough for Anise just to *go*. There had to be trouble of some kind on her way out. And it must have been a lot of trouble, because it was a full year before Anise's parents finally forgave her for *not* being pregnant after she'd told them she was.

Anise was always full of mischief. Mischief and noise and *life*. She never minded if I practiced with my records while she was practicing on her guitar. The more noise the better, as far we both were concerned. When her career started taking off, and she was finally able to buy a Gibson SG up at Manny's on 48th Street, she took the amp from her old guitar and hooked it up to my second-hand turntables in a way that made them work together. I was obsessed with mastering beat-on-beat mixing. It was one thing when the songs used drum machines. But if you wanted to throw something like Eddie Kendricks or Van Morrison into the mix, you really had to work to match the drumbeat from the end of one song with the beginning of the next, so they synced up perfectly.

Maybe it was the overlap between our two separate styles that eventually brought dance rhythms into Evil Sugar's sound. But even then, when people started accusing Anise of "going disco" (her music wasn't disco) and "selling out" (she hadn't), she'd always drop that fifth beat, just to make the music harder to dance to. Just for the fun of making things confusing.

It was because Anise loved trouble so much that she insisted on living with no fewer than three cats. One cat by itself, Anise said, would sleep all the time. Two cats would probably learn to get along well enough and fall into each other's rhythms of silence and sleep. But with *three* cats, her theory went, at least one of them would always be up and into something. Always making mischief of some kind. I guess she was right. Anise's three cats spent a lot of time hissing and yowling at strays through the metal bars we bought on the street from John the Communist to keep other cats (and burglars) from climbing through our windows.

Anise loved those cats like crazy. She was forever brushing and rubbing and crooning to them, or bringing home special treats for them to eat (when, God knows, it was all we could do to feed ourselves sometimes), or making up little games to play with them. She'd wriggle her fingers under a bedsheet for the joy of watching them pounce in mock attacks.

Anise's music lived in her head, but her art lived in her hands. It was there in the way she played her guitar, even back when most of the people we knew in bands prided themselves on *not* being able to play their instruments. But it was also there in the intricate highway of cat runs she decorated our loft with from floor to ceiling and along all the walls. She'd find old boards or wooden planks in the streets and bring them home to sand, saw, and varnish. Then she'd cover them with scraps of colorful material before nailing them up. Sometimes you'd be sitting on the couch when a cat would drop—plop!—right into your lap from a board above your head, turning around once or twice before sinking into a deep nap. Anise would make new outfits for us by tearing apart and re-sewing old outfits, then use the leftover material to make clothes for the cats. Taped up all over the walls beneath and around the cat runs were Polaroids of surly-looking felines in vests or tiny feathered jackets and cunning little hats. Nobody the cats didn't like was allowed into our home, which was also Anise's band's rehearsal space—which was one reason why Anise went through so many different band members in the early days.

Anise's cats loved her right back. There was always at least one in her lap, purring away, whenever we were home. The oldest was named Rita. Anise had found her as a kitten in a junkyard in the middle of a pile of discarded, rusting parking meters. Then there was Lucy, a tuxedo cat with a white diamond-shaped patch on her chest. Eleanor Rigby was Anise's youngest, a sweet calico who could never stand being alone. (No matter how far apart Anise and I were musically, one thing we could always agree on was a passionate adoration of the Beatles.)

One winter night we woke up to all three cats pawing at her frantically, their little faces covered in black soot. The furnace in the hardware store downstairs—which the owner sometimes left on overnight to help us keep warm—had backed up, and our apartment was filling with soot and smoke. We would have suffocated in our sleep if it weren't for those cats. As it was, we ran around the place choking and throwing open all the windows to let fresh air in. After that, Anise doted on her cats even more. *My goddesses,* she called them. *My saviors.*

Still, Anise knew how to take care of herself. She made a point of knowing everyone in our neighborhood. Not just the kids our age, or the older residents who'd lived there forever. She knew the hookers, the addicts, the bums who slept in parks and doorways and always called her "Tinkerbell" when we brought them blankets and warm winter clothing.

"You have to let people know who you are and that you live here, too," she'd always tell me. "That's how they know to leave you alone."

Every so often, though, some new junkie would move into the neighborhood and learn the hard way why it didn't pay to tangle with Anise. One night, on our way to CBGB, a guy jumped in front of us and pulled out a knife. Quick as a cat, Anise snatched a board with an old nail in it off the ground and swung it at him wildly, missing the guy's eye only because he had the presence of mind to duck. Then he ran. Anise streaked after him with the board held high above her head, her six-inch heels for once not snagging on any errant cracks or stones. *"That's right, run!"* she shouted. *"Run, you pussy! I'm a craaaaaaaaaaaazy mother—"*

Anise had the face of an angel, but a mouth like a sewer. She may have looked petite and fragile, but you had to be tough if you wanted to be a girl fronting a rock band on the Lower East Side. I was nearly a foot taller than Anise, yet people were afraid to mess with *me* because of *her* and not the other way around.

Every penny I could spare went into buying records. Between that and David Mancuso's record pool, which distributed demo albums from the labels to New York's DJ population, by July of '77 I had a collection almost as extensive as Anise's. Evil Sugar was taking off by then. They had a manager and a three-record deal with a label, and they were booking proper gigs. *Interview* magazine featured a four-page spread on them with photos of Anise in dresses she'd made from ripped-up T-shirts, and *Rolling Stone* did a big photo essay for their Bands to Watch issue. Anise always had that *thing*— that thing about her that made you aware of her no matter what room she was in. I was still struggling, though. No matter how many demo tapes I put together at Alphaville Studios, where Evil Sugar was recording their second album, once a club owner knew I was a girl he would almost always lose interest in hiring me.

I turned seventeen that summer, and it was brutally hot. Even the cats, who could always be counted on to snuggle up to us at night for extra warmth no matter how hot it was, became sullen. They'd lie on the enormous windowsills and yowl fitfully when there was no breeze to cool them.

That was the summer when I met Nick. It was too hot to stay in our apartment at night, so Anise and I started spending time at Theatre 80 on St. Mark's Place. For two dollars you could see a double feature and enjoy four hours in air-conditioning. We'd sit in the cool darkness and watch the old Hitchcock films and MGM musicals they showed three or four times in a row, until it was so late it was early.

Nick tended the polished wood bar, which dated back to 1922, in the lobby. I would see him waxing it every night, when the crowds were slow. His black hair gleamed as brightly as the wood he polished, so brightly that it seemed to cast light for its shadow. Something about the way his shoulder blades moved beneath the thin cotton of his short-sleeved shirt, and the summer-browned, lightly muscled arms ending in tapering fingers that held the rag and wood polish, entranced me. For weeks, I watched him without being noticed. When he finally looked at me for the first time, with eyes that were a dark midnight blue at the rims and faded to a white-blue at the centers, I was gobsmacked. I had never really been interested in anyone before. Anise saw my face turn red when he looked at me, and she teased me about it relentlessly. It was Anise who sat the two of us down at that bar, who ordered a round of drinks and made introductions. Anise knew everything about attracting attention, but she also knew how to recede quietly into the background and eventually leave unnoticed once I got over my shyness and Nick and I started talking.

I kissed Nick for the first time that night in the theater's basement. It was the night of the blackout, and all ordinary rules seemed suspended. Later we'd hear about looting and riots uptown, but in our neighborhood, people threw parties and played music on the streets. I went downstairs with Nick, armed with flashlights, to look for candles. He kissed me in what had once been the bunker of a Prohibition-era mobster who'd operated a speakeasy where the theater now stood. When Nick took me in his arms, he smelled like lemon-scented wood polish and the heat of the kinetic air outside. For the first time in nearly two years, the music in my head stopped. All I heard was the intake of my own breath in the dark, which paused for what felt like forever when Nick brought his lips to mine.

Later Anise would say that the worst thing she ever did for me as a friend was introducing me to Nick. Those two disliked each other almost as soon as we started spending time together. Nick resented how much of my time Anise took up, and Anise disliked Nick on the general principle that he wasn't *serious* about anything. Nick talked about wanting to be an actor and the one "big break" that was all he needed to launch his career. He'd drag me to tiny black-box productions all over the Lower East Side, but whenever he actually got cast in anything, something always seemed to go wrong. He didn't want to spend as much time rehearsing as the director required, or he'd have a disagreement of some kind with another cast member. Then one day he announced that he was done with acting, that photography was his new passion. I went with him to the small galleries that were starting to pop up in our neighborhood. He especially loved taking pictures of me after I got pregnant with Laura. But his approach was haphazard, and there were weeks on end when the camera he'd spent two hundred dollars on—an enormous amount for that time and place—lay discarded in a corner of Anise's and my loft, next to my mattress. Anise had no tolerance for anybody who wanted to do something creative but lacked the discipline to see it through. Hard work and perfecting her craft were Anise's religion.

"But the cats don't even like him," she would say. Which was true. But it didn't matter to me.

Nick and I were married at City Hall the following summer. I clutched a small bouquet of lilies we'd paid seventy-five cents for in a bodega on our way downtown. Anise was engaged to her drummer by then (the first of what would end up being three husbands and some uncountable number of fiancés), and Evil Sugar was getting ready to go on their first tour. They were opening for the Talking Heads, which unquestionably was a big break. Nick and I found a rent-controlled two-bedroom on the second floor of an old Stanton Street tenement for only $250 a month. Laura was born two years later, and I moved all my clothes, photos, matchbooks, and other mementos of my days with Anise into storage—because once Laura was born, it was like the rest of it hadn't really happened, like it had all been just a lead-up to that first moment when I held our daughter in my arms and she looked up at me with a softer, infinitely more beautiful version of Nick's blue, blue eyes.

By the time she was three and Nick had left for good, Anise was back in New York to give up the loft and move her cats and her band out to LA, which was where they were already spending at least half their time, anyway. Anise was on her way up, while I had a young daughter to support on my own and no clear idea as to how I could do that.

Sometimes, though, things work out the way they're supposed to—or, at least, the way it seems like they're supposed to. One afternoon, pushing Laura's stroller down 9th Street between First and Second, I passed what had obviously once been a record store, now abandoned. Through the dusty windows, I could see a cat who looked a great deal like Eleanor Rigby, clawing languidly at a stack of old 'zines. She turned to look at me, and although I couldn't hear her I could see her mouth say, *Mew.* Then she leapt nimbly from the top of the stack and disappeared around the counter into a back room.

When I tracked down the building's owner, my proposition was simple: If he would let me take over the store, I would give him 5 percent of my first year's gross in lieu of rent, paid monthly, with the option of taking over the lease officially after that. Such arrangements weren't uncommon on the Lower East Side back then, when the area wasn't yet considered desirable by the mainstream and real estate wasn't at a premium. He agreed.

It was Anise who suggested naming my store Ear Wax. With the clarity of hindsight I understood that I'd rushed into marriage with Nick when I was only eighteen because I'd wanted—finally— to have a real family. My father had died of a heart attack not long after I moved to the City, and my mother took their savings and his pension and bought a condo in Florida. She never invited me to visit or asked if she could come visit me, and I never pressed the point.

My marriage to Nick hadn't lasted, but now there was Laura. Laura and I would be a family. Laura would never be left alone in her room to listen to records and wonder why her own mother didn't want to talk to her.

Anise was cleaning Lucy's ears, which were always accumulating a bluish waxy buildup, the first time we talked about my record store. "Why don't you call it Ear Wax?" she said. At first I laughed, thinking she was making a joke about being immersed in ear wax up to her fingernails at that moment. But then she said, "I'm serious, Sarah. Ear Wax is a perfect name."

Ear Wax Re *cords, Ear Wax* Re *cords,* I thought. And I knew she was right.

An artist friend of ours crafted an enormous papier-mâché ear with scratched-up old albums dangling from it, which I hung from the ceiling in the middle of the store. It remained there for as long as I owned the place.

It was easy enough to use the records I'd been collecting in the hope of being a DJ—along with the hundreds of discards Anise donated ("I'd just have to get rid of them anyway before I moved out west," she insisted, as if what she was doing wasn't an incredibly generous favor)—as the nucleus of my fledgling store.

A few of Anise's "cast-offs" were rare imports of the Beatles on mono, and I was able to sell those to collectors right away for a small fortune. I also hired a man named Noel to act as manager. Noel was six foot two of solid muscle and always carried a baseball bat, and he was a walking encyclopedia of artists, albums, and genres. I met him at one of the larger record stores on St. Mark's Place, which he was running on the owner's behalf, and knew instantly that he was exactly what I needed as a woman trying to run a record store in that neighborhood. I lured him away from the larger store with most of the cash from those Beatles sales, and gave him free rein to "staff up" as he saw fit.

Laura and I lived happily in our six-floor walk-up on Stanton Street. There was a bodega downstairs that was open twenty-four hours, making it easy enough to run downstairs if I realized belatedly that I had no milk or peanut butter for Laura's lunch the next day. The Verdes lived two floors above us, and as Laura grew, their second-oldest child, Maria Elena, became her closest friend. Their kids were always in our apartment, or Laura was in theirs.

And then there were the Mandelbaums in the apartment right above ours. Max Mandelbaum drove a cab, and Ida Mandelbaum kept house. They were a gregarious couple, Mr. Mandelbaum's voice so loud and powerful that you could hear it reverberating throughout the building, even when their door was closed. But he never yelled. He was never angry. He adored his wife, even after fifty years of marriage, and she adored him, too. She had a habit of sending him downstairs for a quart of milk every day when he got home, and every day he would grumble about it. "Hush, Max," she always chided him. "You know the doctor says you need to get exercise." When he returned, Mrs. Mandelbaum would say to whoever happened to be there, "He complains, but he likes being nagged by his wife. Better open rebuke than hidden love." And Mr. Mandelbaum would continue to grouse under his breath, but the look in his eyes belied his words.

Mrs. Mandelbaum never really "nagged" him. Her voice was never as loud as his, and her ways were softer. But bright eyes beamed in both sets of faces, always happy to see you and eager to press whatever creature comforts—a soft couch, hot tea, trays of strudel and bowls of hard candies, leftovers from the dinners Mrs. Mandelbaum cooked every night—were available in their small apartment.

Mrs. Mandelbaum delighted in keeping Laura occupied with picture books or lessons on how to bake cookies while Mr. Mandelbaum would accompany me to the neighborhood butcher or baker or fruit vendors. As I made selections, he would keep a shrewd eye on the scales to make sure nobody tried to cheat me. "A young girl like you, alone with a daughter!" he would exclaim. "Someone needs to make sure nobody takes advantage." When I could finally afford to fix up Laura's bedroom, it was Mrs. Mandelbaum who insisted on making beautiful lace curtains from "just a few old *schmatas* I have lying around."

Laura seemed as entranced with them as they were with her, although maybe she wouldn't have loved spending time with them as *much* as she did if not for their cat—a brown tabby with green eyes and a white chest and paws who'd followed them home from the butcher shop one day. "What could we do?" Mrs. Mandelbaum liked to say. "We took her in. Max never could say no to a damsel in distress."

As if the cat knew that Mr. Mandelbaum had been her salvation, she devoted herself to him. She would follow him from room to room, curling at his feet or in his lap as her moods dictated. She was fond of people and had a gentle disposition, although the only person she seemed to love nearly as much as Mr. Mandelbaum was

Laura. Many was the time when I would come to pick her up after a late night at the store to find her curled up on the small bed in what had been their son's bedroom, sleeping on her side with one arm thrown around the soft tabby curled up on the pillow beside her.

I knew, of course, that Laura and I were replacements for the son they'd lost and the grandchild they would never have. Still, it was impossible not to love the Mandelbaums. We needed a family, too, Laura and I.

Every so often, Mrs. Mandelbaum would cup my chin gently in her hand and say, "A pretty young girl like you should get out more. You should find someone to love. People weren't meant to be alone."

"I'm not alone," I would protest. "I have Laura, and the two of you, and my store. How much *less* alone could I be?"

I knew what she meant, though. I thought about Nick, who I couldn't stop loving even though I knew he was worthless. I thought about my mother with her sad, drifting eyes after she lost my infant brother. The Mandelbaums had found the strength to carry on after a similar loss. But the people in my family were different from the Mandelbaums. When we broke, we stayed broken.

The best and worst thing about owning a store is that anybody can walk in. Homeless people came in to get out of the rain. There were those who came into the store three times a day every day because they had no one else to talk to. Or else they were obsessive about checking the used bins for the latest promos and onesies that some music critic had just unloaded. I was more lenient with such people than Noel. I always made sure we had coffee and soda and, when the weather was cold, I stockpiled donated blankets and coats in our basement to distribute. I wanted to be part of a community, but more than that I wanted people to know who Laura was. She couldn't *always* be in the store or at home with me or the Mandelbaums. She had to be allowed to play outside with her friends, but I slept better at night knowing there was a veritable army in place to help me keep watch.

We had plenty of "real" customers, too. Scenesters clamoring for Lydia Lunch and New Order. Kids experimenting with Latin hip-hop at Cuando on Second and Houston checked out our salsa section. DJs traveled all the way down from the Bronx to buy Schoolly D or old-school funk they could remix. A cross-dressing weed dealer—an ardent Reagan Republican with an uptown cabaret act under the name Vera Similitude—was in at least once a week to quote Ayn Rand and buy opera records. I learned that anybody with green hair automatically wanted punk and couldn't be talked into anything else. Suburbanites came for the latest Springsteen or Talking Heads album, and these were the people we'd have the most fun with. They'd break their twenty on the new Bon Jovi and leave with something by Public Image or Liquid Liquid because I'd have it playing in the background. *What's this crazy song? It doesn't sound half bad,* they'd say, before digging into their wallets for extra cash.

Running a record store was like being a DJ in some ways. On weekends, when the store was packed, I had to get a sense of the crowd. I could feel the mood shift depending on what music I decided to play over the store's speakers. If I played the Jellybean Benitez–produced electro cover of Babe Ruth's "The Mexican," every single person in the store would be dancing, and I'd sell all the copies I had in stock.

Whenever Anise was in town, whether to promote a new album or to play Madison Square Garden, she always did a "meet and greet" at my store. In interviews, she said the only place in New York she'd buy music was at Ear Wax on 9th Street. That helped a lot, as did the mentions we started getting in the New York City guidebooks distributed to tourists.

Still, Ear Wax never made much money. Everything I could spare, after paying my rent and handing out well-earned bonuses to my staff, I reinvested. Looking back, this was probably the biggest mistake I made. But at the time I saw the store as Laura's and my future, as our only possible future. Laura was going to go to college one day, was going to have all the things I'd never had. I was going to make sure of it.

Women back then were first starting to enter the workforce in droves and debating the merits of day care centers and nannies. But I was able to pick my daughter up every day after school. I'd bring her back to the record store where she could have a snack, read a book, do her homework. I got to watch Laura grow up, not just in a general sense, but in all the little ways. I could marvel at the glory of her unbound hair freed from the school day's ponytail, or watch one small, perfect hand tracing the lovely shape of her face as she read her schoolbooks. On weekday afternoons, when the store was dead, Laura would choose records for the two of us to sing along to. She would always insist on turning the music down and surreptitiously, fading out her own singing until my voice sang alone.

On school holidays, Laura would come to the store with me hours before it opened. We'd pull albums from the shelves and spread them all over the floor, hopscotching among the squares of cracked tile between them. Nimble and tall—light as a pigeon— she never once brought her heel down on a record by mistake. On the nights when I worked late, Laura could stay with the Verdes or the Mandelbaums, safe in a loving home until I came to collect her. She was a happy child, and I was happy, too. I had Laura, I had my business, I had my music. It was the happiest time of my life.

Even back when the Lower East Side got really bad, when crack invaded in the mid-'80s and you couldn't walk farther east than Avenue A unarmed, even then our stretch of 9th Street was a nice block. Tree-lined and leafy. In the spring, Mu Shu—the cat who lived among the interconnected basements and storefronts of our block, so named because of her passion for Chinese takeout— would leave dandelions at the entrance to the store. Summers she took languorous naps on the sidewalk beneath dappled shade. "Mu Shu's Hamptons," we used to call that patch of sidewalk. Working-class Ukrainian families lived in rent-controlled apartments above the storefronts. Old Ukrainian women would gather on front stoops to gossip at dusk.

In the storefronts themselves, the kids who'd lived there in groups during the '70s, converting them into commune-style apartments, had either moved out or stayed behind to open shops of their own. Small affairs, like mine. A store where one person made and sold leather handicrafts. A clothing shop owned by a jazz musician. When the weather was nice, children played together outside. Laura and her friend Maria Elena often came to play in front of my store with the neighborhood kids, where I could have them within earshot.

Drug dealers and dime-store thugs proliferated on the corners of blocks all around us, but never on our block. Never on our corner. Never where my daughter and her friends played with bottle caps they found in the street while a pretty little calico cat looked on, occasionally snatching one up in her mouth and trotting down the street proudly with it, as if it were a trophy.

8

Prudence

WHEN SARAH WAS YOUNG AND THE WORLD WAS DIFFERENT from what it is today, it could be fun to have no money. That's what she and Anise say, anyway. Whenever they talk about all the Good Times they used to have, one of them always ends up saying, *We were so young then! The world was a different place.*

If you were poor when they were so young, you got to do things like live with your best friend in a huge loft that cost practically nothing. (*Peanuts!* Sarah says.) It would be so big that there'd be plenty of room to set up your DJ table or for your roommate's band to rehearse, with enough space left over to put two mattresses on the floor where you and your roommate would stay up all night talking and laughing and playing with her three cats. You could go to parties or to a type of place called a "club," where friends of yours would play records and musical instruments for other humans to dance to. If you knew the humans who worked there, they would let you eat and drink things for free.

Besides your best friend, you would know other people who did interesting things, like being actors or artists or writers, and all of you together would have fun lying on the grass at outside parks and eating hot dogs (which aren't really made from dogs). Hot dogs cost practically no money at all. Sometimes you and your roommate would save up all your money for one big meal at a restaurant called Dojo on St. Marks Place, where you would get "the works." Or you might go to a place called Ice Cream Connection, where they made their own ice cream from honey and gave their flavors names like Panama Red (which is just regular cherry) or Acapulco Gold (which is peach).

I miss ice cream. Sarah stopped bringing it home, and Laura and Josh never seem to have any. Sometimes I wish *we* were poor, so I could get to have ice cream again.

But we aren't poor, or even broke. At least, that's what Josh is always saying. Like the other day when Laura came home from work with a bag of peaches she bought at the grocery store. Josh asked why she'd bought peaches instead of plums, because she knows they both like plums better. And Laura said, *They had peaches on sale.* He kept saying she should have gotten plums and she kept saying that the peaches were on sale, until Josh said it wasn't like they were too poor to have plums instead of peaches if that's what they wanted. Laura looked upset and confused, like she'd thought she was doing a nice thing by bringing the peaches home and couldn't understand why Josh was making such a big deal about it. Finally, she told Josh there was a fruit stand right down the street, and if he cared *so much* about peaches and plums he had plenty of free time during the day to go out and buy whatever he wanted.

That's when Josh left the kitchen and went upstairs to Home Office, clackety-clacking extra loud on the cat bed/computer thing the way I sometimes go after my own scratching post when I'm angry about something. After he was gone, Laura noticed all the tiny crumbs Josh had left on the counter when he made his lunch earlier, and she got out a sponge and spritzy bottle. She rubbed the counter much harder than necessary to get it clean. Both humans and cats have to find ways to use our extra energy when we get "riled up," as Sarah puts it. It was a good thing I'd jumped onto the counter earlier to eat the bits of meat and cheese Josh spilled when he made his sandwich. If Laura had seen what it looked like *before* I helped clean up, she would have been even more riled.

And last week, when Laura and Josh sat at the dining room table to go over their bills, Laura said how maybe they should try to put twice as much into savings while Josh was still getting money from his old job, even if doing that would make life "a little uncomfortable." Josh told her they had plenty of money in savings, and Laura said, *But for how long?* Josh said, *We're a long way from being broke, Laura. I've been saving for fifteen years. You've* seen *all the paperwork.* Neither of them said anything after that. But Laura got a frown-crease in her forehead, and the skin underneath Josh's left eye twitched. It took a long time of my being in bed with Laura that night before she was able to settle into a real sleep.

Laura's been having a lot of trouble falling asleep, especially since Josh has started coming to bed later than he used to—long after Laura's already been there for a while, with the television flickering some old movie like Sarah used to watch when she couldn't sleep. When Josh finally does come to bed, he sleeps farther away from Laura, so there's plenty of room for me to be there, too, but also so he's touching her less. Sometimes Laura is so tired in the morning that she forgets to do parts of her usual morning routine, like putting on lipstick after her eye makeup, or styling her hair with the gels that live in bottles on the bathroom counter. A few times she's forgotten to take the pill she takes every morning just before giving me my breakfast. She's still feeding me right on time, though, every morning. Occasionally she fills my water too high like when I first came to live here. But now she just sighs instead of pressing her lips together when she sees water spilled from my jostling the bowl.

Ever since the night three weeks ago when they fought about

Josh's severance agreement, things have been different between Josh and Laura. Somebody who'd just met them might not realize anything is wrong because most of the time they're so polite to each other. They say each other's names all the time, and make sure they say "please" and "thank you" after every little thing, the way humans talk to other humans they don't know very well. (*If you're finished with the newspaper, Laura, could you please hand me the business section? Thank you. Or, Josh, could you please pick up some fresh litter for Prudence tomorrow? Thanks.*)

I don't think Laura is as angry as Josh is, because she tries harder to make him talk. She keeps finding reasons to do little things she never used to bother with. If she decides to take a shower after she gets home from work, she brings the phone upstairs to Home Office and tells Josh, *Here's the phone, in case it rings while I'm in the shower.* And Josh says, *Thanks,* without even turning to look at her. Laura waits, as if she expects Josh to say something more since she went to the trouble of bringing the phone up to him. But Josh is silent until, finally, he asks, *Did you want something else, Laura?* Or if Laura says, *I thought I'd order Chinese, if that's okay with you,* Josh just says, *Chinese is fine.* Then Laura will say something like, *Or we could try that new Thai place, if you want.*

Josh likes to tease Laura that you can tell she's a lawyer by the way she negotiates over everything. If he's the one who suggests Thai food, which Laura hates (and I agree, because Thai food is way too spicy for a cat to eat—which means they should never order it), Laura will say something like, *Okay, Thai tonight, but then I get to choose for the next three nights.* And Josh will respond by saying, *Thai food tonight, you get to choose tomorrow, plus I'll give you a foot rub.* And Laura says, *Thai food tonight, one foot rub, and you have to clean Prudence's litterbox for the rest of the week.* And Josh will squint his eyes and draw the corners of his mouth down, and say, *Ooh . . . I don't know . . . I can't decide if I'm coming out ahead or not.* Then they laugh and order the Thai food.

But when Laura suggests Thai food now, which should make Josh happy since he's the only one who likes it, he doesn't say anything except, *Get whatever you want, Laura.*

When I was much younger and had only been living with Sarah for a few months, I used to have a hard time getting my tail to do what I wanted. I would be trying to groom myself, and my tail would wriggle all over the place, pulling itself out of reach of my claws no matter how hard I tried to catch it. I would growl and snap at it, to show it how serious I was. Sometimes I even tried to chase it down, but it always remained just out of reach of my teeth, and all that happened was I wound up running in circles. I didn't get angry at it, exactly. But it was frustrating to see a part of myself doing things I didn't want or expect or understand.

That's what Laura and Josh remind me of now. They seem bewildered and frustrated when they look at each other, like they just can't understand the things this other human—who they thought they were so close with—is doing or saying.

I wish I could talk in human language, so I could tell Laura that Josh is only acting so angry because his feelings are hurt, just like hers. Maybe then she would sleep better at night.

Of course, if she wasn't having trouble sleeping, she might not want me to sleep in the bed with her. And sleeping next to Laura is the best I've slept since the day Sarah left without telling me why.

Today is Sunday and Laura is awake earlier than she usually is on Sundays—so early that I don't have to do any of the things I do on Sundays to *gently remind* her to feed me breakfast at my regular time, like lying on her chest and staring straight at her face until her eyes open, or walking on top of the clock radio next to her head until it starts playing loud music. When Josh hears the clock radio on Sunday mornings, he buries his head under a pillow and says in a muffled, irritable voice, *Isn't today Sunday? Can't you hit the snooze button or something?* And Laura, sounding sleepy, tells him, *I don't think there* is *a snooze button on a hungry cat.*

But today Laura gets up at her usual workday time and cleans the whole apartment. I even hear the sounds of The Monster rampaging in the living room while I'm eating in the kitchen! (I realize now that Laura and Josh use The Monster to make the floors clean. Sarah used to get the same thing done with just a regular broom and rolling thing called a carpet sweeper. It seems foolish to risk all our lives by having a Monster *living in our apartment* just so we can have cleaner floors, although I do have to admit that Laura seems strong enough to control it—for now.) My heart pounding, I leave most of my food uneaten and race for my upstairs room with the Sarah-boxes as fast as four legs can carry me. But when I get there, the door is closed! I meow in my loudest "fishmonger" voice, but the continual shrieking of The Monster downstairs drowns it out. When nobody responds, I jump up and latch onto the door handle with all my front toes, then let the weight of my body hang down until it drags the handle down, too, and makes the door swing open a crack. We had regular round doorknobs when I lived with Sarah in Lower East Side, but here in Upper West Side the door handles are long and skinny enough for me to hold without slipping off.

Josh wanders out of his bedroom—dressed to go outside in jeans, his old sneakers with the dangly shoelace, and a shirt with buttons down the front—in time to see the door swinging open with me attached to it. He laughs. "Poor Prudence! Did you get locked out of your favorite room?"

The Prudence-tags on my red collar make a tinkling sound as I drop to the floor and sit on my haunches, looking up at Josh as he looks down at me. His upper lids droop a bit as his eyes narrow, and I wonder if he's figured out the same thing I have—that Laura doesn't want to come into this room to clean, but also doesn't want to leave the door open for someone to see how this room is dustier than any other room in the apartment. "All right," Josh says, "we'll leave it open just enough for you to get in and out. Okay?" He reaches for the door handle and pulls the door almost-closed. I'm surprised when I have to push it open a bit wider with the sides of my belly as I pass through. Once I would have been able to fit easily into an opening this size. I realize suddenly how long it's been since I last worried about not being fed on time, and started eating all my food as soon as it's put in front of me.

"I'm off to get bagels and smoked fish," Josh tells me. He smiles. "If you're good, you can have some later."

Josh's footsteps thud quickly down the stairs, and The Monster stops shrieking long enough for him to tell Laura that he's going out to get the bagels. She tells him not to forget to bring the shopping list they made last night.

I dart into the room and burrow into my sleeping place in the back of my closet—listening closely to be absolutely sure The Monster isn't going to come in here to threaten me or the Sarah-boxes, but mostly thinking about fish.

Josh's whole family comes over at noon to talk about money, and who's sick and who's well, and who's still married to their husband or wife—although they *say* they're here for a holiday. Josh gives his mother a big hug when she comes in and says, "Happy Mother's Day." Josh's mother hugs Laura a bit longer than she hugged Josh, and rubs her hand up and down Laura's back. "Happy Mother's Day," Laura murmurs, and Josh's mother kisses her on the cheek before letting her go.

Laura came to Sarah's and my apartment in Lower East Side a year ago for this same holiday. She also brought over bagels and fish, along with a bunch of red carnations that Sarah put in a little yellow vase in the middle of our kitchen table. The two of them sort of hugged (whenever they hugged, it was always as if they'd forgotten how), although Laura was less stiff than she normally was when she came to visit us. Her cheeks were pink and her eyes sparkled. She laughed when Sarah tossed the twisty-tie from the bag of bagels in my direction and I leapt to catch it with my front paws in midair. She even smiled patiently while Sarah chattered at her about the weather, and a funny thing somebody at her work had said, and whether Laura had seen any interesting movies lately.

After they finished getting plates and food on the table, I jumped right into the middle so Sarah could arrange some fish on a little Prudence-plate for me. Laura wrinkled up her nose and said, "Ugh, Mom, do you always let Prudence eat on the table?"

Sarah's shoulders straightened the way they do whenever she thinks Laura is criticizing the way she does things. But she just said, "Prudence and I understand each other." She stroked the back of my neck a few times before putting one hand underneath my body so she could lift me gently to the floor, setting my special plate of fish down next to me. The two of them watched me. Then Sarah picked up a fork and started putting fish onto her bagel. She glanced at Laura. "Sometimes I think I'm crazy to love her as much as I do."

"Love is love," Laura said. Even though there was food in front of her, she hadn't touched it. "Who's to say what's crazy?" The corners of her mouth turned up in just the hint of a smile, and her cheeks got pinker. She seemed shy and pleased with herself, like she had the kind of secret it makes you happy just to think about. Suddenly Sarah was looking at her more closely—then she smiled, and her eyes sparkled, too.

Laura isn't pink-cheeked and sparkly today. Everybody keeps looking at her out of the corners of their eyes, trying to seem as if they aren't, and Laura notices everybody doing this but pretends she doesn't. Are they all looking at her because she's the only human whose mother isn't here for Mother's Day? But Josh's parents' mothers aren't here, either, and nobody's watching *them*, so that can't be right. Still, Josh is being nicer to Laura than he's been these past few weeks, sitting on the arm of the couch next to her and putting an arm around her shoulders. She doesn't move away, but she also doesn't touch his leg or look up into his face like she used to.

The dining room table has been set up with a huge mound of bagels in a straw basket I didn't know we had, along with containers of soft cheeses and platters of different kinds of smoked fish. After the *last* holiday, I know better than to jump onto the table and demand some—no matter how tempting all that wonderful fish smells. I look up anxiously into Laura's and Josh's faces as everybody piles their plates with food to take back into the living room. (Josh's father doesn't pile his plate quite as high as everyone else, because Josh's mother tells him, *"Abe,* remember what Dr. Stern said about your cholesterol.") I even rub my right cheek hard against the table leg, carefully scraping my teeth against it to get them extra clean, so everyone can tell by my scent that this is *my* food place right now. But nobody seems to notice how politely I'm waiting. At least the littermates are better behaved than they were the last time. Robert bends down to put his face (too) close to mine and, holding out one hand, says, "Here, kitty. Can I pet you?" But the hand he's holding out doesn't have any fish in it, so I flinch away in disgust, raising my right front paw with the claws extended as a warning.

Once the littermates have their food arranged on plates (and why should *they* get to have fish before *I* do?), they race upstairs to eat and watch TV in Laura and Josh's bedroom. Normally food is *never* allowed upstairs. "That's what I asked them to give me for Mother's Day," Erica says drily. "One quiet meal with grown-ups." Then she sighs. "I was hoping Jeff might send some of the money he owes so I could swing camp for them this summer." She looks at Josh, who's now sitting next to Laura on the couch, but not so close that their arms touch. "Remember how much we loved Pine Crest?"

"Eight weeks in the mountains away from our parents." Josh smiles. "What could be better?"

"Eight weeks in the suburbs with no kids," Josh's mother says, and everybody laughs.

Josh turns to look at Laura. "Did you ever go to summer camp?"

"Me?" Laura seems surprised. She scrunches her eyebrows and turns up one side of her mouth, as if she thinks this question is foolish. "Lower East Side kids didn't go to summer camp. Unless you count roller skating through an open fire hydrant as camp." She grins. "We used to call it urban waterskiing."

"So what did your mother do with you when school was out?" Josh's mother asks.

Laura shrugs. "Mostly I helped out at her record store, or stayed with neighbors in our building. Some mornings she'd take me with her to the thieves' market on Astor Place to buy back records shoplifters had stolen. Then we'd go to Kiev for chocolate blintzes. That's only until I was about nine or ten," Laura adds, in a way that makes it seem like she wants to change the subject. "After that I started taking summer classes to help me prepare for the tests to get into Stuyvesant."

Josh's father's eyebrows raise and he lets out a low whistle. My ears prick up at the sound, thinking maybe he's calling me over to give me some fish. I run to stand next to the chair where he's sitting and rub my cheeks vigorously against its sides. But all he does is say, "Your mother cared about your education. Stuyvesant's one helluva prestigious high school."

"Believe me, I know." Laura gives a short laugh. "Those tests were *not* easy."

"So, wait," Josh says. "You would have been nine in, what, '89?" When Laura nods, he says, "That must have been a great summer to hang out in a record store. You had *Mind Bomb* by The The, *Paul's Boutique,* the Pogues' *Peace and Love.*"

Laura's face as she looks at him is perplexed but also affectionate for the first time in a long time. "How can you possibly know all that right off the top of your head?"

Josh grins. "You knew you married a geek."

"Hey," Erica interrupts. "Didn't *Bleach* come out that summer?"

"That's right!" Josh turns to face Laura again. "What did your mother think of early Nirvana?"

"Oh, I don't know." Laura takes a bite of her bagel, and I watch enviously as the fish goes into her mouth. But when nobody else says anything, waiting for her to answer, she swallows and tells Josh, "She wasn't all that interested in them at first. It wasn't her kind of music. But Anise came into town and dragged her to see them at the Pyramid Club. It was the first time they'd played New

York, and Kurt Cobain got into a brawl with one of the bouncers. That was on Tuesday night." There's a kind of unwilling respect in Laura's smile. "Wednesday morning she called her distributer and had him overnight her a gazillion copies of *Bleach*. By the time the store closed on Sunday she'd sold out."

Josh's father stands and carries his empty plate into the kitchen. I sink to my belly and put my nose between my front paws, disappointed that he didn't think to give me any fish. "The Lower East Side was so violent back then," he says. "Remember, Zelda? Every time you read about it in the papers, it was nothing but muggings, arson, and drug dealers." He comes back to the living room and settles again into the chair.

"You were taking your life in your hands just driving through that neighborhood," Josh's mother agrees. "It's surprising your mother decided to raise a child alone down there."

"Ma," Josh says. There's a warning in his voice.

"No, that's okay," Laura says. "It was different if you actually lived there," she tells his parents. "My mother made a point of getting to know people, so there'd always be someone to keep an eye out for me. I remember one time, I was twelve and riding my bike along Fourteenth and Second, and some older kid tried to sell me drugs. These hookers who knew my mother just *descended* on him." She laughs. "One of them insisted on walking me back to the store so she could deliver me to my mother personally."

Even though Laura's words seem friendly at first, there's a hard, protective sound to her voice. As if she doesn't want Josh's parents to think anything bad about Sarah. This is odd, because Sarah says Laura will never stop being angry at her for the record store or where she decided to raise Laura. *She blames the record store for everything,* Sarah once told Anise. Then she sighed and said, *Actually, she blames me.*

As Laura talks, though, she starts to sound softer and her shoulders relax. The ache in my chest from Sarah's being away thrums and eases as I listen to her, and I hope she'll keep talking about Sarah this way. It's nice to hear different memories of Sarah than the ones I already have. Maybe if Laura says enough of her different memories, we'll have remembered Sarah enough for her to come back and always be with us.

Josh likes listening to her, too. His eyes get shinier and don't move away from her face at all while she speaks. His posture (and Laura's, too) is more relaxed, so that now his arm and leg brush lightly against hers without either of them noticing much—in the old, comfortable way they used to be together before they started being angry all the time.

But his parents look horrified at what Laura has just said, and Laura realizes this. Her face turns bright red, and she gives a laugh that sounds like a dog's yelp. "It was completely different on Ninth west of A, though, where my mom's store was," she adds quickly. "*That* street was always quiet. The street we lived on was nice, too . . ." Laura's voice trails off and when she speaks again, her voice is casual. "How did we get on this subject, anyway?" She looks at Erica, who's sitting next to Josh's mother on the smaller couch. "We were talking about your plans for the kids this summer."

"I have something lined up for them through their school three days a week, but I don't know what to do with them the other two." Erica looks glum.

"I can take them two days a week, if you want," Josh says.

Erica hesitates. You can tell by her face how badly she wants to say yes, but she doesn't want to say so right away. "Are you sure? I know you have . . . other things to do."

"Sure!" Josh says. "I could use some time out of the house, anyway. It'll be fun."

Laura's nostrils widen just a little. She gets up and starts taking empty plates into the kitchen, her fingers gripping them tightly. I follow her and, thinking I *certainly* deserve a reward for the admirable patience I've shown all afternoon, I stand next to the counter and meow at her in the loudest, firmest voice I have. She salvages a small piece of fish from someone's plate and puts it on the floor for me.

I gobble it down quickly—but, really, I deserve better than that, seeing as I've waited so long to try some. When Laura starts scraping the rest of the food from the plates into the garbage disposal, I paw at her leg and meow more insistently. That's when she turns to look down at me and says, "Don't push your luck."

After everybody leaves, Josh carries the plates and platters of leftover fish into the kitchen. The fish goes into plastic wrap and the platters go into the sink. I'm *still* hoping Josh will give me some fish—like he *promised*—but instead he puts on a pair of springy yellow gloves and turns the faucet on. Steam and little rainbow soap bubbles rise into the air. Normally I'd love to jump and try to catch a few, but I don't want to take my eyes off that fish.

Laura comes in with the glasses everybody drank from and sets them down next to the sink. "Good!" Josh says cheerfully. "You can help me dry."

Laura picks up a towel and stands next to him. From the set of her back it's clear that something is bothering her. "What's wrong?" Josh asks, as he hands her a washed plate.

Laura's towel rubs the wet platter so hard it squeaks. "I just think we should've at least discussed it before you committed to taking the kids two days a week." She sets the dried platter into a metal rack next to the sink.

Josh hands her another one. "What's the big deal? I have the time, and I really *do* need to get out. I'm going crazy sitting here alone every day."

Laura's elbow moves rapidly up and down as she dries. "What about looking for a job?"

Josh's laugh is brief and harsh. "Trust me," he says, "three days a week is plenty of time to make phone calls nobody returns and send emails nobody responds to."

"But what if somebody wants to schedule an interview one of the days when you have the kids?" Laura takes the next plate from his gloved hand. "Or what if you *get* a job in a few weeks and don't have time for them anymore?"

"Then Erica and I will make other arrangements. That's a bridge we can cross if and when we get to it." Josh turns off the faucet. The yellow gloves make a snapping sound as he peels them off and turns to face Laura. "Laura, in the next two minutes my parents would've offered to take the kids. At their age they shouldn't be driving into the city twice a week or running around after two little kids all day. My family needs help, and I'm in a position to offer it. I should've discussed it with you first. You're right about that, and I'm sorry. But I really don't see what the problem is."

"I'm your family, too," Laura says quietly, and it occurs to me for the first time, that she's right—Laura and Josh *are* a family. I'd thought of them as being more like roommates—like Anise and Sarah, or like Sarah and me—because their schedules are so different and they don't act like the families on TV shows. But Laura and Josh are a family, and for a moment I'm distracted from the thought of all that fish as I wonder what that makes *me* in their lives. "I'd like to think that I get to be a part of family decisions," she adds.

Josh's face wavers, and I think maybe he's about to say something nice to her. But then his face hardens again. "I'm not the only one around here deciding things unilaterally."

Laura folds the towel neatly in half and slides it through the handle of the refrigerator, where it hangs to dry. "I'm going upstairs to change," she tells him, and walks out of the kitchen.

Josh sighs after she leaves, his eyes roaming around the room until they fall on me, still waiting by the counter. "I promised you some fish, didn't I?" he asks, like it just occurred to him—like I hadn't *clearly* been trying to remind him of this all afternoon! He takes a nice fat slice of the smoked fish out of its plastic wrap and puts it in the palm of his hand, which is shaking slightly. Then he bends down, holding his hand out toward me. "Come on, Prudence," he says in an encouraging voice. "Here you go."

I'm confused, because what does Josh expect me to do? Eat the fish right out of his hand? But then I'd have to touch him! Why can't he just put it on the floor for me, or on a little Prudence-plate (which would be best)?

"Come on, Prudence," Josh says again. His mouth twists. "I'd like to be on good terms with at least one woman in this house."

What house? What is he talking about? Raising my right paw carefully, I try batting at the fish in his hand, hoping to make it fall to the floor. But it stays right where it is.

And that's when Josh does the oddest thing. He starts singing to me, just like Sarah used to. *"Pru-dence, Pru-dence, give me your answer, do."* I look into his face, bewildered. That's when he straightens up and starts moving around the kitchen, turning in circles as he kicks out his feet and waves his hands. He's dancing! He does a funny little dance around the kitchen, dangling the piece of fish between the thumb and forefinger of his left hand. I follow his movements, trying to stay near the fish but away from his feet. Even my whiskers are having a hard time helping me stay balanced as he sings, more loudly this time, *"I'm half CRA-zy, all for the love of you."* Now he throws himself down on one knee with the other leg bent, draping the fish across his bent leg. *"It won't be a stylish marriage, I can't afford a carriage. But you'll look sweet, on the seat, of a bicycle built for twoooooooo!"*

He puts one hand on his chest and throws the other into the air as he holds the last note for a long time. It looks like he's having a good time, actually, as silly as all this dancing around is. Even I have to admit he's kind of entertaining right now. While he's distracted, I come close enough to pull the fish off his leg with my teeth. He strokes my back cautiously as I eat, and I'm so happy to finally have my fish, I don't even try to stop him.

We both look up as we hear an unexpected sound. It's Laura, standing in the doorway of the kitchen. Her lips are pressed together, but this time it's because she's trying to hold back laughter. Her shoulders are shaking with the effort. When she's calmed down a bit, she says, "That was pretty adorable."

Josh ducks his head with fake modesty. "Well, I try."

He stands back up, and the two of them look at each other's eyes. He's breathing a bit harder than normal because of all that dancing around.

Laura walks across the room toward him. "I'm sorry," she says, and wraps both arms tightly around Josh's waist. "About everything. Not just today."

"*I'm* sorry," Josh tells her. For a moment, I wonder if they're going to start arguing about who's sorrier. He pulls back to look into her face. "You know how crazy I am about you." He grins. "I'm even crazy about how much you love your job."

Laura leans her head against his chest. "I'm pretty crazy about you, too."

"Then we're two lucky people," he says, and kisses the top of her head.

I hear the puckering sound of their lips coming together. I continue to eat my fish as the two of them go upstairs to their bedroom. It's dark outside before they come back down.

9

Prudence

THERE WAS ONE DAY IN EARLY JUNE THAT WAS DIFFERENT FOR SARAH from all the other days in the year. She would always spend it listening to the same two songs over and over. The first song is on a black disk from one of Sarah's favorite bands, and in it the man who's singing asks if he fell in love with you, would you (not *you,* but the "you" in the song) promise to be true? The other song is by a woman. In *that* song the woman keeps saying to dim all the lights so she can dance the night away. Sarah never danced when she listened to this song, though, and she kept all the lights just as bright as they always were. She'd take out some dried old flowers from a metal box that she kept in the closet, and lie on the couch with a pillow Anise made for her out of her wedding dress. The pillow is covered in dark marks that Sarah says are water stains it got from being outside in the rain once, a long time ago.

Even though it's not really that pretty anymore—and even

though she only takes it out once a year—this pillow meant a lot to Sarah. She would run her fingers over the material while her music played, and then, finally, she'd stretch out on the couch to nap on it. I'd curl up next to her, nudging at her hand with the top of my head until she started petting me and scratching behind my ears the way I like. I could tell when she finally fell asleep, because her hand would stop moving and rest along the fur of my back. That's when I would fall asleep, too, stretching out one paw to rest on Sarah's shoulder, so we were still touching each other even though we were sleeping.

I found that pillow today in one of the Sarah-boxes. It was stuck under a bunch of rolled-up posters and a pair of small bongo drums Sarah used to let me play with sometimes, laughing and calling me a "hep cat." I had to use all my toes to pry the pillow free so I could lie on it and think about Sarah, and about how she said that if you remember someone, they'll always be with you. But when I opened my eyes, I didn't see Sarah anywhere.

I don't know exactly which day in June was so important to Sarah, so I don't know whether it's come and gone already. I guess it's a holiday just for Sarah and not for other humans, because as we get farther into June the only thing that's different here is the days keep getting longer, and Laura and Josh are running the air conditioner more frequently. In Lower East Side, our cold air came from a box stuck into the living room wall. If I pressed my ear to it, I could hear things happening outside or, sometimes, the sound of birds nesting in it from the other side of the wall. It was frustrating for me, to be able to hear the *cheep cheep!* of birds without being able to get at them. But it was even more frustrating for Sarah, who had to bang our side of the box with her hand until the birds flew away. She said their feathers clogged up the motor that made the cold air come out.

Here the cold air comes from vents up near the ceiling. It blows all the way down to the floor, though, and sometimes the sudden blast when it comes on tickles my ears until I have to scratch at them with my hind paws. On the days when Josh is home and not out with the littermates, he likes to make the air much cooler than most cats (including me) would find comfortable. But when he's not looking, Laura spins a little knob on the living room wall that makes the air warmer. She said something once about how expensive it is to keep the cold air running all the time (even *air* costs money in Upper West Side?), but Josh says that it gets too hot for him on the days when he has to be here.

I keep waiting for Laura to talk more about Sarah, like she did on Mother's Day. I thought maybe Laura would remember the June day that was so special to Sarah, and come upstairs like I did to look through the Sarah-boxes for Sarah's wedding-dress pillow. But Josh is the only one other than me who spends any time in my room, and he only comes in to look through Sarah's black disks for music to play and then put back before Laura gets home from work. I thought maybe he would play one of Sarah's two special songs, but he hasn't so far.

I wish I could figure out how to get Laura to talk about Sarah again. Sometimes when I look at her I get confused and think I'm looking at Sarah. It's what Sarah used to call "a trick of the light" that makes some passing expression on Laura's face, or the angle from which I see the curl of her eyelashes, so perfect and convincing in its Sarah-ness. But I don't know if that's because Laura really looks so much like Sarah, or if it's because I'm starting to forget what Sarah really looked like. I catch myself watching Laura the way I used to watch Sarah—her hair changing colors in the sunlight, her chin that trembles just a little right before she starts laughing at something I've done, her long fingers (that feel nice in my fur sometimes) when she throws me a bottle cap or plastic straw to play with. I've noticed that Laura has more of my scent mixed in with her own, which is even more confusing—because it's *Sarah* who's supposed to smell like me and be my Most Important Person.

Sometimes I catch myself without any pain in my chest at all from Sarah's not being here. I have to remind myself to feel it—even though it hurts—because *ideas* don't mean anything if you don't also feel them with your body. What if I were to forget about Sarah altogether? Already there's so much I can't remember. I can remember the first time Laura ever touched me, and when she first gave me the dress with the Sarah-smell for me to sleep on, and even the first time I met her when I was a kitten. I know I had lots of firsts with Sarah, too, but she's been gone for such a long, *long* time. Sometimes I can remember things about her so clearly, it's like I just saw her yesterday. Other times, no matter how hard I close my eyes and try to think, I can't remember anything at all. I remember the *idea* of Sarah, and all her warmth and gentleness and beautiful singing music, but the memory of the idea doesn't bring any specific feeling with it to my chest or belly.

I wish I could ask Laura how much she remembers about Sarah. Does she remember the way Sarah smells? *I* can, but maybe that's only because the things in the Sarah-boxes still smell like her. They won't smell like her forever, though, and what will I do then? Every day their Sarah-smell is getting fainter.

I've noticed Laura holding the picture of Sarah that used to live with us in our old apartment, and that now lives in the living room here. She'll stare at it for a while before putting it down, and her expression is almost questioning, as if there's something she'd like to know that she thinks she can figure out if only she looks at that picture long enough. If she hears Josh coming into the room, she quickly puts the photo back down and walks a few steps away from it. Is Laura, too, having a hard time remembering little things about Sarah, now that she's been gone for so long?

It was so hard when Sarah went away! But now that I'm losing even my memories of her, it feels like she's going away all over again. Laura's probably the only one who can help me with this. But Laura never talks about Sarah at all.

Two days a week, Josh takes a train up to Washington Heights, where his sister lives, so he can take care of the littermates. He always smells like them when he comes home—like fruit-juice Popsicles and potato chips and too-sweet chewing gum. He also has the good smell of outside air, the way Sarah used to when she came home from one of the long walks around Lower East Side she liked to take in nice weather. Even when Josh left the apartment every day to go to his office, he didn't smell as much like outside as he does now.

Josh likes to take the littermates on what he calls "field trips." At first I was a little jealous, because I know how much *I* would love to play in a field. I've never seen one in real life, but I've seen them on TV. They're big stretches of grass and trees, and even though I can't smell all the wonderful smells I'm sure are there, I can tell just by looking at the TV pictures that there would be no end of things to do or chase or pounce on.

But, other than one time when they went to see Great Lawn in Central Park, the places they go don't sound like fields at all. One day Josh took them to Museum of Natural History, and another time he took them to an indoor place where they could paint their own ceramic plates and pots. In between making phone calls to try and get a new job, Josh also calls humans he knows who have litters of their own, trying to get ideas for new things he can do with Abbie and Robert.

"I thought I'd take the kids down to the Lower East Side next week," he tells Laura one night, after she's come home from work.

Laura's eyebrows come together. "Really?"

"It's not like Manhattan ends at Fourteenth Street," Josh says in a dry voice.

Laura doesn't seem to like this idea. I'm not sure why, though, because going back to Lower East Side sounds *wonderful*. Maybe Sarah is there someplace, waiting for me! And even if she's not— even if she's still doing whatever it is she went off to do—I bet smelling all those familiar Lower East Side smells again would make me remember all kinds of things about her.

I have no way of asking Josh to take me with him if he decides to go to Lower East Side, but I try to give him hints by jumping into the cloth shoulder bag of "supplies"—like games and fruit-juice boxes—that he takes with him whenever he spends time with the littermates. Sometimes I have to push little toys and plastic-wrapped packets of tissues out of the bag and onto the floor to make room for myself (it still surprises me how not-skinny I've become). Josh always laughs when he sees me curled up in his bag with just my head poking out of the unzipped top, but he also always lifts me out of the bag and puts me back on the floor. It was foolish to let Josh trick me with fish and silly singing into not hissing at him when he touches me, because now he's not hesitant about picking me up. If he were, he'd have no choice but to let me stay in that bag and go with him to wherever he takes the littermates. ·

Josh laughs at some of the things I do (as if I were here to *entertain* humans!), but he's also been laughing and smiling a lot more in general. I guess I wasn't paying close enough attention to him before to notice the small changes in his posture and expressions that showed how unhappy he was becoming, being in the apartment all the time. Humans like spending time with other humans. Sarah was always happiest when both Anise and I were there to keep her company. Now Josh's shoulders are straighter than they've been since before he lost his job, and even his face looks different. It's darker from spending time outdoors under the sun, and there are tiny brown freckles on the skin of his nose.

"I didn't expect to love being with them as much as I do," Josh says to Laura one night.

"I'm sure they love being with you, too," Laura tells him with a smile.

Josh and Laura order a pizza tonight, because Josh says he's too exhausted from running around in the heat all day to even think about what they should do for dinner. Laura is tired, too. She's been staying up very late again—later even than she used to when I first came to live here. She isn't spending time with her work papers, and the pink marks on the sides of her nose have begun to fade. (Maybe she's not reading as many papers at her office, either. She doesn't have nearly as many little ink smudges on her fingers as she used to.) Mostly what she does now is put the TV on low and let her eyes go unfocused, as if she's thinking hard about something. She's also started putting little bits of food beside her on the couch and making a *pss-pss-pss* sound that calls me over to come eat them. Lots of times I don't bother moving off the couch after I'm done. I stretch out and settle into a deep sleep, and lately this has become the most restful sleeping I do.

Laura doesn't put any pizza cheese (I *love* pizza cheese!) on the couch next to her as she and Josh eat, but she does drop a bit onto the floor for me. Normally, when a pizza comes to our door, the man who lives behind the counter downstairs calls us on the phone to announce that the pizza's on the way up. He didn't tonight, though, and when the doorbell rang, Laura said, "That's odd, Thomas must be away from the desk." She and Josh are eating the pizza anyway, which I definitely won't do. It's always bad when things are different from the way they usually are, but when the thing that's different is with your *food,* that's the worst of all. So, ignoring the cheese Laura and Josh keep dropping onto the floor (as if they expect me to eat the *next* piece when I didn't eat the *last* one!), I devote myself instead to pushing the little plastic caps from their soda bottles around the coffee table with my front right paw.

"So what'd you and the kids do today?" Laura asks as they eat.

"We went down to Katz's. I had an urge for corned beef." Josh drinks from his glass and puts it back on the table. "Then we walked around for a while and went over to Alphaville Studios on Avenue A." He looks at Laura curiously. "Do you know the place?"

Laura stops chewing, but swallows hard before Josh notices. "Of course," she finally says.

"I figured you would. Evil Sugar recorded their first few albums there." Josh sprinkles garlic powder onto his pizza slice. "I never realized how cheap it is to book studio time there. They even let a lot of the bands leave their equipment set up so they don't have to pay an arm and a leg lugging it back and forth. And they have programs for neighborhood kids who are interested in music. They're good people down there—it's a real asset to the community."

Laura is chewing slowly. She tries to sound casual when she speaks, like she's just asking the questions a human normally would at this point in the conversation, but she doesn't quite succeed. "What made you think of going there?"

"I thought Abbie and Robert might get a kick out of seeing the inside of a recording studio. You know how kids like that kind of thing. I used to know one of their techs, and it turns out he's still there. He must've been there *forever*. He's got this beard practically down to his knees." I try to imagine what a human with no arm and no leg and a long, long beard might look like. Before I can get a picture in my head, though, Josh's cheeks turn a shade of pink so deep, it's almost red. "And," he says in the kind of voice humans use when they're confessing to something they think they should feel guilty about, "I've been looking through some of your mother's old albums. I keep seeing Alphaville Studios in the liner notes."

This time Laura puts the plate with her half-eaten pizza slice down on the coffee table and turns to look straight at him. But before she can say anything, Josh rushes ahead with, "Look, you promised way back in March that we could look through your mother's albums at home. I haven't pushed it. I've been trying to give you space to get things done on your own schedule. But those boxes can't just sit up there *forever,* Laura. At some point you'll need to figure out what you want to keep and what you want to toss or put into storage. And I'd hoped"—his voice gets softer—"that we'd find something else to do with that room."

Why can't those boxes sit up there? Who are they hurting? It's not like Josh doesn't have lots of his own "junk" filling up Home Office. Why can't there be *one* room in this whole huge apartment just for me and all *my* stuff? A spot in the middle of my back stings with an itch, and I turn to attack it angrily with my teeth.

"I don't know, Josh." I see the dark centers of Laura's eyes widen in a flicker of panic. "Things are just so . . . unsettled . . . right now."

"The history of the world is people having children under less-than-perfect circumstances," he tells her, gently.

They're discussing something else now, and I don't understand what it is. All I understand is that if Laura doesn't find a reason to care about the things in the Sarah-boxes, Josh is going to make her send them away. I get distracted, and my right paw—which is still batting at the plastic soda-bottle cap—hits Josh's glass of soda harder than I expected and sends it spilling all over the coffee table.

Josh and Laura both cry, *"Prudence!"* and jump up to get paper towels from the kitchen. I leap to the floor and crouch there. Really, this is *their* fault for leaving a bottle cap right next to a full glass and then distracting me with odd conversations. Still, humans tend to blame cats for things that aren't really the cat's fault. Neither of them scoops me up to kiss my head the way Sarah did that time when I spilled a full glass in Lower East Side, but at least they don't yell at me. They just wipe up all the soda and throw the dirty paper towels into the tall trash can that lives in the kitchen. By the time they're sitting on the couch again, I can tell that Laura has decided to talk about something else.

"So how *was* Alphaville?" she asks Josh—and she must *really* want to change the subject from the mysterious threat Josh had brought up, because I could tell how much she didn't like hearing Josh talk about this Alphaville place. "Did the kids have a good time?"

Josh hesitates and throws her a quick look. But he just says, "They did. Although from what the guy I know there was telling me, they may not be around much longer. The landlord's trying to sell the building. The tenants in the apartments upstairs are up in arms about it."

"That's a shame," Laura says, and there's real sympathy in her voice. "But that's what happens sometimes."

"I don't know," Josh says thoughtfully. "It sounds like there's something sketchy going on. I thought I'd poke around online tomorrow and see what I can find out."

"Is it really that strange? Real estate changes hands every day in this city. It's not like you can do anything about it."

"I don't know," Josh says again. "If there's something shady about the deal and getting press would help them out, it's not like

I don't know a ton of music journalists. That'd be a place to start, anyway."

"But if there really is something 'sketchy' going on," Laura argues, and I can tell she's trying hard to come up with a reason why Josh shouldn't care about this anymore, "wouldn't the music press already be on top of it?"

"Not necessarily," Josh says. "Alphaville's pretty much fallen off the radar over the last decade or so. It's been a while since any major albums came out of that place. Now they mostly serve the community and young bands that haven't signed with labels yet." Josh stretches his arms above his head and yawns. "I'm beat. All that walking in the heat today really did me in. I think I'll go take a shower."

Laura smiles and nods, but as soon as Josh's back is turned, her smile goes away. Then she sighs and pushes her fingers through her hair, the way Sarah always did when she was thinking about something she didn't want to think about anymore.

I can hear the shower running in Josh and Laura's bathroom as I work my way frantically through the Sarah-boxes. I know I can't stop Josh or Laura if they do decide to make these boxes go away, but there has to be *something* I can do. I spin around in jumpy circles as I go from box to box, my plumper belly knocking things out of the boxes and onto the floor. Normally I'd *hate* the idea of things going out of the boxes they're supposed to be in, but this is an emergency. I have more important things to worry about right now.

Suddenly, out of the corner of my left eye, I see a rat on the floor! *A rat!* An enormous black rat with bright-red eyes and a long skinny tail! I haven't seen one (except for in bad dreams) since that day when I lost my littermates, and Sarah and I found each other. I know how easily I can kill mice, but a rat is something else altogether—and this rat is *huge!* I spin around to face it head-on, my fur puffing all the way up, and with the force of the jump I take backward, I knock one of the Sarah-boxes onto its side where it lands with a terrific *crash*! My heart is pounding, and by the sudden brightness of the room, I can tell that the dark centers of my own eyes must have gotten as big as they possibly can.

The rat doesn't move. It just sits there, completely still, not even twitching its whiskers. I creep toward it—with my back still arched and my fur still puffed—and bat at its head with my right paw, taking a jump back immediately. But the rat still doesn't do anything. Once again I creep slowly toward it and bat at its head, and the rat is still motionless. This time, when I hit it, I leave my paw there for a moment. The rat feels strange. And that's when my fur starts to relax. This isn't a real rat at all. It's a fake, made out of something soft and springy.

I hear Laura's footsteps coming up the stairs. "Are you okay, Prudence?" she calls. "What's all the ruckus up there?" If my reaction when I saw the fake rat was bad, it's nothing compared with Laura's. When she comes into my room and sees it sitting in the middle of the floor, her face turns stark white and she screams!

I know that a fake rat can't hurt her, but I jump defensively in front of Laura anyway, letting her know that no rat—real or fake—will ever be able to get close to her as long as *I'm* here.

Laura's shriek of terror is so loud that Josh hears it in the shower. I hear the scrape of the shower curtain being thrown back, and then Josh's running footsteps pound down the hall. "Laura!" he yells. "Laura, what happened? Are you okay?"

Josh runs all the way into the doorway of my room and stands there, dripping wet, holding a towel around his waist with one hand. In the other is the baseball bat he keeps next to his side of the bed. But Laura is chuckling now, breathing hard with one hand on the spot right above her heart, which is probably pounding like mine was. "Good *lord*!" she says. "I thought I saw a rat!" She squats down on her heels, stroking my head with one hand and picking the fake rat up with the other, its rubbery tail dangling down her arm.

"What *is* that thing?" Josh asks her.

Laura turns it over in her hand. "My mom used to get a lot of swag from the record labels. Most of it was silly stuff—like mini lava lamps and key chains—and she'd give it to me. *This,* I be-lieve"—she lets the fake rat hang from her fingers by its tail—"was something she got when they released *Hot Rats* on CD."

"Zappa." Josh smiles and turns to rest his baseball bat against the wall, pushing away the wet hair that's fallen into his eyes. "That was a great album."

Laura stands and laughs again. "Not for me, it wasn't. This thing lasted exactly one day in my room. I woke up in the middle of the night and was sure I saw a rat on my dresser. It took my mother hours to calm me down enough to fall back asleep. The next day she brought it back to her store."

I keep my eyes intently on the fake rat hanging from Laura's hand as Josh puts one arm—the one that isn't holding his towel up—around her shoulders. "You should give it to Prudence," he says. "I think she wants to play with it."

Laura leans her head against his shoulder and looks up into his face. "You think?" Now Josh is looking into Laura's face, too. Without looking away from him, she tosses the fake rat in my di-rection. "Here you go, Prudence," she murmurs.

Josh keeps his arm around her as they leave the room. I swipe at the fake rat with my claws a few times. But silly toys aren't what I'm thinking about right now.

10

Laura

THE WOMAN ON THE SUBWAY WAS MIDDLE-AGED AND FORMIDABLE. Short but sturdily built, she had caramel-colored hair and red fingernails so long they arced gently half an inch from the tips of her fingers. She spoke emphatically to the man standing in front of her. Also middle-aged, tall and slender, his head seemed too large for his frame. It bent slightly toward the woman, like a flower beginning to droop on its stem. *"La gente cambia,"* the woman said, aiming one red nail in the direction of his face. *"La gente cambia."* And then, in heavily accented English, "You don't know me. You don't know me at all." The man didn't do much in the way of response aside from nodding his head dolefully from time to time. Whether because this conversation pertained to him in particular (could they be splitting up, this middle-aged couple in this very public subway car?), or in silent acknowledgment of the fickle mystery of the human heart, was impossible for Laura, seated half the car's length away from them, to discern.

The two of them clung to the steel bar above their heads, the occasional lurches of the train throwing them slightly off-balance but otherwise not disrupting their conversation. All around Laura, seated and standing, people shivered in the too-chilled air-conditioning as they tapped on BlackBerrys (which Laura knew she should be doing, but wasn't) or fiddled with iPods, or stared blankly into the middle distance. The train stopped, and a hot *whoosh* of fetid air from the station entered the open doors along with a black-haired man dressed in a waiter's uniform. It was a muggy July day, and faint yellow circles had begun to form at the armpits of his white jacket. He wheeled a linen-draped cart covered with plastic-wrapped platters of fruits and pastries, pasta salads and sandwiches. *Somebody catering an after-hours meeting*, Laura thought. *Somebody who still has a budget to do things like that.* The people who had to move to accommodate the cart looked at the waiter in minor annoyance, and he returned their looks with a vaguely apologetic expression on his sweat-slick face that said, *Sorry, but I gotta work, too.* Then everybody went back to what they had been doing, the middle-aged woman continuing to harangue the middle-aged man even as one corner of the cart dug into the flesh of her hip.

The woman was right, Laura acknowledged. People did change. Or maybe it was just that, over time, you started to notice different things. She'd been thinking about how dramatically Josh had changed these past few weeks, since he'd become involved in the cause of saving Alphaville Studios along with the apartment building on Avenue A. Except, Laura conceded, with the uneasiness of someone who's deliberately shut her eyes to an unpleasant truth she now has to face, the real change had been happening slowly over the past few months. Once she'd thought Josh exempt, somehow, from the vicissitudes that threatened people like her, whose lives weren't as charmed as his own. Now she realized what she should have seen in a hundred different ways, in small gestures and offhand remarks. Josh was frustrated. The "changed" Josh she'd seen during the last few weeks was merely the confident, energetic, pleasantly busy Josh she'd first met just under a year and a half ago.

She'd been certain his interest in the building would fade after a few days. Instead, Josh had committed himself full-time to the project, making endless phone calls, creating a blog and Facebook pages, sending out a steady stream of emails. He'd pressed his niece and nephew into service, bringing them to the apartment once a week to clip together press releases and informational one-sheets that would be packaged and mailed to reporters, music journalists, city council members, congressmen, anybody who might choose to get involved. Even Prudence had gotten caught up in the frenetic activity, making sudden wild leaps onto the small folding table Josh had set up in his overcrowded home office (he'd had to move a few boxes of his own into their spare bedroom to accommodate it), scattering orderly stacks of papers in all directions. "Look, Prudence is helping!" Robert would shriek, and he and Abbie would collapse into uncontrollable laughing fits—especially when Prudence would accidentally get a mailing label stuck to the bottom of one paw and walk around shaking her paw furiously, assuming an air of injured dignity and refusing to let anybody close enough to pull the sticker off for her.

"It's one of those Mitchell-Lama buildings," Josh had told Laura a few days after he'd first gone there with the children. "You know, those middle-income apartment buildings they started putting up in the fifties."

Laura did know. She and Sarah had moved into a Mitchell-Lama complex farther uptown back in the '90s, when they'd left the Lower East Side.

"Anyway, now the building owner is trying to opt out of the program so he can sell to a developer who'll reset the rents to 'market rate.' Which would basically quadruple or even quintuple what the tenants are paying. A lot of them are elderly and on fixed incomes, or war veterans. There's a cop who lives in the building, and the new rent would be twice what he takes home in a month!"

Laura was only half listening. Of all the buildings in Manhattan, she wondered, why did Josh have to pick *this* building to worry about? She remembered Sarah, on the day they'd gone to Alphaville Studios, adjusting a set of headphones to fit over Laura's ears and saying, *This way we can hear ourselves while we record, so we'll know what we sound like.* Laura had asked, *But won't we know what we sound like just by listening to ourselves?* And Sarah had explained that the way you sounded to yourself and the way you sounded to other people were two very different things.

"The building's property value has been assessed at seven-point-five million," Josh had continued, "and the tenants' association has raised ten million from city subsidies and a handful of private donations. They want to buy the building themselves so they can keep the rents where they are. But the landlord has an offer of fifteen million from a developer, and he's holding out."

Laura had tried to quell the beginnings of panic as she listened to him talk. "It's a terrible thing," she'd said. "But this is just what *happens* in this city, Josh. There's not even any point in fighting it. One way or another, the developers always win."

"And the music studio!" Josh exclaimed, as if she hadn't spoken. "Do you know how many great artists rehearsed and recorded there? Evil Sugar, Dizzy Gillespie, Tom Waits, the Ramones, Richard Hell. And the space is still in use! This isn't just gentrification, this is decapitalization of the arts in New York." He was pacing the room in his excitement. "Clarence Clemons, Nile Rodgers, Dylan, *all* the sessions guys who backed up the big-name performers on their albums and played in clubs all over town. The list is endless!"

It was an uncanny thing, Laura thought, to hear the exact same words her dead mother might have used coming from her husband's mouth.

"But, Josh," she'd tried again. "This is a lost cause. Surely, you can see that. You and I, *we* are *not* a lost cause. *We* need someplace to live, too, and we can't live here forever on my salary alone. The last of your severance is coming up in two months."

"Laura," Josh had replied, and his frustration was evident in the way he said her name. "I've worn my fingers down to nubs making phone calls and sending out résumés. And at this point, nobody's making any major hiring decisions until after Labor Day, anyway. At least this way I could possibly make some new contacts, or maybe it'll lead to something else." Josh had paused to give Prudence, who'd taken up diligent residence in front of the couch, a dollop of tuna salad from his half-eaten sandwich. "It beats the hell out of sitting around here doing nothing."

"Maybe you could try writing again," Laura had suggested. "Isn't that what you did when you first moved to New York? You know people at so many different magazines . . ."

"Oh please, Laura. I couldn't make it as a writer back when people were actually hiring writers. It won't happen for me now when everybody's scaling back." He'd taken her hand and said, "Look, I don't want you to think I'm trying to put the whole burden on you. I *swear* I'm going to find something else. And I know it'll be tight, but we can manage on your salary and what's left of our savings until then. What's that expression? *Safe as houses*? Isn't your job at the firm safe as houses?"

"Yeah," Laura said. "Safe as houses."

White-shoe firms like Laura's had traditionally never engaged in major layoffs the way other companies did. In part this was a point of pride—of maintaining public confidence and public appearances—and in part it was a practical matter. Large cases were apt to spring up on short notice, and then you'd want partners and associates whose skills you knew you could rely on. Sometimes a firm would grow so large and unwieldy that it would collapse under its own weight, sucking everyone into its vortex like a black hole. Typically, though, jobs like Laura's—even during recessions and downturns—had been safe.

But now uneasy whispers and rumors were afloat, tales of large corporate firms like Laura's that were actually laying associates off. Laura wasn't sure precisely when the early-morning phone calls from recruiters had stopped coming in; she only knew that one morning, when the phones were unusually quiet, she'd realized with a start that it had been some time since anybody had called to "feel her out" about her willingness to move elsewhere. At Neuman Daines, the new class of first-year associates, who in the past had always started their employment the September following their law school graduations, had seen their start dates deferred until the following spring. A handful of associates who fell onto the lower end of the billable-hours-per-month scale had been told, in the most civilized way possible, that it would be best for all concerned if they were employed elsewhere within, say, the next two months. Perry had never exactly been a jovial person, but Laura had detected an undercurrent of strain lately in their interactions. She didn't know whether it had to with her personally, or with the firm's larger financial outlook, but whatever its source, it was disturbing.

Nothing had been the same since Josh's company had gone through its own round of layoffs. As soon as Laura had seen the severance agreement in Josh's hand, she'd known what had happened. A "Chinese wall" had been erected around her at the firm. She had been deliberately excluded from anything related to Josh's company, the paperwork the firm was preparing for it, and everything else associated with it. It was foolish, Laura knew, to take such a thing personally. Had she gone to Perry and confronted him with it, if she'd said something like, *How could you not tell me?* she knew exactly what Perry's response would be. *You knew what you were getting into when you started dating a client,* he would say. *You knew there might be complications.* Probably he would have thrown in some pithy quote from the Talmud about choices and consequences for good measure. And of course he would be right. The only thing to be gained by bringing it up would be to appear naïve and overly emotional. Just another woman in business who couldn't separate the personal from the professional.

Still, the thing hurt. Laura would look at her co-workers, particularly the other fifth-years, and wonder who had known what and when. How long before Laura had they known that her home life was about to turn upside down? What had they said about her when her name was mentioned? Growing up, Laura had always had a keen sense of being different—tall and white in an elementary school where few children were either. She had spent most of her adult life trying to fit in, and since marrying Josh she'd nearly convinced herself that this was something she no longer gave much thought to. Yet, as it turned out, it had taken very little for that feeling to come rushing back, to make her wonder if every hushed conversation that ended abruptly when she entered a room had been about her, the oddity, the one who wasn't quite the same as the others, the associate foolish enough to marry a client—something no other Neuman Daines associate had done in the entire hundred-year history of the firm.

Laura remembered a little joke of her mother's, something like, *You're not paranoid if they really are all against you.* Laura didn't want to be paranoid, but she couldn't help noticing that where she'd typically racked up anywhere from 200 to 240 billable hours a month, in the past two months she'd barely broken 160. While technically this wouldn't affect her salary, her bonuses this year would undoubtedly be smaller than in previous years—and bonuses accounted for nearly half of what she earned.

It wasn't that Laura had slacked off or was unwilling to take on the work. Work wasn't being sent her way. It could be that there wasn't as much work to go around as there had been in flusher times. She suspected that some of the other associates might be "hoarding" work, although it was nothing she could set out to discover and prove without making herself appear even more paranoid than she already felt. Maybe Perry wasn't looking out for her the way he used to. Maybe Perry was somebody else's rabbi these days, although she couldn't be *so* far out of the loop as to be unaware of something like that, if it had truly occurred.

Unless, she would think grimly, she was.

Laura had fallen into the habit of staying up late thinking about these things, telling Josh she was staying up to go over work papers the way she always had, but actually turning everything over in her mind. Frequently she found herself encouraging Prudence to join her for company, placing a morsel of tuna or cheese, or some other much-loved treat, on the couch until Prudence was lured into settling down next to her. Once the cat had fallen asleep, Laura would gently comb the tips of her fingernails through the fur of Prudence's back, which was what had first suggested the cat brush she'd spontaneously stopped for on the way home from work today. Only a few months ago (had it really only been a few months?), Sarah must have stroked Prudence in much the same way Laura did now. Laura would look at her long fingers—fingers that, under different circumstances, might have moved with ease across a turntable or a musical instrument or a typewriter—and think, *I have my mother's hands.*

As a child, on hot July days like this one, with school out and her mother busy at the store, Laura had spent a great deal of time in one of the ladder-backed chairs in the Mandelbaums' kitchen with Honey in her lap. Mrs. Mandelbaum would chop a frozen banana into a bowl, sprinkle a teaspoon of sugar over it, then mix it with sour cream taken from what she insisted on calling, to Laura's amusement, "the icebox." Honey would lick the sugared cream from Laura's fingers with her raspy tongue while Mrs. Mandelbaum prepared dinner and Mr. Mandelbaum rested in his overstuffed living room chair only a few feet away, listening to the big-band albums that Sarah scavenged from her store to bring back for him.

Once, listening to an album by the Count Basie Orchestra, Mr. Mandelbaum had closed his eyes and said, "Ah, this takes me back." Calling into the kitchen, "Ida, do you remember this one?"

"Of course I do," Mrs. Mandelbaum had answered. She thwacked a chicken breast cleanly in half with a cleaver. "Norm Zuckerman and I danced to this at the Roseland Ballroom in 1937."

Mr. Mandelbaum grumbled something under his breath that sounded like *Norm Zuckerman* followed by a bad word in Yiddish. But Mrs. Mandelbaum had been unperturbed, her deft hands massaging spices into the chicken as she smiled and told Laura, "Mister Bigshot in there might not have thought much of me at first, but plenty of boys had eyes for me in those days. Believe you me."

"No wonder," Mr. Mandelbaum snorted. "You had the shortest skirts and longest legs on the whole Lower East Side."

"Stop it, Max! You're filling her head with nonsense." Mrs. Mandelbaum slid the chicken into the oven and ran her hands under the faucet. "I'll put the leftovers in the icebox and bring them up later when your mother comes home," she told Laura. "Nothing beats cold chicken at the end of a hot day." She wiped her hands on her apron. "Don't listen to what he says. My mother used to measure my skirts with a ruler before I went out. If they were shorter than two inches below my knee, I had to go back upstairs and change."

"Ah, but those were some knees." Mr. Mandelbaum smiled from his chair. "They still are, you know. Nobody has knees like my wife's." Mrs. Mandelbaum had pretended not to hear him, but a pleasant blush spread across her wrinkled cheeks.

Laura, rubbing her knuckles gently behind Honey's ear, had considered this, unable to imagine what it would be like to have such a strict mother. Sarah had never been especially prone to discipline, had never once raised her hand to Laura or enforced punishments of any kind. "Do you have any pictures of what your dresses looked like back then?"

"Do we have any *pictures*?" Mr. Mandelbaum's voice was always powerful. Sometimes Laura could hear him from the hallway in front of her own apartment, all the way downstairs. But even Honey opened her eyes wider at how loud his voice sounded now. "Ida, bring out the photo albums."

Mrs. Mandelbaum had gone to the linen closet in the front hall, pulling out several thick albums. She'd spread them out on the linoleum kitchen table, and Mr. Mandelbaum came in to join them. Laura marveled at the tiny hats and long beads women had worn back then as Mr. and Mrs. Mandelbaum told stories about this relative and that friend. Finally, Honey had crept from Laura's lap onto the table and sat smack in the middle of an open photo album, rubbing her head against Mr. Mandelbaum's cheek and swishing her tail across Laura's hand. "Honey, in her infinite wisdom, is here to remind us that all good things must come to an end," Mr. Mandelbaum declared. Then Mrs. Mandelbaum had put the albums back in the linen closet and begun preparations for a strudel with Laura's help ("A girl is never too young to learn how to cook," she always said), and Mr. Mandelbaum returned to the living room where he continued to listen to Count Basie until dinner was ready.

Later, after they'd eaten, Laura would fall asleep in the bed that had once belonged to their son, Honey clasped in her arms and purring contentedly. It was from Honey that Laura had learned the trick of sleepily half closing her eyes in a series of slow blinks in order to make a cat fall asleep. At some point Sarah would close the record store and come to carry her downstairs to her own bed, although Laura would be too deeply asleep to remember this part. She'd always slept well with Honey snoring softly beside her.

If she squinted now, sitting on the couch with Prudence, she could almost imagine that it was Honey sleeping next to her once again. The two of them looked somewhat alike, both slim brown tabbies (although Prudence seemed to be getting plumper lately—or was Laura imagining things?) with black tiger stripes. Prudence even had a hint of the same tiny black patch on the white fur of her lower jaw that Mrs. Mandelbaum had referred to as "Honey's beauty mark."

Of course, Prudence and Honey were very different creatures. Honey hadn't been nearly as comical as Prudence, with her funny little airs of self-importance and the peremptory way she was apt to demand food (a thing Honey had never done). And Prudence was far more aloof than Honey had ever been, Honey who was so gentle and who had turned huge, green, adoring eyes upon you the second you reached down to stroke her head. *Sweet as a piece of honey cake,* Mr. Mandelbaum had always said. Laura remembered now, with a sudden shock at having ever forgotten, that Mr. Mandelbaum had also sung the "Daisy Bell" song to Honey—except, of course, he'd sung, *Ho-ney, Ho-ney, give me your answer do . . .*

Honey and Mr. Mandelbaum and everything else she'd loved had been lost to exactly the same inexorable forces Josh was now trying to combat. Mr. Mandelbaum himself had talked about friends forced from their tenements in the West Sixties back in 1959, when the buildings were leveled to clear space for Lincoln Center. It was the inevitable life cycle of a large city. A few tender-hearted people would wring their hands and write piteous op-ed pieces for the local newspapers, and some poor sap would be trot-ted out before the cameras to share his tale of woe for the evening news. But in the end, the buildings came down, the rents went up, and sooner or later everybody forgot. Cities had no memories. Only people did, and even people would forget eventually.

And *this* was the thing, of all possible things, that Josh had chosen to fixate on. *This* was where Josh was putting all his time and energy instead of focusing on what he should have been fo-cused on—himself and Laura and the future the two of them would have together. Laura wanted her life to move in one direc-tion: forward. And here Josh was, dragging her back into the past.

All of it had become so jumbled in her mind that by the time she'd knocked on Perry's office door that morning, she wasn't sure if she was there for Josh, on a pretext to talk to Perry at length about something, or to assuage her own conscience when it came to the dim view she'd taken of Josh's efforts. Probably, she told herself, it was some combination of both.

From her customary seat across from Perry's desk, Laura could see the framed photograph of Perry with his wife and two daugh-ters taken at the older one's Bat Mitzvah two years earlier. Laura had attended alone and been seated with the handful of other peo-ple Perry had invited from the firm. She had been the only third-year associate. Next year, she would attend the younger girl's Bat Mitzvah with Josh. *If I'm invited . . .*

"What can you tell me about Mitchell-Lama statutes and regu-lations?" she'd asked Perry, after pleasantries had been exchanged.

Perry's bushy eyebrows rose. "Are you working on an opinion letter for a client?"

Laura hated lying, knew she wasn't any good at it. "Something like that," she hedged, and felt her cheeks grow warm.

Perry nodded, then leaned back in his leather chair. "Well . . ." The tips of his fingers steepled across his stomach in the professorial air many of the younger associates found irritating, although Laura had always secretly loved it. "Mitchell-Lama is a type of subsidized housing program that was proposed by state senator MacNeil Mitchell and assemblyman Alfred Lama, and signed into law in 1955 as the Limited-Profit Housing Companies Act. There was a large working-class population in New York who needed places to live. Manhattan was pretty crowded back then"—Perry's brief smile contained a hint of irony—"and there was a shortage of affordable housing for people who were teachers, for example, or transit workers, or store clerks. City and government officials all the way up the line wanted to find some way to make affordable housing available to these people. The thinking was that it wasn't in the City's best interests to have a population of only the very rich and the very poor. They wanted a stable middle class who were invested in their neighborhoods in order to generate additional tax revenues, bring crime rates down, et cetera."

"Sounds logical," said Laura.

"It *was* logical," Perry replied. "The problem was that developers would say, *I'm not going to build a building and then have the rent frozen afterward with rent control. Why should I invest money in a losing proposition?* So Mitchell-Lama was created as a solution. The basis was that the city would put up ninety-five percent of the money to erect the buildings. Somebody from the private sector would come up with the additional five percent of the project cost at a ridiculously low interest rate on a thirty-five to fifty-year mortgage, and that would include the cost of the property, building a tenable building on it, and so forth. In exchange for this great deal the City was giving them, the developers would calculate rent by figuring out how much the building would need for maintenance, how much for debt service, and then they would build in a limited annual return for the investors. I forget the exact number, but something like seven percent. There would be *some* profit for the developers, but that profit would be limited so rents for the tenants could remain affordable. The developers knew this going in—it was why they got such favorable terms in the first place. It was a win for everybody at the time."

"At the time," Laura interjected when Perry paused to sip from his coffee mug. "But not anymore?"

"As you know, things change." (Was the look he gave her then meaningful? Or was he merely looking at her? For the life of her, Laura couldn't decide.) "There haven't been many new Mitchell-Lama properties built in the past fifteen years or so. A lot of the buildings that already existed, especially the ones that went up in the earlier days of the program, have long since paid off their mortgages. Property values and market-rate rents have skyrocketed. So now there's a wave of owners and development corporations that want to opt out of the program and flip the buildings, or at least raise the rents substantially. It's not quite as simple as all that, of course. You have to get permission from the DHCR before you can privatize." At Laura's quizzical look, he clarified, "The Division of Housing and Community Renewal. Typically, though, that's just a formality. There's a mandatory process by which the building's tenants have to be notified of a potential privatization and given a chance to protest the opt-out, and to submit any problems with building maintenance and repair that would need to be addressed before the building could be sold. Then there are several different agencies that regulate Mitchell-Lama housing. Not all buildings are regulated by the same agencies, and some buildings are regulated by multiple agencies that have conflicting regulations. Wading through all the bureaucracy can represent hundreds of billable hours and tens of thousands of dollars to a developer's law firm. There are a number of court cases and proposed amendments to the original statutes working their way through the system right now, any one of which could change the game significantly. We've been keeping an eye on them for some of our clients."

"Usually, though, the owners are able to sell the buildings." Laura phrased this as a statement, not a question.

"Almost always, in the end," Perry replied, nodding. "There was one situation back in 2007 with a Mitchell-Lama building up in the Bronx, where the tenants organized and were able to bring enough political pressure to bear that the DHCR ended up denying the request to opt out. That was the only time I've seen it happen, though, in the twenty-five years or so since the buildings started privatizing."

"Thanks, Perry." Laura prepared to rise and leave his office.

"I'm assuming this client you're preparing the opinion letter for is interested in privatizing the property?" Laura nodded, feeling the color rise in her cheeks for a second time. Perry gestured her back down in her chair. "You should know that sometimes, *if* the tenants' organization is very well organized, and if they can generate enough negative publicity for the building's owner, and if they have an attorney who's an ace—someone who can ferret out every problem in the building, every contradiction in the statutes, and who can bury the owners and developers in paperwork and make the whole process even more painful and expensive— assuming a scenario where the tenants' association has the intellectual and financial resources to mount a large-scale resistance like that, then it might be in the owner's best interests to find a way to compromise with them. People don't always like to see their neighborhoods change too quickly, and they'll fight hard to keep it from happening. As the Talmud says, *Customs are more powerful than laws.*"

Laura thanked Perry again and rose. She had been hoping for something—a word, a gesture—that would let her know things between Perry and her were what they'd always been. She'd gotten nothing from this conversation to confirm that wish, but then nothing to contradict it, either. Her hand was on the doorknob when Perry said musingly, "Yes . . . there'd be a lot of potential billable hours for an attorney on either side in something like this." The look he leveled at Laura was inscrutable. For a fleeting moment, it reminded her of Prudence.

Perry had a way of knowing things that nobody had ever told him. Laura wondered if this last statement was meant to urge her on to wring more hours out of this possibly lucrative client she'd hinted at, or if some instinct had whispered that her motivations for asking weren't what she'd led him to believe. Perhaps he was warning her against letting her priorities drift in unprofitable directions.

Not that Laura needed to be reminded where her priorities lay. *At least the tenants have a process,* she thought. *At least they have a chance.*

A chance was more than she and Sarah had ever had.

Laura had spent the past sixteen years of her life worrying about money. The day she and Sarah had been thrown out of their apartment—along with Mr. Mandelbaum and her best friend Maria Elena and everybody else who'd lived there—she'd heard people say how something like this would never have been done to people with money, how it wouldn't have happened if they'd all lived on Park Avenue instead of Stanton Street.

In high school, she'd gone one day with a friend to visit the friend's father, who was a partner in a large law firm much like the one Laura worked for now. Laura would never forget the first time she'd been inside one of those huge, prosperous Midtown skyscrapers. There had been an atrium in the lobby with trees over twenty feet tall, and Laura had been astounded. That there could be trees that big *growing indoors*! A building so enormous, so obviously wealthy, so confident in its own permanence that it could afford the time and money to plant trees within its walls and wait for them to grow—surely the people who worked in such a building could go to and from their offices every day in complete confidence that they would still have homes when they returned to them in the evening. And from that day, Laura had wanted nothing more than to be one of the chosen, happy few who could take such permanence for granted. She imagined opening her eyes one fine morning without even a flicker of memory of what it had felt like to worry about the things that might happen to her if she didn't have enough money.

Laura's philosophy of life was simple. It was that money, money safely in the bank, money enough to pay all your bills, was the most important thing in the world. It was better and more important than youth or fame or having fun or being pretty or anything other than (Laura would grudgingly concede) one's health. Maybe it wasn't more important than love, but even love would crumble in the face of true poverty. *When poverty comes in the door, love flies out the window,* Laura had heard Perry say once, quoting his grandmother. And Laura, remembering the catastrophic days after she and Sarah had lost their home, had known he was right.

Then again, there were the Mandelbaums, who'd always struggled over money, especially after failing eyesight had forced Mr. Mandelbaum to retire from driving his cab. *We'll get by,* Mrs. Mandelbaum would say. *Remember, we're supposed to thank God for our misfortunes as much as our good fortune.* And Mr. Mandelbaum would reply, *Ida, if I stopped to thank God every time I had problems, I wouldn't have time to scratch my own head.* But there would be affectionate good humor mingled with the exasperation in his voice.

People who worried about accumulating a lot of expensive "stuff," or who felt a need to be "fulfilled" by what they did for a living, were people who had gotten used to luxuries that Laura had never been able to afford. Stuff was nice and feeling fulfilled was probably even nicer, but money was more important than either. Without money you ended up the way Mr. Mandelbaum had. Without money you would rot in the streets or in one of those wretched SROs and nobody would care. Laura had no desire to live extravagantly. By living on less than half her take-home, she'd managed to finish paying off her student loans the month before she and Josh were married. Now all she asked was not to have to worry about having enough money to live decently and pay her bills on time.

But these days all she did was worry about money. She'd pace around her office with the door closed, during all of that "extra" time that had once been given over to accumulating billable hours, calculating what she was likely to earn this year with her smaller bonuses, trying to think up a budget that would allow her and Josh to meet their current expenses and leave something to carry over into next year in case Josh still couldn't find a job.

At a certain point, Laura had acknowledged that worrying about these things as much as she did could only be counterproductive and distract her from her work. But even that made her worry more rather than less, until she began to wonder if worrying about worrying was some kind of diagnosable mental disorder.

She thought about her mother, who'd also tended toward obsessive thoughts, although Sarah's obsessions had been of a pleasanter kind. Sarah had sometimes spent whole days listening to a single song—like "Baba Jinde" by Babatunde Olatunji, or Double Exposure's "Ten Percent" on a twelve-inch album—if she was in the right kind of mood. When she was small, Laura had marveled at the intensity and focus something like this required. Now, as an adult, she understood.

The apartment was silent when Laura let herself in after her sweaty slog home from the subway, empty except for Prudence, who was curled up asleep in a box that had once held a ream of paper and was now waiting by the front door for someone (*Me,* Laura thought, a touch resentfully) to carry it to the trash room. Josh was out somewhere, perhaps at some meeting of the tenants' association in the Avenue A building, or at one of the networking events he attended with less frequency as the months went by and they failed to yield any job leads. Possibly he'd even told her about it that morning and she'd forgotten. It wouldn't surprise her at all, considering how snarled her mind was these days.

She went upstairs to her bedroom to remove her watch and earrings and place them in the wooden jewelry box Josh had surprised her with in the early days of their courtship. She'd admired it in an antiques store they'd ducked into during one of their walks. It had reminded her of Mrs. Mandelbaum's jewelry box, which had rested on her bedroom dresser amid framed photos of Mr. and

Mrs. Mandelbaum's wedding, their honeymoon in Miami Beach, the two of them with their son, Joseph, as a towheaded toddler in a Thanksgiving Pilgrim's costume and later as a laughing young man dressed for his high school prom, and pictures of Mr. Mandelbaum in his World War II fighter pilot's uniform. The box itself had been filled with pieces in the art nouveau style that Mr. Mandelbaum had bought for Mrs. Mandelbaum over the years, none of it terribly expensive yet all of it beautiful to Laura's young eyes.

One afternoon, when Laura was ten, Mrs. Mandelbaum had pressed a heavy brooch of silver and onyx into her hand. Laura had tried to give it back, thinking it would be bad manners to accept such a gift, but Mrs. Mandelbaum had said, *Max and I love you as if you were our own granddaughter. This is so you'll always have something to remember us by.* Then she'd fixed the brooch onto Laura's dress and combed her hair before the murky glass of the old mirror in their bedroom. *See how pretty it looks on you?* The two of them had walked hand in hand back into the living room where Mr. Mandelbaum waited with cake and tea things, Honey lying behind him on the back of the couch with one small paw resting on his shoulder. *Hoo-ha!* he'd said. *I had no idea two elegant ladies were joining me for tea.* Laura had blushed with shy pleasure at his praise. The brooch was long gone but Laura hadn't needed it to remember the Mandelbaums, not even all these years later. Not even though she had failed them, in the end.

Of all the childhood places she had loved, the Mandelbaums' apartment had been second only to her own bedroom downstairs from them. She'd loved its sheer lace curtains that Mrs. Mandelbaum had sewn when Laura was still too young to remember such things, and the lovely watercolor wallpaper in deep blues and creams and purples that Sarah had picked out—pretty but not cloying. Perfect for a young girl's room. Laura had been far less tidy in those days than she was now. She'd let dolls and books and clothing accumulate in large heaps until, finally, Sarah would be provoked into one of her rare displays of impatience. *If you don't clean this room soon, I'll . . .* But Laura had liked to let the mess build until even she couldn't stand it anymore, because then she would have the intense joy of cleaning it up. Once she had everything perfectly arranged, the amber of late-afternoon sunlight slanting in through the delicate white curtains (it was important to time the cleaning so that it never started so early or so late as to miss this time of day), she'd walk around touching things and think, *How lucky I am! I'm the girl who gets to live here.*

On her way back downstairs, Laura passed the room she and Josh had intended for a nursery, now filled with Sarah's boxes. Prudence, for reasons Laura couldn't quite figure out aside from a general *Well that's cats for you*, had recently developed the habit of throwing things from the boxes onto the floor. Last night, Prudence had unearthed part of the collection of funny little musical instruments—a harmonica, a Jew's harp, a miniature drum on a stick with tiny wooden knobs attached to it by strings that would hit the drum if you spun the stick around—that Sarah had kept behind the counter of her record store for Laura's amusement.

The harmonica had been Laura's favorite, although she'd never really learned to play it. Sarah, discerning as her ear was, had smiled and never once winced whenever Laura had banged around the store blowing chaotic, discordant "music" through it. Laura had blown a few notes experimentally through the harmonica yesterday while Prudence observed her with grave attention. The noise had startled Prudence away at first, although moments later she'd returned to raise one paw up to it, as if to feel the air Laura blew through its holes or to push the noise back into the instrument.

Today Prudence had somehow uncovered Sarah's old address book, the one Laura had told herself she'd never find among all Sarah's odds and ends after Sarah had died and the question of how to contact Anise, currently touring in Asia, came up. She'd settled for sending a letter through Anise's management agency. In truth, Laura had no desire to talk to Anise. It was Anise who'd first lured Sarah into her Lower East Side existence. And it was Anise who'd abandoned Sarah (and Laura) when that life fell apart.

Lately, though, looking through Sarah's old things with Prudence, Laura had found herself recalling earlier days, when Sarah's owning a record store and living with her in an old tenement had seemed like its own kind of charmed life. Even knowing that Prudence didn't really understand her, speaking aloud about Sarah while Prudence regarded her solemnly had given those memories a substance they hadn't had in years.

Prudence had followed Laura up the stairs and now sat in the spare bedroom next to Sarah's address book, waiting for Laura to put it back in a box so the game of throwing things out could begin again. But Laura's newfound discovery of happy memories was a fragile thing, and thinking about Anise threatened to ruin it. "Not now," Laura said, on her way past the room and back downstairs. Prudence continued to wait with an air of martyred patience that made Laura smile despite herself. "Come on," she said in a softer tone. "Don't you want your dinner?"

Prudence seemed to consider this for a few seconds. Then she stood and, after arching her back in a luxurious stretch (so as not to appear *too* eager, Laura supposed), she trotted into the hallway in front of Laura. The merry tinkling of the tag on her red collar grew fainter as she rounded the corner toward the staircase.

Josh had sounded apologetic a few weeks ago, when he'd moved some of his own things from his office to join Sarah's boxes in their spare room. "I can't even think anymore with all that clutter," he'd said. "And we can always move this stuff into storage if . . ."

He hadn't finished the sentence, and Laura hadn't finished it for him. The last time he'd brought up trying to get pregnant again, Josh had told Laura that the history of the world was people having babies under less-than-perfect circumstances. As if Laura didn't know this—as if that wasn't how Sarah had gotten pregnant with her in the first place. But what was she saying? Laura wondered. That she and Sarah would both have been better off if she'd never been born?

When Laura was a little girl, she'd thought that the saddest thing in the world was a child without a mother. There was a girl in her class whose mother had died of AIDS, and Laura would lie in her bed at night and cry for this girl who she wasn't even really friends with, this poor girl who would now have to live the rest of her life without a mother. Sarah's shadow would appear in the trapezoid of light from the hallway that fell onto the floor of Laura's bedroom, and then Sarah herself would be sitting on Laura's bed, holding her and saying, *Shhh . . . it's all right, baby, it's all right . . . you'll never lose me . . . I'm not going anywhere.* Laura would bury her face in her mother's neck and breathe in the flowery smell of her hair, hair so much prettier than that of any of the other mothers she knew, clinging to her kind, beautiful, loving mother who would never never ever let anything bad happen to either one of them. Only after this ritual of assurance could she fall asleep.

She'd never considered what it would feel like to be a mother without a child. She'd never thought about how many different ways there were to lose a person. She had resented Sarah for so long for not giving up the music and the life she'd loved so she could have given Laura a more secure childhood. And then she'd resented herself for having wanted Sarah to give up what she'd loved, for being angry she hadn't given it up earlier, even after Laura had seen the happy light in Sarah's eyes fade, year by year, as she trudged to and from that dreary desk where she'd typed endless documents for other people who had more important things to do.

And now that Laura was old enough to have children of her own, she was afraid of all the things she couldn't even begin to foresee that might take her and her child away from each other. She was afraid of not having enough money to keep her own child safe, and afraid of the price that would be exacted (because everything had to be paid for in the end) in exchange for the money and the safety that money provided.

She looked at Sarah's picture sometimes, the framed photo they'd taken from her apartment, and wondered how Sarah had felt when she'd first learned she was pregnant. Had she been happy? Had she foreseen a long future of laughter and sunny days together with her husband and the child they were going to have? Would she have done things differently if she'd known everything that would happen?

But Sarah's perpetually smiling face gave no answers. She'd clearly been happy at the moment the photo was taken, her eyebrows arched and her eyes holding a hint of laughter for whoever had held the camera. That was all Laura could tell.

Prudence greeted Laura at the foot of the stairs. Her tail twitched three times and then stood straight up, and Laura thought that she'd never seen a cat with a tail as expressive as Prudence's. It could swish from side to side in annoyance, and puff up when she was scared of something, or puff just at the base and vibrate like a rattlesnake when she felt full of love (as Laura had seen it do in Sarah's presence), or curl at the very tip when Prudence was feeling happy and complacent. This straight-up posture, combined with the series of urgent *meows,* meant, *Give me my dinner now!* Laura obliged her, carefully cleaning the bits of food that had spilled from the can off the otherwise spotless kitchen counter. Josh must have eaten his lunch out today.

Spending so much more time among Sarah's things lately— among the music and picture frames and knickknacks—had made it almost painfully clear to Laura how empty her own home seemed by comparison with her mother's. She had been reluctant to become too attached to the apartment and the things in it—not to *this* apartment and *these* things specifically, but to the idea of apartments and things in general. Looking at the sheer volume of everything Sarah had accumulated over the years, she'd marveled at the courage (for it had been a miracle of courage in its own way, hadn't it?) it must have taken for Sarah to unearth and display old treasures, and even add new ones.

Perhaps it would make her feel more rooted if she and Josh were to finally unpack all their wedding gifts and do something with this apartment they'd spent weeks hunting for together

("Someplace with room to grow," Josh had said, eyes sparkling).
Maybe, if they filled bookcases with well-worn paperbacks and the
glossy hardcovers about music that Josh dearly loved, and decorated bare walls with paintings and prints, maybe after all that
they could rest to admire their work and think, *How lucky we are
to get to live here!*

Except that now there was no telling how much longer they'd
get to live here. Laura knew that if they did end up having to move,
it wouldn't be like that other time. This time they would be able to
pack everything neatly into labeled boxes that would follow them
to wherever their new home would be. Still, she had hoped never
again to be forced to leave a home, and she raged inwardly against
the cruelty of a world that could never allow you to consider anything in "forever" terms, no matter how much of yourself you were
willing to sacrifice for the sake of permanence.

The apartment was stuffy, as it tended to get during the summer when nobody was home to turn on the central air. On swelter-
ing summer nights like the one now overtaking the failing daylight,
she and Sarah had sometimes slept outside on the fire escape, listening to the car alarms and music and laughter and angry shouts
that drifted up from the street. It had been a glorious day when
they'd finally been able to afford a small, secondhand air-
conditioning unit, even though they'd had to wedge it into place
with old magazines to make it fit the roughly cut hole in the wall.

Laura moved into the living room to unlock the clasp that
would allow her to push open the top half of one of the tall windows and let fresh air in. She could see people in other apartment
buildings watching television, many of them unknowingly watching the same show in different apartments on different floors. All
the way down on the street was a cluster of teenagers dribbling a
basketball up the block, and Laura remembered the boys who'd
made basketball hoops out of milk crates in the neighborhood
she'd grown up in, sloppily duct-taping them to lampposts and telephone poles. Across the way the amber-and-white pigeons rested
peacefully, settling in for the evening. Their numbers had grown of
late, and Laura wondered when the mating season was for pigeons,

if perhaps their little group had swelled to (she carefully counted) upwards of thirty because they'd had chicks she hadn't seen, even though she looked at them every day.

As she watched, the black door that led to the roof where the pigeons slept opened. The head of a broom appeared, followed by a dark-haired man in a white T-shirt. The man began yelling something and waving his broom at the pigeons. The startled birds took flight in circles that grew in breadth and number as more pigeons from the roof joined their widening arcs of panic.

Laura didn't know what came over her. There was a part of her mind that watched with a kind of bewildered detachment, even as she pushed her head through the open window and screamed, *"Leave them alone!"* The man must have heard her, even if he couldn't tell what she was saying, because he looked directly at her (the crazy lady in the apartment across the way) as he kept shouting and flailing his broom. Laura waved her fists in the air and continued to scream, *"Leave them alone! Leave them alone!"* Over and over she shrieked, *"Leave them alone!"* until her throat was raw and the man grew tired of his work and disappeared again through the black door. The circles the pigeons made in the air began to tighten and shrink until, finally, a few brave souls were the first to alight. Soon all the pigeons had settled back onto the rooftop, as if nothing had happened to disturb their rest.

Laura pulled her head back through the window and closed it. She discovered small, red half-moons where her fingernails had dug into the flesh of her palms. Her hands were shaking, and she ran them through her hair and took a few deep breaths to steady herself. Prudence was sitting on her haunches in front of Laura, eyeing her steadfastly.

"What are *you* looking at?" she demanded hoarsely of Prudence, thinking that now she really must be losing her mind. "My mother never yelled in front of you?"

To Laura's surprise, Prudence purred and bumped her head affectionately against Laura's ankles. Then she turned and curled the tip of her tail around the bottom of Laura's leg.

11

Prudence

I**T'S BEEN RAINING ALL DAY. A**LL THE WAY DOWNSTAIRS ON THE SIDE-walk, humans struggle against the wind with inside-out umbrel-las that pull them backward or into the street. Some of them finally give up and throw the umbrellas into trash cans with dis-gust. In Lower East Side, our apartment was close enough to the street that I could look out the window and see if Sarah was about to walk in. From this high up, though, I can never tell if any of the humans on the sidewalk is Laura or Josh. I don't know if Laura had any trouble with the little black umbrella she took with her this morning, but she's sopping when she gets home. "Give me a minute, Prudence," she says when she sees me waiting for her by the front door. "Let me get out of these wet clothes first." She leaves little drip-drops of water behind her as she walks toward the stairs.

Somebody left the window open in my upstairs room this

morning, and some of the rainwater has spotted the white curtains and dripped inside. I'm pleased to note, though, that while a little water got into one of the boxes Josh moved in here from Home Office, none has gotten into any of the Sarah-boxes, which live farther into the room. It's more crowded in here than it used to be, but not *so* crowded that I can't still throw little things out of the Sarah-boxes for Laura to find and talk to me about.

The air from outside smells like the rolls of new quarters Sarah used to bring home to feed to the laundry machines in Basement, which means there'll be lightning soon. It also means that the room doesn't have as much of the fading Sarah-and-me-together smell, but that's okay. Listening to Laura talk about Sarah is almost as good as breathing in her smell—my own memories of Sarah seem much more real when Laura tells me about hers.

There are times when she doesn't say much. Once we found a little plastic bag with some old pins—the round, colorful kind that humans occasionally attach to their clothing. Laura picked one out of the bunch and said, "I *begged* my mother to buy me this Menudo pin after I saw my best friend Maria Elena wearing one." Then she laughed. "I think I wore it on my backpack for about two weeks before I got tired of it and left it at the store." That was all she had to say about any of the pins before putting them away again. But other times she'll tell longer stories, or say things that are more about Sarah than other people Laura remembers, and those are the best times of all.

It bothered me at first, throwing Sarah's and my old things out of the boxes they're supposed to be in, because Sarah always said how important it was to keep your past organized. Throwing things on the floor is the *opposite* of being organized. But if I didn't show these things to Laura to make her tell me about her memories, then Sarah wouldn't have a past at all.

Today I found two white boxes while I was looking for things to show Laura—a smaller one and one that's bigger, like the kind clothing comes in when one human is giving another human a present. When Laura comes to sit next to me on the floor, wearing sweat-clothes, it's the smaller box she opens first. "Let's see what you found today," she says. Her voice, which was hoarse for days after she yelled at that man across the street about the pigeons, sounds normal again. When Josh asked her about it, she told him she was in a loud meeting at work and must have strained her throat. Josh has been so busy with his own work lately that he didn't narrow his eyes the way he does when he can tell Laura is saying something not-true. Maybe he didn't even notice how her cheeks changed color. I don't know why Laura wouldn't want to tell him what she did, though, because even things as stupid as pigeons deserve to have a place to live—and they spend so much time on that rooftop that it must be *covered* in their smell by now. Who was that strange man to try to make them leave? I was proud of Laura for defending them, even though it turns out they came right back without her help to where they're used to being.

The inside of the small white box is lined with cotton fluff. Wrapped into the fluff is something made of a smooth, dark-white material that Laura says is called ivory. The bottom part of it is made up of five long teeth, and the top part is shaped like a fan with all kinds of curls carved into it. "It's a comb," Laura says. "My mother had this way of twisting her hair up and holding it with a comb. She looked so elegant and glamorous, I couldn't believe she was really *my* mother." Laura's face used to get so tight whenever Sarah was mentioned, but now it wears a soft kind of smile. Her voice is soft, too. She holds the comb up to the light and says, "I don't remember ever seeing this one, though."

Of course I can't talk and tell Laura so, but *I* remember seeing this comb. Sarah showed it once to Anise. She told Anise that Mrs. Mandelbaum had given it to her years and years ago, to give to Laura on her wedding day. *She wore it at her own wedding,* Sarah said. *She said it was only fitting that Laura's "something old" should come from her.* Sarah told Anise she'd thought about giving it to Laura the day she got married, but ended up losing her nerve because Laura always got so upset whenever the Mandelbaums were mentioned. Anise looked sad for Sarah, and she told her, *You can't spend the rest of your life waiting for a perfect moment to say the things you want to say. You have to do the best you can with the moments you actually get.* It's funny—when I think about the Sarah I remember and compare her with the Sarah in Laura's memories. I remember a Sarah who always knew exactly the right thing to say to me. Laura remembers a Sarah who talked and talked but never said the thing Laura really wanted to hear.

Now she puts the comb back into the little box, and puts that back into one of the big Sarah-boxes, although not the one I found it in. As the days go by Laura seems to be organizing the things we look at together. Some go into boxes with things she probably wants to keep, like this comb, and others go into boxes of things she'll bring to Trash Room someday, like old ordering slips from Sarah's record store, or the funny little drum on a stick with strings attached.

The bigger white box I found is trapped shut with clear tape, and Laura has to slide her fingernail around the edges to get it open. There's lots of crinkly tissue paper (perfect to play in!), and inside of that are tiny clothes, far too small for even the littermates to wear—little knitted sweaters and hats, tiny denim jackets covered in silver safety pins and neon-colored spray paints, and teeny skirts and dresses and ripped T-shirts decorated to match the jackets. The sweaters have the very, *very* faint aroma of another cat, along with a bit of Sarah-smell and another scent that's probably what Laura smelled like when she was younger.

"Oh *God*." The look on Laura's face is amazement. "Mrs. Mandelbaum knitted these sweaters for my Cabbage Patch Doll. And Anise made her these little rock-star outfits." It's when she says Anise's name that I notice something like anger dart behind Laura's eyes and fade again, just as quickly. "I told my mother to get rid of these when I was eleven." She laughs a little. "I *insisted,* actually. I wanted her to know I wasn't a baby anymore." Laura's smile is wobbly. "I can't believe she kept them all these years."

I put one paw tentatively on Laura's knee, waiting to see if she'll make any sudden movements—or try to stop me—as I crawl into her lap to get closer to the little sweaters. I rub my cheeks and the backs of my ears so hard against them—trying to get rid of that other cat's smell and also trying to get that little bit of Sarah-smell onto me—that the clasp of my red collar gets stuck on a thread and Laura has to untangle me. Once I'm freed I rub my head on the sweaters again, trying to re-create some of that good Sarah-and-me-together smell. Laura begins to massage her fingers gently behind my ears. Closing my eyes, I lean the side of my head into her hand and purr. She cups her hand and runs it from the tip of my nose all the way down my back in a good, firm way that makes the skin under my fur tingle.

Suddenly we hear the jangling of keys downstairs that means Josh is home. Whenever he comes home this late, it's usually because he's been meeting with the humans who live in that building above the music studio—collecting their stories, he says. We hear his footsteps coming up the stairs, and Laura moves the white box top so that it mostly covers the little clothes that aren't underneath my head. In another moment Josh is in the doorway with speckles of rainwater all over his jeans, saying, "Hello, ladies."

Josh still comes in here sometimes to look through Sarah's black disks. It doesn't bother me anymore when he does this, because he always washes his hands first and treats them so respectfully. He's looking for music that got recorded at that studio, I heard him tell Laura. Sarah has hundreds of black disks, so it's taking him a while to get through all of them. He never touches things in the Sarah-boxes, though—the ones that don't have any black disks in them—like Laura and I do.

But now he's not here to look through black disks. He smiles like he always does when he sees Laura in here with me, looking at Sarah's things, and tells her, "I picked up a tuna sub at Defonte's, if you want half."

"How did you know I was thinking about cold tuna for dinner?" Laura asks, smiling back at him.

Josh leans his shoulder against the door frame. "You know, it'll be our anniversary in a few weeks. We should do something grand."

"Not *too* grand," Laura says.

"How many first anniversaries are we going to get?" he asks her. "And I'm talking about dinner out. Not a week in Paris." He looks at her hopefully. "Come on. We haven't gone out for a great meal in a long time, and I'll still have a couple of weeks left of my severance."

He says this like it's good news, although from the deepening frown on Laura's face, she doesn't think the same thing. But all she says is, "I'll be down in a minute for the sub."

Josh walks toward their bedroom, and Laura throws the little clothes back into their white box, then tosses the whole thing into one of the Sarah-boxes. "You must want dinner, too," she says to me. Scratching some of the shedding fur on the bottom of my chin, she adds, "And maybe a good brushing later on."

I look back at the Sarah-boxes for a moment. But then— thinking about my dinner *and* tuna *and* a nice, long brushing—I follow Laura down the stairs.

Josh never used to talk about his work very much, but now he talks about it whenever he can find somebody to listen. Laura usually wrinkles up her forehead and changes the subject. Or else she says things like *Mm-hmm* or *Really* in a way that doesn't sound like she wants Josh to keep talking about it. But the littermates ask him lots of questions. Josh brings them here one day a week to help him organize his papers and stuff them into envelopes. I usually help, too, by scattering the papers onto the floor to make sure there aren't any rats hiding in them—I've been extra cautious ever since we found that rat in the Sarah-boxes, even though it turned out to be a fake. Josh isn't always as grateful for my efforts as he should be, though. He acts frustrated and says, "Ah, Prudence, why are you doing this to me?" while arranging the papers back into a tidy stack. But you can tell how happy and relieved the littermates are, when they laugh and praise me for all my help. Occasionally Josh, acting like he's doing me a *favor*, will crumple one piece of paper into a ball and toss it for me to practice my mice-fighting with. Although the littermates have invented an irritating "game"— called Keep Prudence's Paper Ball Away from Her—and they toss my paper ball back and forth to each other over my head, yelling,

"Keep away! Keep away!" until, finally, I jump high enough in the air to smack it away from them and take it downstairs to under-the-couch.

Having the littermates here one day a week is more disruptive than it was having Josh around *five* days a week after he first lost his job. They have a hard time doing the sensible things cats (and older humans) do, like sitting in one spot for stretches of time, thinking important thoughts, and watching Upper West Side through our windows. Their constant movements disturb the air around me and make my whiskers tickle. And they *always* fight with me for my favorite napping spot on the couch. Josh and Laura have learned that a cat's preferred sleep area is her own property and should be respected. But the littermates will plop themselves down on my spot *even if I'm already sleeping there,* which means I have to wake up from wonderful dreams of green grass and Sarah's singing so I can scramble away from their lowering back-sides before I get squashed. Even when I chuff and growl at them, they ignore me. You'd think that such young humans would be *grateful* to have a cat instructing them in proper manners. But never once have they said to me, *Thank you, Prudence, for trying to teach us how to be polite.* If it weren't for the lure of rustling papers in Home Office whenever they're here, I would stay away from them all the time.

They're better behaved with Josh, though. Maybe that's be-cause he's so patient and gentle with them, the way Sarah always is with me. (Although I'm more deserving of gentle patience than the littermates.) If they're sitting at the little table in Josh's office, they'll even raise one hand in the air before asking him questions. I think this must be a good-manners thing that gets taught to young humans. It's surprising to me that the littermates have been able to learn anything that's good manners. But I've never seen any fully grown humans put their hands up before asking something, so obviously *somebody* trained the littermates to do this.

"Uncle Josh," Robert asks with his hand in the air, "how come the people who live in the apartment building have to move away?"

"They don't have to—yet," Josh tells him. "There are rules that say how much money the people who own the building are allowed to charge people for living there. Now they want to change the rules and make the building so expensive that the people who live there won't be able to afford it anymore."

"That's what happened to us." Abbie's face looks solemn. "When Mom and Dad got a divorce, we couldn't afford to live in our house near Nana and Pop-pop anymore. We had to come live in an apartment because Dad stopped giving Mom money."

Josh is putting some papers into a creamy-colored folder, but his hand freezes, the way a cat freezes when she spots something she's going to pounce on. He looks so wary that I think maybe a mouse managed to find a hiding spot in those papers after all, and I peer around from my spot next to Robert's chair, checking to make sure I didn't miss a threat. "Who told you that about your father?" Josh asks Abbie quietly.

The littermates look at each other. Then Abbie says, "Sometimes we hear Mom on the phone, even though she has the door to her room closed." Robert's eyes get big and round, like he's scared of what Abbie just said. "We don't *try* to listen," she says quickly. "It's just sometimes we can't help it."

Josh's eyes turn sad and also angry. But his voice is kind when he tells her, "You and Robert are lucky that your mom was able to find a good job, and that you have Nana and Pop-pop, and Aunt Laura and me, to help her make sure you won't ever have to move away again. But the people who live in this apartment building already have so little money, they wouldn't be able to afford a nice apartment if they had to move. And they've been living in their apartments a long, *long* time. Some of them have been living there since even before *I* was born." Abbie's and Robert's eyes grow bigger, as if they can't begin to imagine how long ago *that* must have been.

"Do any of the people who live there have cats like Prudence?" Robert wants to know.

"A few of them do," Josh says, smiling. "They're worried that if they have to move, they might not be able to find a new apartment building that would let them bring their cats with them."

Well! Imagine that! What kind of crazy apartment building wouldn't *want* cats living there? Who would protect them from all the mice and rats if there weren't any cats? Good luck finding a *dog* to do that as smartly and thoroughly as a cat can! Just when I think I've heard all the ridiculous things humans can do and say, I hear something else that makes me realize there's no limit to how foolish humans can be.

The next time the littermates come over, Josh's father drives his car from his house in New Jersey to go out to lunch with them. I dart upstairs to take a nap on the cat bed in Home Office, but when I hear everybody come back, I leap down and curl up beneath Josh's desk, trying to look as if that's where I've been napping all along. By the time they've gotten upstairs, I'm licking my right front paw and using it to wash my face clean in a lazy-looking way, just to make sure they're completely fooled.

"Whew!" Josh's father says, and settles himself into one of the chairs Abbie and Robert usually sit in. His face looks paler than I remember it being, and there are little drops of sweat-water on his forehead. "The heat's so much worse here in the city than where your mother and I live. It's hard on an old man."

"Are you all right, Dad?" Josh sounds anxious. "Do you need a glass of water?"

"I'm fine, I'm fine." His father waves his hand in front of his face. "Don't tell Mother I got dizzy," he adds sternly. "She worries ever since that scare with my heart last year. I'm seventy-five years old, and she still thinks I don't know how to take care of myself."

"I'll bring you a glass of water, Pop-pop," Abbie says. "Robert and I are thirsty anyways." The two of them run out of the room (the littermates never seem to *walk*), and I can hear their footsteps thudding down the stairs.

"So tell me about this work you've been doing," Josh's father says. "It's all the kids can talk about these days."

"I'm only doing a small part of it." For the first time, Josh seems almost embarrassed to talk about his work. "There are organizations that exist for the sole purpose of preserving Mitchell-Lama housing. I'm just helping a little where I can."

"Show me," Josh's father says. "I'm interested."

"Well . . ." Josh pulls together some of the papers he usually gives to Abbie and Robert to put into envelopes. "I've been writing press releases and sending them out to reporters at newspapers and different websites, letting them know what's going on. And I've been interviewing all the tenants in the building, collecting their stories. I'm writing them up and putting them together with some old photographs they were able to give me. I think showing that side of the issue might be effective." He hands the papers to his father, who begins to flip through them slowly.

"I've also been pulling together a history of the music studio in the building's Basement. It's actually become pretty important in the community over the years. I'm trying to help them reincorporate as a not-for-profit, so they have some legal standing if we're able to get this to a hearing." Josh walks out and goes into my room, returning with a stack of Sarah's black disks. A wisp of Sarah-smell follows them. I have a sudden, vivid memory of Sarah in our old apartment, wearing a long, thin summer dress and standing in front of the shelves where she kept her black disks, saying, *I think I'm in the mood for Betty Wright today. What do you think, Prudence?* But, just as quickly as the memory pops into my head, it pops back out and goes to where I can't find it.

"If you look at the liner notes"—Josh hands the black disks to his father and points to some of the tiny word-writing on their cardboard covers—"you can see how many important albums were recorded there. So I've been putting write-ups of *that* together with photos of some of the bands, and sending it to the editors at my old magazine and some of our—*their*, I mean—competitors. I've also created a website and Facebook page for the building, and we've been encouraging community residents and owners of nearby mom-and-pops, who'll eventually be threatened by the same economic factors, to contribute their own stories and memories. And we've put together an online petition. We've gotten about five thousand signatures so far."

"Some of these photos take me back," Josh's father says. "Your mother and I were buying the house we raised you and your sister in at around the same time this building went up, it looks like."

"Probably." Josh smiles a little. "There are tenants who've been living there since the sixties."

His father half closes his eyes. "When a man has lived in one place for fifty years," he says, "and raised a family there, he doesn't like to leave unless it's on his own terms."

"I wouldn't think so," Josh says quietly.

His father opens his eyes. "You've put a lot of work into this. It must have taken a lot of time to talk to everybody and do all this writing and research."

Josh's face turns a light pink. "I've certainly had the time."

His father sighs and then he sets the papers and photos down on the little table. "I never really understood that job you had. I could see it was making you money, but it never seemed like real work to me. But *this* is something I understand. Helping people who want to keep their homes, I understand. And all this work you've done"—he gestures at the papers—"this is something you can look at and touch and hold in your hands at the end of the day. I'm sure all those people you're calling now think of you differently because you're coming to them *doing* work, not *asking* for work."

"It'd be nice to think so." Josh's smile is lopsided.

"Trust me," his father says. "People always respect a man who works hard and saves his money."

"It's tough to save money when you aren't making any."

"The money will come." Josh's father says it very firmly. "It wasn't always easy for your mother and me, you know. She had to get that job at the jewelry counter so we could send you and your sister to college. But we worked hard and, one way or another, the money always came."

Abbie and Robert come running back with a glass for Josh's father. As he drinks from it, Robert says, "Hey, where's Prudence, Uncle Josh?"

"I think she's hanging out under the desk," Josh says, bending over to check. His sideways eyes look into mine. "Prudence, do you want to come out and say hello to my father?"

I don't, really. But Josh is (finally) trying to introduce me the right way, which means that *not* coming out would be bad manners.

"Well, hello there, Prudence." Josh's father pats my head awkwardly, and I'm relieved when it seems like that's all he's going to attempt to do. "Remember Sammy?" he asks Josh. "You and your sister were crazy about that dog. He could chase cats all day."

I continue to stand there and let Josh's father pat my head, even though I can't help liking him a little less for having one of those wretched dogs that thinks it's fun to chase cats just because they're not smart enough to think of anything sensible to do. Josh's father doesn't know as much about cats as I do about humans, because he says, "I think Prudence likes her Pop-pop."

Josh laughs out loud. "So Prudence is your granddaughter now?"

"She's the closest thing you and Laura have given me so far." His father sounds stern again.

Josh's smile shrinks. "We're working on it, Dad."

"I may be an old man, Josh," his father tells him. "But I can still remember that if you think of it as work, you're doing it wrong."

Josh is in a good mood after his father leaves. He walks around the apartment, humming music under his breath and snapping his fingers. He goes into Home Office and bangs away on the cat bed/keyboard for a little while, but I can tell he has too much energy to sit still for long. Pretty soon I hear what sounds like heavy things being moved around in Home Office's closet, and then Josh comes into my room, carrying a big stack of black disks. I can tell by their scent that these were never Sarah's—he must have had more black disks than I realized, living inside the closet of Home Office all this time.

Josh sits cross-legged and starts spreading out the black disks all over the floor, arranging and then rearranging them in ways that must make sense to him, although I can't tell what the pattern is. I jump on top of one of the Sarah-boxes, to get out of his way, and soon the whole floor is colorful with the cardboard holders for black disks. Then he scooches over to the boxes of Sarah's black disks, and starts pulling out some of those and putting *them* on the floor, looking at the word-writing on each of them and then deciding which ones should go where.

Sarah used to do this sometimes, take out all her black disks and spread them over the floors of our apartment. She was always coming up with new ways to arrange them on their shelves—by what year they came out, or by things she called "genre" or "influence." Once—this is the last way she did it while we lived together—she put them all in what she said was alphabetical order. I can understand Josh wanting to do the same thing with his own black disks, but it's making me nervous to see Sarah's all spread out this way without her being here to supervise. Cautiously, I climb out of the Sarah-box I've been lying in and try to step into the small spaces between the cardboard covers on my way out, but there aren't any, really. Sarah would *never* let me walk on her black disks! The covers feel smooth and slippery under the pads of my feet, but I'm afraid to use my claws to try and get more traction.

While I'm trying to find a good way out, I hear Laura come through the front door. "Josh?" she calls out.

"Up here," he calls back.

The sound of the feet-shoes Laura wears to work comes clicking up the wooden stairs. Her face seems to draw inward when she gets to the doorway of my room and sees what Josh is doing. "What's all this?"

"Don't worry," Josh tells her, looking up with a quick grin. "I know which ones are mine and which are your mom's."

"But what are you *doing*?" she asks again.

"I'm trying to get a visual sense of which of these were recorded at Alphaville, which ones were influenced by artists who came out of Alphaville, which ones use sessions guys who recorded *other* albums at Alphaville." He leans back to rest on his heels and admire his work. "Quite a history for one down-on-its-luck recording studio, huh?"

"It looks like a record store in here," Laura says faintly.

I don't think she's agreeing with him, exactly, but that's the way Josh must understand it, because he smiles at her again. "You know, some of these are worth real money."

"Probably." Laura's lips thin together.

Josh looks up and finally notices the expression on her face. "I'm not saying we should sell them. I'm sorry if that seemed insensitive. It's just the geek in me getting excited looking at all this stuff."

"I didn't think you were." I think she means it, but her lips stay thin.

Josh has decided to change the subject, because the next thing he says is, "My dad was here today. We took the kids out for lunch, and afterward I was showing him everything I've been working on. What he responded to most was the personal side of the story—the people living in this building who'll have to move and uproot their lives. I don't think I've done enough with that part of it yet. I was thinking maybe you could help me."

"*Me?*" Laura looks completely surprised. "How could *I* help?"

"Well, the night we met," Josh says. "You have no idea how moving you were when you were talking about the building you grew up in, and the people you knew there. I know you all had to move when the place was condemned. You have a much better grasp on the emotional side of what these people are facing now than I do."

Laura's face draws even further into itself. Little bumps appear in the tops of her shoes as her toes curl up. When she speaks, her voice sounds funny. "What kinds of things do you want to hear?"

"I don't know." Josh gives a small shrug. "How you found out you'd have to move. How your mom and your neighbors felt about it. What it was like having to move away from your friends and all those people you'd known for years. It doesn't necessarily have to be the bad stuff," he adds gently. "I know you've been going through your mother's things with Prudence lately. That must have jogged some good memories."

Listening to Laura talk about her Sarah-memories has become one of my favorite things. Leaping into the nearest Sarah-box, I helpfully push something out with my nose and paws. This way Laura has something to start talking about. The plastic bag I spill onto the ground holds tiny white-and-blue ceramic cups called a "sake set" that Anise brought back from a place called Japan for Sarah to keep in her record store. They clink against each other as they roll from the bag and around the cardboard covers scattered on the floor. The floor is so many different colors now from all the covers that it's hard to see where some of the sake-set cups end up.

"See?" Josh smiles. "Prudence thinks it's a good idea, too." His smile turns wistful. "You see me with my family all the time. I hardly know anything about what you and your mother were like together. I'd just love to hear you talk about it."

They look at each other for a long moment. Then Laura says, "I have to get out of these work clothes." As her feet-shoes click down the hall, her voice calls back to us, "Let me know when you're ready for dinner."

12

Prudence

AT THE END OF AUGUST IS A LONG HOLIDAY WEEKEND CALLED Labor Day. Humans need holidays and calendars to tell them things cats already know—like when the summer ends, and when the air starts to smell smokier and feel cooler. After Labor Day, the littermates go back to their school and stop coming here.

It's around then that Laura starts getting sick in the mornings. She's been sick *every* morning these past two weeks. My stomach gets upset sometimes, too (and I always try to hide it in some out-of-the-way place, because it's embarrassing when humans have to clean up after me), but Laura's stomach has been upset every single day. After Josh has gone downstairs to start making the coffee, Laura throws up into the toilet in their bathroom—I can hear it from under the door. Then she washes her face and brushes her teeth, and the two of us go downstairs so she can give me my breakfast. Sometimes, when she opens the cans that hold my food, Laura gets a look on her face like the smell of my food is making her feel sick again. Even the way she smells is different—stronger and more sugary since three weeks before she started throwing up.

I don't think Josh knows anything about how sick she's been feeling, though, because if he did I'm sure he would insist she go to whatever the human version of the Bad Place is. Laura probably hates the Bad Place as much as I do, and that's why she hasn't said anything about it.

Still, I wish Josh would notice, because Laura's being sick is also putting her in a bad mood. Ever since that night when Josh spread all the black disks out on the floor of my room, Laura hasn't seemed as interested anymore in coming in here to look through the Sarah-boxes with me. Still, I keep trying to think of ways to encourage her. Like this morning. I find one of the shoe boxes with Sarah's matchbook toys and nudge it out of the big brown box so Laura and I can look through them and she can tell me things about Sarah. It's true that once a few of the matchbooks spill out, I start batting the rest of them around, until there are matchbooks scattered all over the floor and wedged underneath some of the big boxes. But I'm pretty sure that when she sees how much fun it is to bat the matchbook toys around, she'll want to join me.

That's not what happens, though. Laura is walking quickly past my room, but when she sees how the matchbook toys are strewn all over the place, she stops. I nose a few hopefully in her direction, but I can tell she's angry by her hard, rapid footsteps as she comes into the room.

"*No!*" she yells. "No, Prudence! Stop pushing things out of boxes and making a mess! *Why can't you just leave me alone?*" She tosses the matchbook toys back into the smaller box they're supposed to live in, then throws the whole thing into one of the bigger Sarah-boxes. She starts going around to all the boxes and folding their flaps over so that they stay closed by themselves. Then she shoves them around on top of each other until they're all in two big stacks that are so high I can't possibly reach the top. She's breathing hard from her effort, and there are dots of sweat-water on her forehead.

I've never had my feelings hurt by a human before, but now I feel hurt—and also confused. What did I do that was so bad? What was so wrong with wanting to play with Sarah's matchbook toys that Laura had to yell at me and put *all* of Sarah's and my old things where I can't even get to them? How will I remember Sarah enough to make her come back and always be with me if I don't have anything to remember her *with*?

I stretch out all my front claws and scratch at the floor, leaving long, angry slashes in the dark wood Laura cares about so much. I had thought that she and I were becoming close, *almost* like maybe I was a part of the family that's made up of her and Josh. This is what I get for forgetting I'm just an immigrant here, and that *Sarah* is my one-and-only Most Important Person.

Josh hasn't made eggs for Laura in a long time, but this morning is the one-year anniversary of when they got married, and I smell the aroma of scrambled eggs coming upstairs from the kitchen. It also smells like Josh is frying bacon and pouring orange juice—all the things Laura used to like so much on Sunday mornings.

When Laura gets close to the kitchen and smells the eggs cooking, she has to run back upstairs—probably to throw up again. Josh is whistling while he cooks, so I don't think he notices. He scoops the eggs onto plates, and then he puts a little onto a Prudence-plate that he sets on the floor. Laura's face looks much paler than it usually does by the time she comes back to the kitchen to sit down.

Josh stops cooking long enough to come over to her seat with a plate of eggs and bacon. "Happy anniversary," Josh says, and kisses her on the mouth.

"Happy anniversary," she tells him, with a smile that somehow makes her face look even paler. She pushes the eggs around with her fork.

"Are you okay?" Josh asks Laura. His forehead wrinkles in concern.

Laura tries to smile again. "I'm fine," she says. "Just not that hungry, I guess."

"I hope you're hungry tonight. The reservation's at eight, so if you're running late at work we can always meet there."

"I've been thinking." The squeaky sound of Laura's fork scraping against the plate is too high-pitched for humans to hear, but the agonizing squeal of it makes my ears twitch until the left one nearly folds in half. "Del Posto might be a little . . . extravagant for us right now. Maybe we should take a pass."

"Okay," Josh says slowly. He sounds confused. "Did you want to go somewhere else?"

"I don't know." She swallows hard a couple of times, like maybe the smell of the eggs is making her feel sick again. "We can talk about it later, I guess."

"If that's what you want." Laura looks down at her plate while Josh's eyes look at her face, as if he's seeing for the first time that something might be wrong with her. They're both silent until Josh says, "Listen, I've been wanting to ask you about Anise Pierce. I was wondering if maybe you could get in touch with her."

Laura looks up in surprise. "Anise Pierce? Why would I want to get in touch with Anise Pierce?"

"She recorded a couple of albums in Alphaville Studios. We're up to ten thousand signatures on the online petition, and I've got a few media outlets sniffing around. I thought that if someone of her stature came on board, we might be able to nail something down."

"I don't want to get in touch with Anise." Laura picks up the folded paper napkin in her lap and drops it over the uneaten plate of eggs. I can tell already that Laura is going to show her bad mood to Josh, just like she showed it to me upstairs—and I think how much luckier Josh is than I am, because he can talk back to her.

He looks confused again for a moment. "I just think it would really help us if—"

"I already told you, I don't want to," Laura interrupts. "I don't think this building on Avenue A should be your priority right now. We've got things to worry about here."

"What kind of things? What are you talking about?"

"If you want to worry about who can afford to live where," she tells him, "maybe you should worry about where *we're* going to live when your severance runs out next week and we can't afford to keep this place anymore."

Now *my* stomach feels upset, like somebody is squeezing it in their fist. We might have to leave this apartment? How is that possible? Why didn't anybody tell me that something like this could happen? If Sarah doesn't know where to find Laura, how will she know where to find me?

"Oh, come off it, Laura," Josh says. "I know we've lost a chunk of our savings, but we're still a long way from losing this apartment."

"*You* come off it, Josh." Laura's voice gets louder. "I refuse to be the only person around here who worries about work. Do you ever think about what might happen if I suddenly lost *my* job? Do you even *know* how bad things have been at the firm lately?"

"How the hell *should* I know?" Josh's voice gets louder, too. "You don't talk to me about what's happening at your job. You don't talk to me about anything. For months I've been trying as hard as I know how to get you to open up about *something*—your mother, your job, anything at all—but all you do is shut me down. What am I, a mind reader?"

"I didn't realize you had to be a mind reader to do basic math," Laura says. Her voice sounds angrier than it sounded even when she used to get mad at Sarah. "I didn't realize you had to be a mind reader to add the *zero* dollars you'll be earning to our monthly budget and come up with *zero* dollars for rent." Laura is shouting now. She stands up and slams her chair so hard against the kitchen table that it bounces off and tumbles on its side onto the floor. The loud noise and the shouting scare me so much, I skid as I run for under-the-couch. I can still see and hear Laura and Josh, but I feel safer here as I twitch the fur on my back fast-fast-fast. Laura laughs, but it's a kind of laugh that sounds the exact opposite of when a human finds something funny. "And the truly *outstanding* part of the whole thing is that *I* never wanted an apartment this big or expensive in the first place!"

"Give me a break with your revisionist history *bullshit*!" I hear Josh yell. "*We* picked out this apartment together. *We* spent weeks looking for a place where we could start a family. You didn't have one word to say against any of that, but now you turn green every time the subject of having children comes up. Maybe I'm not a mind reader, and maybe I can't do basic math, but I'm not *blind,* Laura."

"How can we even think about having children if we don't have any money!"

"Oh, and you were just *so* thrilled when you got pregnant the first time." Now *his* voice sounds mean. "Your happiness and absolute *elation* were written all over your face. How stupid do you think I am?"

"Don't mix things up! That was then, and this is now, and *now* we *can't* have children without worrying about how we'll pay for everything."

"*Enough already!*" Josh roars. "Everything with you is about money! Stop with the money! We *have* money!"

"Not enough!" Laura yells back at him. "You have no idea how terrifying it is to have no money at all! You don't know what it's like when—" Suddenly Laura stops yelling and is silent.

"When *what*?" Josh demands. "When *what,* Laura? What happened to you that was so terrible you can't even talk about it?"

Laura is silent. When she speaks again, her voice is lower, but it sounds cold. "What happened is that my husband started caring more about strangers, and about playing babysitter to his niece and nephew, than he does about our future."

Josh's voice gets lower, too, but somehow that makes his words crueler. "*You* are not the person to give *me* lessons on how to treat family. You left your mother alone in that miserable apartment you could barely bring yourself to visit once a month. You didn't even take time off work when she died. *Think* about that, Laura. And don't talk to *me* about family."

Laura's breathing gets loud and hard, the way mine does when I'm chuffing. *"What the hell do you know about it?"* Her shriek makes all the fur on my back stand up, and no matter how fast I twitch it I can't make it lie down again. "What do *you* know about me or my mother or *anything*? With your normal, happy, *perfect* family where everybody pulls together and helps each other out and just loves each other *so* much!"

"Do you even hear what you're saying?" Josh yells. "Is *that* what you think? You think there's such a thing as a perfect family? Sometimes my dad's the greatest guy in the world, and sometimes he pisses me off so much I want to *strangle* him, but I won't spend the rest of my life blaming him for everything that goes wrong in it." I hear the sound of Josh's shoes clopping against the kitchen tile as he paces. "Whatever it is you think your mother did that was so awful, get over it! I can practically *hear* you fighting with her in your head, like she's still here and you're still fourteen. *Your mother is* dead, *Laura!* Grow up already!"

Now I realize it—what Josh said before about Laura not taking time off from work. Sarah is dead. Sarah is dead, and nobody ever told me. Sarah is dead, and I'll never see her again. She'll never feed me or hold me or stroke my fur again. Never never never never. No matter how much time I spend with her boxes or my memories, nothing will ever bring Sarah back to me. The ache in my chest from Sarah's being gone rips back open so suddenly that I can't breathe. I curl up in a tight ball under the couch with my nose pressed into my tail, trying to make my ripped-open chest stay together.

"First I'm not grieving enough," Laura yells, "and now I can't get over it. Which is it?"

"Stop with the logic games, Counselor. I'm not your client and we all know you're not my lawyer."

"Maybe *you're* the one who needs to grow up! Stop trying to be the king of community activism and *get a job*. Charity begins at home."

"Do you have any idea how hard it is to get a job right now?" Josh shouts. "Do you have any idea what it's like to watch your profession crumble up and blow away into nothing, and have people telling you day after day how the only job you know how to do doesn't exist anymore? When you're nearly *forty*? Does it occur to you at any point during the fifteen hours a day when you *aren't here* to think about how *that* feels? Or are you too busy totting up in your head *exactly* what you contribute and *exactly* what I contribute?"

"Who's the oblivious one, Josh?" Laura yells back. "When's the last time I worked a fifteen-hour day? Has it ever occurred to *you* to wonder what might be going on with *my* job?"

"No, I don't *wonder* about your job!" It sounds like Josh has slammed his fist down on the kitchen table. I curl into a tighter ball under the living room couch, thinking, *Please stop, please stop, please stop. Sarah is dead. I can't take this, too.* "Just like you don't sit around your office all day wondering what's going on with me. You know what I wonder about? I wonder why I never get to go out to dinner, or make plans with friends, or talk about a vacation. I wonder why I sit around here night after night *alone*. I think about the night we met—we danced, we talked, we had *fun*. We had a lot of nights like that. When was the last time we did any of those things? And I guess we don't have to do anything on our anniversary, either, because another night at home will be such a *blast*! If you ever once came home and suggested we go out and *do* something, I think I'd have a heart attack." I can hear Laura breathe in sharply when Josh says *heart attack*. "I know how important it is to you to make partner. But what are we doing here?"

"That's not fair." Laura's voice has tears in it. "You *knew* how demanding my job was. You told me it was one of the things you loved most about me, and now you're second-guessing it when *my job* is the only thing bringing any money into this house. How can we do any of those things if we don't have money to do them with?"

Josh's voice is quieter now. "What's the point of having all the money in the world, Laura, if we're miserable?"

When Laura speaks again, she sounds hoarse. "I didn't realize I was making you miserable," she says.

"Laura, I—" Josh starts, but Laura doesn't let him finish.

"I have to go," she says. "I have to get to my job while I still have one." She walks to the closet, and I hear her open it to pull out her purse and heavy shoulder bag. Then she walks out the front door, slamming it shut behind her.

The apartment is silent after Laura leaves. The only thing I hear is the sound of Josh pacing and rain pounding on our windows. Josh walks around and around the kitchen and living room, and then he walks up the stairs and back down the stairs and up the stairs again. I hear him opening drawers and slamming them back closed, and once it sounds like he kicks something. Every so often I hear him say, "*Dammit!*" under his breath. I don't think he's looking for anything specific as he walks around and opens drawers. I think he's trying to find a way to feel less anxious. He *must* feel anxious, because I don't think *I've* ever been this upset. I haven't heard humans yell like that since I lived outside with my littermates. The doorbell rings, and I can hear Josh open the door and say a curt, "Thanks," to whoever is there. He walks into the kitchen, and I hear him set something on the counter. Then he grabs an umbrella from the tall stand near the front door like he's angry at it and goes out. The apartment is silent once again.

Sarah is dead. Sarah is never coming back. I'll never see her again. Maybe we were just roommates, but we loved each other. All those times Laura told me things about Sarah, how could she not have told me *this*? And then I have an even worse thought: What if Laura and Josh don't want to be a family anymore because of the vicious words they just said to each other? What if they don't want to live with each other? What if neither of them wants to live with me, either? They might not love me like Sarah did, but if Sarah is really gone forever then there's nobody else in the whole world to care even a little about where I live or what happens to me.

What I should do now is finish my breakfast, like I do every morning. If I do everything the way I usually do, Laura and Josh will have to come back and be happy together the way they usually are. Except I can't quite manage it right now. My chest is hurting and so is my stomach. The hole in my chest from Sarah's not being here has moved down to my belly. Now it's in both places.

It's the new smell from the kitchen that finally draws me out from under-the-couch. There's a bunch of flowers on the counter, arranged in a glass vase. The flowers have little drops of water on them from the rain outside, and the spicy-earth scent of them fills the whole downstairs of our apartment.

I know what kind of flowers these are. They're the same kind as Laura is holding in the pictures from when she and Josh got married.

The smell of the flowers pulls me up. Almost before I've made the decision to do it, I'm sitting on the counter next to them. I remember the cat grass Sarah used to keep for me when we lived together. When my stomach felt upset like it does now, the cat grass would help make it feel better.

Josh must know how upset I am, and that's why he had the man at the door bring flowers for me to eat. He knows I like to eat the things he leaves on the counter.

So I put my whole face into the middle of those flowers and breathe in their delicious smell. Then I start to eat. I chew on the leaves and stems and the soft parts of the flowers themselves. I eat and eat and wait for my stomach to stop twisting around so much, and when my stomach doesn't feel better right away I eat some more . . .

. . . and now there's nothing except Badness. I feel the Badness all over my whole body. My stomach heaves and spins trying to get the Badness out of me, but it doesn't work. I throw up and catch my breath and throw up again, and still I can't get the Badness out. I'm thirsty and try to drink from my water bowl, but the Badness rises up and throws the water out of my mouth as soon as I take it in. It's making everything look funny. Small things look too big and things that are far away look too close and my legs won't work right and my mouth won't stop making water. I bump into things because I can't see them right and they're playing tricks on me, sneaking closer when I'm not looking, on purpose to make me trip over my own feet. All these things are happening, but none of them is making the Badness go away.

I try to meow for help, so that somebody can hear me, like that day when Sarah and I first found each other. But when I open my mouth I throw up again and it just makes me feel dizzier. I try to walk to a cooler part of the room, maybe under-the-couch or down the hall away from the big windows, but my legs aren't working right. I fall over once and then twice, and then I realize I'm not getting closer to where I'm trying to go because I'm walking in circles.

When I lived with Sarah and my belly felt upset, she would stroke my forehead and say, *Shhh, little girl. Don't worry. Everything's okay. Everything's going to be just fine . . .*

But everything's not going to be just fine, because now Darkness comes to work with the Badness. It's like a black sack has been thrown over my head. Except after a few moments, I notice that my body feels lighter, like I don't weigh anything. The closer the Darkness comes, the farther away the Badness feels.

And then, it's the strangest thing. Sarah is here! I can't see or hear or smell her, but I can feel her in the room, like the silent hum when a TV is turned on even if there isn't any sound or picture. *Sarah!* I think. But now the Darkness is going away again, and I know somehow that if it goes, Sarah will go, too. I struggle to keep my eyes closed, to stay inside the Darkness where Sarah and I can find each other.

Sarah! I think. *Don't leave me, Sarah! I knew you'd come back for me! I knew you'd find me again! I knew you'd*

And then everything is Darkness and Silence.

PART THREE

13

Sarah

L AURA TURNED FOURTEEN IN THE FALL OF 1994 AND BEGAN ATTEND-
ing Stuyvesant High School down in Battery Park City. For the
first time, she started taking the bus and subway on her own
every day. Once, this would have terrified me. But Mayor Giuliani
had taken office by then, and he'd started cracking down on things
like graffiti and street crime and the homeless guys who'd come
right up to your car window with a squeegee while you were
stopped at intersections. He got rid of the corrupt cops who for so
many years had taken bribes and allowed the street-corner drug
dealers to go about their business. There was no question that New
York City in general and the Lower East Side specifically were
growing cleaner and safer by the day.

There were mixed feelings about all this on the LES. Nobody
liked crime, of course, and it was a relief to feel that our streets
were less dangerous. On the other hand, we were rather proud of

our graffiti. People like Cortes and Keith Haring were acknowledged as legitimate artists pursuing a legitimate art form. There
were people who grumbled that Giuliani was a fascist. Maybe he
is, I'd reply, but you know what? Drug dealers are fascists, too.
Now there was nobody to menace my daughter and her friends
when they walked down the streets, to tell her which corners she
could linger on and which she couldn't.

"Quality of Life," Giuliani's campaign was called. Many of us
were in favor of it at first. But eventually we came to realize just
how nebulous an expression "quality of life" is. If you wanted to,
you could interpret it to mean almost anything.

Later, after the dust had settled, lawyers and reporters would try
to create a chronology of what had happened on June 3, 1995. We
were able to ascertain a few definite facts—that a concerned citi-
zen's 911 call really had started the whole thing, that there really
were a few bricks that had slipped from our apartment building's
rear façade. Nobody disputed that our landlords had disregarded
necessary repairs over the years. Margarita Lopez, the city council
member for our neighborhood, would later confirm ninety-eight
Class B (serious enough to warrant court action) and Class C (supposed to be repaired within twenty-four hours) violations on record with the City. We tenants had banded together in the past,
chosen representatives, complained formally to the City. But the
City had done nothing for us. All of us living there were old, or we
were immigrants, or we were poor. We worked. We paid our rent
every month and our taxes every year. But, in the end, we were
expendable.

There was money coming to us, the lawyers insisted. Somebody had to pay for what had happened. I attended a few meetings,
but my heart wasn't in it. What difference could it make? And
when we ended up getting nothing, or next to nothing, I wasn't
surprised or even disappointed. We were too broken by then. We
were a group of Humpty Dumptys, and there weren't enough
horses or men in all of New York to make us whole again.

* * *

It was a Saturday morning. Laura moved with brisk purpose through the apartment, wearing a nightgown with a cartoon drawing on it of a girl who stood in the window of a tenement building much like ours. The girl in the drawing had thrown a clock from the window. *Jane Wanted to See Time Fly,* the caption said. It was a child's nightgown, even though Laura had grown so much in the past year I could hardly believe she was the same girl. It wasn't a nightgown I would have worn at her age. But when I was Laura's age, I was already trying to be older. Laura would turn fifteen in only five months. I had been fifteen when I'd met Anise. A chance meeting a lifetime ago, in a secondhand store I'd never intended to go into. And somehow, from that day, events had unfolded one after the other and brought me here. I had a teenage daughter, and this was where we lived.

I wasn't due at Ear Wax until the afternoon. Still, I was up early because Laura was up early, and I sang in the kitchen as I fixed toast and cereal for the both of us. Laura was waiting for Mr. Mandelbaum to return from the cramped, ancient synagogue two doors down from our building. He had gone there to pray every Saturday morning for the past fifty years. Today was different, though. It was Shavuot, the holiday that celebrates God's giving the Ten Commandments to Moses. The Yizkor, the Jewish memorial prayer for the dead, is recited four times a year. One of those times is Shavuot, and Mr. Mandelbaum would be reciting the Yizkor today for Mrs. Mandelbaum, who'd died in her sleep during the past winter.

Mr. Mandelbaum hadn't been the same since. His eyes would roam the room instead of looking at your face when you talked to him. The voice that had once boomed down hallways, audible sometimes even downstairs in our apartment, had faded to a whisper. He would forget to take his medication for days at a time. Even Honey seemed to sense the difference. She had always been close to him, always been "his" cat—his and Laura's—but now she hovered near him constantly. Whenever we went up to see him,

Honey was in his lap or sitting next to him on the arm of his chair. Her soft eyes looked anxious as they followed his every small movement. If Mr. Mandelbaum hadn't remembered to shop for Honey, to buy her food and bring her the little tidbits of turkey she loved from the corner deli, he might not have remembered to shop at all.

Laura and I tried to spend as much time with him as possible. But there were too many hours in the day given to school and to work, too many hours when Mr. Mandelbaum was by himself in that apartment filled with photos of the wife and son he'd lost. Too many hours with only his cat for company. The book Mrs. Mandelbaum had been reading aloud to him the night she died still rested, facedown, on the coffee table where she'd left it before going to bed. Laura had seen him only yesterday, heart torn at Mrs. Mandelbaum's absence from the kitchen where she'd prepared cheese blintzes every year for Shavuot. Laura's idea today was to take Mr. Mandelbaum for a walk, maybe to Katz's for the blintzes they served there. Anything that would keep him from spending the rest of the day alone in his apartment.

But it was pouring outside. Laura fretted at the idea of Mr. Mandelbaum being outside in this weather, fretted also that he might not have remembered to bring an umbrella with him when he'd walked to the synagogue that morning. He was apt to forget such things these days.

It was nine when we heard the knock on our door. Laura, already dressed and hoping it was Mr. Mandelbaum, ran to answer it. I was in my bedroom, just starting to change out of my nightshirt. I heard an unfamiliar man's voice, the upward tilt of Laura's voice responding with a question. "Mom?" she called out. "Can you come here?"

My hands fumbled with the buttons on my shirt. "I'm coming," I called back.

I had missed a button and my shirt was on lopsided. There were two firemen at our door. One of them, the younger one, seemed to notice my shirt but refrained from pointing it out. "Is there anybody else in the apartment, ma'am?" he asked me. Their yellow-and-black raincoats gleamed wetly, and I remember thinking their muddy boots would make a mess in the hall.

"Why?" I wanted to know. "What's going on?"

"We're evacuating the building," the other one said. "Part of the rear façade has been damaged from the rain. There's a possibility the whole building might collapse."

I heard his words, but it was information my brain instantly rejected. "I'm sorry?" I said.

"We're evacuating the building," the older fireman repeated, patiently. "This building is in danger of imminent collapse, ma'am."

"Oh my God." I felt a vein begin to throb in my throat. My mind whirred and skipped, a phonograph needle trying to settle into the right groove. I had a sudden, unbearable image of my daughter crushed beneath a collapsed building, her body broken underneath a pile of bricks and beams. I knew, though, that I couldn't let panic alone, or the sharp pain of my heart thudding in my chest, determine my actions of the next few minutes. I had to force that image away for a second. I had to stop and think.

It's an impossible question to answer in the abstract, what you might take with you if somebody knocked on your door and told you that your home and everything in it could be destroyed in the next few minutes. It's impossible because, when the moment comes, it's always unexpected and you can't think. Only later do you remember things like favorite albums or your grandmother's wedding ring, or the metal lockbox of personal treasures stored on the top shelf of your closet. If you're a mother, your first thoughts go where they always go—to what you'll need to care for your child. Food, clothing, shelter, whatever you'll need in the way of wallet contents and insurance papers to ensure those things are provided without interruption. And so, when my mind stopped skipping, that's where it settled. *Tell Laura to grab enough clothing for a few days*, it said, *while you get your purse, your phone book, and the insurance policies.*

"Quick," I said to Laura, I could hear the rain lashing at our windows. "There's a suitcase on the top shelf of the linen closet. Get it down and we'll—"

"There's no time, ma'am," the younger fireman interrupted. "This building could collapse any second." Laura turned her face up to mine, fear and bewilderment in her eyes, but also trust. Not doubting for a second that her mother would know exactly what we should do.

It was Laura's face that snapped me into decisiveness. "Put your shoes on," I told her. "Hurry!" Without a word, she ran off to her bedroom. Turning back to the firemen, I asked, "Is there truly no time to bring anything else?"

"We'll have it stabilized soon," the younger fireman told me reassuringly. "You'll probably be back in a couple of hours. We're evacuating mainly as a precaution. Just take what you need for right now."

His words eased the knot of panic in my chest, but only a little. The image of Laura in a collapsing building was too agonizing to be dismissed easily.

"Mom," Laura said as she hurriedly laced her sneakers, "what about—"

"Everything's going to be fine." I tried to sound soothing. "But we have to go now."

"But—"

"*Now,* Laura. No discussions."

I wasn't in the habit of speaking to her so sharply. She threw me a surprised look, but finished tying her shoes.

I can almost laugh today, remembering how Laura and I raced to grab keys, wallets, umbrellas. At my urging ("Quickly!" I told Laura, tugging at her arm, *"Run!"*), we bolted down the stairs as if the building were already collapsing around us. We were breathless when we reached the sidewalk.

Most of our neighbors were outside. We whispered among ourselves as we milled about in the rain. "A few bricks fell off the back of the building," the performance artist from the ground floor told me. "Because of the rain. Somebody called 911. They should be able to fix it pretty easily."

It was a comforting thought. Then the police arrived with barricades and yellow tape, and the vein in my throat began to pulse again. All this because of a few fallen bricks? A crowd, larger than the twenty-five or so people who lived in our building, was starting to gather.

It was Laura who first spotted Mr. Mandelbaum, in the thirty-year-old suit he'd worn to his wife's funeral, clutching a small plastic bag in his hand. "We're over here!" she called to him, waving. Laura and I angled our umbrellas so all three of us could fit under them while rain pounded staccato on the fabric over our heads. Laura's face was pale and pinched, but in Mr. Mandelbaum's presence she composed it into a serene expression as she quickly explained what was happening.

Mr. Mandelbaum's eyes swept past the cops, now busily using the barricades and yellow tape to create a perimeter around the building. It stood on the corner, and the barricade extended from all the way around the corner and around back to the narrow alley between our building and the one next to it. Then Mr. Mandelbaum looked up at the building itself. The red bricks rising into gray sky looked every bit as solid as any other building on the block.

For a moment, I was pleased to see his eyes focus in a way they hadn't in months. It was heartening, even under circumstances like these, to see his eyes flicker with life and interest. Then I realized it wasn't understanding that focused his gaze. It was fear.

"Honey," he said.

It's an interesting thing to think about, how rumors get started. How a crowd comes to know something no one individual can account for. When did it happen? When was the moment of certainty? And how was it that we knew for sure?

We had been told that the building could collapse at any second, but two hours later not so much as a single brick had fallen, not one visible crack had appeared in the structure. They had told us we would be allowed back in "soon," but by noon not one of us had been allowed back in. Police officers and representatives from the Office of Emergency Management roamed freely in and out of the building, seeming unconcerned about the dangers we'd been warned of. Many didn't bother to wear hard hats. In hushed voices people asked one another, *Doesn't that seem odd to you?*

Whispers ran among us as we all stood there in the rain, waiting to see what would happen. People talked about SROs whose occupants had been dragged from their beds in the middle of the night and scattered into the streets like cockroaches. The buildings would be demolished the very next morning to make room for expensive new condos and restaurants. There were the squatters who took over apartment buildings nominally owned by the City because the landlords had been unable to afford repairs or taxes. Buildings the City abandoned and neglected until they became crack houses. The squatters would chase out the dealers and addicts, bring in wiring, fix walls and roofs, plant gardens, make the building and sometimes whole blocks livable again. You would see children playing stickball on streets that only a few months earlier no child could have safely walked past. And then one day police would come to chase the squatters out, not letting them take any personal belongings with them. The City would "reclaim" the building and sell it for a profit.

But those people were different from us. The people who stayed in SROs had no formal contracts; they paid on a nightly or perhaps weekly basis. Technically, the squatters had no legal claim to be where they were. *We* held signed leases in our own names. *We* paid our rent every month, as formally and contractually as any millionaire with a Park Avenue pied-à-terre. What had happened to those other people could never happen to *us*.

Maybe it was when Mayor Giuliani pulled up in a Town Car. By then the crowd was enormous. At first people were cheered by the sight of the mayor striding confidently into that building. He didn't wear a hard hat, either. How dangerous could the building be, if the mayor himself was entering it?

But then the murmurs went around again: Why *was* the mayor

here? Why should he concern himself with *us*, with our one little building? Maybe it was a goodwill gesture, an attempt to garner votes in a neighborhood that hadn't supported him in the last election?

But, then . . . why didn't he make eye contact with anybody, or give us even a parting wave, as he exited the building and disappeared back into his car?

One of our local community board members, an architect, was circulating. "Don't worry," he told people. "I went around back and saw the damage they're talking about. Two, maybe three bricks, and that rear wall's at least six bricks deep. There's no way this building is going to collapse."

Few people seemed comforted at hearing this. I noted that. Noted, too, that at some point the crowd had started to lose faith in the idea that whatever was happening here today was a rescue mission. A breeze blew up and I shivered, drawing Laura closer to me.

I don't remember all the events of that day as clearly as I should. Maybe I just don't want to. Or maybe, perversely, too much of my memory got used up in the wrong places. Because the parts I remember most clearly are the ones I would give anything—all the remaining years of my life—to forget. The rest of it comes to me in fragments.

The crowd sighed and surged and swelled and collapsed inward upon itself, only to expand again. Rain fell harder, and people huddled under umbrellas or simply stood motionless and got wet, and then the rain subsided. Faces blurred and shifted around me, as if I were standing still in front of a merry-go-round. The Bengali couple from the fourth floor threaded through the crowd, their three children following them like ducklings in a row. The Polish woman who lived across the hall from us and took in laundry muttered something, to nobody in particular, about the clothing she still had piled up in her living room.

"Five thousand dollars I have in that apartment," Consuela Verde, Maria Elena's mother, said to me. The two youngest of her five children clung to her beneath an enormous flowered umbrella, still wearing their pajamas. Anger and anguish competed for toeholds on the rounded contours of her face. "All our lives, my husband and me worked for that money. All the money we ever have. We no trust the banks. And now these *hijos de la gran puta*"—she spat on the sidewalk—"now they will take it from us. You watch and see."

More hours ticked by. Rain-fed puddles deepened and joined to form small rivers that rushed over feet and carried bobbing, twirling dead leaves toward drains. My stomach churned in time with the movements of the crowd, its anxious circles, the growing sense that something wasn't right. It had been hours since the toast and cereal I'd eaten that morning. Somebody pressed a paper cup of hot coffee into my hand. But my stomach recoiled at the thought of it, so I carefully set the cup down on the asphalt beside me.

Nothing happened to indicate any repairs being made to our building. Why were we kept waiting in the rain? Why, when the building had remained standing for so many hours, couldn't we go in and at least collect a few of our things?

A leg would grow uncomfortable from my standing on it too long, and I'd shift my weight to the other leg. I halfheartedly swung my umbrella around whenever the wind changed direction. Still, I was soaked through. I tried to re-button my lopsided shirt one-handed and succeeded only in making it more lopsided. My purse began to feel too heavy hanging from my right shoulder, so I switched it to the left. It occurred to me that I was long overdue at the store, that Noel would be worried about me. But I didn't want to leave to find a pay phone. The thought faded. Sometimes I decided to count how many people in the crowd had blond hair, how many red, how many brown. It was easy when you could see the tops of everybody's head. I remained within the crowd, so I could hear what was going on, and kept one eye on Laura, who stood with Mr. Mandelbaum across the street.

Laura never left Mr. Mandelbaum's side. He sat on an over-turned orange crate, and Laura held her umbrella over his head so he wouldn't get wet. For hours she stood protectively over him, the tallest woman in the crowd aside from me. Laura's smooth, pale hand against the black plastic of the umbrella handle. Mr. Mandelbaum's knotted hands twisting and untwisting the plastic bag he still gripped. Occasionally Maria Elena went over to talk to her. Once, I think, she tried to convince Laura to go someplace with her. I could tell by the gestures her hands were making. But Laura smiled wanly and shook her head *no,* motioning toward Mr. Mandelbaum. Maria Elena disappeared back into the crowd.

I hovered as close to the barricades as I could without being completely swallowed up by the crowd. People from our building kept approaching the yellow line and the cops standing on the other side of it. They pleaded, raged, argued, wept. Those who didn't speak English, or didn't speak it well, brought their children as interpreters. I tried, too, to reason with the cops. Tension had become a living pain in my chest, but I forced myself to be calm. Years of working retail had taught me to speak calmly, smilingly, to unreasonable people. I had a child, I told them. My child needed clothing. She needed her schoolbooks. So many people had gone into the building all day and come out unharmed. If we could have a few minutes, only a few minutes to . . .

"We'll let you back in," the cops told us again and again. "Once the building has been deemed safe for reentry, we'll let you back in. You have nothing to worry about."

Every half hour or so, I helped Mr. Mandelbaum through the crowd and up to the barricades. I took him from Laura as if we were two parents exchanging custody. I held my umbrella over his head with one hand as we walked. I encircled him with the other, to protect him from being pushed by the crowd. He couldn't be allowed to slip and fall. I had to remind myself to walk slowly, to pace my longer steps to his shuffling ones.

Mr. Mandelbaum's whole face beseeched the unyielding cops on the other side of the barricades. Their eyes never so much as flickered in his direction.

"Please," Mr. Mandelbaum kept saying. "Please let me get my cat out. She's in there all alone. Please let me get her."

More than a few times, I tried to argue on Mr. Mandelbaum's behalf. I circled the barricades looking for different faces, cops I hadn't already spoken to. "He's an old man," I said. "He has prescription medication in there that he needs to take."

Nothing. No response at all.

"Look," I said, lowering my voice to a confidential tone. As if we were allies, partners on the same side of a negotiation. "The man's wife just died. He lived here with her for *fifty years*. That cat means the world to him. Just let him get his cat out. She's a living thing, too." I repeated this sentence often, as if it contained magic words. An unanswerable argument. *A living thing.* "Couldn't somebody at least get her for him? I could get his keys. I keep seeing people going in and out and—"

Finally, one of the cops rolled his eyes. "Lady," he said in an exasperated tone, "we got more important things to worry about right now than some old guy's *cat*."

The crowd continued to grow. It became increasingly restive as the day went on—community board members, friends and relatives, tenants from neighboring apartment buildings swelled our ranks, until there were over two hundred of us and cars couldn't drive down Stanton Street. Jostles became shoves. Murmurs rose to shouts. Chants went up. Who came up with them? How did everybody know to say the same thing at the same time? *"Give us fifteen minutes!"* the crowd howled with one voice, fists in the air. *"Give us fifteen minutes!"* Or else they chanted, *"Mr. Moriarty, stop this party!"* referring to OEM deputy director John Moriarty, who was on-site that day.

I did try to make Laura leave. The Red Cross had set up a relief center a few blocks away, and I tried to send her there. "No," she told me. One hand fell to rest on Mr. Mandelbaum's shoulder. "We're not leaving until we know Honey is safe."

"Laura—"

"No!" Her voice was edged with panic. "I'm not going! You can't make me!"

You can't make me. A child's argument. But Laura and I had never argued. We were as close as two fingers on the same hand, she and I.

Eventually, somebody came to me with a petition. Somebody else came with an affidavit. I signed both. I was told papers were being prepared and notarized at the nearby middle school. A judge had been found who was willing to have the papers delivered to his home on a Saturday. For the first time in the nine hours since our building had been evacuated, I allowed myself to feel hope.

Suddenly Laura was beside me. She held Mr. Mandelbaum's arm. What was she doing here, near the barricades? I had thought, I had been certain, that we'd both understood the terms of our unspoken agreement. She was to remain safely across the street with Mr. Mandelbaum. If he wanted to try talking to the cops again, *I* would bring him over. There was no reason for *her* to be *here.* No reason at all.

Yet here she was. "Fifty years I've lived here," Mr. Mandelbaum was saying now. His voice was no longer a quiet plea. It had gained volume, agitated for the first time. "Everything I have in the world is in that apartment, but I don't care. I don't care! Just let me go to my cat. I'm begging you!" He dragged the wet sleeve of his coat across his face.

The cops continued to ignore him. He was only an old man, after all. They didn't budge for him. Their eyes moved only for Laura, moved up and down, taking her in. A tall, slender, beautiful girl, wearing jeans and a red cotton T-shirt that clung to her body in the rain.

I could see Laura's tight face, the crease between her eyebrows far too deep for a girl her age, as she fought to restrain her own tears. Tears for this man she loved, and the cat she loved almost as much as the man. I couldn't hear her words, but I knew she was adding her own soft, murmured pleas.

A gust of wind came up. It blew Mr. Mandelbaum's coat backward, molded Laura's T-shirt more tightly to her chest. The cops' eyes drifted downward. Sly grins scurried across their faces.

Something uncoiled inside me. It curled my hands into fists, set my heart to pounding so hard I could hear it inside my own ears. My body flooded with a surge of rage so pure and sharp that, for one exhilarating moment, it was indistinguishable from joy.

The crowd roiled again, chaotic now. I was pushed hard from all sides. I struggled to remain standing. I had the wild thought that I had caused this, that my rage had spilled over and seeped into the people around me.

But it had nothing to do with me. I had taken my attention away from the crowd for a second, and in that second the crowd-mind had reached a consensus I knew nothing about.

A crane had arrived.

It rumbled down Clinton Street. Its neck was yellow. Gradually the neck stretched itself up until it rose as high as our building's roof. From the end of the yellow neck hung a brownish gray beak with a row of thick metal teeth, each longer than a man's leg. The bottom half of the beak was a slab. It would catch whatever chunks the teeth tore out.

Large metal containers and lighting trees were maneuvered into place. It had been hard to gauge the day's passage under such a gray sky, but I realized with a kind of dizzy surprise that soon it would be nightfall. There were sounds of machinery switching on and off. Then only the low-gear rattle of the diesel engine of the crane's cab.

The beak opened its maw and poised over the roof, waiting.

The crowd roared and surged and broke in waves against the

police barricades. But underneath the waves, in deeper places, were currents and crosscurrents. Related to the waves, yet unaffected by them.

Word was spreading. The judge was going to issue a temporary restraining order. The restraining order was on its way! Quick as light beams, from person to person, this message was communicated. Somebody shouted it to John Moriarty from the OEM. He took out a cellular phone and made a call. Nodded a few times in response to whatever the person on the other end said. Then he hung up and spoke into his walkie-talkie.

"Do it now," he said.

The rattle of the diesel engine was drowned in a new sound— a loud, continuous hum. People screamed and sobbed. I could hear the wailing of children. For the first time, the police seemed nearly overwhelmed by the force of the crowd struggling to break through the tape and barricades.

"My cat!" Mr. Mandelbaum cried out. Tears coursed thickly down his wrinkled face. "She's a living thing! She's still in there! Please! She's all I got!" The plastic bag he still held twisted convulsively in his hands as he fell, kneeling on the pavement. *"She's all I got!"*

"Laura!" I yelled, bending toward Mr. Mandelbaum. "Laura, help me!" I looked up, and then I fell silent.

Laura wasn't there.

"Laura?" I rose to my full height, stood on tiptoes. Laura and I were both tall. Even in a crowd like this I should be able to see the top of her head. So why couldn't I? I left Mr. Mandelbaum with Hugo Verde, Maria Elena's father. *Watch him,* I mouthed, pointing from my eye to Mr. Mandelbaum. Hugo nodded and leaned down to help Mr. Mandelbaum, still crying, shakily to his feet. I angled through the crowd, turning sideways to slip through crevices between bodies, using my hands to push people out of the way. I no longer felt separate from the crowd, from its terror and frenzy. I was a part of it. "Laura!" I called. "Laura, where are you? Laura, answer me!" I remembered when she was three, when she'd slipped away from me once at a block party. I'd found her that day, but I'd always had nightmares since then. Nightmares just like this. Laura was missing in a crowd, and I couldn't find her. Anything could have happened to her. What if she'd fallen? What if the crowd was trampling her? *"Laura!"* The hard pain in my chest was now a black hole of panic. "I'm your *mother*! Answer me, dammit!"

The crane, fully powered up now, swung back to gather momentum and made its first test swing at the top of the building. The deafening crunch of metal against brick echoed over the heads of the crowd.

Then the head and shoulders of a girl pushed their way through an open window on the third floor. A fair-skinned girl with long brown hair. She wore a red cotton T-shirt. The sky was black now, the clouds had finally thinned, and the girl, the building, the metal containers waiting to swallow them on the ground below, all of them were spotlit by the blazing lights from the lighting trees. They looked superimposed against the black sky. Unreal, dreamlike. The girl waved her arms furiously. "Wait!" she shouted. "Wait, I'm in here!"

"LAURA!" I shoved my way through the crowd again, so hard this time that people fell back as I muscled past them. Dear God, what if I couldn't get to the barricade in time? Already the crane was pulling back, preparing for another swing. Its jaws gaped, glinted in the artificial white light. *"Stop them!"* I screamed. I kept screaming. *"Stop them! Somebody stop them!"* But my screams were swallowed in the crowd. Finally I got to the barricade and clawed at the arm of the nearest cop. *"My daughter is in that building!"*

The cop looked at me and said something terse to the officer standing next to him, who rolled his eyes upon hearing it. The two of them motioned to a third officer to guard their post as they turned and ran into the building. The OEM official barked something into his walkie-talkie, and the crane was still.

Needle-thin raindrops darted silver through the glow of the lighting trees. The crowd, emboldened by the unexpected pause in the crane's movements, flailed against the police barricades with renewed frenzy. My fingers curled, convulsing in rhythm to my anguish. How many more raindrops, how many more seconds, minutes, eternities until Laura was safely in my arms.

Finally, the cops reappeared in the doorway, wrangling a struggling Laura between them. They'd put her in handcuffs, the metal glinting cruelly against the soft flesh of her wrists. My heart clutched in horror. *My child, my child.*

When they reached the barricade, one of the officers unlocked the cuffs and pushed Laura toward me. I stumbled as the weight of her body fell awkwardly against mine, and my arms automatically rose to encircle her. My hands moved from her head to her shoulders, down her arms. Checking to see if anything was hurt, anything broken. "We could lock her up for disturbing the peace," the cop told me. "Keep an eye on your kid, will ya?"

My jaw was so tight it was painful. "Keep your hands *off my child.*" I pushed the words through clenched teeth with enough force to send a line of spittle down my chin. The cop took one look at my face and backed off.

"Mom," Laura was saying frantically. "Mom, I had her! I had Honey! Those cops scared her and she jumped out of my arms when they came for me. She ran under the bed. I know exactly where she is! Tell them! Tell them where she is so they can go back and get her!"

My arm drew up into the air, hand open. It sped down to land across Laura's face in a resounding slap. The force of it rocked her head back and to one side. She staggered, instinctively clutching the shirt of a person standing behind her to keep from falling.

Laura's already fair skin turned white. Chalk white save for the blood-red mark on her face, which took the shape of my hand. Her eyes widened. Raindrops gathered in her hair and spilled down the sides of her face.

"*ARE YOU CRAZY?*" I shrieked. Except I was the one who sounded crazy. And even as I was screaming, even as I struck her for the first and only time in her life, even then a part of my mind was thinking, *Oh, my child, my girl. That you should live to see a day like this one.* I grabbed her shoulders and shook her until her teeth rattled in her head. *"A CAT?"* I screeched. *"You risked your life to save a* cat? *Who cares about the cat! TO HELL WITH THE STUPID CAT!"*

I didn't mean it. Of course I didn't mean it. What I meant was, *Yes, we love the cat, but* you *are more important than any cat.* What I meant was, *Please, if you love me, don't do anything like this again. I couldn't bear to go on if anything were to happen to you.* But I didn't say those things. Not in that moment. How could I? How could I speak calmly when I was gasping for air? When my legs shook beyond my control? When my heart was knocking so hard in my chest, it sent pains shooting through my body?

All I wanted was for Laura to leave. Every instinct in my body was screaming for her to go, to get her away, away, away. Away from the machine with its ravenous metal jaws that wanted to kill something. Had tried to kill her once already. Away from the crowd that also wanted to kill something now.

But Laura wasn't going. She stood there with tears in her eyes, gaping at me as if she didn't know me. Didn't recognize me. The look of perfect trust her eyes had held only that morning was gone. And I knew, as I stood there, I knew I would never see it again. Something had changed between us. I knew it, I just didn't understand *why.* How could my own daughter, the child of my own body, distrust me when I was the only one—the only person in this whole crowd—who was trying to protect her? I felt myself on the verge of hysteria. Clutching her arm, I dragged her through the crowd to where it thinned at the edges. I saw Hugo Verde helping his children and Mr. Mandelbaum into a Red Cross bus. Later I would learn that it had taken people from our building to a motel out in Queens, near LaGuardia Airport.

And then Noel was standing next to me. "I was worried when you didn't show up today. You weren't answering your phone. I came as soon as my shift ended." He stared at me—my face twisted, panting heavily—and trailed off. "Is there anything I can do?" he asked uncertainly.

I put my hand against Laura's shoulder and shoved her, hard, in his direction. "Take her," I gritted. "Take her to your apartment. Take her anywhere. Just get her away from here."

Maybe if Laura had cried, maybe then it would still have been okay. If she had cried, if her face had softened, of course I would have put my arms around her. I would have hugged her close and whispered, *I'm sorry. I'm so sorry, baby. I was scared, that's all. I love you. I love you so much.* And Laura would have hugged me back, she would have sobbed against my shoulder, and I would have comforted her as best I could.

But Laura didn't cry. The tears in her eyes dried without falling. Her lips pressed into a thin line. Noel tried to put his arm around her shoulders, but she shook it off. "I'm fine," she told him.

Noel threw me a look that pleaded for clemency. *Give the kid a break,* the look said. "Come on," he told her softly. "Everything's going to be fine. Your mom's going to stay here and make sure everything is just fine." Placing one hand lightly between her shoulder blades, he started to guide her away from the edges of the crowd.

I watched their backs recede. When they'd gotten half a block away, Laura broke away from Noel and whirled around to face me. *"I hate you!"* she screamed. Hurling the words at me with all the force she had.

Laura's hands rose to cover her face, and she turned to bury both face and hands in Noel's shoulder. Noel's arm went around her. The two of them kept walking until they disappeared from sight.

It took thirteen hours for the crane to tear our building apart, piece by piece, to level it all the way down to the ground floor. For thirteen hours, chunk by chunk, the metal jaws of the crane ate into it and ripped it open. The building never did collapse. Those of us left to watch who had lived here and knew it well weren't surprised. That building had stood for a hundred years.

You could see inside people's apartments as the walls were torn off. The first massive chunk ripped by the crane sent a large

Bible flying into the air. That was the Verdes' apartment. Laura had told me once about that Bible. On the flyleaf they'd written the names of everyone in their family going back four generations.

Furniture looked exposed and naked under the lights, like people caught in the act of changing clothes. Rugs slid into cracks that opened in the floor, dragging couches and tables along with them until everything tilted and teetered at crazy angles, like in a fun-house. Kitchen cabinets were squeezed in the machine's jaws until they vomited up breakfast cereals and silverware, wedding china and plastic bowls for children. Occasionally the white lights would catch a piece of jewelry or a shard of broken glass and beam out to blind me unexpectedly. A tiny blue sweater became snarled in one of the crane's teeth and hung there for an absurdly long time, as if someone were clinging fiercely to the thing, desperate to stop it. Not that the crane cared or even paused. It had all night to complete its work.

I stood there and watched numbly. It was only when the crane had eaten down to the third floor, where Mr. Mandelbaum had lived, that I had to leave. I told myself I was hungry, that I hadn't eaten all day. I went to a diner on First Avenue and sat there with a sandwich and a mug of coffee in front of me for two hours. I took one bite of the sandwich, but the bite marks my teeth left looked too much like the holes gouged out of our building by the crane. My head pounded and my face felt hot, and I bent to rest my cheek against the cool surface of the table.

"You okay, miss?"

A busboy had approached and he hovered, looking worried. "I'm fine." My voice sounded rough, and I cleared my throat. "Is there a pay phone I could use?"

"Around back. Next to the bathrooms." He gestured in the direction of the kitchen. "You sure you're okay?"

My hair fell forward as I bent over my wallet, looking for a few bills to leave on the table and some change for the phone. When I lifted my eyes, the busboy was still looking at me with concern. I smiled weakly. "Just not as hungry as I thought I was."

Someone had etched WORSHIP GOD into the metal of the pay

phone's base. It ate two of my quarters before a third produced the sound of a phone ringing on the other end of the line. Noel answered in the middle of the first ring. "How is she?" I asked.

"Sleeping," he answered. "She passed out as soon as she changed out of her wet clothes. I was going to try to wake her and make her eat something, but I figured she needs the sleep more right now."

"Thank you, Noel." No matter how much I cleared my throat, I couldn't seem to erase the gritty texture from it. I didn't sound grateful, although I was. I didn't even sound like me. "I'll come by for her in the morning."

"Where will you sleep tonight?"

I laughed—a hoarse, barking sound. "Nowhere," I told him.

There was nothing I could do there, but I walked back to Stanton Street anyway. The crane was still at work, and it had reached the second floor. I was there to see its jaws come through the wall of Laura's bedroom, devouring the dolls and board games that had come to live permanently in her closet as she'd gotten too old for them. The curtains Mrs. Mandelbaum had sewn for her. The wallpaper we'd spent days choosing and hours hanging in that room that had once been papered in sheet music. The crane ate it all without pausing.

For years, I waited for Laura to ask me about that night. There were a lot of questions I waited for Laura to ask me, but she never did. I always thought, though, that if she were to ask about why I went back, why I stayed there through the night and into the next morning in the damp, crumpled clothing I'd worn all day, that it would be the one question for which I wouldn't have an answer that would make sense to a practical girl like Laura. I couldn't have explained to her why I stayed, why I had to see all of it—all of our life together—torn apart piece by piece. Why I felt like the destruction needed a witness. Not a witness in the sense that a lawyer uses the word. Not that, exactly.

I stayed for the same reason you would sit up all night by the bedside of a dying friend. Because it was something friendship required of you. And because nothing should die alone.

* * *

The same bus that had brought everybody to the motel out by the airport brought them back the next morning. The police had made a cursory attempt to retrieve some personal effects from the rubble of the demolished building. Waterlogged furniture and clothing, soggy pillows, torn photos, shattered picture frames, pots that held shredded plants, an antique silver hairbrush, yards of snarled tape from the insides of videocassettes, a guitar that had been snapped at the neck, a curling iron, a brush for a cat, endless cracked pieces of china, a chipped commemorative plate celebrating the wedding of Prince Charles to Lady Diana. The things the cops had pulled sat in a wet mound where once our building had stood.

Noel brought Laura back while I climbed the mound, looking through it all, but I made him take her away again. I didn't want her to see this, to see me picking through a pile of broken things on the street like a scavenger. There was only one thing I was looking for, anyway.

It took nearly five hours for me to find it, and it had started to rain again. My hands were torn and bloody by then, and I didn't know if it was dust or tears that had clogged my lungs and made my eyes run. The rest of my former neighbors—those who had even bothered looking through the mound—had long since dispersed. I was the only one left by the time I found what I was looking for. Once I did, I went to find Laura.

In the end, those of us who lived there were compensated to the tune of three nights at the airport motel and $250 in gift certificates to buy clothing at Sears, courtesy of the Red Cross. That was all. Two hundred and fifty dollars for a home. Two hundred and fifty dollars for a life. Tenants with children who asked, *But where will I take my children? Where can we go?* were told they would have to check into one of the City's homeless shelters and remain there for forty days before they could officially be considered homeless and receive government assistance. I don't think anybody took them up on that offer. But I can't know for sure. I never saw most of them again, except for Mr. Mandelbaum—and by the time I found him, I knew he was beyond taking help from anybody. When the building's owners couldn't afford to repay the City for the demolition cost, ownership of the property reverted to the City by default. They sold it to developers for millions. Condos would eventually be built there, starting at $1.2 million for a one-bedroom.

But construction didn't begin immediately. It wouldn't begin for a long, long time.

Laura and I stayed with Noel and his wife and two children for a few days, but it seemed impossible to take advantage of them by staying too long in their already crowded East Village apartment. We spent a few weeks rotating among friends' couches and sleeping bags while I tried to keep my business running and waited for my insurance company to send me a check. Laura was nearly catatonic most of the time, falling into restless sleeps in which she tossed and turned and called out for Honey or Mr. Mandelbaum. And when she wasn't silent or sleeping, she raged at me, demanding the return of some favorite blanket or cherished nightgown that she couldn't try to sleep one more night without.

Sometimes I raged back at her, thinking she was doing this just to torment me, because she must have known how impossible it was for me to restore any of the things we'd lost, how much I would have given if I could have done so. Now I understand that she needed somebody to be angry at, so that anger would give her the strength to fight through and survive those difficult days. Mostly, though, she was exercising a child's prerogative (for she was still a child, even if she wouldn't be much longer) to demand that her mother do what mothers are supposed to do—make everything better.

But I couldn't. I couldn't make anything better. Our resentments grew as the days passed, although I could only guess at Laura's. When we weren't yelling at each other we didn't speak, except when I told her every day how I'd been trying to get in touch with Anise, that Anise would be able to do something to help us, would do it any day now. Anise was on tour in Europe. In those days, most people didn't have email addresses or cell phones. I left messages with her management company, who assured me they were doing everything they could to reach her at each tour stop, although it always seemed as if they'd just missed her before she'd checked out of one hotel and moved on to the next city. They probably thought I was a hanger-on and decided not to bother her.

It was five weeks before I heard from my insurance company, and they informed me that my renter's policy didn't cover lawful acts of emergency demolition by the City. By then Laura and I were staying in cheap hotels on the Lower East Side, and my credit was nearly exhausted. I arranged a "fire sale" at Ear Wax, selling everything that could be sold for whatever price I could get for it to the obsessive collectors who had always been my best customers. At the end of it, I turned the keys and the lease over to Noel. I still had hundreds of records left that were scratched or damaged, or that the collectors hadn't been interested in, and perhaps two dozen that I couldn't bring myself to part with. They weren't worth much anyway (although I don't think Laura, when she saw how many remained unsold, believed that), but now you could probably sell them for something simply because they're old. All of them, along with my personal effects from the store, went into the same storage unit I'd first rented back when Laura was born. Another phase of my life had been boxed up and put away in a dark room, left there to molder and gather dust.

We were living in an SRO up in Harlem—all I could afford at that point, and more accessible by subway to the Midtown employment agencies I had applied with—when we finally heard from Anise in early August. I brought Laura with me to every typing test and every job interview—because where could I have left her?—and that, along with my lack of a "real" address, wasn't helping my job hunt. Most of what Anise had to say about her management company—which, as I suspected, hadn't made much of an effort to pass my messages along—was unrepeatable. She fired them a few days later, and her ousting them in the middle of an international tour over "creative differences" became a minor news item. The new management company she quickly signed with arranged for Laura and me to stay in one of their corporate apartments. Anise offered to do a lot more than that for us, but I refused to take it from her. I knew I'd never be able to pay her back.

Once I had an address, I was able to find a job as a typist at a small real estate law firm. The hourly rate was good, and I learned that if I was willing to work off-hours—late at night, for example— I could make up to double my hourly rate. I was used to keeping odd hours because of the record store, so that suited me fine.

Having a job meant I could finally fill out the reams of paperwork for a two-bedroom apartment in a Mitchell-Lama building in the East Twenties. Only thirteen blocks from the technical boundary of my old neighborhood, but still a world away. We were more or less settled by the time Laura's school year started, although it was Christmas before I could afford to buy us any real furniture beyond the two mattresses I'd used up the last of my credit for when we moved in.

Laura was barely speaking to me those days. When I lost Laura's voice, I lost the music in my head, too. Or it was more like the music in my head *was* my daughter's voice. Laura was my music. It was like living with my parents all over again, except this time the only person to blame was me. I knew the only way I could make things right would be to find Mr. Mandelbaum, to salvage whatever there was left to salvage of our old lives.

I went back to our old neighborhood every night after work, every morning before I was due at the office. I had the photo of Laura and Mr. Mandelbaum that I'd kept in my wallet, and I showed it to people. All the hookers and squatters and street people I'd come to know over the years. Except that there weren't as many of them anymore. How had I not noticed? I even went to the beat cops, the ones I knew from my store. Cops who hadn't been on the other side of the barricades that day. In the end it was Povercide Bob from his usual haunt in front of Ray's Candy Store on Avenue A who—after subjecting me to a twenty-minute diatribe about how the government and the CIA were conspiring to kill the poor, and how what had happened to our building was proof—directed me to a seedy SRO on the Bowery.

I thought (foolishly, I now realize) that if I went to Mr. Mandelbaum with a plan for getting him out of that place, everything could still be all right. I told myself nothing had happened to any of us that couldn't be fixed by time and the quiet order of a clean new home. I called City agencies on my lunch breaks, trying to find a place for him to go. I got shuffled around a lot. Eventually I was referred to the Jewish Home for the Aged, who would be able to find Mr. Mandelbaum an apartment only a hundred dollars a month more than the old place had been. Of course, a hundred dollars a month is a fortune to somebody on a fixed income. But I was making more money now, more than I'd made with the record store. My bigger paychecks, our cleaner, bigger apartment, hung in the air between Laura and me like unspoken accusations. I had to do something. I had to make it right.

The man at the front desk of the SRO pointed me to a room on the fifth floor. How did Mr. Mandelbaum manage to climb up and down five flights of stairs every day? His room was at the end of a drab corridor, next to a large plastic trash can beneath a naked lightbulb. The floors had probably been tiled at some point, although now they were no more than hard puddles of red, blue, and brown.

Mr. Mandelbaum's room contained a single cot and an ancient wooden dresser. A plywood divider separated this room from the one next to it. Mr. Mandelbaum lay on the cot, still wearing the brown suit he'd worn to synagogue the day we'd lost our home. On top of the dresser, an ashtray overflowed. The room stank of smoke, unwashed clothing, and trash from the hallway. I had imagined Laura's joy upon being reunited with Mr. Mandelbaum. It had been the only truly happy prospect I could imagine for any of us these past months. But I knew now as I looked around that I could never bring her to see him here.

"I've been waiting for you," he said dully. He struggled a bit until he was in a half-sitting position, his eyes refusing to meet mine. "I wanted to give you something." His hand fumbled along the top of the dresser pressed flush against his cot. "I bought this for Honey, but I didn't have a chance to give it to her." He handed me a crumpled plastic bag. "Someone should have it."

I accepted the bag and sat down on the bed next to him, trying to think how to begin. "I didn't know you smoked," I finally said. I hadn't meant it to sound like an accusation, but somehow it did. It was the wrong way to begin.

"I don't." He seemed confused. "Ida made me quit thirty years ago. She'd kill me if she thought I was smoking again."

I let it go. "We should talk about what you're going to do now." I tried to sound efficient and cheerful. *Everything is fine,* my voice insisted. *It's all just a question of logistics.* "I've found a place for you to live through the Jewish Home for the Aged. It'll cost a bit more than what you were paying, but I have a good job now. Laura and I can help with the rent. We want to."

He continued to look at the wall. "I lost one home already," he said. "I'm not starting over in a new neighborhood. Not at my age."

"But you can't stay here in this place."

"What difference does it make where I die?"

"Mr. Mandelbaum . . ." I took his hand in mine. "Max," I said gently. "There are still people who love you and need you. I do. Laura does, too. To her you're like . . ." *Like the father she should have had,* I thought. "Like family."

"Every time Laura looks at me, she'll think of that day," Mr. Mandelbaum said. "Better she shouldn't remember. She's still young enough to forget."

Something sharp darted through my chest. *If only she could!* "You're wrong. Laura needs you more than ever now. You need each other. Doesn't she matter to you at all?" My voice became more urgent. "The world is the same place it was three months ago. There are still things in it worth living for."

Finally, he turned to face me. "Oh, Sarah." There were tears in his eyes, and a look of compassion. As if in this moment it were I and not he who needed understanding. "You know I haven't wanted to live since Ida died."

My throat closed in a hard, painful lump. There was nothing I could say.

The hand I held squeezed faintly against mine. I felt how it trembled, cold and papery and crisscrossed with thick veins. The skin slid loosely over the bones of his knuckles, as if there were nothing to connect them.

"As long as I had Honey and my memories, well . . ." He withdrew his hand to pass it over his eyes. "You and Laura will be fine without me," he said. "When they buried my cat and everything that reminded me of my wife, they buried me, too." He turned his face to the wall again. "It's already like I never existed."

Laura had always been a good student. But now all she did was study. She had this grim, determined air about her, like a prisoner trying to claw her way through solid earth. Although maybe that's not as true as I think it is. Maybe Laura gossiped with friends and dated boys and thought about some of the other things pretty teenage girls are supposed to think about. It's impossible for me to know. I worked a lot of late nights, earning as much as I could so I would have something to put away for Laura's college. We didn't see much of each other. We were like roommates, I remember telling Anise once, years later. Like roommates, rather than family. Two people who happened to share a living space because it was convenient and made financial sense for them to do so.

In a way, it was like living with my parents all over again. Our home was silent—no conversations, no music. I knew Laura resented my music, I knew she blamed me for loving it so much that I'd raised her the way I had. She screamed it at me once. It was a month after I'd gone to see Mr. Mandelbaum at the SRO, when I had to tell Laura that he'd died. I had gone to visit him every day after I'd found him, bringing food and soap and whatever comfort I could. I had succeeded so far as getting him to change into the clean clothes that I'd brought. But I couldn't persuade him to leave that place altogether.

It wasn't that Laura blamed me for his death exactly, but that she blamed me for everything—for our having lived in that building in that neighborhood in the first place. "Because of your *music!*" she'd yelled. "Because your music was more important to you than *I* was. You could have gotten a job, you could have asked your mother for help, you could have done *anything* when I was born that would have gotten me out of that place. But you didn't!"

And what could I say? I *had* given up music for her. I'd stopped trying to be a DJ or a performer and went into the business side of it. It was only now, now when everything had ended, that I could see my mistakes. I wanted to say, *I was only nineteen! Only four years older than you are now! Music was the only thing I knew anything about back then.* I wanted to say, *I didn't want to be one of those single mothers who spends all day in an office and never sees her children. I wanted to spend every second I could with you. I didn't just want us to live, I wanted us to have a life. I did the best I could, the very best I could at the time . . .*

I wanted to say those things, but I couldn't. The hardest thing in the world is to admit obvious past mistakes. Not because the admission of guilt is hard (I would have confessed to, would have apologized for, anything at all to win back Laura's love). But because, in light of how stupid you turned out to have been, your defenses end up sounding like nothing more than excuses. Lame excuses, at that.

For years I thought I resented Laura for the guilt she made me carry. (As if I wasn't carrying enough already.) Guilt for things that were beyond my control, for decisions I'd made so long ago (and for such good reasons!) that it didn't seem fair to punish me for them now. For the first time in my life, I craved the silence I'd grown up with. I came to understand my mother better, how a woman could decide that she didn't want to talk to her own child. There were times when I'd catch a look on Laura's face, as if she were about to say something of more substance than *Going to the library. I'll be back later.* Perhaps if I'd encouraged her . . . but I don't know. I never did encourage her. I didn't want to hear her repeat the accusations I made against myself daily. Sometimes I thought there was nothing left inside me but tears, and that if

Laura said the wrong thing I'd put my head down and cry all those tears out until there was nothing left of me at all.

Maybe it wouldn't have mattered anyway. Laura needed to be angry at someone. Who could she be angry at if not at me? The City? The developers greedy for more land they could overprice? Those were anonymous entities, nothing more than a thousand worst-case scenarios Laura blamed me for not having thought enough about. And then one day the anger and silence become a habit. One day it's been so long since you've talked to someone that it's impossible to say the things you should have said years ago.

Maybe that's why I blather so relentlessly at Laura when she comes to visit me now. Too late I realized how insidious silence is. I think sometimes that maybe—by sheer accident—I'll find the one right thing to say, the one thing that will make Laura look at me again the way she used to.

After Laura graduated from college and moved away, she was no longer my legal dependent, and I had to move out of the Mitchell-Lama building. Not that it mattered much to me. That apartment had never felt like a real home, anyway.

I moved back to the Lower East Side. I had to go all the way out to Avenue B—once an unthinkable place to live, certainly for a woman alone—to find an apartment I could afford. It wasn't exactly the same when I moved back (you can never go home again, as they say)—not even remotely the same, really. But it was the only place where I could find traces of what had been, and what might have been if not for one rainy day and a few fallen bricks.

I still couldn't bring myself to listen to my music. But I could no longer stand the silence, either. I started watching a lot of TV. And I went out for long, roaming walks. I felt like a ghost haunting the neighborhood. It was odd to see how much things had changed in eight years. The building where Anise and I used to live was now a luxury high-rise where a one-bedroom apartment started at four thousand dollars a month for only five hundred square feet. A tall silver box divided into dozens of smaller silver boxes, none with any more personality than the other. Lofts the size of the one Anise and I shared now sold for three million dollars, which struck me as something beyond madness. The SRO where Mr. Mandelbaum died was now a high-end boutique hotel. Its lobby bar was thronged at night with young girls who were beautiful and looked very expensive.

But there are still traces of the place I once knew. The DIE YUP-PIE SCUM! graffiti on the occasional brick wall. Chico's *Loisaida* mural on Avenue C. Walking through these streets I used to know so well is like running into a girl you once knew at your twentieth high school reunion, some girl who's had a lot of plastic surgery. She looks older and yet she also looks younger. Like herself and also like a different person from the one you remember.

One day I found myself walking down Stanton Street, where Laura and I used to live. It was raining, and maybe that was what drew my feet in that direction. Where our building had been was now a construction site littered with cement blocks, stacks of lumber and steel beams, and a silent crane. Gaily striped banners proclaimed that luxury lofts were being erected.

I stood there in the rain and looked at it for a while, the way I'd stood in the rain that night, watching our old building come down. I couldn't remember the name of Mr. Mandelbaum's cat anymore, that cat Laura had loved so much she'd been willing to risk her life for her. I tell myself all the time that I'm too young to be so forgetful, even though I have a grown daughter. I'm not even fifty yet. But my memory has become full of holes.

This day wasn't rainy as that other day had been. After one intense, tropical burst, the clouds cleared and the sun was beating down again. Just as I was preparing to leave, I saw something move near one of the cement blocks scattered on the ground.

It was a kitten. A tiny little thing. Probably no more than a few weeks old, cowering behind something solid. The creature looked soaked through. She was trying hard to remain unseen, and for a second I did consider leaving her to her privacy. And yet—surely this was some kind of miracle, wasn't it? That I should find a kitten—one who looked so much like how I remembered the Mandelbaums' cat—on *this* spot, in *this* place? She had the same green eyes, the same black tiger stripes and little white socks on her paws. Surely I was being offered a second chance, to save now what I hadn't been able to save for Laura all those years ago.

And didn't I also need saving? Didn't I also need someone to love? *It was meant to be,* a voice in my head whispered.

I crouched down, holding out my hand. "Hey, kitty," I whispered. "Are you lost?" The kitten shrank back, afraid. *Poor thing!* I thought, and something in my chest that had been hard and frozen for years began to loosen. I reached out to her again, and she seemed to draw herself inward until she was a tight ball of watchful fluff, just beyond the reach of my fingers. It was probably prudent, I told myself, for such a young kitten to be wary of a strange human. As this thought crossed my mind, I remembered Anise's cats, all named for Beatles songs, and I smiled. "Prudence?" I said. "Is that your name?"

The kitten looked at me with enormous, fearful emerald eyes. And then, without thinking about it, I began to sing. For the first time in fourteen years, I found my voice. *"Dear Prudence,"* I sang softly. *"Won't you come out to play?"*

At first the kitten looked bewildered. I wasn't surprised. My voice sounded scratchy, and it was deeper than it used to be. I didn't even sound like me anymore. But as I sang, my voice gained strength and I started to recognize it again. *"The sun is up, the sky is blue . . . it's beautiful, and so are you . . ."*

Timidly, cautiously, the kitten crept out from the shadow of the cinder block. She sniffed my fingers, inching forward, and allowed me to lift her. She was soaking wet, and I bundled her under my jacket, against the warmth of my chest. She pressed one paw, tentatively, softly, to my cheek. I noted what looked like a funny little extra toe.

"Let's go home, Prudence," I whispered. The kitten responded with a series of cheeping mews, as if she were trying to sing back to me.

One day Laura came to my apartment with the news that she was engaged. I was happy for her, of course I was happy for her, and yet I also thought, *My only daughter is engaged to a man I've never even met.* Laura tells me so little about her life. But there was a happiness, a sweetness that seemed to exist despite itself in her blue, blue eyes, so much like her father's. I know my daughter well enough to know when she's happy. And when she invited me to have lunch with her and her fiancé and I met him for the first time, I could see why.

I actually ran into Josh once after that, completely unexpectedly. It was at night, maybe around eleven o'clock or so, during one of my endless walks. One small club I passed had live music playing, and, impulsively, I drifted inside. It was a three-piece acoustic band, performing a cover of Blind Faith's "Can't Find My Way Home."

There are moments when a song hits you in a certain way. You know it's soupy and self-indulgent, but even knowing that doesn't stop the tears from rising. And suddenly I was so tired, a bone-deep exhaustion I'd been feeling more and more lately. I sat down at the bar, needing a moment to pull myself together.

And then, out of nowhere, Josh was beside me. "What a surprise!" he exclaimed, kissing me on the cheek. "I'm here with some of the writers from my magazine, checking out this band. Come over and I'll introduce you. I'm sure the three of you could talk music for hours."

Josh was only nine or ten years younger than I was. Still, he looked like he belonged in this place. Looking around at all the young faces, I was suddenly aware of my age, how far-too-old I was for Lower East Side dives where young artists played in the hope of being discovered. One day you look around and realize everyone in New York is younger than you are. "Oh," I said to Josh.

"That's okay. I was just going to have a quick drink and head home."

"I'll have a drink with you, then." He sat on the bar stool next to mine and ordered a Maker's Mark rocks from the bartender.

"How's your family?" I asked, at a loss for anything else to say. "I'm looking forward to meeting them."

"They're good," he said. "My parents still live out in Parsipanny in the house I grew up in. My dad's getting ready to retire soon. My sister has a house near them, but she's looking for a place in the City, closer to where she works." His face hardened subtly. "She and her husband split up and he . . . doesn't do a lot for their kids. She's basically raising them on her own." Then he sighed. "Oh well. It'll probably make her and the kids closer with each other as they grow up."

"Yes," I said faintly. "It happens that way, sometimes."

There was a mirror behind the bar. The Josh sitting next to me on the bar stool was looking into it. But the Josh reflected in the mirror was looking at me. I turned my eyes down and twirled the straw in my drink a few times.

"Hey," he said. "Did you ever hear how Laura and I met?"

"No." I tried to smile. Tried not to think of all the little ways I'd long ago stopped being a part of Laura's inner life. "I don't think I have."

"She came to my office one day. Her firm represents my company and they had a meeting of some kind. Anyway, I was on my way to see somebody when I saw this beautiful woman near the elevator. She has those *eyes,* you know? And she was struggling with these two enormous briefcases." He laughed. "I mean, they looked *heavy.* Heavier than her, maybe. So, naturally, I went over to help, but she didn't want me to. She didn't just say, *No, that's okay, I can manage.* She *really* didn't want me to carry those briefcases for her. I could tell she was embarrassed. She *cared* about managing those two heavy briefcases on her own.

"For days, I couldn't get it out of my head. Why would somebody care so much about such a simple thing? It wasn't stubbornness, I could tell that, but it was something. I thought about it all the time, trying to figure it out. Finally, I called her office and asked her out." He paused, took a sip of his drink.

"Later she told me it was her first client meeting. Apparently, it's a customary thing for an associate to carry a partner's briefcases when they go to meetings. I said to her, *But that guy you were with was all the way back in the conference room. It's not like he would have seen me helping you.* And she kept saying, *But an associate is supposed to carry the briefcases. That's part of the job. It's what you're supposed to do.* And I thought that I'd probably never met anybody who cared so much about doing the right thing, doing what you're *supposed* to do, all the way down to the little things.

"I couldn't have known it that first time I saw her. But I *did* know it somehow, you know? How sometimes you look at someone's face, and you don't know what exactly it is you're seeing, but you know it's important. Laura thinks she has such a poker face." He laughed again. "I know how hard she works to convince herself she's in control of things all the time. But you can tell when she really cares about something. It's written all over her face." His eyes in the mirror found mine. "I saw it when she looked at you at lunch," he said. "I don't know, maybe you think the two of you aren't as close as you'd like to be. Laura doesn't talk about it much. I have an older sister. I know it can be rough between mothers and daughters sometimes. My sister loves my mother, and the two of them talk all the time. But I never see in her face what I saw in Laura's when she looked at you."

I had to turn my head aside and clear my throat, embarrassed for Josh to see me cry. He was silent as I pulled a tissue from my purse and blew my nose. Then in the mirror, his eyes smiled at mine.

"Let's have one more drink," he said. "I want to toast my mother-in-law this time."

Last week I had chest pains so bad I had to go to the emergency room. After a battery of tests the doctors came back with their conclusions: angina. Also high blood pressure. Who knew? They say it's unusual for a woman my age, but my father's dying prematurely of a heart attack puts me at higher risk. Sometimes these things happen. There are all kinds of things I have to do now to manage my condition. They tell me there's no reason why, with diet and exercise and medical care, I shouldn't live out a normal life span.

That conversation I had with Josh keeps coming back to me. And I know, somehow, that the doctors are wrong. I don't have much time left. I don't mean that I feel sick. I feel fine most days. And yet, as Josh said, sometimes you know a thing when you see it.

Last night I went into my closet and went through some of the things I'd taken out of storage after Prudence had given my music back to me. I pulled out the old Love Saves the Day bag where I'd put a bunch of old newspapers and magazines and, all the way at the very bottom, the crushed metal box I'd managed to find in the wreckage of our old building. I had to struggle to open it. Old, broken things don't like giving up their secrets too easily. Hidden in the clutter of that little box was the red collar Mr. Mandelbaum had bought for Honey on the morning of the day when our building came down. I put the collar around Prudence's neck and told her, "Tomorrow we'll get some tags for you that say PRUDENCE. And maybe we'll have Sheila downstairs take a picture of the two of us together. Would you like that, little girl?" I buried my fingers in the ruff of her neck, and Prudence leaned her head against my hand and purred.

I know now what Laura knew already that day when she risked her life for Honey's—that love is love, whether it goes on two legs or four. Someday Prudence will love Laura. Prudence will love her on those days when it seems as if nobody else does. She'll make Laura laugh when nobody else can even make her smile. Prudence will carry my love for Laura into her new home and her new life. She'll carry my memories back to Laura, too—memories of fourteen years of love and music and a life that was too good to be destroyed altogether, even by that one terrible day. She'll help Laura find her way back into those memories—memories of all of us, of Honey and the Mandelbaums, who loved her also, and of days in a dusty downtown record store when nothing in the world mattered except a mother and daughter who were always happiest when they were together. She'll take with her a love that never died, even if it did change forms.

I *was* meant to find Prudence that day. I know that now, and it seems as if I've known it always.

I've always known I was keeping her for Laura.

14

Laura

LAURA WAS IN A TEN-THIRTY MEETING IN CLAYTON NEWELL'S OFFICE when she got the call. There was a 250-page contract to review for one of their largest clients, and the client wanted notes by the end of the day. The matter was pressing enough that Clay himself had gotten involved.

The phone on Clay's desk buzzed, and his assistant's voice over the intercom said, "There's a call for Ms. Dyen, Mr. Newell."

"What is it regarding?" Clay asked before Laura could say anything.

"It's her husband," Clay's assistant answered. "He says it's an emergency."

"I left my cell in my office," Laura said. Her stomach, which had started to unknot after her fight with Josh that morning as the familiar routines of work took over, clenched again. "He wouldn't call on this line if it wasn't important."

Clay nodded. "Put the call through, Diane." Laura remembered the day she'd gotten the emergency call from her mother's office, only six months earlier. She rose from the couches where she'd been sitting with Clay and Perry, and crossed the room to the ringing phone on Clay's desk. Her hand trembled as she answered it.

"Josh," she said. "Josh, what's wrong?"

"It's Prudence." The anger of two hours ago was gone from his voice, replaced by a controlled panic. "I went out for a walk, and when I came home she was just lying there unconscious. It looks like she threw up all over the place."

Laura, who didn't know what she'd expected to hear, but hadn't expected this, needed a moment to redirect her thoughts. "Is she breathing?"

"I think so," Josh replied. "Which animal hospital should I take her to?"

"St. Mark's Vet down on Ninth and First," Laura responded immediately, trying to control the panic now rising in her own chest. "That's where my mother always took her."

"That's all the way downtown. Shouldn't I bring her someplace closer?"

"What if she has a medical condition they know about and we don't?" *Like my mother did,* she thought. "Tell the cabbie you'll double the fare if he can get you there in fifteen minutes. Triple if he makes it in ten."

"Laura, I—"

"Just *go,*" Laura interrupted. "Go now. I'm on my way down." She hung up and turned to look at Clay and Perry, still seated across the room and watching her closely.

"Is everything okay?" Perry asked.

"My—" Laura stopped, hearing in her own head the words she was about to say, knowing how they would sound to Clay and even to Perry. Squaring her shoulders, she said it anyway. "My cat is sick."

At first, Clay looked more startled than anything else. "What?" he asked.

"My cat is sick," Laura repeated. "She's unconscious and she's on her way to the animal hospital. I have to go meet her there."

Having made this statement, Laura felt foolish for a moment. Not because of what she'd said, or for wanting to rush immediately to the animal hospital. She simply didn't know how to get out of the room. If she'd had a child, and if she'd said, *My daughter is sick, she's unconscious,* she could have left instantly. Nobody would have expected her to do anything else. But this was something different. Instinctively she waited either for permission, as a good underling should, or for the confrontation that would make permission irrelevant and carry her out the door.

"You're kidding, right?" Clay glanced at Perry. Turning to Laura again, he said, "*What* did you say?"

Laura had fought already with her husband that morning. She'd even fought with Prudence who (her heart clutched with guilt and fear) was now on her way to the hospital. *Might as well make a clean sweep of it,* she thought grimly. Aloud to Clay she said, "I think you heard me just fine."

"No, I don't think I did," Clay replied. "Because what it sounded like you said is that you, an associate, are walking out on a multi-million-dollar contract review with two senior partners because your *cat* is sick."

"See?" Laura was gathering her notes and papers. "I knew you heard me."

For one second, Clay gaped at her. It was inconceivable that anybody, any associate, would have the nerve to speak to Clayton Newell this way in his own office. Then his eyes hardened. "Of course I heard you." His voice was wintry. There wasn't an associate in the firm who didn't tremble when Clay sounded like this. "It just never occurred to me that you were serious."

Laura thought of all her late nights in the office, all the times she'd worked twelve, thirteen, fourteen hours, leaving Josh to stew at home, because Clay had dropped some last-minute project on her desk, demanding an immediate turnaround even as he knew— as Laura herself had known—that he wouldn't be in the next morning until hours after the deadline he'd given her.

"Clay," Laura said, turning to face him, "you know how committed I am to this firm. I didn't even take time off when my mother died." She heard her own words echo in her head. *I didn't take time off when my mother died. My mother died, and I came right back to work. As if nothing had happened.* "I've never put anything else first. You know I haven't. Not once in all the years I've been here. But this is something I have to do, and I have to go now."

"Don't throw your commitment in my face like it was a special favor you conferred on us." Clay was angry now. "You were committed and you worked hard because that's the price of admission in a firm like this, and *you* know *that*."

"Clay—" Perry attempted, but Laura interrupted him.

"No, Perry, he's right. I was back in this office one hour after my mother's funeral. I didn't want anybody to think that I wasn't man enough to handle it."

"You could have taken all the time off you needed," Perry remonstrated gently. "We would have given it to you. *I* would have given it to you. All you had to do was ask."

"I know." Laura took a shaky breath. "I do know that. I'm not blaming anybody. But I came back here anyway. And I was back here after my husband lost his job, even knowing that every single one of you knew it was about to happen and didn't tell me. I thought I knew where my loyalties were supposed to be. I made a choice." She remembered the day Sarah's and her apartment had been torn down. *You can't make me!* she'd cried when Sarah had tried to get her to leave. She thought of Josh, who only this morning had yelled at her about how they never went out, never had enough time together, because of her job. She had been outraged, unable to believe that Josh could be so unreasonable as to act as if she had any choice in the matter, any control over the number of hours she spent at the office.

Except that she did have a choice. She always had.

"I made a choice," she repeated. "And I'm making one now." She walked to the door.

"Don't assume you'll be welcome here if you decide to come in tomorrow," Clay said to her back. "I've got résumés for at least a hundred people as good as you are who'd kill to take your place."

"Clay," Perry said quietly. Always the voice of reason. "Don't say things you don't mean."

Laura paused in the doorway but didn't turn around. What had she expected to find in this place, anyway? Had she thought Perry was her *father*? Perry had his own family, his own children. If she lost Josh, if they couldn't get past the things they said to each other that morning, and if she lost this pregnancy like she'd lost the last one . . . If this office was truly all she had left, then what was it, really, that she would have? Some money. A bit of tenuous security, so long as she said *yes* and *no* at all the right times and was properly obedient. Late nights of stumbling home, bleary-eyed, to an empty apartment and a phone that didn't ring once all weekend.

She remembered the day she'd gotten the official offer from Neuman Daines. How proud she'd been! She had called Sarah to let her know, but not in the way a daughter calls her mother to share in the glow of her accomplishments. Just matter-of-fact. *Here's where I'll be working. Here's where you can reach me if you need me.* Except that Sarah *had* needed her. And she had needed Sarah. It wasn't confusion over phone numbers that had kept them apart.

"She was my mother's cat, Clay." Laura's voice was no longer argumentative. "She's all I have left of my mother."

She didn't wait to hear if Clay or Perry responded. She walked out.

In the back of the cab that sped down a rain-slick Park Avenue, Laura pressed her right foot impatiently against the floor as if there were an imaginary accelerator beneath it, willing the car to go faster. When it slowed down behind another cab making a turn, Laura leaned forward and said desperately to the driver, "Go around him, go *around*." She knew, somehow, that this was her fault. She'd yelled at Prudence only this morning. *Why can't you just leave me alone?* Laura's stomach lurched in agony, and she pressed her hand, cool from the rain outside, against her forehead. If this *was* her fault, if she had done this to Prudence somehow, then surely she could undo whatever it was, if only she got there quickly enough.

When had it happened—how long had it been since Prudence, nearly unnoticed, had crept into that place in her heart once held by Honey, a place she had kept resolutely closed for so many years? Prudence with her black tiger stripes and dainty white paws. Prudence waiting patiently outside her bathroom when she was sick in the mornings, then following at her heels, turning in eager circles as Laura prepared her morning meal. Prudence sitting up with her night after night, purring melodically next to her on the couch, her only comfort—the only reason she was finally able to fall asleep—on so many nights during these past few months. Laura thought about Prudence's peremptory, guttural meows as she demanded some treat of tuna or cheese. Why hadn't she given those things to Prudence from the first day she'd arrived in their home? Why had she needed to be asked? She had known the things cats liked, that made them happy. And she had known how it felt to lose Sarah.

The taxi passed a green apartment building awning, beneath which a woman held the hand of a chubby, diapered infant, clearly in the early bowlegged days of learning to walk. Laura thought of Prudence's funny little kitten waddle in her mother's kitchen, Prudence rising on fuzzy, unsteady legs to snatch some treat or tidbit from Sarah's outstretched hand. The cab was racing down Second Avenue now, past Baby Bo's Cantina. Sarah had loved their quesadillas. They'd been a Sunday ritual for her, along with the fried plantains she'd known Laura enjoyed and had made a point of having when she knew Laura would be coming over. Laura had noticed when Sarah stopped bringing the quesadillas home, sharing the sour cream and pulled chicken with Prudence. But she hadn't thought to ask why.

A garbage truck turned a corner to emerge and stop in front of

them. The cabbie slammed the brakes, flinging Laura—still leaning forward—against the Plexiglas partition separating the front
seat from the back. Rubbing her forehead, she was about to make
another impassioned plea for him to go *around* the wretched thing,
but the driver was already looking over his left shoulder and sliding into the next lane. They made better time after that, easing into
the rhythm of the lights and making it through a few yellows at the
last possible second. St. Mark's Church, where she and Sarah had
gone every New Year's Eve to listen to all-night poetry readings,
flew by on their right. At Second and Ninth they passed Veselka,
where she and Sarah had sometimes treated themselves to borscht
in the summer, mushroom-barley soup in the winter. The restaurant and the church remained, but Laura would never go to either
of those places with her mother again.

With one loss, Laura realized, others multiplied. Suddenly she
wanted her mother with a desperate want that sat on her chest and
wouldn't let her breathe. She wanted to feel her mother's arms
around her, to press her face into the graceful bend between her
mother's neck and shoulder and inhale the comforting scent of her
mother's hair. More than anything, she wanted to hear her mother
sing. She hadn't heard Sarah sing in sixteen years, not since that
June day when Laura was only fourteen.

But she would never hear her mother sing again. For the first
time since Sarah died, Laura truly understood—*felt* all the way
down to the pit of her stomach—the awful finality of the word
never. She would never hear Sarah's voice again. She would never
have her mother's comfort again. She hadn't felt the loss as deeply
as she should have because Prudence had been there, a living piece
of her mother that was still with her. And now she didn't know if
Prudence would survive the day.

For months Laura had been unable to cry for her mother's
death. For one dreadful moment, she felt herself on the verge of
breaking down completely, right here in the back of this cab. She
bent forward to put her head between her knees, willing herself to
hold it together.

With a squeal of rubber against wet pavement, the cab skidded to a stop. "Twelve dollars, miss," the driver told her. Laura handed him a twenty from her purse and hastily murmured, "Keep the change." She drew the jacket of her suit over her head to protect it from the rain as she ran from the car and down the short flight of metal stairs to the basement-level entrance of the animal hospital.

The waiting room was tiny. Blond-wood floors and recessed lighting created what probably had been intended as a warm, comforting atmosphere. But it was the kind of gray, rainy day when even lighting the lamps seemed to enhance the gloom rather than dispel it.

As Laura shook the rainwater from her jacket, she saw Josh pacing the small room. He had turned a stranger's face to her that morning. It had been like that other day all over again, when her mother had turned on her with a stranger's eyes and slapped her across the face. Worse than seeing their home destroyed, worse even than losing Honey and Mr. Mandelbaum, had been seeing a person she didn't know wearing her mother's face. It had seemed impossible that she and Josh could ever again speak to each other kindly, with love in their voices, after the things they'd said.

But Laura could see at once that all that had been put aside, at least for the moment. Josh's face was as taut as her own, his eyes red. "Josh," she said. She quickly crossed the room to where he stood and, without thinking, put her hand on his arm. She felt the warmth of his skin beneath his shirt. "Josh, what happened?"

"It was the lilies," he said, and Laura's heart turned over at the haggard look on his face.

"What lilies? What *happened*?"

Josh sank onto one of the benches in the waiting room, wooden benches that suggested festive outdoor activities where people might bring their dogs, and that held wicker baskets containing magazines like *Cat Fancy* and *Best Friends*. "For our anniversary, I went to the florist who made your wedding bouquet. I had him make an identical one. It was supposed to come before you left for work today." He gave a mirthless laugh. "Nothing this morning has gone the way I'd planned."

Laura felt tears sting her eyes. "Oh, Josh," she murmured, and sank down onto the bench next to him.

"Prudence ate some of the lilies." Josh seemed to address this to the bulletin board with flyers for lost dogs and kittens for adoption that hung on the wall across the tiny room, unable or unwilling to look her in the face.

"Okay," Laura said, confused. "Cats eat plants sometimes."

"Yes," Josh said. "But lilies are *toxic* to cats. There's something in them that shuts their kidneys down."

"But she'll be okay, right?" Laura willed Josh to look at her, but his eyes stayed fixed on the wall. "You got Prudence here quickly and they'll be able to . . . to fix her, won't they?"

Josh's hands rose to cover his face. "I don't know. They're still working on her. Nobody's been able to tell me anything yet." Josh rose and began pacing the room again. When he finally turned to Laura, his eyes were outraged. "Why doesn't anybody *tell* you something like this? There should be a . . . I don't know, a *manual* or a warning label that gets sent home with every cat, with a picture of a lily in one of those big red circles with a line through it. I didn't know." His voice was ragged. "I had no idea. I would *never* have let those flowers into our house if . . . if I'd . . ."

"You couldn't have known, Josh," Laura said, softly. "I had a cat growing up, and I didn't know, either. You did the right thing. You brought her here, and that's the best possible thing you could have done for her."

Josh nodded, although he looked unconvinced, and came to sit by Laura once again.

The minutes ticked by, marked by an oversized clock above the reception desk, until Laura was so tense from the *ticktock tick-tock* she thought she might scream and hurl the nearest blunt object at the thing. Twice she walked over to the reception desk and asked, in a hushed voice, if there was any word yet about Prudence Broder? The first time, the dark-haired woman—wearing blue scrubs and a nose ring—pressed Laura's hand and said, "I was sorry to hear about your mother, *mamí*." Laura was unable to respond beyond nodding and leaving her hand in the receptionist's for a moment. As she returned to her seat, a black-skinned man in a white *guayabera* walked in with a large green parrot perched on his shoulder. *"Hello, this is Oliver. Hello, this is Oliver,"* the parrot squawked. "Hel*lo*, Oliver," the receptionist greeted the parrot in a cheerful, trilling voice, and the three of them—man, woman, and bird disappeared through a swinging door into an exam room. The receptionist returned in time to welcome a large woman carrying a tiny dog of indeterminate breed, wearing a pink sweater and attached to a rhinestone-studded leash. "Dr. Luk is waiting for you and Pancake in exam room three," the receptionist told the woman. "You can go on back."

Laura rose and walked to the reception desk again. Was there anything the receptionist could tell them? Any news about Prudence at all? "Dr. DeMeola is with her right now." The receptionist's voice was so sympathetic that it made Laura's heart lurch, certain the news could only be bad. "She'll be out to update you as soon as she can." Laura nodded once more and returned to her seat next to Josh. She tried flipping through one of the magazines in the basket next to her, but page after glossy page filled with photos of other people's happy, healthy cats did nothing to ease the knot in her stomach. Finally, she gave up and tossed the magazine back into its basket.

"You never told me you had a cat when you were growing up," Josh said suddenly.

"Well, she was our upstairs neighbors' cat." Laura smiled wanly. "But we were close. She . . . died. When I was fourteen."

Josh's long legs were stretched out in front of him, and Laura studied his jeans. They'd come home one Sunday afternoon to find Prudence sleeping comfortably on them where Josh had tossed them across the bed, and Josh hadn't had the heart to make her move. There were a couple of snags where Prudence's claws must have caught them. "I had a cat when I was a kid, too," Josh said after a moment. "For about five minutes."

"What are you talking about?"

"I was fifteen. I had my first after-school job at a Sizzler near our house, but I didn't have my driver's license yet. So my dad would come to pick me up at the end of my shift. One night we found this cat, sitting in the middle of the street. He had been hit by a car. He was just kind of wagging his head, you know? People were honking and honking at him, but he wouldn't move. I got out of the car and wrapped him up in this blanket we kept in the trunk. My father drove to the nearest emergency animal hospital as fast as he could."

Josh shifted slightly, leaning his head back to rest it on the wall behind their bench. "I remember holding this cat, his eyes were open and staring up at me, and he was panting so hard. He must have been in shock. The whole time my father was driving, I kept thinking, *Don't die. Don't die. Don't die.* When we got to the hospital, the vet on duty examined him and said he could save the cat, but it would cost a lot of money and the cat would need a lot of looking after while he was recovering. My dad explained that he wasn't our cat, and that we couldn't take him home with us because of our dog. That's when the vet said that maybe the best thing to do would be to euthanize him, so at least he wouldn't suffer anymore."

Josh fell silent. Laura didn't know if the pity choking her throat was for the cat in the story, or for the boy Josh had been—the boy who was now a man and still didn't understand why there should have to be such a thing as suffering in the world.

"But I thought, *no.* I thought if I could go home and call all my friends, surely one of them would offer to take him. I had a girlfriend, Cindy, and she had cats, and I thought maybe her parents would agree to take him. My father wanted to euthanize the cat while we were there, but I talked him into taking me home and letting me try. I thought I at least had to *try.*

"Of course," Josh continued, "I couldn't find anybody who was willing to take on the financial burden of some cat they didn't know who might require all kinds of long-term care. I called everybody I could think of, but they all said no. I guess it was stupid of me to think someone might take him. I was only fifteen, what did I know? My dad called the vet hospital and told them to go ahead and euthanize the cat. But they couldn't do it without my dad coming in to sign some paperwork first. And my dad, who'd been working all day, was so angry. Here it was, nearly midnight, and he had to drive all the way back to the animal hospital. I was in my bedroom on the phone with Cindy, and my father came in and yelled at me for all the trouble and inconvenience I was putting him through, and to tell me how selfish I'd been.

"Cindy could hear him shouting. I don't think I've ever felt worse. The cat was going to die. I'd made all this extra work for my father, and he was yelling at me. And my girlfriend could *hear* him yelling. You know how the most embarrassing thing in the world when you're a teenager is for your friends to hear your parents yell at you." Laura, who had only ever been yelled at by Sarah once, and never in front of her friends, nodded anyway. "When he left, Cindy said, *Listen to me, Josh. Listen to me. You're a good person. You're a* good *person, Josh, and you did a good thing. Don't listen to what your father said.*" He shook his head. "I don't think I ever came as close to hating my dad as I did that night."

"I can understand that," Laura said softly.

Josh looked up at her. "My parents were having money problems then, although they didn't tell us at the time. That's why he was working such long hours, why he was so tired at the end of his day. He worried about me so I could have the luxury of worrying about a stray cat." He held her gaze. "I can see where you might think I was doing the same thing now, letting you worry about money so I can worry about other things. That's not what I've been doing, but I understand how it could look that way."

Laura was silent for a moment. Then she said, "You never told me that story."

"No," Josh agreed. "I guess I try to only tell you the good ones." His left hand plucked at the folds on the sleeve of his sweater. Laura saw the glint of his wedding band as it caught the light. "There are a lot of stories you haven't told *me*. I wish you would."

Her chest and throat were so heavy with tears that wouldn't

come out, she could hardly speak. She looked down at her own hands. "What if my stories aren't good?" she whispered.

He laughed. The sound incongruous in the humid air of the waiting room. "What do you think, I got married so I could hear *interesting* stories for the rest of my life?" Laura lifted her eyes to his face and saw that he was smiling at her.

Josh slid closer to her on the bench, putting one arm around her shoulders and drawing her to his chest. She rested her head in the curve of his neck and smelled the familiar scents of his aftershave, of their home. "She'll be okay, Laura," Josh said, and Laura didn't know if he was trying to convince her or himself. "Prudence is tougher than we give her credit for. We'll take her home, and she'll go right back to throwing things on the floor and bossing us around." Laura tried to laugh, although it came out sounding strangled. She felt Josh's hand stroke her hair. "We love her too much for anything bad to happen to her."

"That doesn't always matter." Laura's voice was still thick. "Sometimes love isn't enough."

"This isn't one of those times." He kissed the top of her head, murmuring against her hair. "You'll see."

The door behind the reception desk swung open and a young woman with curly brown hair wearing a white coat emerged. "Mr. and Mrs. Broder?"

"Yes," Laura said, rising quickly to her feet.

Josh rose, too. "How's Prudence? Will she be okay?"

"We've done what we can for her. We had to induce vomiting for a while." At the look of dismay on their faces, the doctor added gently, "It *is* very unpleasant for the cat, but it was necessary. What we want is to stop the toxins from the lilies from getting into her system and reaching her kidneys. We have her on an IV fluid drip right now, to flush everything out and give her kidneys some extra support. We also have her on a charcoal drip, to coat her intestines and help prevent any further toxins from being absorbed. We've drawn some blood, but we won't get the results back until tomorrow." She paused, the hint of a frown creasing her forehead. "Prudence is unconscious right now, which is unusual. We're not sure what's causing it. I'd feel a lot better about her odds if she were awake." She hesitated, then looked at them. "Generally, with lilies and potential kidney problems, we like to keep them here at least three days. There are also some additional tests we'd like to run, and that can get a bit expensive. If money is an issue . . ."

"Money's no issue at all," Laura said. "Do whatever you have to do for her. Can we see her?"

"Typically we don't like to bring people back into the tech area." The veterinarian looked at Laura and Josh, and Laura knew how much anxiety could be read in their eyes. "I'd feel a lot better, though, if Prudence was awake. Her vitals are shakier than they should be just from the lily toxicity. I think it'd be okay if one of you came back. Sometimes their moms can do more for them than we can." Touching the sleeve of Laura's jacket, she added, "We were all so sorry to hear about your mother, Mrs. Broder. Sarah was a good soul. Everybody here really liked her."

"Thank you," Laura murmured. Giving Josh's arm one last squeeze, she followed Dr. DeMeola back through the swinging door and up a narrow flight of stairs. At the top of the stairs was a large white room filled with kennels. Prudence lay in one of them, as still as something dead. Laura could barely even see the rise and fall of her abdomen as she breathed. Her front legs had been shaved for the insertion of drips and tubes, and the flesh that had lain hidden beneath her white socks was pink and vulnerable-looking. Laura couldn't remember the last time she'd seen Prudence without her little red collar, and the fur of her neck looked naked without it.

"I'll leave you alone with her for a few minutes," Dr. DeMeola said, unlatching the door to Prudence's kennel and walking noise-lessly out.

Laura crouched down to bring her head closer to Prudence's. In a low voice she said, "Hi, Prudence. Hi, my sweet girl." Tears rose in her eyes as she saw how silent and still Prudence remained. "The doctor says you'll be just fine in a few days, and then you can come home. But we'd all feel better if you'd wake up and say hi to us." She waited for a sign that Prudence could hear her, a tiny meow, a twitching paw, anything. But Prudence remained utterly still.

Laura brought her face to the fur of Prudence's neck, whispering into it, "I'm sorry, Prudence. I'm so sorry I yelled at you this morning. I don't really want you to leave me alone." Laura began to stroke the fur of her back, combing her fingers through the way she knew Prudence liked. "I couldn't stand it if you left me. Please, Prudence. Can't you try to open your eyes for me? Just a little? Josh and I love you so much. Please don't leave us, Prudence. You don't know how much of me you'd be taking with you if you did."

Laura looked down at Prudence's still, silent form, and thought of her mother, of the way Prudence had nestled in Sarah's arms and given her the love Laura herself had always felt, even after she'd lost the words to tell her mother so. She had wanted to get past the wall of words Sarah had put up between the two of them, had desperately wanted to say something *real*. But everything she tried to say to her mother ended up coming out wrong. Why was it that, with a cat, issues of love and trust could be so straightforward? Was it because a cat could love you for your better self, the self you wanted to be and knew you could be, if not for the endless complications of human relationships?

Their moms, the vet had said. Was she a "mom"—could she be a mom to the baby she was carrying? For she realized now that she wanted this child, even if she was pregnant only because of the two or three morning pills she now realized she had forgotten to take a few months back. She wanted her child and she wanted Josh, even if he never worked another day in his life. And she wanted Prudence. She'd lost the Mandelbaums, and Honey, and her mother. Laura couldn't bear to lose one more thing that she loved.

It was Sarah who'd been a mother to both her and Prudence, who would have been a grandmother to this unborn child. It was Sarah who should be here right now, for all their sakes. It wasn't fair . . . it wasn't fair at all . . .

For all of Laura's young life, before all the things that had gone wrong between her and her mother, the most comforting thing in her small world had been the sound of her mother singing. She reached down to stroke Prudence's head, and suddenly she heard a voice that sounded like her mother's issuing from her own throat. *"Dear Prudence,"* she sang. *"Open up your eyes . . ."* Then she stopped, the threat of more tears choking her throat shut. She imagined her mother standing next to her, holding her hand and adding her voice to Laura's, the way they'd sung together in that music studio when Laura was a child. Laura sang now, and could have sworn that she heard her mother's voice singing with her here in this room. *"The wind is low, the birds will sing . . . that you are part of everything . . ."* Then Laura bent to kiss Prudence's forehead at the spot where her tiger stripes formed a little "M" above her eyes. "Dear, dear Prudence," she whispered. "Won't you open up your eyes?" Laura's voice was her own again. Desperate now, she pressed her lips to Prudence's ear and murmured, "Come on, little girl. My little love. Open your eyes for me."

And Prudence did.

15

Prudence

THERE'S A TALL GREEN PLANT THAT LIVES NEXT TO THE LIVING ROOM window leading to the fire escape. The sunlight through the window today is brighter than usual, so bright I have to squint my eyes. That doesn't make the game any less fun, though. This is Sarah's and my favorite game.

Sarah is walking from the bedroom to the kitchen. She passes my hiding place inside the plant, and the rustling sound of leaves as I crouch lower makes her head start to turn. The movement is so small only a cat would notice it. I know she knows I'm here, but she keeps walking.

Just as she passes the plant, I leap out and pounce on her ankles. Sarah pretends to be very surprised by this. She thinks I don't know that she knew I was about to pounce, but pretending is what makes this game fun for both of us. Now my paws are wrapped around her right ankle, my teeth on the skin of her heel (although

I don't press down in a *real* bite). "Oh no!" she cries. "It's the deadly attack kitty!" I switch and wrap my paws around her left ankle. But Sarah knew I was going to do this, because she's already bending to her left to scoop me up in her arms. "Who's the vicious kitty?" she says, in the voice she only uses when she's talking to me. "Who's my brave little hunter?" She brings my face closer to hers, and I press my forehead against hers. She knows I don't like being held in the air for very long, though, so she puts me back down on my own legs. She shakes off some of my fur that got onto her hands and says, "I think somebody could use a good brushing. What do you think?" From a drawer in the kitchen, she takes out the special brush that's only used for brushing my fur, and the two of us settle on the couch with me in her lap.

The brush-bristles against my skin feel nice, and Sarah's hand following the movement of the brush down my back feels nicer. Sarah's smell is even more wonderful in my nose than it usually is. *I knew you weren't really dead!* I think. *I knew you'd come back to me!* I don't know why I think that, though. Whoever said anything about Sarah being dead?

"Don't leave," Sarah says. "Please don't leave us." Her voice sounds different, a little deeper than normal maybe, and I wonder why she's asking me to stay. Where would I go? And why is she saying *us*? There's only one of her. When I look up at her, her eyes are full of sorrow. The skin of her forehead puckers just a little above the inner corners of her eyebrows. But the brush feels so comfortable, and Sarah smells so warm and safe, that my eyes start to close before I can think any more about that. I feel a purr start in my throat, spreading its warmth into my chest.

That's when Sarah starts to sing. Her singing voice also sounds different, like maybe it's the voice of someone I've heard talk before, but who I've never heard sing. This is strange, because singing is almost the first thing I ever heard Sarah do. The voice is Sarah and not-Sarah at the same time. Still, it's a voice I know I could listen to forever and be happy. It sounds the way love feels.

Prudence, the voice sings, *open your eyes.* I don't want to open them, though. I'm too comfortable and sleepy. But the voice keeps singing and saying, *Dear, dear Prudence . . . won't you open up your eyes? My little love.* It's so insistent that I have no choice. I have to fight with my eyelids, which have become heavy and stubborn. There's a powerful light over my head, hurting my eyes and pushing my eyelids down. I finally pry them apart, and it takes a moment to focus and see things around me clearly.

When I look up, it's not Sarah's face I see. It's Laura's.

"Dr. DeMeola!" Laura cries. "She's awake!" The blurry shape of a familiar-looking woman drifts through my vision, somewhere behind where Laura is standing. Laura's smiling, and there are tears in her eyes. I don't realize I'm on my side until I feel her hand start to rub gently behind my right ear, the one that isn't pressed against whatever it is I'm lying on. There are bad smells in this place—scary smells—but Laura's Laura-smell is stronger than they are as she continues to stroke behind my ear and down the length of my body. I try to lift my backside the way I usually do when my back is scratched like this. But my body won't move when I tell it to, so I blink once at her, slowly, instead.

Laura brings her mouth close to my ear and murmurs, "Don't scare us like that again, little girl. We need you to stay with us. Can you do that, Prudence?" Her eyes look into mine, and I recognize her expression. It's the one I used to see on her face sometimes when she looked at Sarah. I used to wonder what that look meant, but now I know. Her eyes are filled with love.

My throat is raw and scratchy. It feels like something bad happened to it. But I'm still able to answer with a faint *Mew.*

"Good," Laura murmurs, and she kisses my forehead.

From the cage they make me sleep in (I have to sleep in a *cage*!), I can smell nervous cats all around me. They stand and pace, hoping to find some warm new corner or a way to get out they haven't discovered already. Their movements disturb the air and make my whiskers tickle. At night, when most of the humans who work here have left, some of the cats cry out, wanting their own humans to come and take them home. But I never cry. Sarah is never coming back for me.

There are whole chunks of pink skin showing on my front paws, where my beautiful white fur used to be. One of the stabbing people here shaved the fur off so they could attach dripping tubes. Sarah was the first one who ever said my white paws looked like human socks. Now, with so much of the fur missing, they don't look like socks at all. I lick and lick at the spots where fur is supposed to be and think, *This is what happens when the human you love dies. Pieces of you go missing.*

But Laura will always come back for me. I saw it in her eyes when she sang to me and woke me up. When I think about Laura singing the *Dear Prudence* song, the hole in my chest from missing Sarah begins to fill. There's something growing there. Soon it will fill up the whole space.

For three days I'm forced to live here, and every day Laura and Josh come to visit me. A woman with curly hair unsticks my front paws from the tape that fastens dripping tubes into them, and then she wraps me in a strange blanket that doesn't even smell like me and carries me into one of the smaller rooms where Sarah brought me once a year to get stabbed with needles. The room smells like the metal of the high table where needles get stuck into cats. It also smells like Laura and Josh fresh from being outside, sweating slightly under their coats and forced to stand too-close when the stabbing lady comes in to tell them how I'm doing. She says I'm not really sick, that they're making me stay here "just as a precaution." A precaution against what? It's being locked in a room with sick cats all the time, away from my own food and special Prudence-bowls, that's going to make me sick if anything will. I try showing Josh and Laura how little they should trust the stabbing lady by hissing at her every time she comes near me, but that just makes them laugh and say things like, *Look how feisty Prudence is! She'll be better in no time, won't you, little girl?*

I recognize this stabbing lady—she's the same one who once agreed with Sarah that my front paws looked like socks. Josh keeps standing, but Laura sits cross-legged on the floor next to me and strokes my back while I lick. "It'll grow back, Prudence," she says gently. "It'll all grow back." She hums the *Dear Prudence* song while she pets me. Her humming voice sounds so much like Sarah's that I stop licking my paws and walk into her lap, sitting on my haunches and pressing the whole side of my face against her chest. Her arms come around me and one hand rubs the good spot underneath my chin until I purr.

"Sweet girl," she murmurs. "Who's my little love?"

Sarah's eyes looked sad in my dream because she knew she had to stay in that place, without me, just like I have to stay here without her. But Laura's eyes smile as she looks down at me now. "You can come home with us tomorrow," she says, as her fingers keep finding good places beneath my chin. I know now that "home" is wherever I live with Laura.

I don't think I've ever been happier to get into my carrier than I am the next morning when Josh and Laura come to pick me up. The humans at the Bad Place remember to put my red collar and Prudence-tags back on me before I leave, and there's no more tape on my front paws. Just the faintest little fuzz of white on the pink skin. Even from inside my carrier and cuddled up with the old Sarah-shirt that Laura put in here with me, the air outside feels cold and scrapes against my furless spots. It hasn't rained since the day I got sick, but the little patches of dirt around the trees in the sidewalk still smell damp. This is the time of year when leaves change color and start to fall off trees. Sometimes Sarah would come home with red and orange leaves clinging to her hair or coat, and she would put them on the floor for me so I could roll around on them while they made crunching sounds and broke up into little pieces. The pain in my belly when I think of Sarah flares again, until I look through the bars of my carrier and see that Laura and Josh are holding hands.

Laura is the one who holds my carrier as we leave the Bad Place. I've been living high in the air in Upper West Side for so long, I'd almost forgotten how things look and smell down here on the streets. Laura must have stepped right near where a pigeon is sitting, because one flutters up past the bars of my carrier with a gurgling coo. I can hear the squeaks of mice, too high-pitched for humans to notice, burrowing into soft dirt, and cars speeding by on the streets. A woman walks quickly past, talking into a tiny phone. Her voice goes up at the end of every sentence even though it doesn't sound like she's asking any questions. *So I said to him? I was, like, if you think you can treat* me *that way? You've got the wrong girl.*

The bricks from the buildings here smell older than they used to, and I can't decide if that's because I've been away from Lower East Side for so long, or because I've gotten used to the newer, bigger buildings in Upper West Side. I realize that I'm not an immigrant anymore—that Upper West Side is the country where I live now. Laura stops in front of one building and says to Josh, "This is where my mother's record store used to be." The vibrations from her chest when she speaks travel down her arm and make the walls of the carrier hum. The shop she points to has tiny clothes in the window, probably for human infants.

"This is a nice block," Josh says.

"It always was. The guy who used to own this place sold chess sets he made"—Laura points to another window—"and there was a candle shop next to that." Her arm sweeps back, to her left. "And down there, on Second Avenue, was Love Saves the Day." She's silent for a moment. "I think I heard it's a noodle place now."

Josh puts an arm around her shoulders, bringing my carrier closer to the side of her leg. "Did you want to pick up some lunch there?"

"Nah," she tells him. "Let's get something Prudence likes. Maybe tuna sandwiches."

They walk to the end of the block, and Josh puts his arm in the air until a yellow-colored car pulls over next to us. All three of us get into the backseat and Laura settles my carrier onto her lap. I think about tuna sandwiches the whole way home.

※　※　※

It's funny how a place you know well can feel so different when you come back after a long time. Part of it is realizing how bad I smell now (like the Bad Place) after smelling all the things at home with my regular Prudence-smell. But the whole apartment looks bigger in some places and smaller in others, and just *odd* in general. Maybe it was being with Sarah in our old apartment while I was sleeping that makes everything around here seem different than it used to, and like I was away for longer than I was. Still, it's good to be home. First I spend long moments re-marking my scratching post (I didn't have anything to scratch on at the Bad Place). My Prudence-bowls are filled with food, exactly where I left them. I'm even happy (only for a moment) to see that awful blue mat with the fake-happy cats resting beneath them. When I jostle the water bowl, it's because I can only drink moving water, not because I'm angry about the mat anymore.

Laura and Josh must have gone shopping while I was staying in the Bad Place, because now the living room floor is crowded with store-bought cat toys. There are little toys that look just like mice—with fur and everything—that squeak when I bite them, and balls with tiny bells that roll in all directions and remind me of the jingly toys Sarah brought home when I first went to live with her. Josh and Laura remembered to save the big paper bag the toys came in, and I crawl all the way into the back of it, holding one of my mice in my teeth and swiping out at their feet with my front paws whenever they walk past. There's also one toy that's like a long stick with feathers—like the ones from Sarah's bird-clothes—dangling from a string at the end. Laura holds the end of the stick over my head and drags it around while I try to catch the dangling feathers. She laughs when I stand up on my hind legs and bat at them with my front paws, until I wonder who's supposed to be enjoying this toy—her or me?

They also brought home something called catnip, which looks a little like the cooking herbs Sarah used to make our food with but smells *so* much more wonderful. Josh sprinkled some on the living room floor, and at first I was just breathing its smell in and noticing how nice it was. Then, the next thing you know, I was rolling around on my back and all I could think was, *This is soooooooo gooooood*. This, of course, is not a dignified way for a cat to behave. I was able to recover a little bit of dignity when Laura walked by while I was rolling around, and I leapt at her ankles. She seemed as delighted with this display of feline hunting skills as Sarah ever had. She even scooped me up the way Sarah used to and asked, "Who's my happy girl?" I rubbed my forehead against hers just the way I used to with Sarah when we lived in Lower East Side.

Days pass, I'm not sure how many. Laura doesn't go to her office during the day, and she doesn't read any work papers at night. Now she spends a lot of time napping, and I nap with her. Sometimes we nap together in the big bed upstairs, and sometimes we fall asleep on the couch until Josh comes to throw a blanket over us. He's always very quiet, trying not to disturb us. He seems concerned about making sure Laura is getting enough rest, even though she isn't getting sick in the mornings anymore.

She and Josh talk and watch movies and go out to lunch on days that aren't even Sundays. Last night, they went out together to celebrate some sort of word-writing about that building on Avenue A. "We got a story!" Josh kept saying. "A story in *The New York Times*!" But he didn't say how *many* times, or times *what*, so it was hard to know why it was such a big deal. It must have made more sense to Laura than it did to me, because she put her arms around Josh and said, "I'm proud of you." The skin on her forehead didn't even tighten the way it used to whenever Josh mentioned that building.

Later that night, after they came home, Laura told Josh a story about when she was fourteen, and the apartment building she and Sarah were living in got torn down. I was lying on the back of the couch, behind Laura's head, and she reached one hand back to press my face close to hers when she talked about what happened to Honey the cat.

Josh was sitting at the other end of the couch. His eyes never left her face, and he moved closer when she got to the part about Honey and Mr. Mandelbaum, taking her hand and squeezing it tight. "I'm sorry," he said when she was finished talking, and pressed her face to his shoulder. "Oh, Laura, I'm so sorry. But you *must* know," he squeezed her hand harder, "you have to know that nothing like that is ever going to happen to us."

"How can you know that?" Laura's voice sounded like she was ready to cry, even though she didn't. "How can you possibly know what's going to happen to us?"

Josh exhaled loudly through his nose and let go of her hand, running his own back and forth across the top of his head. "You're right. I don't know for sure. There could be a fire or a flood. Or a freak tornado could flatten New York. But we have resources. And we have each other." Laura was staring down at her hands while Josh said all this, and he fell silent until she looked up into his face. "Nothing like that is ever going to happen to us, or to our child."

Laura didn't say anything. She leaned her head back against the couch, her hair brushing against my whiskers, and Josh put his arm around her again. He held her until her eyes closed, and she and I both settled into a peaceful sleep.

Two days later, at breakfast, Josh's forehead is knotted, like he's thinking hard about something. He fiddles with the twisty-tie from the loaf of bread he made his toast from, and when I stretch up one paw to reach for it, he drops it onto the ground in front of me so I can pick it up and toss it into the air. I chase it into the corner behind the kitchen table, where it tries to hide from me. Laura and Josh watch. "I have to tell you something," Josh finally says.

Laura's body stiffens a little. "Okay." Her voice sounds deeper than usual, the way a human's voice sounds when they're nervous but trying not to sound that way.

"I've been getting a lot of calls since the *Times* article came out," he tells her. "Magazines and other papers that want to do follow-up stories, things like that. I've also been hearing from a lot of the artists who've recorded in the music studio over the years. Some of them are pretty big names." He pauses. "Anise Pierce called last night after you went to bed. She read the article, too. She wants to come out here and help."

Laura's left hand, which has been resting in her lap, rises onto the table. She drums two fingers against it. From underneath the table, where I'm sitting with my twisty-tie, I can hear the light *thump thump* of fingers against wood. "Anise," she repeats. "Anise Pierce wants to come *here,* all the way from Asia, to help save a music studio she hasn't set foot in for thirty years." I think Laura may be asking a question, although I can't be sure. Her voice doesn't go higher at the end of what she says the way human voices usually do when they're asking a question.

"She's in California now," Josh tells Laura. "She got back a few weeks ago. To be honest, I think she wants to come out here to see you more than Alphaville."

Laura doesn't say anything right away, although I can see her toes curl up inside her socks. At last she says, "You said yourself that all kinds of people have been coming forward since the *Times* article ran. Do you really need Anise's help?"

"Maybe it would be good for you to see her again," Josh says. "How many people knew your mother as well as she did?"

"Let's talk about it later." Laura pushes back her chair and stands. "Right now I want to do some grocery shopping, and I'm not sure I have anything to wear outside that still fits me."

Laura has been getting fatter lately, probably because she sleeps a lot more and stopped drinking coffee. She pauses in the doorway and, without turning around, says to Josh, "You can call Anise and tell her to come if she wants."

Laura walks up the stairs, and I follow her. If she's unsure about what clothes to wear, she'll want my opinion, the way Sarah always did.

For days Laura attacks our apartment. She moves everything around on counters so she can scrub every little corner, pushes rugs out of the way to sweep away whatever bits of dust might be hiding there, and stands on ladders so she can wipe shelves and the tops of furniture too tall for a human standing on the floor to see anyway. Blue liquid from a spritzy bottle makes rainbows in the sunlight when she stands near the window to clean, but it smells fake sweet and falls onto my fur when I get too close. I squint my eyes and let my mouth hang open, trying to keep the stink of it from invading my nostrils. Even The Monster gets taken from its special closet. I hide in Home Office—which is the one room Josh told Laura she isn't allowed to clean—until The Monster is safely back in its cave.

"Maybe we should hire someone to do all this," Josh says.

Laura is lying on her belly on the floor of their bedroom, half underneath the bed as she tries to get rid of something called "dust bunnies." I see little balls of fur and human hair, but nothing that looks like a bunny. "We don't need to hire somebody," Laura says. "It's not like I'm busy doing anything else these days."

Josh has been standing in the doorway to the bedroom watching Laura chase the invisible bunnies. Now he turns to leave. "Anise Pierce isn't going to look under the bed," he says over his shoulder.

"Yeah? Thanks for letting me know," she says in her "dry" voice.

By the time the doorbell rings the next night, the apartment is so clean it doesn't smell like anybody lives here. I'm busy rubbing my Prudence-smell back into the living room couch when Josh opens the door. Laura is seated on the couch with her back straight and her hands folded in her lap. After spending a lot of time deciding what to wear, she finally put on a pair of jeans and a soft, light blue sweater that's big enough to hide her growing belly. I think the color of the sweater looks beautiful with her eyes.

There's the sound of Josh saying hello and Anise's familiar voice, deep and raspy, answering him. Then she walks into the room behind Josh. Seeing her face again and smelling her Anise-smell makes memories of Sarah and our old apartment fill my mind so fast, I have to lie down for a moment and feel the cool wood of the floor against the skin of my belly. I see Sarah and

Anise singing along to black disks and talking about The Old Days, Sarah telling Anise about Laura and Josh back before I knew that, someday, Laura would become my Most Important Person. I remember Sarah holding me in her lap while she told Anise there was something wrong with her heart, and Anise saying, *You should tell Laura, Sarah. She'd want to know. She loves you more than either of you realizes.*

Laura stands, and Anise and Laura look at each other for a long moment. I can tell from the way Laura's eyes widen that she's remembering things, too. "My God," Anise finally says. "You look just like her. I'd forgotten."

"Not the eyes," Laura replies. "She always said I had my father's eyes."

Anise's laugh is loud and hoarse-sounding. "We won't hold that against you." She crosses the room in only three long steps and wraps her arms around Laura. She seems to grow taller, so that all of Laura is folded up into her hug. "I'm sorry, baby. I'm so sorry. It's a terrible thing to lose your mother, especially when she was so young." Anise's eyes over Laura's shoulder are shiny with water. "I still can't believe she's gone." She pulls back to look at Laura. "I'm sorry I couldn't be here for her funeral."

Laura takes a step back from Anise. "I know how hard it can be to reach you when you're overseas."

"I have a cell phone now," Anise says. "I don't think you would have had trouble reaching me, if you'd really wanted to."

Anise looks at Laura, who seems to shrink a bit until it looks almost like she and Anise are the same size. Anise's words sound like an accusation, but then she smiles and adds, "You must have gotten your stubbornness from your father, too."

Laura doesn't seem to know what to say to this. Josh, who's been standing there watching them asks, "Anise, what are you drinking?"

"Just some tea with lemon, if you've got it," she tells him and Josh disappears into the kitchen.

"Have a seat," Laura says, and Anise perches on the shorter end of the couch. Now that she's closer to me, I realize how familiar she smells. There was a hint of this same smell on the bird-clothes Sarah kept in the back of her closet.

Anise notices me sniffing her leg and grins. "Prudence!" Putting one hand beneath my nose, she says, "It's a long time since I've seen you, baby doll." She begins petting me almost before I know what's happening, but her fingers are so skilled they find all the good places behind my ears and under my chin that I'm helpless to protest. I fall to the ground and flip onto my back, sad when Anise pulls her hand away too soon. "Look at this apartment," she says, her bright eyes darting around the room. Then she laughs. "Sarah must have *hated* this place."

Laura laughs, too, in an unthinking way that seems to surprise her. "You're right," she tells Anise. "My mother said buildings like this look more like hotels than homes. But then," she adds, "I remember her complaining about how hard the stairs in her building were on her knees whenever it rained."

"It stinks getting older," Anise agrees cheerfully. The little lines around her eyes crinkle as she smiles again. "Your whole life you're young, and that's all you know how to be. That's all you *remember* being. Everything anybody says to you starts with, *You're young. You're young so you don't know any better. You're too young to know what being tired feels like.* And then one day they stop saying it. You realize it's been years since anybody called you young. These days everything people say to me begins with, *At our age. At our age, who has the energy to run around Asia with a rock band?*" Josh has returned with two cups of tea, handing one to Anise and the other to Laura. Anise sips at hers and says, "I don't think I'll ever be the grown-up your mother already was at nineteen, but she also had a gift for staying young. That's tough to pull off. I appreciate it more every day."

Laura drinks from her teacup, too, but doesn't respond to this. Josh walks across the room to fiddle with something next to the TV, and music fills the room. Anise is also silent for a moment, then says, "Is this Sarah's copy of *Country Life*?"

Josh looks surprised. "It is," he tells her. "How did you know?"

"Because I gave it to her." She puts her teacup down on the

coffee table. "Before I moved to California. You always recognize the crackle of your own records."

"We have a bunch of her records and things upstairs," Josh says. "You guys should look through them."

Laura's face tightens. But Anise says, "I'd love that, if it's okay with you?"

She looks over to Laura, who hesitates before nodding and putting her teacup on the table next to Anise's. Standing, she says, "Come on. I'll show you where everything is."

My fur prickles as I follow everyone into the room with the Sarah-boxes. I haven't been in here since before I got sick. Even now, knowing that it doesn't matter if everything in them stays in the right place because remembering things won't bring Sarah back, it's hard for me to watch Anise take things out.

Still, it's nice to hear her talk about Sarah. She has memories that are different from Laura's and mine. She exclaims over the box of matchbook toys (*I can't believe she kept them all these years!*) and tells Laura stories about the places she and Sarah used to go and the things that happened to them there. She also tells Laura stories that Laura is too young to remember. "We had your fourth birthday party at Ear Wax. You wouldn't stop trying to rip up record covers, and it drove your mom nuts. She was always so patient with you, though. More patient than I would have been." She looks through Sarah's collection of black disks like they're old friends. "I remember *you!*" she exclaims a few times. Laughing, she pulls something from one stiff cardboard holder. It's not a black disk, but a colorful one that looks just like Anise except smaller! The cut-out is Anise holding a guitar and throwing her head back with her hair flying around behind her. There's a hole right in the middle that lets you put it on the special table Sarah had, just like the black disks. "I always told your mom these picture disks would never be worth anything," she says to Laura. "But she insisted on holding on to them."

"She put most of this stuff into storage when we moved into

the apartment on Stanton." Laura shakes her head. "I could never figure out why she kept it all."

Anise's eyes narrow in confusion. "Why does anybody keep anything? To help you remember." Then she looks around this room, which is still empty except for the Sarah-boxes, and doesn't say anything else until she sees the black garbage bag with the bird-clothes. "No *way!*" she says happily. "*Look* at all these! I made most of these for your mom, you know. We had disco outfits for when we went to her kind of clubs"—Anise makes a face—"and all these little punk-rock-girl clothes for when she came with me to the places where I played." She holds up a shirt that looks like it's been clawed up, held together with silver safety pins. "Did you know your mom was a drag king for about thirty seconds back in the day?"

Laura has been sitting cross-legged on the floor with me in her lap, watching as Anise looks through everything but not doing much herself. I feel her surprise in the sudden slight movement of her arms and shoulders as she says, "Wait, what?"

Anise laughs. "*Nobody* wanted to give a girl DJ a break back then. It used to kill me to see Sarah spending so many hours at Alphaville, making audition tapes nobody would listen to. So one day I came up with the idea of dressing her like a guy. Neither of us had much in the way of a chest"—Anise looks down at her own skinny shape—"and she was so tall anyway that all it took was some clever needlework. In the clothes I made, and with her hair up under a hat, she looked like a very pretty boy." Anise's smile is gentle. "I never saw anyone as beautiful as your mother who was so completely unaware of how beautiful she was. Like it was nothing. The first time I met her was in a store where she was trying on dresses. She came out of that dressing room looking like a model, but you could tell just by looking at her that she didn't see it when she looked in the mirror." Anise makes a funny face and sticks out her tongue. "I thought *somebody* should tell her what a knockout she was."

Laura's voice is hesitant. "So why did she stop? Being a DJ, I mean," she adds, when Anise looks confused. "She talked about it sometimes, and even when I was a kid I could tell how much she loved it. Why did she give up the way she did?"

Anise's eyes widen. "Because of you," she says. "Because once you came along, nothing else was more important. Not even her music. She used to say *you* were her music."

Laura's fingers have been stroking my fur, and the pressure from the tips becomes a bit harder, as if her fingers are curling up. I start to purr, hoping it will ease her tension. "But then, why did she have that record store? Why did she raise me in that neighborhood?" Laura is starting to sound angry. "Why did we live the way we did if I was more important to her than anything else?"

"Go sing that sad song to your husband. *My mother didn't love me enough.*" Anise looks as mad as Laura just sounded. "You forget—*I* was there. What kid was ever happier than you were? What kid ever had a mother who *adored* her the way your mother adored you?" Anise's hands rise into the air and start making gestures. "Your mother gave you a *family,*" she insists. "She gave you a *life.* Isn't that what every parent wants, to give their children what they never had? Do you think I can't tell what *you're* hoping to give your children just by looking at this apartment?"

"You haven't seen me in fifteen years." Laura's voice is low and sharp. "You don't know anything about me or what I'm trying to do."

"Don't I?" Anise's voice doesn't get louder, exactly, but it sounds more powerful. "I know you've been letting one *horrible* day roam around in your head like a monster you can't kill and won't ever let die. And yes, I know how bad that day was for you," she adds when Laura takes a breath as if she's about to interrupt. "Bad things happen and people spend months and *years* trying to recover because they don't get the kind of help from friends that your mother did. Help she didn't get from those grandparents of yours, who you don't even remember because they never cared enough to meet you. You had the Mandelbaums for grandparents and that girl who lived upstairs—what was her name? Maria something?—for your sister, and Noel from the store and everybody in the neighborhood your mom made a point of knowing so they'd all look out for you. You had a mother who picked you up at school every afternoon and built an entire life around being able to spend time with you. And she was lucky, because not everybody has the chance or the resources to do what she did."

Laura doesn't say anything when Anise's rush of words stops. I look up and see the skin of her throat tightening, like those times when she wanted to say something to Sarah, but couldn't.

"Look," Anise says. "It's not my place to tell you what you should think of your mother, Laura. But don't ever think she didn't give you enough. Sarah gave you *everything*. She gave you a family. And here you sit—smart, successful, and happily married, so she obviously did *something* right. I don't think you'll ever know"— Anise leans forward and touches Laura's hand—"how proud of you she was."

Laura's touches the tips of her fingers lightly to Anise's, then moves them through my fur again. I press my forehead against her arm and think about what Anise said, about Laura and Josh, and about how Sarah gave me a family, too.

When Laura speaks, her voice sounds almost as hoarse as Anise's laugh. "I still haven't cried for her." She raises one hand to run fingers through her hair, just like Sarah used to. "I don't know what's wrong with me. But I can't. I haven't been able to."

The inside corners of Anise's eyebrows rise, making her face look softer. "Sarah would have been proud of what you and Josh are doing for Alphaville and the people who live in that building."

"It's just Josh." Laura clears her throat. "I haven't done anything."

Anise smiles and tilts her head to one side. It's the way she used to look at Sarah sometimes. "You will."

Later that night, after Anise has left and it's just Josh and Laura and me sitting together in the living room, Laura tells Josh, "I'd like to help with what you're doing for this building on Avenue A."

The corners of his eyes push up in a smile. "Really?"

Laura starts to smile, too, and her voice sounds casual, but her eyes are still serious. "Why not?" she says. "Sleeping twelve hours a day is completely overrated."

Just when I finally think I have humans figured out, I realize again what mysterious creatures they really are.

16

Prudence

THE PHONE RINGS WITH TWO SHORT RINGS INSTEAD OF ONE LONG one, the way it does when the man who lives in the lobby downstairs is calling to say someone is on their way up to see us. Laura looks up in surprise from where she's sitting on the couch with me on one side of her and a stack of papers bigger than me on the other. On the coffee table are a lot of thick books that Laura went to get from her office one night. Josh is out at a meeting, so it's just Laura and me by ourselves in the apartment.

"Yes?" Laura says when she answers the phone. After a pause she says, "Of course, send him up." Then she runs to the little bathroom in the short hallway near the front door, where she pulls a brush through her hair and splashes cold water on her face. I stretch and walk over to the entrance of the kitchen, which is also next to the front door, to help Laura in case this surprise is a bad one. She's patting her face dry when the doorbell rings.

"Perry!" Laura says, as she pulls the door open. "What a surprise!" There's a smile on her face, and she reaches out one hand to hold the stranger's for a moment, but her eyes are cautious.

Perry's eyes aren't cautious like Laura's, but they look at her closely without seeming to. When he says, "You look good. Better than good, actually," Laura's face turns pink. The lids slide closed over his eyes so briefly it almost isn't noticeable, as if Laura's face changing colors has confirmed something he suspected. "May I come in?" he asks.

"Of course." She leads him into the living room, where he sits on one of the chairs facing the couch. "Can I get you anything?"

"A glass of water would be nice," he says, and Laura walks into the kitchen to get it for him. Now I'm standing near the other entrance to the kitchen—the one that opens onto the dining room table and living room—and from here I take a closer look at Perry. Some humans, when they see a cat, immediately want to pet her and say something like, Come here, kitty, come here. Some humans look annoyed (especially if they're allergic), and some humans don't even notice cats at all. Perry doesn't do any of these things. He sits in his chair, his shoulders and spine held in a way that looks alert yet completely comfortable, with the kind of control that cats have mastered but that humans rarely can. He looks right back at me with his dark brown eyes, and in them I see a hint of amusement.

I notice his outfit, which is a jacket that matches his pants, both of them made from a material that looks wonderfully soft, yet doesn't bunch up or wrinkle the way a lot of humans' clothes do when they're sitting. Around his neck is a piece of dark yellow material that some of the human men on TV wear, although I've never seen Josh wear one. His shoes are black and perfectly clean, what Sarah would have called "immaculate." I can tell why it used to be so important to Laura to make Perry happy with her work, and suddenly I'm glad the fur on my paws has grown almost completely back.

Laura walks into the room with two glasses and hands one to Perry. The two of them talk for a while. Laura says the names of humans who work at their office and asks how they're doing. Both of them seem to know, as they sip from their glasses, that Perry didn't decide to visit us so he could tell Laura that her assistant got her hair cut too short, or that someone named Greg keeps making everybody look at pictures of his new baby. But Perry seems comfortable and not like he's in a hurry to say his real reason for coming.

"So how's Josh?" he asks. "I don't think I've seen him since your wedding. I was hoping I'd get to say hello." His voice is deep and strong without being loud. It's so deep that listening to it starts a faint rumble in my chest, like a purr coming from outside my body.

"He won't be back for a couple of hours," Laura says. "He's working on a project, and there was a meeting he had to go to."

"Ah, yes. The Mitchell-Lama on Avenue A. I read about it in the *Times*."

Laura laughs. "I always forget you know everything," she says. "Yes, he's meeting with the owners of the music studio in the building's Basement. They're incorporating as a 501(c)(3) so they have a firmer legal standing if it comes down to a hearing. Josh is helping them with the paperwork."

Perry nods. "You'll forgive an old friend for prying, but what are Josh's plans after this whole thing is over?"

"If things go our way"—Perry's eyebrows rise when Laura says *our*—"we're hoping that, eventually, he might be able to help them raise enough funds for their community outreach programs to justify some kind of paid position. If not . . ." She spreads her hands in front of her. "Who knows? It's tough out there right now. We're trying to take things one day at a time."

Perry tilts his head at her. "You say I know everything, but I have no idea why you haven't been back to the office in nearly four weeks."

"I'm taking a leave of absence," Laura says slowly. "If you check with HR, you'll find the paperwork properly filed and authorized."

Perry leans forward. "Come on, Laura. I always thought you

and I could talk to each other like people. Of course all the paper-work is in order. That's not what I'm asking you."

Laura squares her shoulders and straightens her spine. "To be honest, I'm surprised to hear you'd *want* me to come back. I thought Clay made himself fairly clear about that the last time we spoke."

"Clay knows how good you are as well as I do," Perry tells her. "People get overworked sometimes, and tempers flare. We all know how it is in this business. Everybody at the firm wants to see you come back. Actually"—Perry smiles—"you've become some-thing of a legend. Like the man who shot Liberty Valence. You're the associate who told Clay off in his own office and lived to tell the tale."

Laura's smile is teasing. "I see. You want me to come back so you can prove Clay didn't have my body dumped in the East River."

He looks her in the eye. "We want you to come back because we think you have a great future with us."

"The kind of great future that might include a raise?" Laura's smile gets wider, although her eyes narrow as she looks at Perry.

"A raise, yes." Now Perry is smiling, too. "A raise big enough to justify that Cheshire-Cat grin? Probably not."

"A bigger expense account might get me to come halfway." Laura's voice still sounds playful.

"So we're negotiating now? I may know of a corner office that's about to open up. Normally we'd save it for a new partner but . . ." Perry laughs. "We could probably work something out. If you're serious."

Laura's face is friendly, but her smile fades. "I don't know, Perry. It isn't *really* about Clay or my salary or which office I'm in or any of that. I took time off because I needed to think about where my life is going. I don't know if I want the same things I wanted a few years ago. Right *now* I want to help my husband save this building. You know," she adds, "it was your idea."

Perry looks startled for the first time. "*My* idea?"

"Don't you remember?" Laura's posture relaxes, and she leans back a little. "When I came to ask you that time about Mitchell-

Lama buildings, you were the one who said that an attorney who was an ace with paperwork, and who could ferret out all the contradictory statutes and building maintenance issues, might be able to force the owners to the negotiating table."

"I see." Perry shakes his head. "Hoisted by my own petard."

"Anyway," Laura continues, "this just seems like the right thing for me to work on now. And after that, I truly don't know. Things are . . . changing in my personal life. A position with a smaller firm might be a better fit."

"I suspected as much," he says. "Is it too early to offer my congratulations?"

Laura's face turns light red again, although it's hard for me to know why she seems embarrassed. Usually, congratulations are things humans like to hear. "We won't start telling people officially for another couple of weeks." Her voice is hesitant. Then she smiles and rests her hand on the swell of her belly. "But no, it isn't too early."

"Arrangements can be worked out," Perry says. "Flextime, reduced hours for a while. We've done it before." Laura opens her mouth like she's about to say something, and he insists, "I just want you to think about what you'd be giving up. You'll never see the kind of money with a boutique firm that you'll be on track to make with us in a few years."

One corner of Laura's mouth turns up in a half smile. "I know," she says. "But money isn't everything."

Perry nods his head again, just a little. He sips one last time from his glass, then stands, running one hand over the front of his jacket. Laura stands, too. "I should be getting back." With a sigh he adds, "It's the end of the month, and I don't think anyone in our group has submitted time sheets yet. They can't all be like you."

They've reached the front door when Perry stops and says, "I almost forgot. I was hoping I'd get to meet the famous cat who started all this ruckus."

Laura looks around and spots me sitting on my haunches near the entrance to the kitchen. "Hey, Prudence," she says. Lately she's been talking to me sometimes in the same kind of special voice

Sarah had when she talked to me. That's how she says my name now. "Would you like to come over and meet my friend Perry?"

It's only when I get closer to them that I realize Laura is taller than Perry, although neither of them acts like she is. It's also the first time I notice the smell of Perry's cologne. Usually I don't like artificial human-cologne smells, but Perry's is different. His smell is deep and rich, like earth, and other animals, and flowers that only send their odor into the air at night. He smells so good that I find myself rubbing my head against his ankles without waiting for him to put his hand down for me to sniff, and then I squeeze between them until I walk all the way through to the other side, where I rub my head some more against the backs of his legs.

"Wow," Laura says. "I've never seen Prudence act so friendly with someone she doesn't know." She smiles in a way that lets me know she's joking when she adds, "Maybe she wants to follow you home."

Perry also smiles down at me and notices where some of the white fur from my chest has rubbed off on the legs of his pants. He laughs and says, "It looks like I'll be taking some of her with me." He bends to put one hand under my nose, and I lean my whole head against it. "She's a beauty," he tells Laura.

"She's perfect." Laura's voice is more serious when she says, "We almost lost her. Someone was looking out for us."

"I don't doubt it." Perry stands up straight so that he's looking at Laura again. *"Every blade of grass has its angel that bends over it and whispers, Grow, grow."*

Laura's eyes look shiny, and without warning she reaches out to put her arms around him. "Thank you, Perry," she says in a choked-sounding voice. "For everything."

He puts his arms around her, too. "You can always call me. If you change your mind about coming back to us, or if there's anything else you ever need. You know that, right?"

Laura takes a step back and nods. Perry kisses her once on the forehead, and then he leaves.

* * *

Laura has been more tired than usual in the mornings because she doesn't drink coffee anymore. But she seems alert at breakfast this morning when she tells Josh, "I have a meeting this afternoon with the attorneys representing all the different sides in this thing. I'm hoping we'll be able to start formal negotiations."

Josh looks startled as he puts his cup of coffee down next to his plate of toast. "Are we at that point already?"

"Well . . ." She rests one hand on the stack of papers she was reading while Josh made his toast. "I have a complete list from the tenants of every unaddressed maintenance and repair issue. There are about two hundred, actually." She makes a face. "And I've noted every statutory regulation that would be violated by the proposed deal between the landlord and the development corporation wanting to buy the property. Mostly because the regulations are so contradictory that nobody could be in compliance with *all* of them." She rubs the corners of her eyes beneath her reading glasses with the thumb and first finger of her right hand. "Honestly, I don't know who writes this stuff. Luckily for us, though, all the confusion works in our favor. You said the property's been assessed at seven and a half million and that the tenants have raised ten through grants and loans?" Josh nods. "The development corporation's offering fifteen. We'll offer eight and try to convince all parties that a prolonged legal battle would be more painful and expensive than the property's worth."

Josh pushes his plate of toast away, then puts a piece on the floor so I can lick the butter from its top. "So you're saying this could all be settled today?"

Laura makes a *pfft* sound. "No. We just want to get the ball rolling and show them how serious we are about fighting this thing. We'll let the landlord talk us up to ten million if we have to. Hopefully either the development corporation will drop their bid or the landlord will decide it's better to take our ten million now than spend months or years fighting for the development corporation's fifteen."

Josh still looks doubtful. "What about a DHCR hearing? The

City paid for ninety-five percent of that building. Technically they get a say in whether or not it's converted out of the Mitchell-Lama program."

"They do have the right to a say in it, and as a matter of principle maybe they should exercise that right more often," Laura says. "But as a matter of practice, they generally don't. The problem with a hearing is that it's a one-shot, yes-or-no thing. And if our side gets the *no,* it's game over." She pauses to take a sip from her glass of orange juice. When she starts talking again, her voice is gentle. "I know you have this romantic idea of a big hearing and cheering crowds, but realistically a compromise is nearly always the best solution. The landlord gets more than the property's technically worth, the tenants gain all the rights and privileges of ownership, the community gets to retain affordable housing along with the programs and services the music studio offers. This would be a good thing for everybody."

Josh stands up to dump the rest of his toast in the trash and give me a nibble of cheese from the package on the counter. "You're right," he tells Laura. "I guess I've been working on this so hard for the past few months, it's hard to think of my part in it being over."

Laura looks surprised. "But it's not! It's more important now than ever for you to keep up the pressure on the publicity front. That's what'll convince the landlord he might lose at a hearing if he were to turn us down flat and walk away from the table. Every news camera and article in the paper is one more reason for him to question the strength of his position."

I never knew that a human you actually *know* could end up on TV. But a week after Anise came over to visit us, there she was on our TV set, along with a bunch of other humans who Josh said were famous musicians. They were in a room with no windows and lots of musical instruments, and Josh and Laura were there, too! They were standing in the background, while a man with a microphone talked to Anise and some other people. Laura and Josh were already home when the show came on, and it was weird to see them here in the room with me and also tiny versions of them on the TV screen at the same time.

After that the phone rang constantly for weeks. People were calling Josh to talk about doing more TV shows and newspaper word-writing about the building, and the people who own the building were calling Laura to talk about what they should do with it. Laura was hardly at home at all those few weeks, because she was always out at meetings with the humans who live there and with other lawyers. Finally one day she came home with the news that the negotiating was over. She was still taking off her coat and hanging it in the front closet when Josh came down the stairs with an anxious look on his face. "Well?" he asked.

"It's done." Laura's voice was very serious, and Josh's face went white. "The owner's willing to take nine from the tenants' association. The developer dropped his bid. The lawyer for the tenants' association and I have to get some paperwork going to make it official, but . . ." The smile on Laura's face was wider than just about any smile I've ever seen. "It's over."

Josh made a loud *whoop* sound and grabbed her in a hug so big it nearly lifted her off the ground. I don't think Laura likes being lifted off the ground any more than I do, because she almost lost her balance and swatted at Josh's shoulder a couple of times until he put her down. "We did it!" Josh yelled.

"*You* did it," Laura answered. "The tenants' association did it. I just kind of swooped in at the very end." The way she says this makes me imagine her with a pair of wings, circling in the sky like a pigeon. I don't think that's what she really means, though, even though it's what she said.

The two of them went to a party that night that the people who live in that building threw to celebrate, and they're still celebrating now a week later when Josh's parents and sister come over with the littermates for another special holiday dinner. Josh spent two whole days cooking a huge turkey, and by the time his family gets here I think I'll go crazy if somebody doesn't give me some of that turkey right away. It's unbearable to watch Laura and Josh talk to everybody and pour drinks and bring out little plates of smaller foods as if there wasn't a *whole turkey* sitting in the oven just waiting for someone to eat it! I make it my job to stand in front of the oven and meow at everybody until they remember the most important part of the day. Once everybody is (finally) sitting down to eat, they all go around the table to say what they're thankful for. I'm thankful that this time they put some turkey and other foods on a little plate for me *before* everybody sat down.

That's when Josh announces that Laura is going to have a baby. I guess that explains why she keeps getting bigger. I'm surprised at how excited Josh's parents are, because it sounds like Laura is only having *one* baby. If she were going to have five or six at the same time, *that* would be a really big deal. But having only one baby at a time is just typical of the inefficient way humans do most things. And it's probably better for me if Laura's litters are only one baby at a time, because it will be easier for me to teach one baby proper manners than it would be if there were a whole bunch of them.

"Let me ask you something," Josh's mother says. (Josh's mother likes to begin sentences by saying, *Let me ask you something.*) "Do you know yet if it's going to be a boy or a girl?"

Laura and Josh smile at each other. "We'd like to be surprised," Laura says. "Sometimes surprises are a good thing."

"It could be a Martian, so long as it's healthy," Josh's father says. "You and I didn't find out until we were in the delivery room," he reminds Josh's mother.

"You've thought of names, though," she insists.

"A few," Laura answers. "If it's a girl, we'd like to name her Sarah."

"That's the right thing." Josh's father nods. "And if it's a boy, you can still name him for your mother. Samuel is a fine name you don't hear very often anymore."

"Dad," Josh's sister says, "I'm sure they can pick a name themselves."

"We should go through our address book tonight," Josh's mother says to his father. "If it's a boy they'll make a bris. We need to think about who we'd invite."

"There's plenty of time for that, Zelda," Josh's father tells her. Winking at Josh, he adds, "Your mother's looking for an excuse to call everyone she knows with the news."

"I'm just so excited!" She stands up and walks around the table to hug Laura. "Listen to me. If you have any questions, or if something doesn't feel right, or if you want someone to go to the doctor with you, you call me or Erica. We've had four babies between us."

"Do you think Prudence will like the new baby?" It's Robert who asks this, putting one hand up in the air. Abbie adds, "Will she, Uncle Josh? She didn't like us very much when she first met us."

"That's true," Josh's mother said. "Sometimes cats and babies don't get along."

Josh laughs. "I think Prudence is going to love having a baby to boss around."

"What do you think, Prudence?" Laura asks. I'm sitting next to my now-empty plate, waiting to get someone's attention. It's only polite, at a holiday dinner, to refill somebody's plate for them once it's empty. Seeing that Laura is looking in my direction, I stalk back into the kitchen and sit in front of the counter where the rest of the turkey is waiting. I can worry about the baby and whether or not I like it when it gets here, but the food you like should always be eaten while it's still in front of you.

The people who live in the building that Josh and Laura saved in Lower East Side don't have to move, but we do. Laura and Josh say that this apartment is too expensive for us to live in while Josh still can't find a job, especially now that Laura is going to work at a smaller law firm that pays her less money. Once this idea made Laura's face and shoulders knot up with tension whenever she and Josh talked about it. Now she seems happy, though. We're moving to a place called Greenpoint, which is in a country called Brooklyn, and Laura says that she'll be able to come home on time for dinner every night. Our new apartment will have an upstairs and a downstairs, like this one has, but it's at "ground level" with no lobby and no man to open doors. Laura and Josh even say it has a little backyard with a high fence and that I can go outside with them sometimes! Too much change all at once is never ideal, but the thought of staying with Laura and Josh and also getting to lie outside in sunlit grass sometimes *almost* makes me think that *this* move might be a good thing.

For now, though, we're all living in a mess, as Laura puts it, throwing lots of things away and packing up what's left into boxes. Having so many boxes around is by far the best part of moving. Boxes are just about the best place to sleep, because they're small and safe and when you're in a box, you can see whoever is walking up to you before they can see you. My new favorite thing is to crouch down low inside a box and wait for Laura or Josh to walk by, and then leap out at them. Sarah used to pretend to be surprised when I would hide in the big plant and do this to her, but I think Laura and Josh are surprised for real when I spring at them now. Which just goes to show why a box is such a perfect hiding place for a cat. "It'll be nice when we unpack at the new place and get rid of these once and for all," Josh said last night while I hung on to his left ankle with both paws. I think about how much time I've spent in boxes—I've been in boxes all the time since I've been living in Upper West Side. I'll miss them when they're gone. But sometimes you have to put your memory-boxes away, so you can start living your future.

It's cold outside now, and the pigeons on the roof across the street almost blend into the snow. I wonder if Laura will miss them. She says we'll be living in our new home by New Year's.

New Year's is another made-up story—like hours and minutes—that humans tell themselves. Years don't begin and end because everybody gets together at the same time and says they do. Years *really* start when important things happen to you. When you're born. When you find the human you're going to live with forever. Your life begins when it becomes important. Like the day when Sarah found me. I've been counting my years from that day ever since.

Laura and Josh have brought all the Sarah-boxes downstairs into the living room so we can look through everything and decide what to bring with us and what will be left behind when we go. The Sarah-smell of them fills my nose and goes straight into the part of my mind that still dreams of her sometimes. Laura and Josh are dividing everything into three piles—a "yes" pile, a "no" pile, and a "maybe" pile. Josh put all of Sarah's black disks into the "yes" pile right away. Laura put things like Sarah's address book and bongo drums into the "no" pile. The matchbook toys and bird-clothes are in the "maybe" pile. "I hate to throw them away," Laura says, "but it's an awful lot of stuff to take with us."

"We could put everything in storage for a while," Josh replies.

Laura's face is doubtful. "I guess. We'll probably need to rent a storage unit anyway. How is it that every time you move, you end up with *more* stuff instead of less?"

"I think it's a law of physics that things in closets and boxes expand over time." His voice sounds very serious when he says this, but there's a grin on his face.

"Speaking of things expanding . . ." Laura says, and scoops me out of a box. "Somebody's put on weight these past few months." I think how unfair it is for Laura to say anything about *my* weight when *she's* the one who's getting bigger every day. But her eyes sparkle the way they do when she thinks something is funny, so probably she isn't really trying to insult me. She puts me on top of a stack of black disks, which surprises me because Sarah *never* let me touch her black disks. Josh looks surprised, too. But Laura just laughs and says, "Well, Prudence *is* coming with us, isn't she?"

The stiff cardboard holders the black disks are kept in feel cool and smooth beneath my belly, and I'm happy to lie here for a while. Suddenly Josh jumps up and says, "I almost forgot!" I hear his footsteps going up the stairs, and then he comes back down holding the Love Saves the Day bag. "I put this in my room after I found Prudence shredding everything in it one day."

Shredding! I remember that day. It was one of my first few days living here, and I just wanted a comfortable place to fall asleep with my memories of Sarah!

I try to fix Josh with my best indignant stare, but he's already sitting on the floor with his arms in the bag. "I think this is just old newspapers and stuff," he tells Laura, and puts the bag in the "no" pile. But I remember, now, that I found something else in the Love Saves the Day bag that day. Leaping from the pile of black disks, I dive into the bag headfirst and start pulling out all the old newspapers. (This is where having "extra" toes comes in handy.) Laura and Josh are laughing as more and more of me disappears into the bag, but when I get to the metal box in the bottom—the one Sarah took my red collar from the day she gave it to me—it's too heavy for me to pry out. I pull and pull at it, my back straining so hard that it arches up and almost rips the thick paper of the bag.

Laura finally notices what I'm doing and reaches into the bag to help me. When her hand and my head come back out, she's holding the box. It's crushed and dented, and I remember how difficult it was even for Sarah to open it. I can't see Laura's expression, because she's looking down, but she holds the box in her hands and turns it over and over for what seems like a long time.

"What is that?" Josh asks.

"This is from our old apartment." Laura's voice is hushed. "I always assumed it was lost the day they tore it down."

"Do you know what's in it?" Josh looks curious and then concerned when it takes Laura a few moments to answer.

"Not really." She's still turning the box around in her hands, looking for a way to open it. "How did she even get this back?"

"It looks like it's been through a war," Josh says. "Let me get a hammer from the toolbox and see if we can pry it open."

"I think I can get it." Laura slides a finger into a tiny gap between the crushed lid of the box and its body, using her other hand to flip up the latch that holds it closed. She strains against it for a moment, and just when Josh is reaching over to help her, the box flies open. Laura's hands shake as she starts pulling things out. There are some red satin ribbons, and an old, balled-up T-shirt with a funny picture of a fake ear with black disks hanging from it and word-writing across the top. Laura says the word-writing spells EAR WAX RECORDS. There are also photos of a very young-looking Sarah standing next to a man who looks a little like Laura. Sarah is holding a baby and smiling at us. In another picture that's creased, like it's been folded in half, a young-looking Laura is hugging an old, old man.

Josh has moved over so that he's sitting behind Laura now, looking over her shoulder as she finds a small velvet bag that holds a plain gold ring. "This was my mother's wedding ring." Laura looks up at Josh. "I don't think she ever got over my father. She never dated. And every year on their anniversary, she'd pull out old records and listen to 'their' songs."

Josh puts his arms around her. "That's the trouble with romantics. Once they fall in love, it's for life." But he doesn't look like he really thinks this is "trouble," as he kisses the top of Laura's head.

The last thing in the box is a small plastic rectangle with two holes punched into either side. "A cassette," Josh says. "What's on it?"

"I . . . I'm not sure." Laura lifts it from the box and looks at the front and back of it, but there's no word-writing on it. "She made so many mix tapes back in her DJ days. This could be one of them, or . . ."

She doesn't finish the sentence, so Josh says, "Let me get my cassette player. It's in my office." Josh runs to the stairs again, and I hear the sound of things being moved around above our heads in Home Office before Josh comes running back down holding what looks like a black radio with a window on the front of it. It's dusty, as if it hasn't been used for a long time. He presses a button to make the window open and, taking the tape from Laura's hand, drops it inside.

First there's a sound like a long *sssssssss*. Then music starts playing. A voice that sounds like Sarah except a little higher says, *Are you ready?* A little girl's voice says, *But I can't sing as good as you do.* Sarah's voice says, *We'll sing together. Just try.*

"Oh my God." Laura's voice is a whisper, and one hand rises to cover her mouth. "We made this together, at Alphaville Studios. I was only a few years old."

Sarah's voice hums a little, like she's trying to show this younger

Laura what the tune should sound like. Then both of their voices sing:

Winter is over
Gone is the snow
Everything's bright
And all aglow . . .

Hearing Sarah's voice now is like being there again the day we found each other. Sarah's singing was my first beautiful thing, the thing that all the other beautiful things in our life together came from. It's the sound of cold nights cuddled up under the covers together and sunlight shining butter-gold on Sarah's hair through the windows, and the hand that used to stroke my back when something frightened me. It's the sound of feet-shoes coming up the stairs at the time of day when I knew Sarah was coming home and I'd wait for her in that little ceramic bowl by the door. It's the sound of Sarah's voice saying, *Who's my love? Who's my little love?* and knowing the answer to that question even though I couldn't say it to her in human words. My first beautiful thing. It's here in this different apartment in a whole different country.

I know now what Sarah meant when she said that if you remember someone, they'll always be with you. Sarah is here with us now. As I listen to her sing, I know that she never left.

The water that fills Laura's eyes makes them look darker, until they're the same color as Sarah's eyes were. When her hands rise again to cover her whole face and her shoulders begin to shake, I know it's because this is the same for her as it is for me. Sarah's voice was Laura's first beautiful thing, too.

It's the sound of Laura sobbing that makes Josh and me go over to her at the same time. Josh's arms go around her again and I crawl into her lap. It's harder for me to get comfortable there than it used to be, because her belly has gotten bigger, but I press my forehead against her chest anyway and purr as fiercely as I can. "Look," Josh whispers. "I think Prudence remembers, too."

The three of us sit together like that until Laura's shoulders stop shaking and one hand falls to stroke the top of my head. In the light from the window, I think again how much Laura's hands look like Sarah's. Outside, on the rooftop across the street, the white and amber pigeons huddle together against the cold air and prepare to take flight. One after the other they throw themselves into the sky. Soon, though, they'll flutter back down again and return to the place they know is home.

Author's Note

On January 24, 1998, a century-old tenement building still in use and located at 172 Stanton Street was demolished by the City of New York following a 911 call reporting damage to the rear façade during a rainstorm. Some two dozen residents were evacuated early that morning without being allowed to gather any personal belongings. Firefighters and city officials assured them that they would be allowed to return within a few hours. Mayor Rudolph Giuliani entered the building without a hard hat at approximately eleven AM, but ultimately residents were not allowed to return before demolition commenced eight hours later.

Whether or not the building was in danger of imminent collapse is a question still hotly debated. Witnesses say that it had to be leveled to the ground over a thirteen-hour period and never collapsed on its own. Today, luxury condominiums occupy the site.

The events portrayed in chapter 13 of this book, while inspired by eyewitness accounts and newspaper articles about what happened that day, are a fictional creation and not intended to accurately depict real events. The characters in this book are also fictional creations and do not represent any actual persons who occupied 172 Stanton in 1998 or at any time in the building's history.

There was, however, a real "Honey the cat." Honey was one of two cats and a parrot living in the building on the day it was demolished, whose owners were not allowed to retrieve them. Neither the cats nor the parrot were ever seen again.

Acknowledgments

This book would not have been possible without these books:

Alphabet City, Geoffrey Biddle
Last Night a DJ Saved My Life, Bill Brewster and Frank Broughton
Alphaville: 1988, Crime, Punishment, and the Battle for New York City's Lower East Side, Michael Codella and Bruce Bennett
Street Play, Martha Cooper
Blackout Looting!, Robert Curvin and Bruce Porter
Hot Stuff: Disco and the Remaking of American Culture, Alice Echols
All Hopped Up and Ready to Go: Music from the Streets of New York, 1927–1977, Tony Fletcher
Making Tracks: The Rise of Blondie, Debbie Harry, Chris Stein, and Victor Bockris
Love Saves the Day: A History of American Dance Music Culture, 1970–1979, Tim Lawrence
Please Kill Me: The Uncensored Oral History of Punk, Legs McNeil and Gillian McCain

Resistance: A Radical Social and Political History of the Lower East Side, Clayton Patterson and Jeff Ferrell
Tompkins Square Park, Q. Sakamaki
New York Rocker, Gary Valentine
Naked City: The Death and Life of Authentic Urban Places, Sharon Zukin

As well as the newspaper article:

Andrew Jacobs, "The Angry Urban Refugees," *The New York Times,* May 10, 1998

This book would also have been impossible without the following people who allowed me to interview them about motherhood, music, record stores, lily toxicity in cats, life in a law firm, Mitchell-Lama housing, and everyday life in and around the Lower East Side in the '70s and '80s: Dr. Tracy DeMeola, Richard Finkelstein, Jim Kiick, John Kioussis, Andrea Kline, Manny Maris, Lorcan Otway, Clayton Patterson, Binky Philips, Dee Pop, Tony Sachs, Jay Wilson, and several female attorneys who wish to remain anonymous.

And, last but not least, my deepest gratitude goes to:

Michele Rubin, superagent and "author whisperer." My editors Caitlin Alexander—the first person to fall in love with Prudence—and Kate Miciak, who offered far more patience than I deserved as I raced to cross the finish line, and whose insights and feedback made this book better than it has any right to be.

Anise "Anise's to Pieces" Labrum, for ten years of true friendship and crazy stories better than any I could have made up, for flying from Napa to New York a week before my wedding—with a broken arm!—to sew my wedding dress, and for allowing me such free use of her name, talents, and persona.

Peri Stedman, the woman at whose thirtieth birthday party I was introduced to one Laurence Lerman. I told you I'd work your name into the next book I wrote!

David and Claire Berkowitz, my grandparents and the inspiration for the Mandelbaums. I was lucky enough to have my grandmother living with us for twelve years of my childhood, telling me stories she probably doubted I'd remember. God was very good to me when he gave me two mothers.

David and Barbara Cooper, my parents and the greatest cheering section any daughter who wanted to be a writer could have asked for.

Laurence Lerman, the world's best husband and my first editor, who read (and then re-read, and then re-re-read) every word of this book as I wrote it, whose brilliant suggestions occasionally made me wonder if I should turn the writing over to him, and who put up with me during the many, many months when I was utterly unbearable. Also Ben and Saundra Lerman. Nobody ever had better parents-in-law.

Melanie Paradise, a great friend, greater cat guardian, and this book's first reader aside from my husband and editors.

Rhoda Palmateer, in loving memory. Rhoda's love saved the day for many hundreds of cats and kittens who otherwise would have languished on the streets or died in shelters. Your extraordinary heart will always be missed.

Everybody who read *Homer's Odyssey,* took the time to email me, followed Homer and me on Facebook and Twitter, and whose daily encouragement kept me going when I was positive I wouldn't be able to finish this book.

And, finally, Clayton and Fanny Cooper-Lerman—the most adorable kittens ever (aside from Homer, Vashti, and Scarlett, of course)—for the frequent and necessary laughter breaks during the last few weeks of writing.

PHOTO: © ROBERT CALDERONE

GWEN COOPER is the *New York Times* bestselling author of
the memoir *Homer's Odyssey: A Fearless Feline Tale, or
How I Learned About Love and Life with a Blind Wonder
Cat* and the novel *Diary of a South Beach Party Girl*. She
is active with numerous animal welfare organizations.
Gwen Cooper lives in Manhattan with her husband, Lau-
rence. She also lives with her three perfect cats—Homer,
Clayton, and Fanny—who aren't impressed with any of it.

www.gwencooper.com